THE
FIFTH
HEAVEN

Translated from
the Hebrew by
PHILIP SIMPSON

THE JEWISH PUBLICATION
SOCIETY OF AMERICA

Philadelphia · New York · Jerusalem
5745 · 1985

THE
FIFTH
HEAVEN

A NOVEL

RACHEL
EYTAN

Originally published in Hebrew under the title
Ba-raki'a Ha-hamishi
Copyright © 1962 by Am Oved Publishers, Ltd., Tel Aviv
English translation copyright © 1985
by The Jewish Publication Society of America
First English edition   All rights reserved
Manufactured in the United States of America

Library of Congress Cataloging in Publication Data

Eytan, Rachel.
   The fifth heaven.

   Translation of: Ba-raki'a ha-hamishi.
   I. Title.
PJ5054.E9B313   1985   892.436   84-26128
ISBN 0-8276-0248-0

Designed by Adrianne Onderdonk Dudden

CONTENTS

Resh Lakish says,
The Heavens are seven
and they are:
Curtain,
Firmament,
Clouds,
Abode,
Refuge,
Foundation,
Paradise . . .

REFUGE,
where hosts of
Ministering Angels
chant hymns
by night . . .

And are silent,
by day
for the honor
of Israel.

Tractate 'Hagigah'

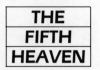

THE
FIFTH
HEAVEN

1
HERETICS
AND BELIEVERS

It's a pity that we are not water. Water bears everything in silence. Dov Markovski looked at the crescent of sea opening up before him at the foot of Allenby Street, the grey jacket folded under his left arm and the suitcase gripped in his right hand.

He felt a painful need to clear his mind before going to see Senya Wolfson. Those stupid words, the cruelty thrown in his face that very morning—he must wash them away with a torrent of other words, a great many words.

As he strolled aimlessly along, he found himself drawn into a group of Australian soldiers. They were somewhat unsteady on their feet, leaning on one another as they lurched toward the sea, the sea impervious as metal. Even at this early hour of the morning, their clumsy gait showed they had been drinking. He felt a twinge of revulsion that was immediately replaced by a narrow stream of envy: the freedom of these ruffians, their blissful unconsciousness, was like a breath of fresh air.

Unexpectedly he found himself in the center as they crowded around him, brushing lightly against his body and prodding him with friendly little jibes, hoots of laughter, and ironic congratulations. He broke away from them finally in spite of their loud protests and gestures of invitation and drifted toward a shop window, waiting for the wave of alcohol to pass. As the last of them went by, they turned back and waved their broad-brimmed hats. On their faces, the faces of callow youth, were expressions of good-natured camaraderie. Against his will he smiled at their capriciousness and followed them with his eyes, as if to compensate for not accompanying them further in their tipsy march toward the sea.

He turned to the shop window, criss-crossed with protective tape. Olive wood camels, souvenirs, inkpots, embroidered Slavic shirts. It all rose again to the surface of his mind.

Just that morning Kashka's second wife had worn an embroidered blouse exactly like that one, with the bouncing tassels on the front, looking as if it were a holiday. You might have thought for a moment, or been tempted to think, that it was she herself who invented the precious aphorism that she threw at him over breakfast, polishing and rehearsing it for a long time in her muddled brain before slapping it in his face.

Deep down in his guts he still felt the wound to his pride. When a woman hurts you, your own bitterness becomes the poison on her arrowheads.

A picture of the morning still in his mind: sitting at the table in Kashka's kitchen, separated one from another by her husband, who bolted his food hurriedly before leaving for work. Like a fool, Dov sat facing Regina and the omelette that she had fried for him, and he watched her determined jaws as they munched the portion of spinach that she ate daily to fortify her milk supply.

Her full breasts pressed through the transparent fabric of the blouse, the tassels bouncing against them.

The baby was asleep in the next room and Kashka's eldest daughter had left the house, immediately after her father. Some sense of expectancy hung in the air between them, so he imagined to himself, as if something was about to happen, without any effort or expression of willingness but of itself, as a continuation of the idle shuffling of the morning, with bare feet and limbs uncoordinated from sleep. In the three weeks that he had lived in this house, Kashka had not hesitated to go out every morning and leave him at home with his wife. It even occurred to Dov to suspect that he might be intentionally leaving her in his hands. Sitting like this, facing each other in the kitchen, whose tiny cell-like window had at last been reached by the sunlight, she swallowed the last leaf of spinach and suddenly raised her chin from the plate, saying in Russian, without hesitation or preamble: "Listen, Markovski, you can't make bread out of ideologies." A brief and witty sermon on the exploitation of the proletariat.

She is like a tame goose, always carrying a volume of Plekhanov under her wing as evidence, to prove that she is worthy of Katriel Hermoni. Then she tries, as it were, to blur, to soften what she has said. She lowers her eyes to the stove. But he is already packing his shirts into a suitcase—how theatrical! The omelette lies intact on the table, and the door slams behind him!

The glass of the shop window is cool between the strips of blackout paper. Inside the window are the moving reflections of long-haired girls. They mince along in noisy groups, wooden clogs bound to their ankles with colored threads, to the seashore, to loiter by the coffee houses, watched by the wide-eyed young Australians.

Your comrades—how they love to see you marching at the head of the procession with the flag in your hand, first to be arrested in the May Day demonstration. They love to listen to your lectures in the club while furtively glancing at their watches, and then to leave you, naturally, to pick up the papers, the books, and put the benches back in their places. They are happy to meet you at a street corner and pass the time of day with you, to glean fresh information from you, since you are familiar with the newspapers and you have all kinds of facts at your fingertips, to hear you singing fervently, eyes closed: "We shall create a new world, oh listen!" All of that! But to see you in the morning, every morning, at their table, to let you inhale the trivia of their existence, strip away the covering of varnish with those gimlet eyes and probe the cracks while you're still affecting the good humor of a natural member of the family? Alright, so you organized a strike—big hero! For a day or two, welcome to our bosom and we'll pinch your cheeks in high spirits and look at you, our eyes moist with pride. But to sit facing you like this for a week, two weeks, three, and to see reflected in you the recurring wave of our petty hostilities, of coupling at night and evenings of boredom? While everything that passes within us is forever locked away within you, stuck to your brain cells, and your seismograph is endlessly writing our true history?

For three weeks he was in and out of the Employment Office. Day by day he climbed the stairs until he knew, to the point of tedium, every stain on the wall, and he saw how one manly fellow out of twenty was chosen for work worthy of an insect. And when he began lecturing to them, the unemployed, all he achieved was a paralyzing sense of anger at their impatience, their lack of response, their smoking, their furtive grins and banal conversation, their scribbling with pencils on the dirty walls . . .

He found his reflection in the glass, abnormally tall and broad, his neck stretched forward like an inquisitive hen. He turned away from the window in bitterness and fixed his gaze on a house opposite, on a second-floor balcony. Mock-Corinthian pillars, an ornate, sentimental Star of David, and in the center—Senya Wolfson's balcony.

His meeting with Senya did not turn out the way Markovski had visualized it.

He was careful to leave the suitcase in the secretary's room. A bit seedy, but a real secretary! Very good! The steady clicking of a typewriter. He felt rebellious, as if this was an encounter with authority.

Senichka rose noisily to greet him. A light of "Here Comes the Bride" shone in his eyes as he ran from behind his big desk and leaped at him with open arms, drawing him into the smell of ironed starch and the stiffness of two fountain pens in his breast pocket: "Dear Borinka! You're here! And I was sure that you'd been deported." And standing back a little, clutching him with outstretched arms and a look of compassion: "How thin you've grown! Starving you, starving you, eh? They've squeezed you dry and left just a drop of spit. No, no, for God's sake, just don't get started . . . sit down, sit down."

He did not even attempt a reply, but it was as if he smiled inwardly, an unexpected sense of relief propelling his body into the big soft armchair.

"And how glum you look! The agony of ideas, delightful! Like the creasing of the face at the moment of ecstasy—delightful, but the scars remain . . ."

At once, without hesitation, he offered him Scotch—genuine, original stuff that he had only just acquired. Proudly he drew a charming flat bottle and two glasses from his middle drawer, and, with the open drawer still butting against his stomach, he poured the drink into the glasses, carefully matching the level of liquid in both, and, holding out the bottle as if to convince his guest of its quality, he said offhandedly, in English: "Keep it."

Suddenly Dov realized, with self-hatred, how deeply he needed just such a Senichka.

It was as if the door of the balcony, open onto the street, was touched by the balconies of the houses opposite, as if the people inside them were floating above the treetops. There was the sound of eternal, unrequited craving, cars changing gear, the trudging of strangers at the foot of the building, and the staccato babbling of sparrows. "There's a war on!" he said to himself once or twice, like a brief chorus. "There's a war on!"

Again he leaned back in the armchair and studied the English label on the bottle. Any moment now his friend would come up with a witty toast.

And so it was. "Sieg Heil to Comrade Molotov!" cried Senya. He assumed an expression of liberal moderation. In their early youth they had often drunk together in secret.

The drink shocked his stomach. Alarmed, Senya raised an eyebrow: "Well, what's new?"

He murmured something, with a touch of pride, about a short-age of resources in the resistance movement, as if to say: "You see! We're hungry! We're hungry too!" A small lie, as in fact he had only been hungry for twelve hours, but it was plausible enough, and it had the desired effect.

He waited for the protest with a kind of childish joy. And it came. "What a thing! My poor Boria! I'll call the secretary at once and have her pick up something from the Tnuva coffee shop. What an idea, coming to me early in the morning and enticing me with hugs and kisses into giving a fellow a drink on an empty stomach! Right away, I'll . . ."

"Alright, alright, calm down," he replied, hardening his heart. A pleasant vibration throbbed inside him.

"Well, then, are you on holiday today?" inquired Senya, calm-ing himself with difficulty and taking his place behind the desk, again offering his companion the bottle: "Keep it."

He took off his glasses and wiped them. The handkerchief was dirty and he was ashamed of it. For a moment he stared at the lenses and then answered offhandedly, but again with unrestrained pride, that this was "unpaid leave."

Senya was silent for a moment but then cried joyfully: "Ah,

Boria! My hero! Now I remember, of course, in all the news-papers! Congratulations, a real American-style strike! For three days the whole of Palestine was gasping to smoke Patron cigarettes, an entire cigarette factory standing to attention and saluting Boria Markovski! And then—chop-chop—unpaid leave! And the whole country is again exhaling putrid smoke—cheap and putrid! A contemptible technique." He nodded his head like an old doctor observing the all too predictable relapse of a drug-addicted patient.

Two rings from the telephone. Senya grabbed the receiver. On hearing the name of the caller he grimaced comically at his companion, as if secretly conspiring with him against whoever it was on the line. With obvious reluctance, he talked about quan-tities, building materials, and development sites, at the same time impatiently combing his hair with the fingers of his left hand.

It seemed that the years had not aged him since he last saw him, before the outbreak of war; they had just smoothed away a few rough edges with the touch of their striped wings. Those penetrating clownish eyes inviting conversation, that upper lip, always tensed capriciously, as if about to tell some new and ex-traordinary anecdote. Even in high school, Boria had been the nearsighted prodigy, with his loyal attendant Senya opening for him the doors of good Zionist households and wreathing his head with a crown of genius. When they met again in Palestine, Senya was in his junior year at the Herzliya High School, close to his father's table, whereas Boria, a sterile autodidact, was one of those national heroes who study after a day's work. During that period they sometimes met in the local branch of Working Youth, but then they were all poised for some traumatic new schism, and the two of them were on opposing sides, each stamping on the other's fingers.

Later, when we, "all the heretics and all the believers" (this was how Senya put it when he decided to turn his back on party politics), were howling and growling in the stifling cellar of the Ararat Café, arguing with bored women who were pretending to be bohemian about Bernstein and futurism, about revisionism and internationalism, this "treacherous raven" (as he called himself) was tending his father's camels by the Yarkon. And now—a telephone, tweed suit, a secretary, Scotch! Of course, of course, we despise him, interpreting his actions in the least favorable light, and he is always presented as a shining example of the narcissistic apostate.

As he spoke smoothly into the receiver, and then played with the coils of the cord instead of listening, Senya offered him an open packet of Players to show that he was not neglecting him.

For a whole week he had wrestled painfully with his pride before coming to see this "raven" of his, but this morning, deciding that this degradation was no worse than what had gone before, he made an effort to dispel it.

Now hold on there, Borinka, don't try to pretend that we did not loll around the club not too many years ago, arguing in a half-flippant style that concealed a powerful faith, dividing the offices of government between us. Tweedledum for Prime Minister, Tweedledee for Minister of Heavy Industry—and we were already discussing the question of whether the Foreign Minister should visit the capitals of the world in a top hat or not, when the waves of the "Internationale" were breaking on the shores of Palestine. And then—the clicking of cameras, Ribbentrop and Molotov embracing, baring twin sets of teeth on the pages of the world's press.

The receiver was replaced in its cradle. Senya sighed with relief and at once raised his eyebrows in an expression of compassion: "So, they've given you the boot, my Marxist Hercules. Kashka, naturally, all those ambitious dwarves—but you . . ."

"As I remember it, Hercules was never renowned for his intelligence," said Dov scornfully.

"That's exactly what I meant!" When his quips misfired, Wolfson was always able to extricate himself with dignity by means of pure bluff. "They have found that they have time for 'weak links,' " he said with professional scorn.

"Is this the time for witty recriminations? The bear grumbled at the bees when he put his shoulder to the full honeycomb," Dov replied, drawing on the well-worn proverb.

"The bear!" said Sashka pityingly. "The bear! Some miserable beggar from Rehovot with ten acres of orchard! The bear! For years he bent down and spat into every hole for irrigation, working his orchard with a slipped disc in his back—ha ha! Lord of the manor! Some beggar with a rundown workshop for tin cans—an 'international concern'!"

"It's a fact that there was a strike," Dov replied without pleasure, "and the workers supported us. Which means it was necessary."

"But management got a compromise out of the valiant bees within two days—to its own advantage," Senya laughed. "What enviable fighting spirit!"

"There was pressure," he murmured with great weariness. The combination of cigarettes and Scotch had set his stomach on edge. Wolfson took a deep breath, as if testing the flavor of what he was about to say.

"There *was* pressure! The feeblest nonentity from the Labor Union understands that we are standing on the threshold of great prosperity, that Palestine—Eretz Yisrael—is going to be the central army base of His Majesty's prestige in the Near East. Ask me! For pity's sake, you're yellow, dying, a leaf in autumn . . ."

Dov did not respond.

"When that *nudnik* arrives, tell him to wait," said the boss to the secretary, who had stopped her typing for a moment in the reception room. "It won't hurt him to stew for a while in that tasty juice of his. We're going out to eat! Afterwards we'll gobble him up!"

The "we" was music to Dov's ears, but at the same time he did not forget to take his suitcase with him. Senya snatched it from him, weighed it once or twice in his hand, and smiled.

At the table, which faced onto the street (Senya liked to be seen in public), the contractor directed jokes and flirtatious gallantries at the elderly waitress. As soon as they entered she came hurrying toward him in her orthopedic shoes and stared into his eyes with a concentrated gaze that penetrated the depths of his fastidious stomach, fanning its embers into life. Then she leaned over him slowly, as if they were plotting some delicious mischief together.

"And with your imitation chopped liver you can feed the rest of the cavaliers!" he called after her in convoluted German, full of mistakes. She turned to him with a smile and pressed two fingers to her heart in a gesture of promise.

He tried to stop himself from sniffing the food, ashamed by his flooding saliva and the turmoil in his throat. He had not known that such food still existed. Lately he had seen it only in cartoons featuring the black market. He pulled himself together and with practiced humility dug his fork into the roast liver and the steaming fried egg. Everything seemed blurred and tiny against the white tablecloth and the napkins in their laps.

Senya began describing his business dealings, as if it was his duty to give chapter and verse, to prove that there was somebody who was doing something. He tried to revive in his heart the feeling of their youthful hideout beside the lake, where long ago they used to spy on the girls bathing, Senya raping them with his mouth, one after another.

At this hour of early afternoon the commercial nerves of the street were drawn tight, softened only by the shapes of the tired women coming up from the sea, string-bags swinging in their hands, wet-haired children trailing behind them, munching popcorn.

"I go into the bar with Major O" says Senya. "A perfect gentleman, even the badges on his shoulder say: 'After you, Sir.' All for the sake of courtesy and respect and the anti-imperialist struggle. No man in this land will say that I'm a traitor, a dirty collaborator. On the contrary, it's as if they're all winking at me and know what I'm up to: bribe a cock and he'll even lay eggs! Major O goes out of the bar hopping on both legs, flushed to the coxcomb, a sweet rustle in his pocket and his head. And the British Empire—may its name be wiped off all the atlases! It's like they say in the Talmud: you can get it all from contractors! Major O isn't risking anything, all he has to do is give the go-ahead to some inflated building projects, with doubled and quadrupled estimates for construction materials. Just a little blood-letting from the veins of the government into the wallets of the chosen people! Afterwards, when it's all over, he can return to England and go into The City and Mrs. O can preside over afternoon tea and tell her friends about 'Poor Major O,' how he suffered from the Oriental climate when he was building all those camps, and you'd never believe how quickly the washing dries under the Middle Eastern sun . . ."

Dov laughed, but Senya lifted a finger and pointed solemnly at the fried egg on the table: "There you are! That's your world picture! In the middle, the yolk—fine, pure, whole. And all around it—disgusting, shapeless, burnt! That's the way they fry things here, the bastards! It oozes about, chaotic, evil . . . but, my dear boy," not allowing Dov to interrupt, "it goes into the stomach—mish-mash! It all goes! Your fine yolk goes! It all gets mixed up with pepsin and acids and satisfies your ravenous stomach."

Gradually Dov began to feel irritated at this self-confidence, all these clever proverbs, the gyrations of the waitress, who was now looking at him too with affection as she brought the second course and said in German-Hungarian: "All friends of Herr Wolfson are friends of mine!" And now Senya was interrogating him as if he were a prodigal son returning in penitence.

"I'm sure you're content with your lot," said Senya, patiently peeling off the golden skin of the goose, as if in the crudest, most unimaginative of caricatures, "a romantic, making sacrifices, persecuted at work. Where were you until you remembered that I existed? Did Kashka take you into his house? He must have mistaken you for a woman," he said scornfully and dwelt for a while on the finer qualities of his leader. Then he added, in a fatherly manner: "And why didn't you come to me straightaway? I could have used my influence, put things right . . . and I'm sure, I'd stake my life on it, that if the British were making arrests now, you'd want to be the first to be clapped into handcuffs! And how humiliating it would be if they didn't lead you, our martyr, in full view, the whole length of this street! Brother Bear, Brother Bear, haven't you always preached the importance of humor in the class struggle?"

Something stirred within him, something that angered and shamed him. He felt he no longer had that violent initial opposition, that rigid hostility; it was a pathetic yearning that he felt toward this man, his closest friend. He knew that he should take courage and defend himself.

For a while both were silent, but Senya is never simply silent. In his silence you feel his thoughts flowing rapidly into some hidden cup until it is filled to the brim, and then he speaks again.

"The clever thing, Borinka," he felt his friend's hand on his arm, "the clever thing is to be neither too dry nor too wet. If you're dry, you'll be broken; if you're wet, you'll be washed away."

This proverb (another proverb!) immediately halted the softening movement within him. He looked around him. The waitress was the only woman in the place. The tall, dark room, full of scraps of conversation both loud and soft, a mixture of tongues and perpetual smoke, was a fashionable meeting place for men of the world: tradesmen, agents, small and average salesmen— these were the people who spent the whole day cramped at the café table, not moving from it except to answer the telephone or go to the toilet. He fanned the flames of revulsion within him and felt slightly relieved.

When the old Hungarian woman brought the "real" Turkish coffee, setting the delicacy on the table with a display of ceremonious affection, Senya sniffed it, narrowing his eyes in a gesture of provocative suspicion, then said a "well" of resignation and indulgence. He waited until she had moved away and gently clasped Dov's hand to the tablecloth.

"And I'm not going to let you die on bread and butter!" he said, with a grin of compassion.

Dov knew that he should be grateful, but he felt the reverse. He looked at Senya, who was filling his mouth with the last morsel of poppyseed cake, once again pouring his thoughts into the hidden cup.

Suddenly he snapped his fingers in the air. "Don't you have some experience in children's affairs, education, working youth?"

"The children I know best are you and me," said Dov.

"Well then, you're an expert," laughed Senya. "Yech! This coffee should be eaten." Then he unfolded his suggestion in a manner ranging from thoughtful embarrassment to noisy enthusiasm. "And anyway, for this job there's no need to be a Makarenko.*"

Stunned, Dov began building a house of matchsticks on the stained tablecloth, bending over his work as if nearsighted.

"Isn't the idea to your taste, Borinka?" Senya Wolfson asked anxiously, staring intently at his face.

"My taste is crude, as you know," Dov replied coolly, addressing the match that he laid crosswise on the table, to form the roof gutter of a farmhouse. He decided he wanted no more advice from Mr. Shmuel Wolfson.

"The Talmud says: 'Buy yourself a friend.' You're a beggar, Boria."

Once more he was in the sticky delta at the lower end of Allenby Street, advancing slowly toward the heart of the city. Crowds of girls passed him again in the same narrow but constant stream, driving on toward the sea. The sharp rays of the sun impaled

---

* A revered Soviet educator.

him, the winter jacket burned under his arm. He let it drop and slung it over his suitcase.

"It's all useless," he thought. Watching the people around him, he felt a certain bitter relief in not knowing a single one; nobody was forcing him to speak, to inquire after his health, share an opinion, wink at him knowingly. All the army camps in Wolfson's hands, all the threads between his fingers, all the sympathetic, dismissive smiles. Suddenly a daring thought flashed into his mind, sending a thrill through his chest: He's afraid! Senya Wolfson is afraid, afraid of the "Evil Eye," of those who will pass the word that Senya Wolfson the contractor sent him, "the Marxist Hercules," to pluck golden apples in the sacred garden of King George VI.

All at once the business took on a new, gratifying, comprehensive significance, part of a damnable human phenomenon. The degradation was a confirmation of the theoretical distinctions.

"Ass-licker, quisling, toady, bribe-chaser! 'Phone me during the week! *Phone me!*' The big boss, official telephone and private telephone. With him, eat fried chicken; without him, carry on, gnaw at the backbone, probe the social perversions of Mamushka Wolfson!"

Carefully he synchronized his watch with the clock in the square. A long time, far too long, was left until the evening, until the obligatory session of the Central Committee. At Kashka Hermoni's house, naturally.

Within the course of one day everything had collapsed and given way beneath his feet, and there was nothing except him, the street, the suitcase, and a heavy weight of depression.

There is a saying that Katriel Hermoni never tires of repeating to all hearers, on the rostrum of the committee and in the pages of our newspapers: "An ordinary man may be a fool or a scoundrel, a pack mule or a leech, sensitive or crude, but when he walks with the masses, in their direction, all his qualities and deficiencies disappear at once. When he is with the masses, with the proletariat, he marches together with them to greet the higher, Socialist man."

Kashka Hermoni appointed himself long ago, with a touch of humor of course, to the Ministry of Education of the Socialist Eretz-Yisrael—a second Lunacharski.* With a sense of admiration, they say that, with his intellect, he could even interpret the views of a revisionist on the run from a Siberian labor camp.

That evening the last string of the harp of the past was snapped. A dim silence without anticipation and without implication. Dov's ribs felt the hard floor beneath the blankets. He pulled the sheet up to his chin and his feet were exposed. He pulled it down with his feet and his neck was exposed. He turned his face to the wall.

Kashka's daughter Maya tossed about in the gloom on the sofa opposite, and at that moment he heard the anxious, urgent sucking of the baby.

He would have done better to have gone down to the nearest bomb shelter, to lie down on the public bench, wrap himself in his jacket, and sleep well in the stink of ashes and stale excrement.

Kashka had spread the bedding on the floor for him with his own hands, as if nothing had happened, as if he didn't know about the progress of his second wife in the sphere of philosophy. He, Dov, had been afraid to refuse, lest Kashka see this as a petty bourgeois reaction to what had happened at that evening's meeting.

He remembered the neighbors who had hammered on the ceiling, and in spite of himself he laughed. "You can argue as much as you like, but quietly! Quietly! For God's sake, let us get some sleep! Sleep!"

He was disgusted with the image of himself that he had projected that evening. Preaching all those unrehearsed words, those immature emotional statements. He had seized on trivia and made

---

* First Minister of Education in Soviet Russia.

them the central points, and the others had taken hold of them and rushed away into side tracks, into abstract theorizing, evading the things that really mattered.

He should have sat quietly beforehand in some avenue, rehearsing, constructing an idea with proofs, evidence, conclusions, solutions; but instead he had rushed like a lunatic from street to street before drifting into some matinee performance in a hall full of children.

With a pang of hatred he remembered the scorn in Regina's haughty eyes, suddenly opening wider as she came in with the sheets, to help her husband lay out the bedding on the floor.

Until now nobody had understood why Kashka had exchanged his first, beautiful wife, with her roots firmly planted in the Palestinian soil, for this new immigrant with her provincial expression, her artificial intellect, and the deliberately pathetic statements with which she sought favor and acceptance: "Me? I'm a simple woman, I'm a proletarian!" Meaning, everything that Katriel Hermoni does, he does for my sake! Dov knew that now he was thinking about her and the morning in order to dispel from his mind Kashka and the evening. He was always so impatient in debate, passionate and impassioned, while all the others were still cool and sober. He went over their words in his mind, trying to understand them, to find in them an understanding of himself, a vague, conjectural justification.

From the start Kashka had succeeded in presenting him as a stage comedian, bathed in the rosy light of ridicule:

Dov: "But we know that the Soviet advance came to a halt in a certain place!"

Kashka: "The conquest of Eastern Poland by the Soviets only came about, and I'm surprised at you, Comrade Markovski, in order to block the advance of the Nazis."

Dov: "But it halted! Did it halt or didn't it? It halted! Everybody knows it, we aren't blind and deaf!" A hasty, emotional outburst, sounding comical.

Kashka (with all the venom under his tongue): "*Everybody?*
And who is this 'everybody,' may we ask, and what is the 'certain place'?"

Dov: "The advance was broken off on the *exact* line that was agreed with Hitler in the first place!"

Again he felt that ceaseless throbbing in his gut, horror at what he had said, a sense of ruin, his despairing cry—"It was the conquest of Eastern Poland that enabled the German army to turn to the Western front!"

The uneasy silence that followed, the raised eyebrows, something in the air that boded ill, the flash of the guillotine in Kashka's eyes and the restrained reply, the reverse of what he had expected, that air of calm authority.

"First of all, my dear Boria," he said, "Why do you have to try out your new tunes on my ear?" All the cards in his hands. All of them laughing with relief, enjoying the dialogue, the collective wisdom sharpened into one arrowhead, all turning their backs on him with contrived emphasis. "I don't know where this new information of yours comes from, Comrade Markovski, but what *we* know is that your conquest, in double quotation marks, has been accomplished without any red stains unless we count the red flags with the agreement—whether you like it or not— with the full agreement of the Poles! Each and every one of us desires such a conquest for himself—and at once."

And his voice again, a faint buzzing from a fearful void, a crushed head peering out from the ruins in search of an ally: "It may be convenient to think so!" (The throbbing in his gut.) "But the battle for Grodno! The battle for Grodno! A battle in the very heart of the city! Who was fighting? Eh? Angels from Heaven?" (Would *nobody* tell him who had been fighting whom, and why?) "And the Soviet fleet chasing the Polish submarine that escaped from the Baltic?"

Kashka, with emphatic scorn, with a knowing grin toward the others, replied: "We certainly didn't know that our Odessa was populated by such enthusiastic Polish patriots, and you, Markovski, our oracle, can you be sure that these warriors were workers, proletarians? Were they? Did they appear—outside *your* sources of information—anti-Nazis?" Like an experienced orator arguing from the public stage with a heckler, Kashka went on: "And does he still, *still* not know what brought the Red Army into Poland?" He turned to the rest of the company, as a sign that Dov was no longer worthy of individual attention. "The good tidings of the revolution! Distribution of land! The transfer of industry into the hands of the workers! The formation of soviets!" All Kashka's fingers clenched with the tension of these stirring achievements. "All of this makes no impression on Dov Markovski. He must be blind, deaf, and dumb! But what makes him excited? What makes him shit in his pants? Some ship in Grodno! Some woman that nobody's ever heard of, a dockyard whore! Without even a work permit!"

The admiring grins of the whole company and a sudden outburst from Grisha, demands for "fundamental clarification," the mistakes of the past, hints of impending ostracism. "I ask myself," says Grisha, "what has suddenly happened to Comrade Markovski, what *catastrophe* has befallen him, that he's suddenly lost all ability to distinguish the trivial from the crucial, to tell plus from minus?"

And Dov's own voice: "The ship is not trivial!" (That's the way they always seize on details when the whole is too heavy to bear.) "It's true, the Red Army brought this and this and that, but there are other things, other things, that it can never provide! It's a symbol! I'm choosing my words carefully, but I feel, I sense, that this revolution imposed . . ."

"Imposed? Feel? Sense? *Imposed!*" shouts Kashka rising from his seat, the stunned hypnotized glances fixed on him as if he were a dangerous lunatic about to jump from a high roof. "*Imposed?*"

His own voice: "This revolution that came from outside will

be exploited first and foremost as a new experiment in Stalinism! And don't pretend you don't know perfectly well what I mean."

"No! We don't know, but Sir Wolfson apparently knows well enough!" It was Grisha's voice, provocative and threatening. How did they manage to know, and from where?

The movement in the room, hasty rising from seats, angry shrugging of shoulders, even out-flung fists, and the voice: "We can't allow this to go on!" Wolfson's name repeated endlessly, pale threatening faces, stunned, embarrassed, confused. And suddenly the sense of instantaneous, momentary clarification, as if he had been working for a long time on the solution to a crossword puzzle and now, suddenly everything comes together, becomes clear. The picture is complete for a moment but then immediately blurred; a strange relief followed by a sense of oppression ten times worse than before. He hears his voice crying out plaintively into the sea of angry faces, into the rancorous eyes, that all the achievements of the Socialist Movement are going to hell, that there is no longer any opportunity for criticism, that cases are being judged before they even come to trial! And suddenly the knocking from upstairs, the voices of the neighbors from their windows: "Let us get some sleep, you swine!" And all eyes look to the ceiling, as if God himself were coming down to judge the case of Boria Markovski. The comical gesture of Kashka, pushing his head down between his shoulders to protect himself from the knocking, but at the same time stretching out his hands with the equanimity of a conductor: "Let him say his piece—it's healthier for him and more so for us." The silence that suddenly reigned, and Kashka's voice glided over the stillness.

"All of us admire sincere feelings," he began, "and Boria knows as well as anyone that we don't despise sentiment; without sentiment there would be no comrades prepared to sacrifice so much. But let us suggest to Comrade Markovski that he weigh matters on the scales of science and not the grocer's scales. Let us keep our emotional delicacies for the brighter days to which we all look forward no less than Comrade Markovski does—and we, at least, know what we are looking forward to! History is not at all interested in the sensitive spiritual machine of Markovski, the subjective individual . . ." His voice gaining in pitch and emphasis as if he were lecturing to an audience of beginners on different approaches to the perception of reality. And again, his offer of help for a fresh analysis "to put the engine back on the rails," the necessity of bringing the matter before the Secretariat, and a few words on "agents of British Intelligence."

Finally, turning suddenly to Grisha as to a man whose reliability was never to be doubted, Kashka's voice announced: "The next item on the agenda—the movement against foreign imports."

The voice of Senya Wolfson: "Stalinist fanatic!"

The voice of Kashka Hermoni: "Subjective idealist!"

And he himself craving to burst into Chaliapinesque laughter.

The baby began to howl. The light came on without warning, and he turned his face from the wall. When his eyes cleared he saw Regina in a white gown, two big yellow blotches on her swollen breasts. When she glanced at him he closed his eyes and breathed heavily. Suddenly the baby's crying stopped. Then there were the sounds of sucking and moans of contentment. The springs of Maya's bed creaked. She was awake too.

From the next room came the sound of rustling newspapers. Kashka was not asleep either. That evening, it seemed, he had lost Kashka as well. He turned his face to the wall again. The swellings in the white plaster bulged before his naked eyes and his ears took in the efforts of the suckling woman, hardening her heart toward the man, now a stranger to her, who lay wrapped in her sheets on the floor. Tomorrow she will hasten to throw them in with the dirty laundry to wash away the stranger's scent.

He began to sink into slumber. Tomorrow he will enlist—and that will be that! He will stand in line, baring his chest for a doctor whom he does not know, be given a bed, a number. Every day a marching drill, canned bully-beef, sunburn, orders, just orders, not worth thinking about. The High Commissioner and Moshe Shertok will address the passing parade. The British sergeant will bark an order, and the soldiers will clamber onto the trucks. They will sing "Here is a marching wall of steel, like steel is our spirit in battle." On the bench, opposite him, will sit some boy soldier from Hadera or Haifa. They will sit thus, facing each other, as their bodies absorb the rolling of the truck. They will stare into each other's eyes in silence, until they reach Kantara, Cairo . . .

His friends will sit on the bench in the club and look at his regular place beside the lecturer's stand. Someone will say: "Already at the time of the Moscow trials he was so unstable, even then we noticed something."

And a woman's voice, Regina's, complacent, sanctimonious: "And now he's gone and joined the imperialist front."

And suddenly Wolfson's voice, like the voice of a cheerful prewar travel agent: "What I recommend for you is fresh air, Swiss scenery, close to God Almighty."

Again the sight of the comrades in the club, staring at his regular place, and somebody saying maliciously, in a fake bass voice: "Well, yes, Boris Isakovitz has gone to the people."

He was trapped. He had never felt it, and yet here he was, trapped, as if he always had been trapped, a captive lion cub in the eyes of those whom he had taught to believe. Ah, Boria, Boria, you subjectivist porridge you . . . how you would have liked, muddlehead, how you would have liked everything to be always vibrant, at the beginning of its bloom, refreshing the eye, open to the light, and the heart—a kind of political mollusc— to spill without shame, without hindrance, into the festive streets.

Now, completely awake, he heard in the darkness the regular breathing of the children.

He slipped outside quietly, into the night. And until dawn he roamed the streets of the awakening city.

The voice of Wolfson on the telephone: "Borinka? I *knew* you'd call!" (Another blow.) "Come around, I'm waiting. Where are you?"

He called the office from the restaurant opposite. He felt humiliated in his betrayal, as the others had seen him last night, and he could not rid himself of this external evidence, like a sudden emptiness, a vacuum dragging all toward it.

2
THE BEAUTY
AND THE OFFICER

Senya rang the bell with mischievous ferocity. On the ancient door, with its studs of polished brass, was screwed a copper plate bearing the name of Yehiel Wolfson.

"Who's there?" came a weary, suspicious voice, accompanied by the sound of a slow shuffling of feet.

Some twelve years had passed since Dov heard the voice of Batya Wolfson in Odessa.

"*Bonjour, Madam!*" cried Senya with the air of an impatient suitor. "Are you alone?"

Senya's mother appeared in the doorway, smiling apprehensively at her son. All the splendor that Dov remembered had fled from her body to be replaced by a corseted matronly corpulence. She looked worried. Suddenly she noticed the guest. "And who is this?" she inquired, as if asking after a child, and at once she became confused. "My God! It's . . . How he's grown! And the glasses! He's a real adult."

Astonished, she studied the tall body of the guest, then said reluctantly that there was already somebody visiting, a lady from "up there," who would soon be on her way. Would they mind leaving and coming back in a quarter of an hour? But Senya winked and burst into the house, his mother following, still with obvious reluctance.

In the drawing room, beside the big oval table with its ancient and ornate Russian-style cover, sat a blonde woman in her early twenties, watching them with an eagerness that disappeared as soon as she had greeted the son of the house. It was obvious that she knew him, because Batya Wolfson glanced at her sharply, as if to ask what she meant by such a cold gesture of welcome.

"Frie—da!" cried Senya in delight. "What perfect timing! Mamushka has a special talent for collecting pretty girls," he explained to his friend.

He waited for her to reply, but she lowered her head slightly, as if contradicting him with dignity.

"Well, sit down, sit down," said Batya angrily, not averting her gaze from the girl's face. While she questioned her son about his latest activities, totally ignoring the two guests, Dov sat staring at the girl's face, which previously, at a distance, had looked ridiculously blurred. Her expression was rather too serious, too emphatic, the fair hair, almost albino, drawn back firmly behind her ears and fastened at the nape with an unfashionable double clasp, an arrangement proclaiming, like the caption to a portrait: "I am beautiful, but I don't admit it!" Her yellowish blouse, padded at the shoulders and several sizes too large, with the letters "F.A." embroidered on the bust in European script, made her look like an immigrant. Everything about her invited change, modification, rearrangement.

"This is Frieda Auerbach," said Senya, seated beside his mother, hinting that he had noticed his friend's preoccupation. He felt in his soft hand, the hand of a cigarette worker, the shock of her hard touch.

"My childhood buddy!" added Senya, walking toward the girl, who leaned on the arm of the antique chair. "This is Boria M., Professional Revolutionary!" He spread his lips wide with an air of lightheaded insolence. Dov felt as if Senya had shaken him and turned him inside out, like the gizzard of a chicken.

"I'd like you to meet," he smiled, overcoming his annoyance with a theatrical bow toward Wolfson, "my impresario!"

Senya adopted the expression of a father surprised at the cleverness of his offspring, and at once he turned to the girl as if handing over his treasure to her safekeeping.

"You'll have ample opportunity to know him. You'd have to crack open dozens of men like me, like safes in the Anglo-Palestine Bank, to find one heart like that of Boria Markovski."

"Thank you for saving me the trouble," the girl replied. He heard her voice for the first time. Her voice was too clear. Her eyes, set some distance apart, flashed at him for a moment, at Dov. He took this as a sign that she shared his grievance.

Batya Wolfson, apparently ignoring this Hebrew conversation, and deprived of her son's attention, began asking the guest about the health of his parents, sincerely sharing his regret that they had stayed behind in Odessa and asking how he had managed to come to Palestine alone. All the while, her eyes kept watch on the other two.

"Mamushka," her son's voice interrupted her, "how about some tea?" Dov felt disappointed when she stopped asking him questions and rose obediently to her feet.

When she had disappeared into the kitchen, Senya hurriedly informed the girl that she had probably guessed for herself that he, Boria, his good friend from childhood, the one and only Boria, would be joining them "up there." And at once, with mockery in his eyes, he announced them betrothed.

The girl's reaction suggested that she did not like the idea. He preferred this conclusion to the interpretation of her expression as a sign of disappointment. Senya drew two cigarettes halfway from his pack.

She declined the offer. "No, thank you, yours are too strong for me." That lucid voice again, as if she were determined to show her strength. Senya bared his teeth, winked at his friend as if understanding a profound hint, then turned to her with his most charming expression. Boria hurriedly produced a crumpled pack of Latif. His was accepted immediately, plucked out with a chewed fingernail.

"Angel cigarettes," Senya smiled again, consoling himself with a display of wit and offering her his lighter, "but fire from Satan's furnace."

Markovski stood up to look for an ashtray. Some of the furniture he remembered from his childhood, from the Wolfsons' big grey house. Here it looked foreign and dejected between the bare walls.

As he rummaged through the sideboard with its intricate black wood engravings, he felt a sweet shudder that he could not account for. He looked again, and saw a small, yellowing picture hung above the mirror. He took it and examined it closely. Then, in Odessa, the figure in the picture had seemed to him that of a mature woman and now it seemed the image of a young girl.

Senya was already standing at his shoulder.

"She was the most beautiful woman in all Poland."

At that moment Batya Wolfson came in carrying a tray and saw at once what was going on.

"Stop it, stop that!" she cried in Yiddish, hastily putting down the tray on the table. "Give it to me at once." She rushed at her son and snatched the old photograph from his hands.

"Why? Why?" he cried like a protesting child. Then, putting on the expression of a sulky infant, he grabbed the picture back and clapped it between his hands, while she stood resisting him helplessly.

"The most beautiful woman in all Poland!" Batya Wolfson turned to the girl, to whom the words had been addressed, looking perplexed.

"She's still beautiful now," said Dov. He regretted it immediately; the words sounded impertinent.

"Oh, Borinka, oh, what are you talking about?" cried the son, giggling as he bore his plunder beyond the range of his mother's flailing arms. The childish demeanor of "the great contractor" was amusing and embarrassing at the same time. "Mamushka, come on, seriously now, relax, sit down, drink some tea, come on now."

Batya Wolfson obeyed again. She sat down at the table and distributed the cups in silent anger, her lips trembling slightly.

"What she has now," the contractor turned to face the girl with an air of enthusiasm, "all that is left to her now are relics, just tiny relics of a rare, wonderful beauty. Mamushka, the tea's going cold! Here." He handed the photograph to the girl, his mother still quivering with resentment. The photograph was very old, mounted on thick cardboard, but the ornate monogram of the photographer stood out fresh and clear. Unconsciously Dov leaned over the girl's head. Formality eased as they looked at the image of the young woman from the past, whose curves were well defined in spite of her thinness. His eyes studied the high bosom, the lean profile turned slightly to one side with a touch of ingenuous narcissism, the virginal eyes that still did not know the power of their beauty . . . Suddenly he felt that he was trampling crudely on a pure and untouchable world.

Batya Wolfson could not resist the temptation to join the group clustered around the photograph, as if wishing to discover how she had looked then through the eyes of others.

For another moment they gazed in silence, in a strange idyllic serenity, at the shiny satin blouse, at the long plait of hair hanging down to the waist, at the thin body leaning with aristocratic ease on an old garden fence, stumps of classical pillars on the painted background of a dense romantic grove that rays of sunlight were trying to pierce, paper flowers scattered in "natural" fashion on the ground.

"Well?" Senya ruined everything with his voice. Batya Wolfson withdrew at once as if caught red-handed in an act of indiscretion. "Doesn't it drive you mad? Now, Frieda, you'll understand what happened to the saliva glands of the Russian officers," Senya teased. "It doesn't matter, Mama," he roared, "We shall pay respect to history!" Again he gestured at the tea cup while she still ground her teeth. And by himself he began to sip. "This is tea!" he announced.

"Do you understand?" He turned his attention to the girl. "All the officers used to swarm around her shop with tongues hanging out. They were ready to throw down and burn at her feet all their medals and fine uniforms."

Batya Wolfson, who still did not have the courage to protest, was shaking her head incredulously over her glass of tea, her lips set in a bitter grimace; but from time to time her aged eyes looked up, unconsciously, to pluck the flowers of her guests' admiration, whatever they might be.

"The grandparents on her side I never knew. The story is shrouded in mystery. But they had a very distinguished shop that sold all kinds of *tsatskes*. How do you translate that? Hey, Boria, you're the brains around here."

"Dry goods," he replied cautiously, knowing that his friend needed no help from him but was trying to draw him into the story.

"Dry goods! Exactly! But not just any old dry goods store. This was a *magasin*, a gallery *à la Paris*! Eh, Mamushka? Lacework from Switzerland, isn't that right? Carpets from Bukhara, Armenia? Slippers from—well, from where, Mama?"

His mother said nothing, but brooded angrily. "Izmir!" said Boria, feeling sorry for her.

"Izmir!" cried Senya like an advocate presented with the evidence that will prove his case. "Izmir! *Haute couture*! And the clientele—no riffraff. Their customers were the generals and equerries of Tsar Nicholas." He rose from his seat with a ceremonious gesture. "The Emperor of all Russia, King of Poland, Prince of this, that, and the other . . ." He paused to give the girl time to laugh. "They used to come once a year, in summer, to hunt game in Spella, at his *dacha*, next door to Mamushka's township. But where did they go for their hunting, the Gentile breed? To the forests? What did they want with dark forests if they could visit a real *magasin*—*haute couture*—and inside, such goodies as these?"

"Senichka!" hissed Batya Wolfson, but immediately she pursed her lips. Senya ignored the interruption.

"But this one? This one was an idiot. To look straight into their eyes and offer hot porridge for their breakfast—no! This one didn't know how to exploit what nature had given her." He smiled, seeing the face of the girl, which for a moment gaped at him like the face of a deaf mute. "Do you understand? Instead of that, she lowers her modest eyelashes, rolls her sleeve down to here, to the wrist—Heaven forbid that any Gentile equerry should lust after her elbow . . ."

"Oh, Senichka!" Dov murmured in mounting discomfort.

"Oh? Why do you say 'Oh'?" he protested, with a pretense of astonishment and anger. "Isn't that exactly how it was, Mama?"

Batya Wolfson shrugged her heavy shoulders and let them droop, helpless when confronted by this shameless son of hers, but her eyes revealed the childish anticipation with which she was following his story, momentarily forgetting to protest.

"That's how it was, exactly! Just so! But," he raised his voice as a hint that he had at last arrived at the punch line of his story, "but there was one officer there, a very handsome fellow, the kind any woman would swoon over. His eyes—like two wells of Kvass . . . Is she laughing? Look, she's laughing! How do I know all this, eh? And his legs—a little bent, like this, not from the

English disease, Heaven forbid, but from riding, an honorable deformity. The little Jewish heart from the *shtetl* going clinkety-clank in time to the clatter of the spurs."

The girl winced from time to time, angry and embarrassed, and Dov felt sympathy for her.

"And what did the officer want?" He stretched out his hand, great sadness in his eyes, enjoying the girl's discomposure. "Well, what did the handsome man want? Tell us, Mama! She still hasn't gotten over it yet! If you won't tell us, I will! He asked for one thing only. The Tsar was holding a banquet, as he did from time to time, in the palace of Spella, a place strictly out of bounds to the local people, and here was the officer with his eyes of Kvass and reverent manners, standing on the other side of the counter and appealing to her in a trembling voice: would Miss Batya Yakovlevna be so kind as to come with him to the banquet, so that he could present her to the Tsar and the court? He only wanted to show him what rare flowers bloomed in these provincial forests. She had nothing to fear, and if she was afraid, the lady could come with a friend or a sister—no need even to dance, just to be presented, show themselves. And when this foolish girl turned down her sleeves to the wrist, the officer pleaded: 'And if the honorable Miss Yakovlevna gains favor in the eyes of the Tsar, her *magasin* will receive a concession. The whole town, the whole area, the entire district! If she will only come . . .'

"All of this with reverence and perfect manners. Where were you then, you girls?" He turned to Frieda. "But she, Miss Ya-kovlevna, turns her back on him, stoops over some drawer full of rags, because this was, to be honest about it, nothing but a dingy little shop, begging your pardon, Mama. Since she was a child she'd heard people gossiping . . . Just once to peep at, to see the Tsar, the royal palace, taste champagne, dance a quadrille, she, she alone, the only one out of all the *shtetl*, she, with her rags and buttons . . ."

Batya Wolfson was nodding her old head slowly and mournfully, entirely forgetting that there was an audience present. Senya stealthily drew the girl's attention to this movement. She winced and narrowed her eyes.

"But our officer," he went on, "has a wolf's blood in his veins! He doesn't give up! Every day he arrives and buys a handkerchief, a napkin, another handkerchief. He's building up a museum of handkerchiefs! And selling—wretched Jews have no choice but to sell! Until one day, when there's nobody about, the poor fellow can't resist—really, Mamushka, you played a cruel game!—and he takes the girl's little hand as she gives him the thirtieth or fortieth handkerchief and—woe, alas—he kisses it! And what a moustache—like Chinese silk! And she, what does she do? With her free hand—God have mercy—she slaps his cheek!

"Afterwards there's the usual commotion, groveling apologies from the heads of the community, panic, everyone paralytic with fear, and there are even some who secretly complain about the girl's brazenness. In the end, the end, who knows what the end would have been if my late father, who was, Borinka, let's not deny it, a coarse man—with no charming manners, without any style or distinction—who happened to be there at the time on business, had not snatched her up, taken her by the hair and dragged her off to our Odessa, to our timber business, to a nice mother-in-law with a matron's wig."

Batya Wolfson groaned softly, and her head, lost in oblivion, resumed its earlier nodding, as if immersed in a prayer of devotion.

There was a stunned silence. But Senya, like a wagon driver who lets his horses go for a moment on a downhill stretch, giving them their heads for a while, took a firm grip on the reins again.

"And that officer? Think about it! He could be a doorman now, Borinka, in the Grand Hôtel de Paris, or a chauffeur on the Alexander Bridge. She always had a sense of history, my Mamushka! Well, how about that?" He turned to Frieda.

"Of course," she replied, with a surprising sharpness in her tone, "if that hadn't happened you wouldn't be alive!"

He caressed her with his eyes and then closed them, as if sampling a vintage wine.

Dov, who had been entranced for a moment by the strange magic of the story, glanced quickly at the old woman, flooded by waves of memory:

"And if she were given the whole thing to relive, if it were possible, would she have gone to this castle of Spella?"

At the same time his eyes took in the strained expression on the girl's face and the contented smile of his companion.

The old woman blinked, shuddered, then stared into space, but suddenly, as if grasping an answer from the depths of the distant past, she wagged her heavy chin at him in pathetic entreaty and sneered. "Look at him, please, just look at him," she snapped. "Look at him, my clever boy, this cunning . . . You shouldn't have told them, Senichka, you shouldn't have!"

"How profound!" commented Senya, his laughing eyes watching the girl. "Well, what do you think?"

"But he knows how to tell a story," said Frieda Auerbach dryly.

An appetite for tantalizing gossip was bubbling to the surface of Dov's heart, an instinct to sniff out discreetly the meaning of what was going on around him. The mother had now recovered her composure. She gave her female guest a sharp look that said clearly: you've heard enough.

It was not hard for Dov to guess that in fact Batya Wolfson did not know how to handle this girl, who ought to be submissive to her, except that life in this land had become so confused and so adrift from its normal framework that it was no longer possible to judge the hierarchy of people. Furthermore, he had the impression that in a sense this Frieda reveled in Batya Wolfson's hatred and was even at pains to cherish it in her own way.

The old woman was now making an effort to erase everything and restore herself to her rightful place. For a while she returned to a display of interest in her son's business dealings, inquiring about some building development in Herzliya and asking what had emerged from his meeting with the city architect. And throughout this conversation she lashed her guests with looks of pride, as if to say: "So, you see?"

Senya wriggled and fidgeted in his chair like an overheated cement mixer. Instead of absorbing the fire of his mother's pride, now so insistent, he tried to distract her by offering her cakes, removing an invisible hair from her dress.

"What about our Boria?" he said suddenly. "Just imagine, he's got the urge to work in your institution."

The old woman shuddered and stared at her son's laughing eyes as they flitted about the room.

"Boria? How is this, Boria? What is this, Boria? Have you gone mad— *up there*?"

"Isn't the place respectable enough for him?" he asked carefully, bending toward her.

"The place isn't respectable for friends of my son!" she exclaimed.

"I'll confirm that!" said Frieda calmly.

Batya Wolfson clenched her jaws and her face grew pale.

"It seems to me that the two of us, Mrs. Wolfson and I, have already settled the business that we needed to discuss," she said, rising to her feet, her eyes shattering every bone in the body of her patroness.

He saw her standing up for the first time. To him she looked pretty and radiant, and he could see that her breasts were firm, although her blouse and skirt were too big for her, as if she had borrowed them. Hurriedly she snatched up her handbag from the chair, an old-fashioned handbag adorned with a string of white beads. "I've finished," she said to Dov, who felt himself woven, against his will, into a new web. She wished him, only him, a "Happy New Year." Unconsciously he wished that she would not go yet. His eyes were drawn to the motion of her body, which was a little stiff, as if she did not like to move her limbs freely in their presence, and he noticed the worn heels of her shoes. Wolf-son jumped up and opened the door for her, in the style of a trained doorman. As she passed him Dov heard him say: "But you haven't finished with me yet." The commonplace words disturbed him. Then Senya accompanied her as far as the stair-case.

"She has no diploma," said Batya Wolfson after a long silence, angrily swallowing the dregs of her tea.

"But she's pretty," said Senya, who had come in with the air of a man returning after a long journey. "She just needs a bit of polish." He looked to his friend for confirmation. "But that's what money gives you."

"So brazen, no diploma—like a *rebbitzin*" said Batya Wolfson. Senya clicked his tongue.

"Impudence succeeds even against God," he said. "The Mon-tessori madam was better, huh? Mama had a woman like that in her house once—*bitte schön, danke schön*, at twenty pounds a month, no less—but her 'cases' suddenly stopped getting up in the morning. Mama baked cakes in her honor and sang her praises twice a week in front of the guests: 'A Ph.D. from Switzerland!' "

"Don't you interfere," said Batya Wolfson.

"I wish there was something to interfere with," he replied, opening the sideboard and bringing out apples. He bit into one and threw the other to his friend.

"When there's no Eve, what's the use of an apple?" he com-plained, the apple between his teeth, challenging his mother.

"A peacock, a peacock, just like his father," said Batya Wolfson. "A female passes by his tail, and already he's full of eyes."

"What will I have to do there?" Dov asked Senya as they walked again down the little street, in the shadow of the balconies. For some obscure reason, Batya Wolfson stopped resisting him. With two words of agreement she had taken him onto her "staff," and with one she determined the scale of his salary, paying no attention to the protests of her son. All this time it seemed to him, to Dov, that the three of them were playing some game that had no connection with the real world.

"Thread the annual budget of Batya Wolfson on a cord and hang it round your neck," replied Senya with the same light-hearted mockery. His experience in deciding the destiny of important things had equipped him to evaluate the significance of minor details.

"All that business with your mother . . . ," said Dov.

"She kills herself for money to legitimize bastards, and in the process she defiles herself. Every day of her life she courts humiliation." Senya sounded sincere. "Did you see?"

Dov was unwilling to probe and ask why her son made no effort to help her.

"It won't be easy for you up there," said Senya, and he laughed. "There won't be anyone to strike against! But of course *she* will be there! Try to put a finger between her teeth!" All of this in a tone of easy, noncommittal scorn. "Just now I'm jealous of you," he said suddenly, "but only for this minute, sixty seconds—and that's all."

Noon lay heavy on Allenby Street, but the cafés were already packed with customers. Business had never flourished as it did now. Since the bombing, the people had taken to the streets in force—dancing, public entertainments, imaginative French hair-styles—like a firm of undertakers celebrating after a funeral.

"GERMAN TROOPS INVADE ROMANIA IN FORCE. HAS ITS CONQUEST BEGUN?" asked the headlines of the morning paper.

"No news," said Senya, curling his lip. Suddenly his expression changed, and he started to laugh. "Some day I'll tell you how I bought timber in Romania. The story will drive you mad. Of course, it won't do you any good."

When Maya Hermoni entered
the bathroom of the hostel carrying a worn kitchen towel (one of
those that Regina had set out for her, accompanied by indignant
and repetitive protests at the "sacrifices" that she was making),
everything that had gone before was wiped away from her heart.
All that remained were her blurred and flickering impressions of
the morning journey with her father to the new place, her question
about the cornstalk, which her father was unable to answer, his
hesitant, hypocritical smile, seeking to secure both her acquiescence and his own peace of mind, his goodbye kiss, his haste to
leave, and the strange relief that descended on her when he went
and left her here, with her possessions.

All this, together with all the days of her past, rapidly shrank
and contracted into one tiny, motionless point. The new place

suddenly opened up before her, expanding with her perception of every new feature.

In the room, much of it obscured by dense clouds of steam, she noticed the blurred shapes of a number of girls, some dressed and some naked, all of them watching her, she sensed, and judging her.

Now was the time to say something pleasant, to gain sympathy with some witticism that would transform her at once into one of those girls who stood there watching her. The thought of belonging to them appealed to her with a special force, but she could think of nothing to say. She stood still for a long moment, absorbing the soft, steamy gloom. From the little window, above the bath, a milky light penetrated the room. Her nostrils caught a whiff of paraffin, mingled with the scents of soap, urine, wet walls and shoe polish. At that moment of nervous adjustment she became aware of the monotonous and menacing racket that filled the room.

Suddenly the face of a girl came into clear focus. She saw damp hair and heavy freckles, then another four or five faces. They were engrossed in attending to themselves, as if she did not exist. Because of the constant noise, their conversation was like a mime show. One of them stood up in the bath to soap her legs, another was standing on tiptoe on the wooden mat in front of a small mirror. All this activity exuded a powerful sense of freedom, of expertise in the ways of the world.

She stepped forward cautiously, not knowing how far she was allowed to walk in shoes, until she found a peg where she hung her embarrassing kitchen towel among unfamiliar gym shorts and shirts. The hook startled her; it was carved in the shape of a long-haired man, his mouth wide open in a roar and his eyes staring with menace. She averted her gaze from the terrifying face on the peg but could not help looking back at its fearful eyes. Hurriedly she took off her dress, using it to cover up the holes in her towel, and she felt eyes staring at her back. She slowed her movements down, anxious to make a good impression. She stripped off her undershirt, but then her courage failed her and she did not dare take off her briefs. It would be embarrassing and strange to be seen completely naked before they had heard her voice. She felt the lump of silence growing and blocking her throat. Desperately she tried to dispel the lump by saying something clever and witty, but the words would not come. She decided that she must move into the center of the group. She peeped at the bath and saw that it was vacant. Cautiously she turned and paced toward it. She bowed her head and curled up her toes, pretending to concentrate on the warm, glimmering pools of water that lay in the hollows of the concrete floor, still wearing her underpants and waiting for the words to come by themselves to her tongue.

As she stepped into the tepid water of the bath with its dark film of fresh dirt, she relaxed a little, for now she stood partially hidden in the gloom. The window, half of it blinded with a cardboard covering, was above her head. The din in the room grew. Now she noticed the source of the noise: near the bath, in the corner, stood a primus stove—a Goliath of a stove—and on top of it was a giant black steaming cauldron. Suddenly, above the roaring of the stove, a cry went up in the room, cutting through all the vapors, straight to her, to her heart. It was happening at last.

"Hey, new girl! Do you want to wash your dirty underpants at the same time, new girl?" An anonymous hoot of laughter, soaked in steam.

She bent down and looked at her underpants as if she had never seen them before. Against her will, a crushed, threadbare sound emerged from her mouth: "Oh, I forgot!"

"What was that? What did the new girl say?" asked the same strident voice that had called to her before, from a distance.

"Ohiforgot! She said Ohiforgot!" answered another voice, close to her body.

"Oh and woe, I forgot!" screeched the first voice.

A kind of savage gaiety swept over her from all sides, as if she were a tree and all at once they were stripping off her leaves.

Suddenly an ominous silence filled the room, as if she had fallen into an abyss of silence, to the end, to the bottom, to a space inhabited by whispers and shuffling feet. Only afterwards did she realize that it was the stove that had stopped roaring.

She came to a hasty decision and, turning to the wall, she bared her buttocks toward them, her hands trembling.

"New girlie!" asked a voice from nearby, trying to imitate the ringing distant voice. "What have you got there, there, down below?" She froze where she stood, expecting obscenities. These terrified her more than anything else.

"At the side, new girlie, here, at the side!" The voice insisted impatiently.

Immediately she remembered and she felt a slight spasm of relief.

"It's nothing," she said, turning her face toward the dense crop of freckles, toward the curious, greedy eyes. Her voice rang out clearly. "When I was little I sat on a pair of scales. I went into a grocer's shop and sat on the scales. They were on the floor. This is a mark from where the pointer cut me."

A hand reached out and probed the little scar roughly. She felt sure that this scar added to her prestige.

"Did you hear that?" It was the lively, strident voice again. "They bought the new girl in a grocer's shop. They weighed her. A penny a pound!"

With her hand still on the scar, the girl who was probing it roared with laughter in Maya's face, as if this was the cue that she had been waiting for. Her laughter aroused a chorus from the others.

She could have put on a brave face, lashed out with her tongue, but, just as it had been in her confrontations with Regina, she could not bring the words to her lips. Instead of this came the clear, despairing realization that she could not hope to float and rise on a wave of sympathy.

She fixed her pupils on the bright eye of the window, seeing through her tears the little cloud that floated there, like a fish. Giggles and whispers broke in waves upon her back.

After a pause she braced herself, took a deep breath and, without moving her body, turned her head and in a cool voice asked the big freckled girl who had touched her: "Tell me, how do you get water here?"

The freckled girl looked startled. In silent confusion she peered about her as if seeking help.

"How?" The lively, strident voice answered her instead. She still did not know the source of this voice. "How? With your hands, new girl, with your hands, a penny a pound . . ."

She realized that this derision was quite pointless. She heard the croaking laughter of the freckled girl and it sounded false, artificial.

She decided to ask no more questions and instead to assert the independence that she had brought with her to this place. Her glance fell on a tin can that stood at the foot of the stove in a little pool of water. Another hand beat her to it.

It was the freckled girl who snatched the can, put it like a crown on her wet black hair, stuck out her tongue and began gyrating in front of Maya with lewd and clumsy movements. Maya stretched out her hand angrily and this was the signal for the start of a new game, a hectic game of running and chasing up and down the little room, of taking the can from head to hand and from hand to head. She felt the challenge in the air, but a cautious feeling warned her to stand aside. She turned and bent down over the low brass tap.

The tap grunted, gave a deep groan, and, as a token of its sympathy and complicity with the others, spat one unfriendly mouthful of cold water over her knees and stopped at once.

The familiar, repugnant blockage returned to her throat. Rising from her stoop, she looked again at the one eye of the window. The little fish-cloud was tattered and threadbare, as if the evening shadows had been playing with it, chewing out its guts bit by bit, spattering it with crimson and violet splashes and leaving it to a slow dissolution.

Another sudden decision, a special, wonderful act of strength. Quickly stepping past the girls who gyrated in front of her, paying no heed to their ugly grimaces and flashing teeth, she leaped toward the peg, took hold of her dress, and made a show of examining the fabric closely. Again her eyes met the eyes—she had forgotten them—of the man carved on the hook, eyes popping out of their sockets. Now she focused on them without fear because she already knew their expression, and at the same time she remembered the instructor who had received her. The blonde girl had seemed to her like a new end, a safe harbor where she need not fear casting anchor.

Suddenly a light came on, and with it a new commotion began. She saw a pale bluish light from a carbide lamp, like those of the falafel sellers in the town, but without the cheerful bustle around the vendors' stalls. Mysteries gave way to other mysteries. The girls, who had previously been endowed with a kind of alien potency by the twilight gloom and the reflected flames of the primus stove, seemed to her now, in the space of one heartbeat, ugly, withered, and apparently confused by their exposure. The frightening shapes all around turned into dirty, peeling walls. The sky outside grew dark at once and blinded the window's other eye.

"Blackout! Close the window, you moron!" cried an agitated voice.

Immediately the tall freckled girl jumped onto the rim of the bath and blocked out the window with a blackened shutter.

Under the carbide lamp sat two girls whom she had not noticed before, busily polishing shoes. A third stood by and watched them as they worked. Her fear suddenly melted away. Her own shoes needed cleaning, and she decided to stay there and polish them, as the others were doing. The shoe leather looked as if it had been chewed and its sheen was preserved only at the back, above the heels. (She heard Regina's voice, indignantly responding to the list: "High boots, new ones! What next—a sable fur?")

She approached the three girls, her own shoes in her hand. They seemed harmless enough, working at a pleasant job, not threatening in the pale light. And again she was charmed by the air of freedom that radiated from them, perhaps because of their steady polishing movements, perhaps because of the massive tin of polish into which they dipped their rags again and again, as if it were a never-ending box of wonders that would always be re-filled, no matter how much was taken from it.

The polishers looked at her for a moment, but then, as if to order, they dropped their heads to their work. Only the girl who was standing went on studying her with that special, prolonged, feminine look that she had seen on Regina's face when a well-dressed woman passed her in the street.

She interpreted their silence as a sign that the novelty in her was already wearing off. She stood facing them and felt the first stirrings of a sense of belonging.

She noticed that one of the girls was even smearing the soles of her shoes. She suppressed her astonishment, deciding that this must be the custom and that she should do likewise. Her attention was drawn to this girl's special movements. They seemed to have some peculiar significance of their own, expressing pleasure and delight. When the polishing was completed, the girl buffed the soles with a big brush. The two other girls stared at her in wonder. Maya realized that this was not usual, after all, and that they too were bemused by the procedure. Eager to get to work, she looked around for spare brushes but found none. The meticulous shoe-polisher was watching her as she searched, but she said nothing. Holding out the shoe at arm's length, she examined it carefully. Apparently she was not satisfied with her work, since she was now smearing the sole for a second time with that murky liquid that gave out a strange, rubbery smell. The delight of the two girls was out of all proportion to its stimulus.

The limbs of the girl who was polishing were so thin and so finely planed that every joint stood out. Her movements were smooth, fluid, delicately fastidious. On the middle finger of her right hand gleamed a gold "heart" ring, and it seemed that while moving her arm she was making an effort not to dim its radiance, even for a second. A ring is never to be obscured! Her thin, short, blonde hair was damp and formed a little kiss-curl above her left eye, held in place with a barrette—a touch of conscious femininity. The whole of her face—narrow, delicate, and slightly angular—gave an impression of a kind of arid purity.

"Hey, new girlie!" Maya recognized the voice at once. "How are you? What smart shoes you've got, new girlie!"

"They didn't have time to buy me new ones," she answered. She felt gratified by this calm reply, restraining the desire to hide the shoes behind her body, out of the other girl's range of vision. The oppression returned and blocked her throat.

In the town the children had not mocked her clothing. Only the adults ever mentioned it, and always with the object of inciting her. She glanced at the shoes of the other girl, the quiet one, and was surprised to see that they were as tattered as her own, with gaping cracks in the soles.

She knew that this was the moment to say something sharp and provocative, but again she suppressed the competitive instinct, which was foreign to her nature. "Well, when will you be finished?" was all she said.

The girl seemed pleased at the question. She smiled calmly and, with extraordinary laziness, she inflated her nostrils. "I'll only be finished when these shoes o'mine are p–ure gold," she drawled. "Do you know what p–ure gold is, new girl?"

She knew that the other two would yell with laughter at this. And yell they did, as if the previous laughter around the bath had been only a tiny foretaste of the great dish that was set before them now. She sighed impatiently and turned to go out.

"New girlie!" The voice pursued her, ringing out through the laughter of the others. "Why don't you want to polish your wonderful shoes?"

The dormitory was lit by three paraffin lamps. She found the bed set aside for her, looking expectant. Now she was standing in a room of cleanliness. The floor had been washed and the moisture still showed in its dim crevices. She remembered that it was Sabbath eve. The beds, about ten in number, all sagging in the middle and not one of them like its neighbor, a wondrous flock of strange beasts covered with tattered piebald blankets, were pushed close together and glistening between them, like white bones, were the chamber pots.

A few of the girls from the washroom were moving about in the spaces between the beds, sorting out their possessions. She felt a slight twinge of uneasiness when she found that the freckled girl, the one who had touched her scar, had the bed next to hers.

The pain of her previous humiliation was again dissipated by a delightful sense of independence, the joy of belonging to this great institution, this team life. She hurried to her bed. The worn old blanket that she had been given had a pleasant feel to it, as if it had lived a good and long life in this place.

Suddenly, without realizing it, she was already deep in conversation with the other girls, hesitantly answering their questions. She still knew nothing at all about them, except one—they called her "the Quiet Loony"—who lay wrapped in her bed, without moving, at the far end of the room beside the window. "She's the queerest case we've got," Yaffa, the freckled girl, told her, her eyes sparkling with happiness. "Her mother's in the loony bin too. When the children go past the loony bin she gets up, stands at the window behind the grille and shouts: 'Good children, children of Israel, write a letter to the King of England, so he'll know what the Jews are doing to me!' "

Another, smaller, girl was bubbling over with joy as she solemnly announced, "The Quiet Loony's sheet is the flag of the hostel because every morning they hang it on the balcony to dry."

They were joined by another two or three girls from the spaces between the beds, all of them good-natured and curious, eager to uncover her past, glad to be telling a stranger about things they were familiar with. All these stories were exciting and somehow reassuring. As the light and friendly gossiping went on, she suddenly felt that she wanted to unburden herself of the funny incident that had happened to her in the washroom. Her indignation over what had occurred increased as she noticed how eager they were to share the details. She told the story and then, feeling quite relaxed, made the lighthearted comment that she, the one with the "golden shoes" was "a cunning little bitch who thinks she's really something . . ."

Then it happened! It took her a moment to realize that she had made a terrible mistake. Yaffa, the big freckled girl, clapped her hands over her ears as if she had heard something blasphemous, and it seemed that every freckle was quivering on her cheeks. The other girls were dumbfounded. As if from deep inside a lonely sealed cell, into which she had been thrown at one word of command, she heard Yaffa's strident voice, full of importance and indignation, telling her that "Bat-Sheva is the best girl in the place, the . . . cleverest in the place, the most . . .," and "the cunning little bitch—that's you, you!"

"Farting bitch!" yelled another, animated voice. She saw the door opening and *that girl*, Bat-Sheva, standing there.

Now everything happened quickly, and already she was standing on the bed that she had not yet slept in, being violently buffeted from all sides. The room was full of girls and flying limbs. And then the pinching and shouts of "Get her down! Finish her off!" And the blows to her stomach, her chest, her thighs, a relentless hail of body punches.

In the middle of all this she was dimly aware that she was lying on the bed with her dress rolled back above her head. She told herself that this was she herself in this place, that she herself was kicking with all her strength, lashing out, but all her strength was as nothing, empty kicking into empty space. And suddenly a yell—a yell of astonishment and delight combined, an answering chorus of panic, a whirlpool of friction, warmth, and bodies. Suddenly she was released from the stifling prison of her dress. In a flash she saw the faces of the shrieking girls, standing back, held by the force of something known only to them. Shattered by exhaustion and shame, she lay for a moment stretched out on the bed, her mind blank, until the realization dawned that for some reason, unclear to her but not to the others, she was free. She jumped off the bed, or was pushed from it, and stared at the place where the others were focused.

"Fire! That's fire!" she heard herself shout as she bent down to look. Under her bed a little flame was climbing higher, gathering strength, licking at the mattress. She also saw the source of the fire—a little comb, all in flames, every tooth burning away prettily. "Assholes!" shrilled the voice of *that* girl, Bat-Sheva. There was no fear in the voice, but a kind of relief. "Get some water, quick!" And with her own hands, exulting in a spirit of cheerful recklessness, she pushed the bed out of range of the others. "The mattress, idiots! The mattress!" She was screaming with laughter at the prank and she laughed with all her mouth at Maya, as if including her in the general merriment.

Some of the girls rushed forward and turned the mattress over, and they kicked at the burning patch while Bat-Sheva stamped on the comb. Someone had already fetched water in a bucket, and they tipped the water over the mattress, squealing joyfully with every dowsing.

A shout was heard from down below. The bucket fell to the floor. There was a stampede to the door. She was left alone beside the scorched and upturned bed, seized by disbelief and a sense of guilt, as if she were to blame for all this. She looked up and saw the closed shutters, hanging loose on their hinges like the mouths of old men. For a moment she sat on the floor beside the charred mattress, but then she stood up and began a desperate attempt at dragging it toward the bed. Then she heard a new voice, and she saw a girl who looked different from the rest, a model child, very neat and cheerful. Her face reminded Maya, for an instant, of the face of a hunting dog, except that the next moment she was sure that she did not exist at all, in her starched white blouse, her bright muslin collar, and the neatly pressed khaki shorts on her cylindrical legs.

"Come on, let's do this quickly, before the staff see it," said the girl. "They'll kill you otherwise!"

She did not ask who the "staff" were. It was all a miracle, clear, self-explanatory.

The girl—a stranger with a different kind of strangeness—set almost everything to rights. Maya could not stop staring at her skillful hands, at her swift movements.

"Look at all the bed bugs that have been burned," the girl grinned, pointing at the floor. As the mattress was put back in its place, tiny dark bodies came showering down, one after another.

The hole in the mattress was "not too bad," the girl said as she stuffed a rag into it. Together they pulled and lifted it onto the worn metal rods, the hole uppermost, "so that the straw doesn't fall out and nobody notices."

"Don't be afraid of that one," said the girl. "If you show her that you're scared or you give in to her too easily, you've got no chance."

These words awakened a new fear in her, deeper than before. She understood that "that one" had a power that everyone recognized.

"This place is called 'the Fifth Heaven,'" the girl added, "and you will soon learn why."

"Now you must go downstairs to eat," she told her. "Don't tell the staff anything. I'll stay here and wipe the floor. They call me Margarita, and I don't live here."

She obeyed. She still did not understand everything, only the paralyzing fear that pinched at her stomach as she groped her way down the dark unfamiliar staircase to the new, unfamiliar place, hearing the clatter of plates and the voices of children, boys too.

Everything was slow and fast, repellent, alarming and engaging, here and not here, the pleasure and the pain of the new suffering that awaited her here—wondering was this really her, or someone else?

"I think I told you it's against the rules to be late here," the voice of the blonde instructor greeted her above the smells of strange food, tin plates, and the eyes of unfamiliar boys.

4
MARKOVSKI'S ARRIVAL
IN KIRYAT SHKAK

From the moment that Dov Markovski leaped down, bare-headed, from the platform of the bus—before the stop, a contemptuous leap, perfectly timed, a light hovering in mid-air followed by three braking shuffles on contact with the ground—he had been the object of unwavering attention.

His appearance, it seemed, imposed upon all the religious inhabitants of Kiryat Shkak a special and urgent obligation to stare at him, to understand or remember who he was. Who in the name of God was this bare-headed fellow with the crumpled jacket under his arm, with the suitcase and the shirt unbuttoned at the chest, and what business brought him here?

He stood for a long moment in the dust at the edge of the main street, among grape stalks, sun-scorched scraps of newspaper, melon skins, and wood shavings, as if on the bank of a river that he must cross. With a kind of provocative glee, he inhaled the critical looks of these orthodox people, and with them the dust of the street, its molecules drifting in the rays of the early morning sun, and the bold, stifling scent of salted herring, chickens, and old sacks.

He was seized by an uncontrollable desire to laugh as he watched the passersby, imprisoned by their clothes and their beards. He felt like a rebellious young colt among old and tethered mules. He looked at the women. The men strode past them with an air of indifference, as if they already knew them all and had grown tired of them all, swaying along with their baskets and pregnancies, their geometric head scarves, kerchiefs, and matrons' wigs, elbows hidden and legs encased in heavy stockings. He listened to the Yiddish-Polish melody that passed between them, a fat in which his Russian guts were instantly fried.

Two women passed close by him, glancing at him furtively and nudging one another in the ribs, as if they suspected him of plotting to offend their modesty. He watched them in amusement. They made their way toward one of the Arab peasants who were filling up the morning street with their little beasts, laden with boxes, and their uninhibited cries: "Gra–a–apes! Gra–a–apes!" The two women were thrusting bodies and arms shoulder-deep into the boxes on the back of one of the donkeys: "How much is this, do you hear? Do you hear?"

Their voices were drowned by the haggling cries of the other shoppers. Then the shorter of the two, the one with the head scarf, suddenly and deliberately withdrew, standing to one side and angrily waiting for the gloomy fellah to admit defeat.

Then it was back to groping in the box, sniffing at the Arab with what was left of her dignity, the others giving her support and exchanging suspicious comments as she rejected, one after another, every bunch of grapes chosen for her by the "Araber." He stood there barefoot in the dust in his broad peasant trousers, waving his discredited scales in the air above their heads.

Suddenly the fellah grew tired of all this and, snatching up the laden pan of the scales, he threw it furiously into his box: "Go home, lady, go home!" The woman in the head scarf, not in the least offended and quite indifferent to his anger, boldly thrust her hand once more into the box, pulled out the bunch of grapes that she fancied, and with the other hand took a firm grip on the pan; by this time the fellah was helping her.

Nearby stood a little peasant boy wearing a colored cap and long khaki trousers, stroking the donkey's mane. From time to time he would turn around, slowly and silently, and he would stare at the women and at his father with wide, bright brown eyes.

Markovski detached himself effortlessly from these sights. A wave of childhood memories assailed him, but everything looked grotesque and distorted under this scorching sun, in the stifling heat that sprawled beneath the shadows of the trees, facing the khaki-painted bus that was now honking morosely to disperse the crowds of suicidal Thursday shoppers.

He crossed the street to the tiled pavement opposite. At once a familiar, sweet smell came to his nostrils. He looked up to find the source of the smell and saw that he was standing at the foot of a long white building, different from all the rest. It was a cigarette factory—the longstanding competitor of his Patron company—and even the short tiled pavement was meant only for the factory, like a special honorific carpet spread out on the grimy dust.

The gate suddenly opened, releasing a great gossiping swarm of women and girls in blue overalls. The sight was so familiar to him that a sudden flash of comradeship impelled him toward one of the girls. He groped in his pocket and pulled out the piece of paper. The dusky girl glanced at him and at the paper, shy and a little alarmed, and then grinned brightly at his smile and at another, older woman who joined her at once. "What do you want, eh?" asked the old woman, staring at him suspiciously.

He asked where he could find the address on the paper, feeling like a fool.

"We don't live around here," the old woman declared. "We have no business here. At seven the bus brings us here, at four, home again."

The girl scrutinized him closely for a short moment. He glanced in a friendly way at the down on her dusky lip until the old woman dragged her away, to the kiosk. He watched them as they went. For a moment pictures of the Patron factory came back to him, the lectures that he used to give the women there, before work and during the morning breaks, that scornful feminine air of aloof self-assurance, their perverse misunderstanding of his interest in them, their impatience for him to go and leave them to finish their salads in peace.

To the left of the factory, where the pavement was once more licked by dust, he looked in a bookshop window. Here were sacred books, pious books, silk prayer shawls, and calendars for the Jewish New Year.

As he walked into the shop, he thought he saw a woman's face smiling at him from between the newspapers hanging in the doorway.

Once inside, the din from the street subsided respectfully.

In the fragrant dimness of a genuine bookshop—a scent of glue and old leather bindings—he made out with difficulty, against the background of books, the black beard and shiny black frock coat of the proprietor, who was arranging bundles of New Year cards on the counter in front of him.

"Prayerbook for the New Year?" asked the bookseller, peering at him shrewdly through glimmering spectacles.

In the agreeable spirit of provocation that had taken root in him, Markovski asked hurriedly for the one newspaper that he was sure would not be stocked here.

The bookseller came to life at once, as if he had been expecting him here for a long time, armed and ready to confront him. "A wise heart to his right and a foolish heart to his left," he frowned, glancing up at his books, as if looking to them for confirmation.

"We are all foolish, except the heartless," Dov replied happily. He felt the stirrings of a vague sense of affection for this bearded man, who had already found the text that he needed to prove his point and was intent on showing him the place where it was written, really, black on yellow; then he led him to the door to show him which magazines he considered fit for buying and selling.

Dov looked up and was dazzled by the blinding light that shone through the treetops. Putting on an expression of piety, as if quoting a forgotten text and copying the bookseller's tone, he said, "Thus have our wise men taught us: 'Even the most righteous of the righteous, is not given authority over sexual affairs.' "

"Eh?" The bookseller jumped as if bitten by a snake.

Markovski gestured with the back of his hand at the face of a movie starlet whose smile gaped out like an open wound from among the kosher morning papers, and he grinned at the bookseller, a grin of complicity, of willingness to assist him in his transgressions.

"That's for the sluts from the *fabrik*," replied the bookseller without embarrassment, pursing his lips dismissively toward the factory. "And the chickens from the yard, you still haven't taken to the slaughterer?" his voice boomed on in Yiddish, without a pause. "Idle child! Sabbath eve and she's sitting there, just sitting there!"

A little girl wearing a long dress and knee socks stood up from a bench that leaned against the nearby dingy shop. She turned her head slowly toward Markovski and bared a pair of inquisitive rabbit-teeth, then groaned an elderly sounding groan. "Well, go on then, go on!" cried the man.

Suddenly Dov remembered the purpose for which he had entered the shop. Although he knew that he would have found his way without assistance, he liked the idea of chatting to the people of the neighborhood, an unnecessary but enjoyable pastime. But when he asked for directions to the children's hostel, the bookseller's face changed at once. Until now there had been concealed in this face, between beard and eyes, a restrained note of respect for the learned "*goy*", but now every bristle stood on end, and he spoke with undisguised contempt:

"I should have realized at the beginning that you were keeping a bastard of yours *up there*," he rattled on in Yiddish, growing more and more excited. "It's a new custom of yours, you Bolsheviks, copulating in tents and throwing your bastards away on us! A city of refuge for Bolshevik bastards!" He grabbed him roughly by the shirt and went on: "And how do you know, how can you be sure that this bastard came from your body, eh? In your tents fetid drops trickle without shame from vessel to vessel . . . and I'm surprised that you have the audacity to come this way, Sir, seeing that all your friends, all the other Bolsheviks, do not dare show themselves in the main streets but search around for all kinds of roundabout routes to take them there secretly, to their bastards. Only last week they pulled one of those women of yours out of a well in someone's backyard, screaming her head off. The saintly lady was creeping around from backyard to backyard so people wouldn't see where she was going, and she fell into a hole."

What a wonderful turn of phrase this bookseller has, Markovski thought happily, a regular Sambatyon! And as the other went on talking, he felt the indifference and sense of fortuity dissolving within him, giving way to a certain fascination for "that place," so full of mysteries and human suffering. He remembered Frieda. At once he interrupted him and tried to explain to him, the wonderful bookseller, why he had come. The latter scratched his beard and looked at him with incredulous astonishment, frowning and chewing something between his teeth. Then he led him out into the street and simply showed him the way to the "shrine of idolatry."

"Mr. Bolshevik," he murmured close to his ear, "come back in a few days from now and you will find the paper that you asked for, but please come discreetly, when there's nobody else in the shop. There will just be a little extra to pay for the order."

He turned to the kiosk to buy cigarettes and again his eyes fell upon that young Carmen, leaning on the fence and now surrounded by a thin carpet of sunflower seed shells, over her eyes a fine veil of insubstantial, idle imaginings, absorbed in the process of splitting the seeds that she carried on so assiduously. She looked at him, at Dov, straightened up at once, shaking off the shells that had clung to her overalls, and, as she did so, smiled at him with an air of lazy comradeship. "Have you found it, Sir?" she asked.

He nodded cheerfully and raised his free hand to show which way he was going.

"Why 'Sir'?" he called out. "Call me 'comrade'!" She did not reply, but went on smiling lazily until he had finished buying the cigarettes.

As he walked past her once again, he could tell that she was still smiling at his back, and in spite of himself his movements became clumsy.

A number of women standing in the doorways of the nearby shops had been observing with interest the little conversation of gestures between him and the girl, and they were now sharing it between themselves.

All the way up from the village street to the top of the hill Markovski was scrutinizing his surroundings. First he turned his attention to the seedy little shacks, which had climbed, with such strength as they could muster, out of the grimy dust to this dwarfish height, hiding their shame with panels from tea chests, tarred paper, layers of newspapers and cardboard, leaking steady, respectable streams of sewage water into the street. Inside the shacks people haggled loudly over bargains or beat their children in the doorways.

He skipped over the streams of sewage that flowed in rivulets to the delta of the main street. In a careless moment he soiled his shoes. He looked around for a piece of paper or a leaf to clean them with. Beside one of the shacks stood a number of tall trees covered with some kind of white blossom, abundant and exotic, which attracted his attention. He hurried toward the blossoms, looking up in joyous curiosity, but then saw that they were a mass of feathers, white chicken feathers.

From some hidden source he heard a loud chorus of chickens, screeches of death and cries of final confession. And out of a yard nearby came an urchin, dressed like the young Boria Markovski, pushing a shabby creaking perambulator that contained a squabbling mass of live feathers. Immediately behind him came a crowd of women and children carrying hobbled fowls, heads down and blood from their lolling necks dripping on the path, blinking with their upturned eyes and some still croaking weakly as the blood drained out.

Then he noticed the ground about him. It was moist and dark, saturated with blood, and the fences, fashioned out of planks from old boxes, were all freckled with splashes of dried blood, fresh on top of old.

In the middle of the slope the houses opened out suddenly, the little shacks now crouching at the feet of taller buildings, allowing more and more space to a distant landscape that peered out from between them in strips of greens and blues. And with the landscape the people opened out as well. The air grew sharper. There was a lot of warmth in it, like the onset of a European autumn. A black shape hurried toward him. As it came closer, he saw it was an adolescent yeshiva student, with black hat and dangling earlocks. Running down the hill and gaining momentum, in his efforts to catch up with and overtake a woman who was strolling down the slope, the boy almost collided with Dov.

"Where's the children's hostel around here?" Dov called out to him, just to try and stop him.

The yeshiva boy waved at him dismissively, dodged nimbly out of his path, and went racing on, dragging his whirling feet between the flaps of his heavy coat. "Donkey! Donkey at Tammuz-time!" Dov called after him, enjoying his own feeling of irresponsible superiority.

From within one of the big houses came the thin voices of young children. He paused for a moment to listen, thinking this was the place. Young voices, three or four years old, were singing in Hebrew carefully and very slowly, as if tasting every word, the prayer of praise *Adon Olam*, following a few seconds behind the gentle voice of a woman: *"B–li re–shit, b–li tach–lit . . ."* He knew at once that this was not the place. He heard a shutter opening above his head. His eyes made out the shape of an old woman. He waved her a friendly greeting, grinning at her curiosity. The shutter closed abruptly. For a brief moment he marveled at the cloistered world into which he was about to be thrown.

He continued his climb toward the summit. The curtain of buildings cleared away as he advanced. Beyond the levels of the hill a new landscape spread out before him. The plain of Sharon, sober and clean, basking in the sun, a flat geometric board of yellow and brown, its pattern marred only by a deserted Bedouin encampment, darkening toward the horizon, upon which white water towers vibrated in the air, like a procession of tightrope walkers. He put down his suitcase in a rustle of pale summer vegetation, craned his neck, scratched his forehead, and stretched out his arms to the sky. He felt a vague sense of conceit, descending from the bright expanse above him or oozing from the tops of the cool pine trees.

Only now did he become aware of himself and start to ridicule this "naive fascination" of his. He never would allow himself to feel happy and say: "Stop! Seize the moment! Look, I'm ha–ap––py!" Immediately the thought came to him: "So what? This is the end! This mediocre finality—it's the summit!" and at once the sensation would pass. These thoughts went through his mind now again and again, as his ribs stuck to his shirt and his lungs gasped in the fresh, sharp air, the scent of the pine trees, but for all his efforts he could not rid himself of the invasion of pleasure.

"You slept eight hours last night," he lectured himself, staring at a clump of heavy-shadowed trees whose name he did not know. "It's simple, you drank real coffee this morning. It's only gut happiness, gratification of the body." He stepped down from the crevice of rock, moved two paces forward, and put the suitcase down again. He craned his neck to watch a flock of birds wheeling above his head in smooth circular tranquillity, not moving their wings. When he looked to his left, toward the West, he saw at his feet a small deep gully—like the offspring of a natural disaster, filled with a weird growth—the shuddering inspiration of a valley of ghosts. Giant skeletons of dead gourds crouched there in the white light of the sun, great wounded agaves, half withered with drooping leaves, and above them—in their rhythmic circular flight—the little rings of birds.

Only now did he narrow his eyes against the tall building, which loomed up before him with dazzling whiteness out of the darkness of the height, on a big plateau of flat rock.

In a flash the oppression returned to his chest. He knew that this was definitely the place. With the oppression he came to himself again, settling into it comfortably, as if this was his old bed, with all its familiar hollows.

As he approached the house he saw that his eyes had misled him. The frontage of the house, which from a distance had looked different from all the others, standing out in its shimmering whiteness, turned out to be bare of whitewash. A long fissure, like a big canal, gnawed at the building diagonally, and he saw several deep clefts running in zigzags into the walls themselves, as if someone had hacked at them with a chisel to force a way into the house.

The hostel seemed uninhabited, and for a moment the hope flashed through him that it had been deserted, closed down.

The yard was as squalid as those further down the hill, and its dust was dead. Half a loaf of stale bread lay in the center, flanked by an ornamental flower bed of empty tin cans, egg shells, a twisted shoe, and some old exercise books. Beside the broken fence lay a low heap of limestone rocks and uprooted weeds, a sign that somebody had decided to start clearing up the mess. The path of solid concrete that led from the gate to the front door of the house had been broken and he slipped on it once, when he looked up at the staircase. Above his head, in the doorway, suspended like a tooth about to drop out, a light socket quivered on a precarious lead.

As he began to climb the stairs he heard voices. Hurriedly he tucked his shirt into his trousers, made sure that they were buttoned, and smoothed back his hair, the unique forelock that was his pride and joy.

Right there in front of him, on the landing of the stairs, he saw the girl, Frieda.

She stood sandwiched between two young boys who danced around her, using her body as a refuge and each trying to snatch the other's cap. She herself was howling out loud in a kind of simulated terror, which amused and excited the two little urchins to the point of ecstasy.

Suddenly, like a coiled spring, she snapped upright, her whole body rigid.

"Oh, hello," she said without enthusiasm. "Is that you?"

"Yes, I myself," he smiled, plucking up courage. "I've been *hired* at two pounds a month, to serve as Lord *High* Treasurer." He could tell at once that she was not responding to the witticism.

The two children also froze for a moment, staring at him with all-knowing eyes.

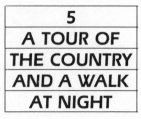

All that is to be done from now
on is to inhale air surreptitiously into the lungs.

On one of her first nights, "new girl" lies awake on her bed,
everything within her laid bare, straining to absorb what goes on
in the strange darkness. From deep down inside her she sends
out probing rays into the corner of the room.

There, in that corner, is Bat-Sheva's bed, the point upon which
all their secretive glances are focused, the source of all joy and
pain, doses of delight, degradation, fear, and compassion. And
from the darkness comes Bat-Sheva's voice. "Now it's Maya's turn
to take a tour of the country," she announced.

Maya froze. But Bat-Sheva called her by her name, not "new
girl," and the voice sounded benevolent. She felt a slight relaxing
within her. The fears, the terrors, the imaginary horrors that Bat-

Sheva's presence had aroused in her since her first day, now turned into one clear and somehow reassuring command, a command to be interpreted and obeyed.

From the other beds rose whispers of anticipation.

"Come on now. It's fun!" said Bat-Sheva's voice.

From all around her loud voices assured her of the thrill that awaited.

She groped her way to the floor, advancing slowly, lest she stub her toes on an iron bedpost, stumbling over shoes, a heap of clothes. Suddenly it seemed to her that she had been walking for hours, without a pause, on the bed of a dark sea teeming with sinister life. She bent her body forward, her hands blindly seeking a path between the beds and the voices. Before her eyes floated a strange gold filament, tiny red balls spilling from the open mouths of sacks, round rings, diamond-shaped rings, yellow rings rising up at her out of the gloom, streaming, rolling, swelling, and disintegrating before her eyes.

"Where are you?" she asked in the middle of the sea.

Suddenly, when she knew that she was already beside her, right beside her, she felt as if her stomach had been slit open, as if she had been drawn up on a hook to writhe in the air.

"Do they know in Tel Aviv about touring the country?" asked the other's voice, with a hint of alluring confidence.

All that she had she would give—just to know!

"Yes," she murmured apprehensively. "Yes, but not very well."

"Then why are you standing there like that, eh?" said the voice. An emaciated hand gripped her hand and pulled her toward the bed. From the other beds expectation rose in silent waves.

The bony claw guided her hand to a naked back and left it there.

She felt carefully, fearfully, the smooth, strange, skeletal back. Revulsion set her guts on edge.

"Come on, draw the map!" said Bat-Sheva's voice.

"What with?" She could not disguise her uncertainty.

"I thought you said they know in Tel Aviv."

"But not *very well*," she said, choking with fear. "So what with?"

"What with?" Bat-Sheva imitated her voice and amplified it until it became once more that voice in the shower room: "With your father's finger!"

From the other beds howls of laughter bombarded her. She could not understand what was so funny. Soon she would learn that in this place the words "your father" or "your mother" were the crudest and most suggestive of expressions, obscenities surpassing even the customary crudities of children.

"Get that finger moving!" said Bat-Sheva's voice impatiently, but with a note of dismissiveness. "Trace on the west side the coast line of the Mediterranean, then the Jordan on the backbone, then Lake Tiberias and the Dead Sea on the popo!" Soon she would learn that only Bat-Sheva had a "popo"; the others had "asses."

"But surely you don't expect me to keep it there!" Maya responded, affecting what she hoped was a lewd tone of voice.

From the beds came an emanation of malicious delight. Again rings floated before her eyes. A ring flashed and burst—plink! Laughter swept around her. Then the voice, sticky and sweet as toffee, saying; "If not, then goodbye!"

She mumbled some words of apology and leaned sideways, uneasily, over the smooth back that her fingers had begun to study. Obedient to the instructions, she drew the map, by guesswork.

Now came the essence of the thrill: "A train from Tel Aviv to Tiberias." She must pass lightly over the back with two fingernails, from one imaginary point to another, keeping precisely to the prescribed distance.

"A fast trip from Jerusalem to Haifa." A rapid, synchronized movement of the balls of her fingers and her forearm, starting at the cleft of the "popo."

"A crazy cyclist." She must turn a series of little figures of eight with a gentle finger along the whole length of the highway.

Bat-Sheva gave orders and groaned in turns, gurgling and shrieking with pleasure, writhing lightly under her fingers. Quickly she learned that a sting on the thigh, a pinch of skin between fingernails, was the voluptuary's signal of a deviation from the route. A pinch of flesh with the full fingers meant a major disruption of traffic. Later these pinches prevented her, when her eyes were closed and her fingers weaving, from sinking into slumber.

In the nights that followed she grew accustomed, like the others, to the fitful and attentive sleep of the woodland beasts.

Bat-Sheva's bed was not like the other beds. Hers was a magnificent couch that had materialized in this place from another world, from some pampered nursery, with high inlaid boards, one at the head and one at the foot, painted with a face and a body, the recurring and constantly changing portrait of a girl in a long pleated dress, shielding and unconsciously complementing the form of the bed's occupant. Her long, wispy hair was tied above her brow with a broad ribbon, and between her motionless hands a big wooden wheel was supported on the ground, reaching to her shoulder. The rust sent out its fingers from cracks in the enamel, but it did not detract from the strange charm of the girl. Tradition had it that the bed had stood here in its empty anticipation until Bat-Sheva came and redeemed it, in those faraway mysterious days, the fine secret days of the hostel.

Even the music of the bed was different. The music of superb springs, without the inevitable rasping of worn metal ribbons.

On one of the first nights she felt in her restless sleep that some movement was afoot in the room. She stirred herself and became aware of a cautious process, the creaking of springs, the rustle of pillows. She saw the girls closest to her sitting on their beds wrapped in woolen blankets. And then Bat-Sheva's voice was heard, saying clearly, "I've got to go!"

The shrouded forms rose from their beds and moved hurriedly toward the exit. She saw that some of the girls were staying in the room, still asleep. Full of apprehension, Maya hastened to follow in the footsteps of the awakened. Now she saw Bat-Sheva pacing at the head of the procession and the shrouded girls following her, barefoot, in a line that stretched the whole length of the corridor, and more behind them, from the other room, straining to catch up with the front of the column.

Suddenly Bat-Sheva stopped, turned, her face in darkness, just the blanketed silhouette framed in the pale light from the open window. The others waited.

"Yaffa! You shithouse queen, who told you to come, anyway?"

They all stopped moving. Yaffa, who had woken up late and missed the start of the procession, came running up from the rear, and it was the sound of her running feet that drew attention to her. Because she had not had time to wrap herself in a blanket, she stood shivering in her underwear pathetically hunching her head between her shoulders, trying to inject into the soft mumbling of her rusty voice a ring of normality, even a note of flattery. "It's not like that," she pleaded, "I've got to go, really . . ."

"Every time I have to?" whispered Bat-Sheva.

"Yes! No, it's not like that. I just . . . I've got to go. My tummy's bursting, it hurts . . ." She clasped her lower abdomen between her hands in a clumsy, artificial gesture.

"Then go and do it in a bucket!" bubbled Bat-Sheva.

Yaffa did not move, but stood and waited for a change of heart from the mistress, rubbing her stomach feverishly. On her face, ugly in the distorting light of the moon, was a look of entreaty.

"I told you to go piss in a bucket."

Maya felt nausea mounting inside her, as when for the first time she touched Bat-Sheva's bare back.

Yaffa shuffled a little where she stood, making as if to go but waiting there in the gloom until attention might be diverted from her. She knew from experience that the risk of leaving was greater than the risk of disobedience.

Bat-Sheva's attention was diverted. Now she chose a companion from among the hopeful girls. After she called the name, she canceled it and chose again. The second choice waited for a moment—perhaps she too would be dismissed and escape exposure to shame—then detached herself from the group, adopting the expression of one in harmony with her fate and all illumined with inner, festive light. She slowly padded after Bat-Sheva toward the "boudoir." They both disappeared. The others moved forward silently and stood like a guard beside the locked door.

Six or seven girls, wrapped in blankets that gave off a sour smell, stood motionless in the grey moonlight, like elderly chickens with drooping wings and spindly legs, deep in thought, attentive to the sounds arising from behind the door of the toilet. A stream of liquids in the pan, secret whispers, boding ill, suppressed laughter. For a long time they stood there idly, in consuming anticipation, some starting to fidget, others to dance, restrainedly. The flushing water—a moment of excellent opportunity to whisper plots—and finally the redeeming click of the bolt. The girls roused themselves.

From the cubicle the chosen one emerged into the pale light, uneasy happiness in her bleary eyes and behind her Bat-Sheva with her pure face, bare to the bone, and her benevolent smile.

"Tell me," she whispered to her companion, as if reminded of something important that she meant to say before, inside, "why, when you're doing it, does your pee whistle?"

The outrageous openness, the unrestrained profanity, filled Maya with a sick sense of dread.

The face of the companion withered at once, like Yaffa's face. Stunned, defeated, staring at the others in hatred, in protest at the charge but not daring to deny it. The others stared back at her, still silent and aloof, careful not to make the mistake of showing malice before the final, decisive, development.

"So who gave you a whistle down there!" said Bat-Sheva with her benevolent smile. "Even outside they could hear it whistling. Isn't that right, Mayakins, wasn't it whistling?"

All eyes were turned toward her, as if she were about to pass sentence both on the companion and herself.

"I couldn't hear properly," she said, disgusted at her fear and lack of experience. Which would be the mistake: agreement or rebuttal? "My ears hurt, so I didn't hear much."

"You're lying! Of course all the girls heard it, clearly," came a voice from the distance, the hoarse voice of Yaffa. "It's just as if they put a whistle there!"

Bat-Sheva transferred her fixed smile to her companion, savoring the desperate appeal in her eyes. At once all the voices began quietly babbling, repeating again and again, "Whistle, whistle . . ."

"Stinking parrot!" grated Bat-Sheva, her face taking on that sharp-beaked expression of hers, but still careful not to raise her voice, lest she rouse the "staff." "Who invited you here anyway, Yaffa, you shithead? How could you have heard it if she hadn't? Well?"

The others hurriedly pretended that they had never confirmed the sound of the whistle, all rallying around the insulted companion, shielding the pure, quiet truth from the accusation. Through Maya's limbs spread a swooning sweetness of relief.

"Come on!" Bat-Sheva commanded her companion, paying no attention to the others.

Now all were seized by a new confusion, the confusion that always recurs at this time, when Bat-Sheva has completed her business and they too have no choice but to go in, unable to return with her before the obligatory act, abandoning her to the hands of one of them.

Some of them changed their minds at once, suppressing their needs and returning with Bat-Sheva and her exonerated companion, who was now doubly dangerous. Only those most in need stayed behind, scared, chivvying one another with hatred and angry despair. Maya slipped cautiously out to the balcony, sat on the end of the furthest railing, afraid lest the whole house be aroused by the voices. But everything stood still in its drowsy peace.

Then she ran back to the plot-infested dormitory.

6
MARKOVSKI
IN HIS ROOM

I n the early days of the institution this little room had served as a clinic. Remnants of its past were the white stand in the corner for bandaging leg wounds, a pale-colored doctor's table, and a white closet bearing a red Star of David, once a medicine chest but now a filing cabinet. Inside it he could see the black files of which Frieda had spoken yesterday, between scrubbing the dining room floor and going to hang out the laundry in the yard.

Flinching inwardly at the sight of the black files that awaited him, and putting them out of his mind, Dov was at once drawn to the doctor's desk. His nose was tickled by the bitter scent of the peeling paint, which he inhaled almost with delight as he sank into the white wooden chair, idly experimenting with the feel of the seat before planting his elbows on the table and his fingers in his hair. An animal yearning was awakened in him, the sensation that always assailed him at the sight of a writing desk, especially a heavy and old one, ready to imprison your whole being in a wooden cage, arousing a mighty sense of industry, of willingness to work patiently, page upon page in a ripening heap; and even when you depart from it, it awaits your return, constantly calling you back.

Dov always saw a writing desk as his final, proper place, and the rest—convoluted and wearisome obstacles—as his way of attaining it. He saw himself in an ideal state of true and fitting peace, in a short pause for thought between sentences, thumbnail lightly tapping the lower incisors and pen resting between finger and thumb.

The world needed, indeed was waiting for, the words still stored up in him, in Dov. He foresaw with pleasure the great struggles that awaited him when he should succeed in attaining that final pose: daytime at his desk; nighttime in contentious talk. There would be debates with political columnists and arguments over his articles in the clubs, in the artists' cafés, in the labor forums, in symposia; and afterwards, perhaps, an abridged compilation of selected extracts, possibly in a small private edition, without preface or commentary.

No, as Heaven was his witness, he had no desire for glory, just a cool appreciation of clever Markovski's essence, recognition of Markovski's philosophical system. Just a name, only a name, without the body residing in some cozy clique, without the mouth laboring ad nauseam with self-publicizing. Just a name, a name of somebody working in purity, distinct from any association, a name to stun, to alarm, to dispel complacency. Suddenly someone will rise from his seat and cry: "Who is this, who wrote this?" And perhaps not even Markovski, maybe a pen name, a fresh subterranean flow from within the dunghill. Stretching his legs beneath the table until they touched the wooden board at the back, he closed his eyes and rubbed them with his fingers under the glasses. These ponderings, borrowed from his public time and his public persona, aroused in him a mild sense of guilt. He was glad that he had no newspaper and was thus spared the temptation of reading it. Without any enthusiasm, like a maid before a full sink, he remembered the files, glanced behind him, and was at once drawn to the window.

The room set aside for him was on the ground floor of the hostel, which suddenly seemed to him like a glorious stronghold, standing like a giant among the stunted shanties that sprawled on the slopes of the hill and the flanks of the valley of the ghosts— like the one he had seen yesterday on his arrival—with big wash-tubs hung beside the sunken doorposts, with the bristly climbing burdock and the broken tin fences. "The files, the files," Dov again reminded Boria, marveling at the pitiful sight. Why is it that, of all things, the sight of poverty inspires in us poetry, delicate feelings, the urge to eternalize it, to ravage its entrails. From squalor there radiates a strange and wonderful warmth, the internal combustion of rubbish; or perhaps this is the emberlike warmth of the tiny struggles that turn every single detail of this petty life into something to be burned with eternal fire, so that the thought of existence itself is not to be neglected even for a moment, seeing that if your mind is distracted, then every-thing . . .

He hurried to the medicine chest, pulled out a file at random, trying to guess who was knocking at the door, and struck an artificial, somewhat casual pose. As he had hoped, Frieda came in, and without smiling. For a moment she flashed him that special look of hers from under the brow, a look of sober percep-tiveness that changed at once to a superficial efficiency, shaking herself free from an existence not hers. In her hands she carried a twig-broom, worn down to the strings that held it together. With a hint of aloof affection, which for some reason reminded him of a deportation order, she asked his pardon and added that this was her job, implying, ironically, that *yours* is immeasurably more important, of course. In order to dispel all this, he calmly let out a neigh and creased his mouth, to impress upon her that her scorn was matched by his own. His groan was intended to tell her something about his true inner nature, to show that he was not satisfied with this subordinate spiritual existence; but it sounded, not to his advantage, like the hypocritical loud moan of a retiree who despises laziness.

Frieda put on a blank expression, evidently directed at him, hurriedly leaned the broom against the bandaging stand, and deftly retied the strings of her apron behind her back. Now a waist appeared and the matching contours of hips, which she moved stiffly again, as if hesitating to reveal the whole range of her movements to him, as she leaned on the broom and pushed her head into the interior of the desk. Suddenly she stopped and straightened up, her eyes lacerating his face. He stared back at her as if he were a stranger caught taking a short cut through a private garden. "It seems I'm disturbing you," she said.

"Oh, no, no," he replied, and smiled, "I used to do this work every evening in my club. " He pointed to the broom.

She put the chair back in its place, noisily.

"Everything here is ultra-modern," he said in an attempt to make conversation. "I see that the experts wrote these files with real professional enthusiasm," inviting her to hang her complicity, her mutual feeling, on this ironical hook. "Every case a curriculum vitae with all the spiritual *Untervelt*. And all of it in Oxford German," he added, addressing her back as she moved toward the window. "At long last a little peace!" Again he tried an unconstrained approach. "A school is, in spite of Rousseau and everything else, an ingenious invention!"

"The noise that the children make here is no more annoying than the chattering of the adults," Frieda retorted.

A feeling of urgency impelled him to soothe her strange aggressiveness, to bribe her with words.

"Yes," he said, "I also have noticed that the children here have an unusual power of attraction, of fascination I should say!" He followed her movements with his eyes, searching for some slight hint of empathy. He studied her face, which had looked up at him for a moment, but found in it no positive response. "No, no," he said, determined to elicit from her the reaction that he wanted, "this isn't the idealization of poverty, but the fervor of the wounded and deprived who are forever seeking, with eager desire, the end, some truth. They have the capacity to love. Surely, from the whole of this ghastly business there peeps out some unadulterated humanity, some totally different expression. No, no, it's not offensive at all. These bald patches, ringworm scars, and iodine stains, the faces constantly searching for satis- faction—somehow they resemble the privations of sanctity. Even their preening has nothing ugly about it . . . the little girls adorn- ing themselves with rings of silver paper, the fancy curls of those rescued from baldness, as if in this place they learn to value their good fortune anew every day."

"I've already been told that you have an unusual gift for words," she interrupted him as she swept the rubbish out through the door and closed it behind her, quietly, as if anxious not to disturb him further. He stared through his glasses at the blurred, dirty panel of the door. Not allowing the setback to defeat him, he fixed his gaze on a file, on the German words: "Parents divorced at age two. Custody given to the father. Oedipal relationship. 'Lemel' School. Bedwetting to age seven."

The hinges creaked again. Frieda, it must be, coming back to smile and soften the blow.

"Do—ov?! Got any nicotine around here?" A voice rang out, fresh and self-indulgent. Shoshana, the nursery attendant, filled the room, licking her painted lower lip with satisfaction and look- ing at him with the eyes of a young girl who knows no restraint. "I'm dying for a smoke."

"Listen," she said, "you've been dealt a wild card, getting pushed into this office for half a day. You've no idea what it's like, getting mixed up with this gang. In theory, maybe it works," she added, looking at the file. "How did you get here? Must have been Wolfson's influence . . . an old friend of yours, so they say . . . I'm sure you've noticed the only way to get into this Holy of Holies is by influence. Frieda's a friend of his too. As a building contractor he's well-heeled enough. Works with the British. There's just one thing that puzzles me . . ."

This slow, relaxed style of speech was, to Dov, the identifying mark of daughters of the long-established first colonies in Palestine. Freedom of movement, arising from the natural awareness that everybody knows her and has loved her since the day she was born. She will always be a young girl, until those older than her have died off.

"And how did *you* come to be here?" He decided to take an interest in her story (her improved opinion of him might somehow infiltrate to the one who insulted him).

"Me?" Again she moistened her lower lip. "You can believe it or not," she said, stretching out her hand, "but I'm here out of idealism!"

"Idealism, just idealism!" he cried, as if delighted that at last he had met somebody whose purity of mind astounded him. He hurriedly offered his cigarettes when she put two fingers to her lips to remind him. He looked good-humoredly at her clean, rosy fingernails as she inhaled smoke and sucked the insides of her cheeks, like a little girl gulping down a soda.

"You should buy your cigarettes at the kiosk down there at the bottom of the hill, in the village square," she said, puffing the smoke. "They supply on credit, so you can get a better brand." As she spoke she lisped slightly, with a sort of pampered delicacy, pronouncing the last word somewhere between *brand* and *bwand*. She giggled simply as if aware of her subtle charms.

"Yaffa Matosevitch," she said in a friendly way, glancing into the file. Unlike Frieda, she had plenty of time to waste. She gave off a faint whiff of soiled diapers. "The commonest type of case here," she said. "Someone put the idea into the Wolfson woman's head of setting up a new organization with the payment of fees. What we lack now is just this—a man's voice. Controlling fifty kids like these with our twittering voices, can you imagine it? Only Pani-Paula's bass baritone is still worth anything here."

He was entranced by her gossipy tone, her breathless account of the last psychologist who had vanished from the place some three months before. And with him—who would have believed it—the kindergarten teacher!

"Middle-aged he was, the face of a German or a Czech. He didn't even know the teacher's name. He always called her 'Fraulein.' But he called all of us 'Fraulein.' I'm sure there was nothing between them. We've heard that they opened a private institution. They will make money. From places like these you can make money these days. These days you can get the children of actors, singers, and even the most famous poets—but the Wolfson woman buries herself with "social cases"; even soldiers' children she doesn't have. And for how long can she milk her 'Old Man Slonim'?"

"A business that only brings in money is too damn poor, according to Henry Ford," said Dov, and he laughed alone.

"Where did he write that? The titles of books I remember perfectly, but the writer's name—unless it's a funny one—always escapes me somehow," she said, affecting the casual ignorance of the aristocrat.

A moment later he found himself caught up in a lecture on the Industrial Revolution, the assembly line, and its psychological influence on those dependent upon it. She shook the cigarette ashes into the lap of her apron.

"Are you really comfortable holding the file like that?" she asked, and then, as he laid the file on the desk, it was if she examined his face for the first time.

"Who is this 'Old Man Slonim'?" he inquired, to forestall any intention she might have of practicing physiognomy on him.

Her eyes lit up at once with a gossipy delight. "Why, I can't believe it! Haven't you heard? You must be as dumb as a spoon!"

"A spoon?" he grinned. "Why a spoon?"

"How should I know? That's what the Sabras say," she stressed with modest pride, a hint of 'Let no stranger eat of holy food.' "One of the Wolfson woman's inventions, her discovery, except that with her it always turns out like they say: 'Even when she falls on her back she breaks her nose.' " She smiled with childish malice, exposing fresh rosy gums.

"Why do you people hate her?"

"Hate her? Who told you that? Anyway, it's not true, maybe just Frieda does, but my feelings about her are *quite* different. I don't know exactly, but I don't feel *hatred*. Frieda, now she really *does* hate her. That girl is one big principle, anyway. After the Wolfson woman visited us the last time she said, 'It's impossible for a person to take so much trouble over something without feeling any emotion.' Do you understand? It seems strange, perhaps, but the Wolfson woman, if you knew her, really does devote her life to all her 'social cases'; yet the moment she comes here— first thing—she insists on clearing all the children out of the way. And it's the same with this Slonim. She's terribly concerned for him. For three years he's been in her hands. When he came here she gave instructions that he be bathed, his underwear changed every day, we were to call the doctor every time he felt the slightest thing, and she wanted detailed bulletins on his state of health. Suddenly, one bright day, this dying man, after lying up there in the attic for nearly two years without lifting a finger for himself, appeared downstairs in the kitchen and beat the oven with his stick. Pani-Paula told me afterwards that she nearly fainted when she heard those awful knockings. You can imagine what it was like, suddenly finding this terminal case standing behind her in a black cloak, and with that long white beard of his. Then he yelled at her, saying that from that day onward he wanted 'every day fresh bouillon with a roll and white chicken—no cheating.' I ran down to the village to telephone. Two hours later the Wolfson woman was already here. When she came down from the attic she looked like her own grandmother. Then she lost her temper and went right off her rocker, and for the first and last time we saw her in a real state, shouting: 'The Litvak, the thief! He's cheated me, ruined me! How dare he feel well, how dare he! And what a color he has on his cheeks, like a *shiksa* on her wedding day! Now he'll gobble it all up, interest and all!' She went right on yelling. That way, incidentally, she gave away her secret, which everyone already knew anyway. I'm sure he's doing his best not to snuff it just to spite her. You understand what an arrangement this was? They all knew that on the day of his death there'd be a resurrection around here. You even hear the kids saying: 'Lend me a red crayon. When the Old Man dies, I'll buy you a new one.' "

"About three years ago he came here—like all of them—to die in the Holy Land. His wife was already dead. Somewhere the Wolfson woman got the whiff of a deed on a site in central Tel Aviv. They say his bank account's healthy enough. They brought him in here on a stretcher, to a 'pension with special treatment.' His doctor didn't give him more than half a year. The Wolfson woman gave him, apparently, three months. They say that to start with she had a free hand to draw money, and she really was able to plug a few holes with repayments. Now he's sitting pretty; he's handed over the rights to an attorney and she receives an allowance for his support. God knows how, and you can believe it or not, but he knows by heart all the prices of food in the market. Now we have to make sure he doesn't dare come downstairs. You can see why, Heaven forbid, at his age he should break an arm or a leg on the stairs. She's simply afraid that if he comes down some time he'll go into some synagogue and a rabbi will grab him by the beard and tempt him to leave his money to a yeshiva or something like that. After all, a yeshiva has a lot more prestige to it than a home for bastards."

"Are *you* waiting for him to die too?" asked Dov. Her story both entertained him and jangled his nerves.

"Me? I've nothing to complain about. He's a nice enough old

man, I suppose, and he knows a lot and keeps his hands to himself. But just you try going up to the attic three or four times a day with a full tray," she said earnestly.

Shouting was heard, the protests and tears of a little boy.

Shosh fled at once, stubbing out the cigarette butt in the doorway.

7
BETWEEN HER
AND THEM

Under the cork of silence Maya's story is sealed, fermenting.

The stories of all of them, some tasteless and some obscure, have already been wrung out drop by drop or swallowed at one gulp, and Maya's story is sealed.

"This is the double-Nelson," Bat-Sheva explained almost gently. Two hands gripped Maya's shoulder from behind, the elbows pressed forward. Yaffa kicked her in the crotch. "Give it to her in the gut, shake up her food," said Bat-Sheva.

"Yaffa," Maya gasped, "if you don't leave me alone . . ." Protest and threaten as much as you like, no one will lift a finger to help you; the prospect of a new and racy story excites their imaginations.

It was Maya's own tongue that had first set the trap. When she saw the splinters of the windowpane that had been broken in the evening's rumpus, she said suddenly to one of the girls with a sort of pride: "That reminds me of my stepmother." This was the first time that she had used this term, a simple phrase evoking in the heart a sweet sense of importance.

"I'll only tell you about my stepmother if you leave me alone!" She must lay down conditions in order to salvage her dignity. She would show them she could still lay down conditions! Maya's arm returned slowly, joint by joint, into the burning shoulder socket.

"But all of it! The glass as well!" warned Bat-Sheva, pulling up her silk underpants, which had slipped off during the fracas.

Again she didn't really want to tell, wanting and not wanting. She was aware from the start of the tragic beauty of her story and the impression it made on others. Here the one whose "sufferings" are most intense stands the best chance of melting the barrier of suspicion and hatred. Her prestige would improve, just as in the hospital the greatest prestige always goes to those with high temperatures and terminal diseases.

"We'll put together my bed and Hedva's," Bat-Sheva commanded. "You lie in the middle and tell us, and you can't move until you've finished."

She watched them at work, savoring the importance of the moment, like an actress waiting for her props. Suddenly she felt afraid, afraid of the tedium of her story. When the words rose to her tongue they might pale and lose their flaming colors. The words would be lost, for they would not want to hear them a second time, and she would be lost with them.

The girls sprang excitedly onto their beds, their eyes fixed on her. Maya stepped over Hedva's body, lay down between the two girls, and waited for their instructions.

"Okay, start quacking!"

"It's impossible, when you're so . . ."

"So what? Get on with it! The stepmother! The glass!"

"It'll have to be slow. It must come to me."

"As slow as you like. You can even stammer if you want."

Maya stared into the lamp, stumped for the words that were going to come out all wrong, because of Bat-Sheva.

"It's just," she garbled hurriedly, "I was just sick. My mother came to visit me and there was a fight. That's it, that's all."

"Is that all? yelled Bat-Sheva, half sitting up. "She says that's all! You wanted to get out of a beating, did you?! This isn't good enough . . ."

She couldn't have endured another of those double-Nelsons.

"Sick," she said hastily, trying to revive within herself the sensations that had overcome her then. "People were beating each other."

"How were they fighting?" Bat-Sheva demanded. "You're not getting out of this!"

"How should I know? They were fighting!" Everything went cold again. "I had a temperature of about 103 degrees, and suddenly I got water poured over me and I was cold. The water and the fever made me shiver and all around me people were yelling."

Bat-Sheva clicked her tongue in dissatisfaction: "Double-Nelson hold! *What* were they yelling, eh?"

"My stepmother stood beside me and said to me: 'Your mother's wicked! Your mother's wicked! Say that your mother's wicked!' And I stood in my wet pajamas, trembling with cold. There was broken glass on the floor from the vase, the hands of the big clock were bent, the face was ripped, and I stood there on the wet bed and shouted as loud as I could, together with my stepmother: 'My mother's wicked! My mother's wicked! My mother's wicked!' "

"Who broke the glass?" asked Bat-Sheva, breathless at last in her eagerness to know.

"I lay on the bed. I slept for a while and woke up and dozed off again. Suddenly I saw my mother beside the bed. I closed my eyes so the dream wouldn't stop. Suddenly I heard the voice: 'Mayinka, I heard that you were very ill. I came running to you straightaway. I don't give a damn about *them*! I have the right! I have the right!'

"Suddenly there were two mothers beside the bed, one of them a stepmother, shouting in Yiddish: 'This is my house!' Then they both shouted: 'This is my house!' They started throwing things at each other and yelling. Suddenly the room was full of people, neighbors and relations. My father too. One of my uncles tried to grab my mother. (No it wasn't like that, not so *quiet*. There was a terrible noise, shouting, people running, chasing, scared and twisted faces, furniture overturned, a deep well of suppressed emotions turned upside down.) I saw my mother standing, high above the rest, on a table, throwing something. And then I felt cold. I started to shiver and then I saw that the bed was full of water, all green, and the window and the clock and the flower vase were broken. My mother shouted: 'That's my vase! My clock! I have the right!' I started shouting too, but I couldn't hear my own voice. They all chased her out to the balcony and she was still shouting 'I have the right!'

"I saw our neighbors gathering in the yard opposite. They were shouting something too. A woman was crying 'Police!' " —the sublime intoxication of the words swept her along—"and then they threw my mother off the balcony." Tears choke the gullet, as is necessary in such cases. How can they know, the tears? "This uncle, who threw her out, didn't know her at all, and when she fell into the yard he shouted something terrible at her."

"What did he shout?" Bat-Sheva whispers close to her ear, her body motionless.

"Something absolutely not true."

"What?" insists Bat-Sheva.

"Don't take it to heart," a soft voice pipes up suddenly, one of the smallest girls, who can barely explain where bread and water come from. "Every man who beats a woman calls her a whore. I've seen that men always shout 'whore' at the woman they're beating."

"But my mother isn't. She isn't at all."

"That exactly what he said," said Bat-Sheva.

"My mother is just beautiful." For a moment the thought occurred to her that it would perhaps be better if she were a whore. Maybe that way she'd be more important, like Ketzele's mother.

"What's a whore?" Yaffa's voice chimes in from the far end of the room, feigning innocence.

"What you'll be if you go on being so retarded," replies Bat-Sheva.

"You mustn't talk about that, you mustn't," says Yaffa in a quavering voice. "God hears everything."

"God Himself wrote about that with His own finger," says Maya triumphantly. "In the Torah."

"A whore is a woman who betrays the Jewish people," somebody cries nearby, "like in the song 'Yankee Doodle went to town riding on a lady.' Does your mother go with the English too?"

"No," says Maya. "With no one else either!"

"How do you know?" Bat-Sheva sat up on her bed. "None of us can be sure exactly what our mothers are doing, except me, and that's because she lives nearby. You all have no way of knowing if your mothers are whores or not."

The light went out.

For a long time they lay in the dark, arguing hotly about the nature and conduct of whores. Sleep plucked Maya away from the conversation and Bat-Sheva's nudgings brought her back to new words.

"So how did it end?" asked Bat-Sheva, gripping her shoulder. "You haven't told us how it ended."

Maya continued in a sleepy voice and her tongue stuck to her palate. "Then my stepmother stood beside me and told me to shout: 'My mother's wicked!' Only the clock was broken and the vase. Let me go to sleep."

"You can sleep tomorrow. Why did they beat her? Come on, tell us why they beat her."

"Because she's my mother! I want to sleep!"

Maya hated women, all of them. To start with, she detested the young ones who used to come to the house once her mother had gone. They looked alike and all of them swooped on her with their swollen arms, with their special smells, a feminine smell of armpits mixed with soap, or perfume blended with a breathtakingly bitter skin smell. Or perhaps this was the smell of the inner body of a grown-up woman. And every one of them treating her, Hermoni's little girl, as if unable any longer to hold back the floodgates of their affection. All those squelching, lip-smacking kisses, with sidelong glances at her father; that fervor to scatter about her, with the ring of proof, the sparkling coins of their love; all those cries of wonder and stifling embraces as they pressed her nose into the soft recesses of their bodies, thinking that they were thus transporting her to the highest peak of delight. All those secretive voices, the gloomy whispers, like the rumbling of their intestines: "And what is your mummy doing now? Does-she-come-here-or-do-you-go-to-her?" (That's very important for them.) "Well? Well? And is it true that she's planning to marry?" (That too is very important for them.) "I saw her walking with . . ."

It seemed to Maya, that all these big-limbed women had made up their minds, as if they had discussed it between them, to refresh with living spiritual water the dry, neglected channels of her heart.

When Regina came to stay their visits suddenly stopped. But now, when she met one of them in the street, the woman would present to her a little double chin awash with grief, breathing compassion all over her and trying to draw from her lips confirmation of the slanderous rumors about her father's new wife.

"My child, how bad, how neglected you look. She's starving you, of course, that bitch."

These encounters awakened in her, to her own annoyance, some momentary sympathy for her stepmother, and then, deliberately, she would exaggerate, rolling out her praises and her fine deeds. A wondrous delight would overtake her to see that chirping leech purse her lips and radiate dissatisfaction.

Regina she hated, to the extent that an eight-year-old girl is capable of concealing her hatred from the eyes of others.

When she came to their house at the outbreak of war, she was an immigrant, a polite and aloof lodger, from a good family— so she announced morning and evening—without a single word of Hebrew in her mouth, something which awakened in Maya an impression of stupidity and boorishness. For some time she lived thus, with her manners. And suddenly, all at once, her talents were revealed: cooking the borscht that was her father's favorite food, sewing, darning socks, polishing a bathtub to perfection, and singing. And then it also transpired that she came from a proletarian family. Now even her name was a cause of vexation and resentment.

When she went on her errands to the shop, the grocer would trample on her feelings by saying, "Tell Mama there are no grapefruits today!" The tax collector, standing between them, used to ask "the daughter" to translate and explain to "Mama," who didn't understand a word of what he was saying, or was pretending so for her own convenience, that "they'll cut off Mama's water supply if she doesn't pay." Once when they went out to buy her woolen underwear, and she didn't like them because of their length, the salesman said with his Ashkenazi accent, "Mama always knows what's best for her daughter."

Convinced that they were all mistaken, she concentrated her efforts on correcting them with the subtlest of hints. In public she took care to pronounce with exaggerated emphasis the name *Regina*, but no one paid any attention to nuances of the tongue in these hard times. Later it occurred to her that they all knew, knew perfectly well, but they had united against her because they were grown-ups and therefore Regina's natural allies, so that in the end she would be forced to accept her as a mother. Sometimes she wondered, trembling in front of the mirror, if there really were in her face any points of similarity to the foreign features of that swarthy woman.

Only later did she learn to declare, when her enemy was not present, "She isn't my mother at all!" The change that this announcement effected in the faces of people created within her a new range of sensations. The world was then divided into three types of person. The obtuse: those who correct themselves and say "aunt." The straightforward: those who give the impression that they are mourning for a mother who has died on her, and their alarming implication—that an orphan is *entitled* to a stepmother. And the sharp-witted, at two levels: those who affect embarrassment and those who affect gossipy enthusiasm. Those who affected embarrassment were the ones she liked best; they were the reassuring proof of the lack of urgency in the business. To them she would hastily add, in a manner of total offhandedness: "My real mother lives somewhere else." The gossipers were useful to her; they were the microbes responsible for spreading the truth, but their voluptuous interest in her was something that existed for its own sake, and she found it insufferable.

Maya became aware, vaguely, that the "stepmother" is created by the stepchildren themselves. And if she is not "wicked and unkind," they will strive to turn her into a witch, so long as they have another mother in the background. The more that Regina courted her, the more Maya treated her with hostility. On no account would she let her take the place of her mother in her heart or in her life. Every brief smile was taken as a criticism, and every expression of generosity as implacable malice. Were it possible to rationalize the child's feelings toward her, they would be expressed as: "I want her out of here! Let her disappear, not exist! Let her not show herself! Let her not pretend to be good! How dare she try to use me as a means of finding favor in my father's eyes! How is she suddenly part of the family, this stranger? How have all the things that used to be mine suddenly become hers?"

In the beginning, when Regina was eager to penetrate into the life of Katriel Hermoni, she took pains to make allowances for his daughter as well. But the daughter was incorrigibly wayward, not at all as she had imagined, with her own heart still brimming over with excellent intentions. When it became clear to her that this was the way Maya meant to go on living, she refrained from obligatory kindnesses and, from the anniversary of her establishment in the house, began to address the girl as "you filthy little slut." The more Regina's animosity grew, the more gratified Maya became with the awareness of bitterness and pain. The legends and stories were not told in vain; she had a genuine stepmother.

Little by little she dropped out of walking together with Regina, as otherwise it would be impossible to deny her motherhood.

And the woman seemed to be glad of the change. Naturally, it gave her no pleasure to be seen in public with a sulky, petulant child who bears witness, so to speak, to her cruelty and adds years to her account. Also her tatters and grime were not such as to arouse the esteem of those who knew the truth.

From now on Maya had nothing but contempt for those who are the willing slaves of their mothers. She enjoyed the sweet sense of freedom that is the lot of abandoned children. The town, the time, the vendors' stalls, the petty items pilfered from them, car accidents, bathing in the sea in total solitude, the markets and the nights—all these were hers. In the evening she would make her way home by the light of the bluish blackout lamps to find cold and tasteless food on the kitchen table. Swarms of ants surrounded it, and she gladly left it to the ants.

Regina did not dig around in dustbins, and for this reason she never came across the pointed notes of the teacher: "I would like to draw to your attention the fact that your daughter is neglected and is not doing her homework." They had almost stopped seeing each other.

And there were other women.

On the third floor of the Hermoni house lived Katriel's sister with her husband, a shrewd food wholesaler who, according to

Katriel, "has clearly proved the truth of Napoleon's dictum that an army marches on its stomach."

From the end of Passover to the evening of the day after the feast of Sukkot, Aunt Vera would go out on the balcony each day, the taste of an agreeable afternoon nap on her lips, to entertain a friend or a neighbor with a light repast of tea and small delicacies, to talk about "that's life," and to enjoy the gusts of wind coming from the open expanse opposite.

The apartment on the third floor always repelled Maya, with its cherished silence, its "don't touch" furniture, and the red display candles that were never lit.

Once, in the summer, in one of those afternoon hours when it was forbidden to disturb the peace of all these new immigrants with their Prussian manners, she was hanging on the garden gate, pushing it with her stomach one way and idly submitting to the motion that carried her back, pushing and letting go, pushing and letting go, while the hinges of the gate cried out for help. Suddenly the sound of scolding came from above (a contribution to her enjoyment)—"What is this, a workshop? Stop that at once!"

Maya instantly recognized the voice of her father's other sister, the one from Haifa, who had apparently come for a visit. She looked up, continuing with the delightful discordancies, and saw, sure enough, the heads of them both—Aunt Vera's head and the head of the Haifa woman—peeping out from under the awning like a pair of balcony cacti.

"Ah, Mayaka, is that you?" called the Haifa woman. "Come upstairs, Mayaka!"

She liked the Haifa woman slightly because she lived a long way off, and when she came visiting she divided her attention equally among all her relatives.

Her stomach warmed at the thought of the rare opportunities for gluttony that awaited her up there on the balcony. She jumped from the gate and hurried up the stairs, bruising the toes of her bare feet as she ran. Before she rang the bell she noticed how dirty her toes were. She spat into her hand. The spittle did a good job of cleaning her toes and her grimy ankles.

The light filtering through the red awning gave a soft rosy hue to the white cloth and to everything that was on it. A different kind of freedom dominated in this place—the private, aristocratic relaxation of women who pamper themselves, who know their own worth and sacrifice delicious sweetmeats to themselves.

Her eyes, like two hooks, were caught—one by the slices of dark brown liverwurst patched with whitish stains, and the other by the puffed pastry cakes, so brittle, sure to melt at the first tickling contact with a licking tongue. She adopted an expression of indifference, as if these things were commonplace to her, but she could not stop herself from swallowing noisily.

The Haifa woman eagerly thrust a finger under the girl's chin and turned up her face, studying it with eyes that narrowed as if strained by the sunlight. Now the auntly questions would come. They came. She answered the three of them: "Yes. Yes. Yes."

"Lovely," said the Haifa woman. "Really lovely."

Then the finger dropped. The Haifa woman took a slice of bread, so thin that the bread itself could have been the condiment, and laid on it a lump of butter, still hard from the refrigerator. As she crushed the butter with a shiny little knife, a smell like that of a sumptuous kitchen wafted through the air. The aunt squashed the butter where it needed squashing, rounded it when it needed rounding, near the brittle crust, until she had covered each tiny pore of bread. Maya suddenly felt a powerful urge to sink her teeth into the place where the butter had spilled into one of the pores, but the Haifa woman now lifted up two slices of liverwurst, extracting them neatly from their shining pack, and at once, with the expertise of a restauranteur, slapped them down on the bread. She laid it all on a white earthenware plate, which she pushed to the corner of the table. She did all this in solemn silence and with self-conscious willingness, while Aunt Vera followed her actions with the eyes of one who sees a disaster unfolding and can do nothing.

"Take it! Enjoy life!" said the Haifa woman to Maya, who stretched out her hand.

Suddenly a bitter feeling of revulsion swept through her. Only now did she sense that in this agreeable family scene there was something shameful and false, as if they were "buying her" at the cheapest price. Her head shook in refusal, as if the sandwich disgusted her.

"Why?" asked the Haifa woman incredulously. "Oh, perhaps you don't eat non-kosher?" she grinned.

"All that they do for her is no good," said Aunt Vera in Russian.

"But this is *good*," insisted the Haifa woman. "Just take a tiny little taste and you'll see that it's good."

The word "good," pronounced with a twisted and guttural "g", so that it sounds like "ghood," aroused in her a clear and decisive disgust, disgust at this handsome woman and her obtuse complacency.

Her saliva bubbled and her tongue became heavy. For fear of revealing what was in her mouth, she drew her shoulders up to her neck in an ugly gesture of refusal.

"Do you know what?" said the Haifa woman happily, as if a message from Heaven had fallen into her hands. "First of all, *our* little girl will drink something, and then she can eat. Her mouth is terribly dry."

Again that obstinate, ugly grin. The aunts looked at one another briefly, almost abruptly, and at the sight of these exchanges of weapons Maya felt an acute appreciation of herself take shape in her heart: pride that she was not to be tempted even by sweets wrapped in gold and a sense of vindictiveness because they were fussing around her almost in hysteria.

"Ah, strange creature!" said the Haifa woman fiercely. "When you were little, when you just saw me a long way off, you used to shout, 'Come, come!' So I'd take you in my arms. You were much more lovable then."

"Just ask her!" said Aunt Vera in Russian. "Try leaving her here on her own, and she'll polish off everything you see on the table. She's become so, so . . ."

Maya put on an expression of blank incomprehension and moved to the rail of the balcony. She bowed her head under the awning to watch the children playing in the empty lot. From time to time she turned an ear to her aunts' conversation—they might say something about her or her mother—but they were already engrossed in more agreeable matters.

"I know ex–act–ly all the dirty places in the apartment. Every day they have to be gone over again. My western window—the maid cleans it three times a week, but that's not enough. Every day! Do you believe me? Every day!" said Vera in the loud, indignant voice of a persecuted saint.

"Every time the same places get dirty," said the Haifa woman. "Do you think I don't know it?"

"Beside the fridge," said Vera, "I could go out of my mind! And Shimon, how does he open the fridge? How many times do you think I've told him not to open it *like that*?! One hand he puts on the handle—that's alright. But the other hand al–ways, without exception, he puts on the wall to the left. It's a crazy habit that I'll never cure him of. *This* he brought from home! Just imagine what a big stain of dirt is made on the wall. Twice a week I have to go and clean it—it's impossible, it's crazy— every time he opens the fridge he leaves a handprint."

"Always when everything's been cleaned and the house is spar- kling," the Haifa woman broke in urgently, "I ask myself: When some stranger comes to the house, does he too notice how clean it is, or is it just me that notices? Look at Hayya Gruber, who lives opposite me, the one who works in Food Control, always coming and advising me to go out to work. There are jobs, the men are in the army . . . Anyway, she's a pretentious sort of woman, everything she says, always 'I this' or 'I that.' Just take a look at her electric outlets! All the outlets in her apartment are as black as pitch, but the point is—she's working!"

"I clean outlets with burdock bristles," said Vera.

"I think steel wool . . . but these days you can't get it . . . my grocer promised . . ."

Maya saw the neighborhood children climbing on the big sycamore and hanging from it a hammock and a swing. She longed to go down and join them, but a stronger desire kept her rooted to the balcony. She listened to her aunts' conversation out of a morbid compulsion. She expected them to talk about her mother and her father, but the Haifa woman, who was considered to be "a woman of the world" because she had married a Canadian doctor, spoke of her experiences in Haifa.

"The most charming man in Haifa is the barman at the Neptune Hotel. What a marvelous person! When you go to the bar, he first asks you, in English, 'How much?' Meaning: 'How much money are you prepared to invest in drinking?' When you tell him, you can see his mind working, all the wheels turning for you, as he figures out what combination he can make to give you the most possible. 'Usually,' he says, 'that would be enough for two drinks, but for you I'll make it three, possibly even four.' There are some people!"

Aunt Vera sniffed uneasily. Maya turned for a moment and saw her finger screwing in her nostril, and then she drew it out and examined it for a moment. At last the sniffing stopped.

"I don't want to grow up any more," said Maya to herself. "I don't want to grow up into a woman."

She saw that her aunts' attention was completely distracted from her. Unable to restrain herself any longer, she stealthily snatched one sweet from the table, said a hurried goodbye, and went out.

For a long time she sucked the candy under the sycamore in

the hammock, sucking and taking it out of her mouth to look at it, hastily, trying not to swallow it until she had squeezed all the goodness out of it.

Before Regina invaded the house the spare room was rented to a Polish virgin from a small township, thick-fleshed and delicate of feeling, a God-fearing teacher called Bluma.

At the hour of greatest loneliness, the hour of twilight, the hour when delicate strands are drawn out from deep within her, entwining and interweaving nervously between the darkening leaves of the mulberry and the lattice of the fence, reaching out to the earth fragrant with the scent of each individual grain of dust, to the chirping of sparrows, hidden from sight, the brief chirping of slow exchanges of thought before sleep, then returning at a bound to her innermost being with a painful jolt, the hour when children of the neighborhood stand relaxed on the balconies or in the frames of windows, chewing in lethargic silence their evening meal of fresh bread with red mulberry jam, the shadows of their mothers hovering behind them as they stand and watch the world stretching out its familiar shapes—at this hour she used to feel the anguished need to cling to someone for support, to escape from the world that was melting before her eyes and leaving her in isolation, alone with the shadowy courtyard and the chirping of the sparrows.

Then she would hurry to Bluma's brightly lit room.

Possibly Bluma was ugly, possibly not. Now Maya remembered only that some heavy, almost unbearable heat used to emanate from her; but the slice of bread that she cut for her from the loaf that she kept in the closet, among the white pillowcases and sheets, had a different taste, a full taste. And when Bluma quavered in her thin soprano voice, "Under your cradle, my gentle son," her eyes used to spill hot tears on the hands of the girl, or so Maya imagined. Bluma spoke of "marriages made in Heaven," of the "sanctity of the family," of "moral corruption" and "disappointment," and she taught the girl to recite the prayer *Shema Yisrael* each night before commending her soul to God. "And you'll see how good you will feel," she promised.

Since then, when Maya huddled herself up in her bed in the empty apartment, she would hold in her hands the little prayer book that Bluma had secretly given her, sniffing the special aroma of its worn pages, staring entranced at its strange, peculiar symbols, at the little word printed in the corner of the page, the word that would return in big letters on the following page, with joyful consistency, as if a miracle had happened. Then she was aware of the wonderful peace that clothed her body in this veil of separation from the world. She used to read to herself slowly, tasting the lovely words one after the other, scarcely sensing any connection between them but with a growing absorption that blunted her loneliness, her fear of thieves, the distant wailing of jackals and the rustling of bookworms and bugs.

One evening, as she was murmuring to herself the prayer *Milifana'i Micháel*, she became aware of a movement around her, and voices, as if the angels Michael and Gabriel really . . . Alarmed, she looked up from the book, her body frozen under the sheet. Around her bed she saw her neighbors from the second floor, Aunt Vera, some young woman, a friend of her father's, and her father himself, who until now had been absent from the house. There he was too, suddenly, amid this strange company—no knowing how—clutching his stomach and laughing, clutching his stomach and roaring with laughter, convulsively. Suddenly there came a howl of tearful mirth: "Ha, ha! Help! He–elp! Oh, oh! Kashka's daughter is reading the '*Shema!*' I'm dead! Dying! Oh, aagh! Kashka Hermoni's daughter! I can't believe it!"

This was the neighbor from the second floor. Maya slowly realized what was happening around her: the word "*Shema*" constantly repeated, the outbursts of laughter, all the cheerful faces. And she realized that she had committed some act of irreparable stupidity, a pointless folly. Then she burst into tears. All rushed toward her, slapping her shoulder in playful reassurance. Some-body stroked her back, but the laughter went on, until she too was laughing with them through her tears, just so they would stop.

A few days later, in the afternoon, Maya saw the figure of pious Bluma, with her wobbly, gooselike gait, walking through the dust of the alley in the wake of the porter's handcart. In her mouth there lingered for a moment the genuine taste of the slices of her bread. She was glad that Bluma's back had disappeared around the corner of the street.

It seems that she became aware of the crystallization of her hatred on that "Sabbath of the pajamas." It was Sabbath breakfast, and they were dining in the "salon." Ever since the girl was evicted from there they had called it the "salon." Framed extracts from Pasternak were hung on the wall, and on the new sideboard stood a black plaster bust of Beethoven. Katriel Hermoni was an admirer of Beethoven because he did not bow to the Emperor.

When the ceremonial cocoa had been drunk—to honor the father's return at the end of a week's work out of town—Regina handed her husband a clumsily wrapped parcel, her face the face of a slave girl anxious to please her master.

Katriel shook the parcel while she followed his movements as if her fate were about to be decided. The pajamas, which she had been painstakingly sewing for days, were revealed. Katriel's face was, indeed, like the face of a king whose will has been satisfied. He pulled the pregnant woman toward him and kissed her lips, a "foreign," grown-up kiss that set Maya's stomach on edge.

Suddenly the father seemed to remember the daughter. His face clouded for a moment, and, as if fulfilling a necessary and important obligation, he bent over her and, with those very same lips, kissed her on the cheek. Her guts turned over in disgust. From this moment on she would be unable to endure her father's kisses.

As he stood up from the table, tensing his replenished stomach,

Katriel glanced at both of them, as if folding them together in one look, and distended his lips in a smile of conciliation, as if believing that with an equitable distribution of kisses he had at last caused the flowers of love to blossom on the complex family root. Then, eager to show gratitude to the industrious wife, he stripped the upper half of his body, revealing to both of them the white torso of a laborer, sunburned at the arms and the neck, firm and blue-veined, and carefully put on the pajama top. Regina hurried to him, pulled away the fragments of white threads from the wings of the collar, and slapped it with her hand to put it straight, fixing her eyes on her husband's face as if searching for something.

Her sharpened perception informed the girl that deep down in his heart her father already detested this woman who was striving so hard for his good graces.

She returned to her chair and stealthily sucked up the bitter dregs of the cocoa, listening attentively to their Russian conversation, waiting to hear some key word. But the fountain of their talk quickly ran dry. Regina turned and went to the kitchen, slammed cooking pots around and raised her voice in song. She prided herself on her voice, a high-pitched voice, with grating passages between the high notes and the low, like a sheet-metal saw—an operatic voice inviting parody. The desire to imitate Regina's singing stuck in her throat.

Katriel himself, all gentle Sabbath lethargy in his new pajamas, now asked for "complete silence," because he was "preparing a lecture." He sat down at the old desk and began humming to himself a bright, lively Ukrainian song that once, in a moment of willingness, he had translated for her:

My neighbor has a little house,
My neighbor has a pleasant wife.
I, poor man, have neither house
Nor spouse to cheer my life.

In one of the closets Maya found a white card. She was always rummaging in closets to discover the secrets of that woman. The white card was headed "Prepare for Childbirth," and under the title was a detailed list of different kinds of diapers and garments to be assembled in readiness for childbirth. The word "childbirth" seemed to her, suddenly, the crudest, most grating, most disgusting word of all.

They brought the screaming thing home. The father smacked his lips at it, cavorted like an idiot around the new crib, and even drew the silent Maya toward it, saying with paternal resonance, "Here he is, your dear little brother."

She stared silently at the yellow bandage bound between his thin, waving legs, and at the other yellow bandage tied around his protruding tummy, and she smiled. To conceal her scruples, she even dangled her fingers above the infant and her father rewarded her with a smile of relieved satisfaction.

Regina came in from the kitchen in a full dressing gown, looking swollen and disheveled. She changed the baby and a ghastly smell filled the air. Then she took him to her body, crouched on a chair, and, in full view of the girl and her father, bared a heavy, ugly breast, its nipple abnormally large and dark. Pursing her lips, she squeezed the nipple, drew from it a few thin sprays of milk, and then thrust it inside the yelling mouth, moving it about between his lips until they clamped on it.

Maya ran out and was violently sick in the shade of the mulberry tree.

Regina guarded the screaming bundle jealously. "*Nicht*, don't touch!" she scolded incessantly. "*Du!* Don't look at him from behind! You want to give the child a squint?! That's what you want."

As the other woman in the house, Maya was obliged to hang up the diapers and perform chores. She liked going out on errands because they gave her a brief spell of freedom, but they were still somehow sullied, as they were done for the benefit of Regina and her son—"your brother"—and not only "your brother" but "the bearer of the name and true heir to the house of Hermoni," as his mother never tired of repeating.

Now Katriel, arriving home after a week's absence, was explaining in his typical oratorical style how overworked Regina was and how Maya ought to respect her since she cared for her too, for Maya, while her natural mother wanted nothing more to do with her.

When she did not respond to his haranguing, he would turn on her with the full force of his rage, raising his voice to a ludicrous high-pitched howl with Regina backing him up from the kitchen: "She's been corrupted, corrupted!"

Maya's feet were still set firm in a domain where hidden meanings are attached to words. The mouth became a treacherous instrument that must be bridled; every word that is uttered bears the threat of disaster, and every word withheld is a world of silence and deliverance. Maya found herself a hiding place in the shade of words left unspoken.

One day Regina's fury boiled over. Maya could not explain even to herself how it happened that she brought home only the stalks of the expensive early grapes that were intended for the baby. On the way she pinched a few of them, just to see if they were ripe. At home Regina pulled out of the bag a few pips hanging weakly from the stalks, withered, like her tears.

The blows were a real pleasure to Maya. There was a sort of heart-filling wholeness in this hatred that they nourished.

Sometimes, in a sudden surge of paternal instinct, Katriel would indulge simultaneously in concern for his daughter's education and in speculation about her thoughts.

There was in Maya a secret longing to give in to this fatherliness, to rush through the door that he opened for her. But she had learned from experience not to put her head through the transparent window: her head would be smashed on the glass barriers of disillusion.

"You should be grateful for what you have . . . there are other children . . . orphans . . . unfortunate . . . concentration camps . . . slum neighborhoods . . ."

"I have a different mother," she told him once, emerging for a moment from the shade of the unspoken words.

The light—and the regret—dazzled her.

"When you grow up you'll understand," replied Katriel, with the melancholy of a grown-up to whom everything is clear.

She wanted to ask him why he didn't love his second wife either, but she held back again.

Once she made a birthday request that her mother be allowed home. She knew that there was no importance in what she was saying; her request was meaningless and the picture that had been torn out could never be stuck back in its place. It was just a part of the cruel and competitive game that the two of them had to play.

"When you grow up you'll understand," said Katriel.

She didn't want to grow up. Growing up meant recognizing and solving and creating new problems, knots, whole mountains of them, knots tangled by the impulses of others.

Sometimes he responded to the nagging resentment of his wife, her constant lament that in a moment of weakness she had been trapped into taking responsibility for this little monster, and then he would seize his daughter (surely out of weariness, utter weariness), drag her into the bathroom, and, in an outburst of desperate anger, beat and thrash her until he drew tears.

She understood by now that her weeping had become the ticket with which he bought his portion of tranquillity from her stepmother! Maya was careful to keep the price of the ticket high, until the tears escaped her control and fell, while *she* waited, listening, outside the door.

When her screams reached such a pitch that there was no

further need for them, he would leave her alone to calm down. And when she was gasping, choked by dry belches and tearless groans, seeking to prolong the delight of her spent weeping, he would come in again, lock the door behind him and—all conciliation now—try to win back her love.

"Yes, yes" was her hurried answer to his question "Well, are you going to be a good girl?" for she could not bear his embraces and his self-abasement before her, the meaningless self-abasement of one whose sin and repentance are both preordained.

Within the apartment itself, in the third and farthest room, there had lived for some time a pair of elderly relatives, a childless couple.

Aunt Feiga Levin took the new order as a personal and unforgivable insult, since from the day that Katriel's first wife left him, she, Feiga, had been the mistress, bearing the yoke of the household and controlling her nephew's finances.

After Regina's invasion, the Levins shut themselves away in their little room, coming and going by the rear entrance, and nursing their resentment.

Valentine Levin, whom behind his back everybody called "Valentino" or "Vaselino," a worn-out dandy with long limbs and greasy hair, strutting about on Sabbath afternoons in a top hat, with gloves and a walking stick, used to drag the girl into the cheerless room where the couple lived and there sit her down on the threadbare sofa facing a portrait of His Majesty King George V, framed in gold. Vaselino was a loyal supporter of the monarchy, and this was a cause of never-ending friction between him and Katriel Hermoni.

He used to look in turns at the king and at his stringless balalaika that hung on the wall, "corrupting" her in a magician's whisper. "Girl! Don't eat any food that *she* cooks . . . all the food is full of microbes . . . after she goes to the toilet she doesn't wash her hands, she wipes her ass, infects the food. Hey, hey, are you going to see your mother? Tell her everything right away, every-thing, tell her what she's doing to you, that gypsy thief . . ."

His stumbling speech was hateful to her, but she cherished his company because he too had been outlawed by the confederacy of aunts on account of his idle and hedonistic nature. Valentino sided with her mother because she was prettier than Regina and because she was a *"blondinka,"* and because she wasn't wandering around here, between the walls of his house.

All this time Feiga Levin would be filling the air of the little room with the stifling smells of soups cooked on her tiny stove, and occasionally she would feed "our orphan" thick and oily bean soup, asking her *"Goot? Goot?"* while Maya forced herself to swallow the vile broth, scooping it up with a flat Russian spoon and assuring her that it was good, just so Feiga Levin would go on hating Regina.

The whole house was whispering. The walls seemed impreg-nated with whispers and "scandals." The father took to staying away longer from the house, returning to it irritable and impatient. His quarrels with Regina grew more violent, reminding Maya of his quarrels with her mother in her early childhood. During these altercations, which began with the frenzied exchange of senseless insults and ended with plates lying smashed on the floor, the daughter stood pressed against the wall, digging her nails into the plaster and trembling with hatred and delight, until the father disappeared behind the door and she heard the woman's subdued whimpers as she gathered up the broken crockery. These whimpers enraged her, made her confused, and opened up something inside her. She enjoyed seeing Regina in her wickedness, her incoherent stupidity, but not in tears. Weeping was somehow a desperate appeal for justice.

At such times she would run to Valentino. Once she found him, after such a "scandal," dancing with joy, his thin legs skip-ping around the blazing stove as he held his silent balalaika in one hand and plucked at imaginary strings with the other, the top hat on his head. When he saw her he stopped for a moment and blew kisses at her in celebration of a shared victory. Then he winked at her, pointed toward the kitchen whence came the sound of Regina's desperate sobbing, listened for a moment with eyes half-closed, as if hearing a delightful melody, joyfully slapped his chest, raised the balalaika, and "plucked" it again, hopping on his toes on the tattered carpet, moaning in nasal imitation of the woman's sobbing: "O–oh, o–oh, o–oh."

On one of his first nights at the hostel, Dov Markovski went out, in an open-necked shirt, to stroll around the neighborhood. He went alone, although Shoshana had invited him to join them, the three women. "After the children's bedtime," she informed him with some excitement, "there will be 'reinforcements from outside' "; this was a visit she had been expecting for a long time.

That summer of 1928, a dozen years ago, when he arrived in the land of his dreams, he felt as if something was ripped apart inside him. And since then it had never healed. Then everything lost its softness, its depth, its vision, everything was exposed; he was struck by a blast of cruel light and with it the first stirrings of regret. The flowers were alien, nameless, with no burden of memory; the trees, his own age or younger, were like a temporary decoration. Although he was only sixteen years old, he could not be reconciled to the new landscape and was left with a bitter and permanent streak of alienation. Over the years his picture of the Ukraine had turned to a lost, heart-draining memory, sweet and whole.

Now he summoned the comforting darkness of the night, which cloaked everything in a shroud of illusion. He went out from the gloom-filled courtyard and proceeded slowly, groping his way along the unfamiliar route that he hoped would lead him to the lip of the hilltop, bowed, obstinate but full of curiosity, like the man who has wept bitterly for the woman he loves and now goes to meet the unknown spouse imposed on him by the marriage-broker. For a moment Frieda's scornful smile flickered through his mind. If she could see him now, blind in the dark! The pale rays of light, filtering weakly through the cracks in the blackout screens over the windows of the houses, were gradually extinguished, one after another, as if blown out by somebody patroling the neighborhood while the night was still young.

He climbed higher, and, stumbling on an outcrop of rock, he spread out his overcoat and sat down. For a long time he stared into the abyss before him. From the furthest reaches of the barely visible plain that sprawled at his feet, rose the darkness—the light, limpid, floating darkness of the void and the viscous bulk of another darkness, hinting at the shapes of things.

The ground resembled a gigantic tortoise, lying supine, spread-eagled and helpless, in expectation, under the flickering sky of war.

There was a kind of sweet, painful enchantment in staring thus at the frightful, desolate void, its stillness suddenly invaded by the freshening wind from the North.

For a moment, recognizing his reflections, he felt gratified by them, but when he found that he had sunk unawares into the very heart of the darkness, he was suddenly afraid and his heart froze for a split second. In a momentary flash of clarity, he felt a cold and crushing awareness of the deepest depths of the earth, the yawning immensity of the globe. His nerves—fully stretched—had a fleeting, shuddering sense of the line that passed from the center of the earth through the tightly packed layers of substratum, tracing its path to him, to his shell-like body, stuck to the very edge of the little rock. An all-consuming loneliness, the isolation of a husk confronted by the scale of the universe and confronted by darkness.

But only for a split second. He shook himself, hurriedly felt his chest. Cautiously he inhaled the new smells of the night: a smell of strange leaves, a smell of dry dust, and the distant sickly smell of carrion. Suddenly his ears were opened to the sounds coming from the distance, approaching and receding, as if the night were transferring its voices from one vessel to another: the sound of a fretful car dragging up the slope, the clink of a chain, a brief, frightened twitter close at hand, a rapid movement among the bushes at his feet, and, above all this, the hypnotic, vibrant, stubborn password of the crickets. Finally, the murmur of people, fragments of laughter, and a woman's voice.

His initial sense of self-wonder now seemed ludicrous and excessive. He retraced his steps, already bored and impatient to return, trampling underfoot the dry, rustling undergrowth.

From the house arose the ringing voices of the women, awakening in him a new excitement.

In the doorway of the brightly lit dining room, he was greeted by the basso profundo of Pani*-Paula, the cook (or "estate and inventory manageress," as she insisted on being called), a voice both attractive and repellent, with its contrived tone of aristocratic grandeur. At once his excitement was extinguished.

"Ah! Mr. Markovski! Come in, come in! Didn't I tell you all that our partner would come in the end? And where has our

---

* Polish for the title "Lady."

esteemed friend spent the whole evening, if one such as I may be permitted to ask? Of course he's been reading the books he brought with him, mountains of books . . . I tell you . . ." She spoke in a tone of extravagant and ironical respect, alternating Polish with Yiddish. He cursed himself for having told her once, in an unguarded moment, of his fluency in Polish. And how did she know what he had brought with him?

With an unwilling smile, he murmured a few pleasantries. His eyes, which had become accustomed to the darkness, now took in the spectacle of the long table, the worn tablecloth, the playing cards stacked in the circle of light shed by the oil lamp, and only then the surrounding shapes, shrouded in smoke. Suspended conversations hanging in the air, the silence of a group of convicts scrutinizing the new prisoner. He felt a twinge of uneasiness and understood why when his eyes fell, suddenly, on the promised "reinforcements." The eyes of a stranger glanced at him obliquely, in cold appraisal, from under the Australian bush hat, the strap dangling casually against his chin. He felt he must justify himself.

He thought of the three stories of the silent house, three stories imbued with the breath and the stink of children, that stood between him and his books, between him and the article awaiting completion on his writing desk.

The hat—only the hat—was the reason for his aversion, a man sitting in a closed room at night in a hat, just because it suits him. And his moustache, and because Frieda is at his side.

"Mr. Markovski," Pani-Paula's voice harangued him in Polish, as if she were the patroness of a salon, "won't you be more comfortable if you play sitting down?"

He replied deliberately in Hebrew, declaring that he had come in only for a moment, and that urgent work awaited him elsewhere. He was aware of the dishonesty of his words and knew they would be interpreted as arrogant self-importance. His eyes strayed again to Frieda. Her eyes, level with the sentry's shoulder, looked at him again with the same challenge.

"Ah, work!" said the cook, with an emphasis that dismissed in advance whatever he was supposed to be doing.

"Do—ov! Come and sit down—here." This was Shoshana, who pulled out one of the chairs nearest to him with a kind of natural grace and slapped it with her hand, smiling a gum-revealing smile of affection, radiant with pleasure at the generous deed itself rather than the thought of his proximity to her, or so it seemed to Dov.

He assumed the air of one submitting with dignity and sat down, cursing himself, then remembered to smile gratefully at this picturesque creature, who now exuded a faint smell of scrubbing soap. At once he turned his gaze to Frieda, as if apologizing for staring so long at her friend.

The cook—a childhood friend of the Wolfson woman—shuffled the cards expertly, snapping the two halves of the deck together with a sound like the swift ripping of cloth. Then she murmured the numbers as she dealt out the pairs of cards to the players, as if throwing nuts to monkeys. Her body was all of one piece; the only moving parts were her arms, her wrinkled gizzard, and the cigarette hanging from her lower lip.

The "estate and inventory manageress" was a type familiar to Markovski: a strain of aging women who have lost out on the days of their youth. The Party was full of them, aggressive creatures who adopt the manners of cunning conspirators, penetrating through your eyes to the marrow of your spine, seeking thus to defend themselves against the revulsion that their bodies inspire and against new disappointments that they no longer have the strength to bear.

The obscenities constantly on her lips had earned her the nickname "Bloody Mouth," but even more impressive were her sudden silences, cutting off your words with prolonged sarcastic stares, as if at this moment, this very moment, she has cracked open the dark vessel of your thoughts, exposing all its putrefaction. What a dangerous creature to minds consumed by self-love! The few who found the key to the narrow, twisted passage that led to her heart were, as is normal in such cases, the very ones who meant least to her, whom she despised in her heart.

Rumor had it that in her youth she had been married "to some *goy.*" This was at the height of World War I, but the man failed to return to her warm embrace, sinking instead into the cold waters of the Vistula, one of Marshal Budonny's bullets in his back and Hetman Skoropacki's flag flapping gestures of farewell about his body. She arrived in Palestine a widow and a semilegal immigrant, bringing with her proud memories of the days when she prepared French cuisine in one of the fashionable restaurants of Warsaw.

Dov picked up his cards and began to sort them. The detestable triviality of the proceedings stuck like glue to his fingertips.

"Wow," the voice of Shoshana shrilled beside him. "People are strange! Haven't you introduced yourselves yet?!" Her voice had the strident tone of one determined to have a good time, whatever the price. She herself took no part in the game but leaned against the back of a child's chair, her thighs crossed and slanted far to one side at an oblique and charming angle, the blue pleated skirt folded above her knees, which were exposed like a pair of babies' heads, one peeping out from beneath the other. To her right, on the floor, lay an embroidered cloth bag from which trailed a strand of the knitting yarn that had occupied her attention all evening.

"*Duce*! Yosef! Hey, what's the matter with you?" she cried eagerly, putting down her knitting in her lap. The guest looked up with deliberate laziness. They made their introductions like representatives of enemy camps meeting by chance on neutral ground, or so Dov imagined.

Before returning to his former position, the sentry* tossed his hat behind him, without resorting to a backward glance. It landed,

---

* One of the Jewish youth who served as volunteer guards for the rural settlements of Palestine during the period of the British Mandate.

neatly, on the window latch, and his youthful locks were revealed.

Dov recognized the surge of uncompromising hatred that swelled in his heart. The three women watched the young man's movements as if they were being offered a rare delicacy. Suddenly they seemed ridiculous to Dov, a trio of cheap metal ornaments that had just now been polished and burnished, revealing all the sharp lines previously hidden by dust and verdigris.

"Do you know why they call him 'Duce'?" Shoshana raised her voice, apparently so as to be heard by the sentry too.

Pani-Paula began cursing over the extinguished stub of her cigarette.

The game began at last.

Dov's cards were bad, and he made no effort to play well. The others troubled him. Three or four new forms had invaded his life all at once, and if he allowed them, they would melt into his bloodstream, diffuse themselves in the channels of his brain, wring his neck, and boil him in their pan of tepid water.

The cook, her little finger thrust deep into her mouth at the point where her jaw bones met, a place where, apparently, a tooth was missing, was totally absorbed in a practical exercise, chewing her finger incessantly.

The sentry was alternately singing and humming, with the equanimity of anticipated victory, a song from a film that everyone in town was rushing to see. "Mama darling . . . Mama darling, Mama, oh Mama . . .," he crooned, raising and lowering his voice according to the play of the cards.

Frieda handled her cards with perceptible slowness, her brow wrinkled. He did not know what intentions to attribute to her, but he felt a vague presentiment of disappointment. The neutral Shoshana glanced from time to time at his cards, giggling a friendly warning, endlessly licking her lower lip with a broad, hedonistic motion, naively confident of her charm. Once or twice she rose from her seat with a lively toss of her limbs to measure her knitting on the back of the sentry, who was engrossed in his cards and his scheming.

The game dragged on, and again he seemed to hear Kashka's voice, drunk with incisive proofs, a voice like the creaking of wooden benches: "Spokes in the wheels of the Revolution . . . people like a certain well-known comrade . . ." Confusion had hit him when Kashka had informed him that he was about to send his own daughter, Maya, to this place, this very place, and she was already here, although Katriel Hermoni still chose to ignore *his* presence here. His wandering thoughts returned to the dim lamplight. Here he was in a strange place whose existence he had never imagined, and his thoughts were distracted against his will by the repetitive victory cries of a fat woman seated beside him, at the same table, picking out cards and laying them down, apparently without any break between one hand and the next, and the noisy bids of the others, people with whom he would never, of his own free will, have chosen to associate.

His eyes came to rest again on the girl, on Frieda, perhaps to remind himself of the reason for his tarrying here. Her face dim in the lamplight, she seemed engrossed in a painful prayer.

"Perhaps you'll explain to me," he cried suddenly, just to hear the sound of his own voice as he picked up another stack of cards. Frieda immediately raised one eye and an eyebrow.

"Why should people put so much effort into assembling a dynasty of castrated kings?" At once he realized his mistake. They had been waiting for this!

"Aha! You have a choice, Comrade Markovski!" Paula trumpeted like an excited elephant. "Of course you're an expert in the matter . . ."

Shoshana laughed in astonishment, eager to show him her affection and unaware of the web of hostility being woven about him.

"I tell you, they have no lower half!"

"Let's get on with the game!" said the sentry calmly, throwing down a card.

Pani-Paula carried on in her Polish Yiddish, which grated in his guts like a metal file.

"We've all heard it before, a great expert! Play the joker! That's typical of your sort, throwing away the king and playing the joker, eh? But how to play, they don't really know."

"Let's get on with the game!" the sentry stressed pleasantly and returned to his visceral song.

He felt obliged to react as if he were enjoying the jibes of the cook and looked at her with a smile of appreciation, but she at once pulled in her double chin and fixed him with one of her piercing stares.

Late in the night they finally totaled up the scores. The cook had made a handsome profit. With an emphatic disregard for the congratulations of the other players, she picked up the lamp from the table and commanded Shoshana to accompany her to the kitchen.

This last month they had stopped using electricity and also started saving oil, Frieda explained to the two men. She giggled helplessly when the sentry commented on the staggering stupidity of living in such a frugal style without any attempt at escaping, then came up with a proposal to set up a weather vane on the roof and operate a private generator. He struck his temple and declared that the only thing this place lacked was simple intelligence.

Dov found in these words an explicit reference to himself.

The two women went out and took the circle of light with them. The room was left in semidarkness and there was an awkward silence, soon broken by noises from the kitchen, the clattering of tin plates and the loud instructions of the cook. The sentry said something to Frieda's silhouette, something soft that sounded like Italian, and then he asked her to scratch his back.

"No, not there, what's the matter with you? Under the ribs! Now lower down." The next sound to be heard was his playful sigh of relief.

Dov felt a spasm of uneasiness and found himself listening intently to the two of them, until the sentry complained in a loud voice that the "spoil sports" were coming back with the light.

"*Du-u-ce!*" Shoshana's voice rang out, accompanied by the smell of coffee. "Sau-sa-ges! There are sau-sa-ges!"

In the circle of light that was restored to its place, the tin plates were noisily distributed, piled high with sliced sausage, segments of various cheeses, pickles, and biscuits, and on the tray beside them a challah loaf resembling a homemade cake and a metal pot giving off the aroma of real coffee.

The sentry, whose presence in this place was still a mystery to Dov, rubbed his hands together with an air of total freedom and, letting out a childish hoot, swooped on the refreshments.

"I say, you're in luck, *Duce!*" cried Shoshana. "Only yesterday the Wolfson woman was kind enough to send this . . ."

"That's what you think!" The cook set her double chin quivering. "That great public-spirited woman. One kilo, that's all! And that *grand dame* act of hers when she comes here . . ." At once she went into her "Bloody Mouth" routine, all the while passing plate after plate to the sentry, her expression saying: "Eat, eat—until you burst!"

The guzzling was at its height, the women analyzing the taste of the food with great percipience. Dov refrained from eating, until Shoshana thrust a sandwich into his hand. At the sight of all this eager consumption he felt a strange sense of guilt at his unwillingness to share the others' pleasure.

"Health to the Wolfson woman!" cried the nursery attendant, in a youthful Sabra voice, attempting again to spread gaiety all around her. "In spite of everything, health to her!" And as she raised her coffee with a toast—"For the poor children!"

"And health to Reb Shulmanitski!" Frieda followed suit. Her

voice, amplified with an effort, had a hoarse and strident quality that did not suit her at all, and from the look on her face it was clear she was afraid she might be unable to match the natural delight of the others.

"An expensive butcher he is!" Paula contradicted angrily. "He'll get what he deserves!" She shook her head as she slapped a rosy segment of sausage onto a slice of the challah that she had baked herself.

"*Duce*! Chee–eese!" sang Shoshana.

"*Cholera*!" The cook went on with her stream of Polish cursing. "Expensive butcher—I wish they'd smoke his shmuck the way he smokes this sausage, hang that cat's tail of his on a hook for all the Carmel Market to see. Ugh! One kilo! Stink of cats!"

"Hallo, *Duce*! Pickled cucumber?" sang Shoshana.

"I hope all his life they write him recipes like the recipe of this *cholera*," said Paula.

Dov listened, making an effort to tie the words together.

With the outbreak of war and the drying up of funds from the Belgian diamond merchants who had been the patrons of the establishment, the Wolfson woman overcame her scruples and went out every few weeks in a hired taxi on a crisis mission to tour the haunts of the wholesale food suppliers in the lower reaches of the Carmel Market. She used to pass from shop to shop, dressed in elderly elegance and with her insistent cry: "For the poor children!" The more wary succeeded in fending her off with pretexts of wartime shortage, but she, ever persistent and with an expression of reproach on her face, fished out from among them four or five who took pity on the old woman wandering in the ways of strangers. These "fish" were already struggling in her big basket, from time to time donating to the "poor children" sacks of grouts that had become slightly mildewed, flour teeming with beetles, wheatmeal, misshapen lentils, and broken biscuits from the bottom of the carton. Sometimes, adopting a more aggressive approach, she forced one of them to hand over a few slices of cheese. As for Shulmanitski, an acquaintance of her late husband, his cringing excuses were no use and he was obliged now and then to toss into her bag, with the expression of one casting pearls before swine, a few kilos of cheap sausage.

It was obvious to any unprejudiced observer that these scraps of sausage, suspicious in color, which arrived now and then in the pantry of the "estate and inventory manageress," and the odd slice of sheep's cheese, which needed soaking in milk for several days before it could be eaten, could not by any means satisfy the ravenous hunger of forty or fifty "poor children." So, for self-explanatory mathematical reasons, these delicacies fell into the laps of the members of the staff, who after all had not many pleasures in their lives.

"These imbeciles," Paula tended to explain her economic policy, "just don't realize what they're eating. They're used to eating whatever garbage is given them. It's a miracle stomachs have no windows—a miracle."

Dov became aware of all this at a later stage, but now he listened in amazement to the names being thrown about the room one after another, between every bite and gulp, and he stared at the cheeks of the cook, bulging with food and rosy with contentment.

"*Duce*," Shoshana licked her lower lip again, eager to catch the sentry's eye, "enjoying your treat?"

The guest stuck out his lips like a duck's beak.

"This—is this all there is?" he responded weakly, as if fainting from hunger. "It's never possible to tell with you if you're being serious," Shoshana countered with that hackneyed statement beloved of infatuated girls.

"That's right," he agreed with a sigh and turned eyes full of healthy masculinity toward Frieda. "You should just see what I do with the fridge at Yosef's mama's house.

Paula stopped munching, swallowed, and stared at him, expecting an insult.

"A full fridge—oh, yes!" he added, glancing around him. "And when I've finished with it, all that's left is a desert! An empty, Arctic desert!"

"Lord's Miracles!" cried Paula. "What a good boy!"

"What *desert*?" asked Shoshana, like a schoolgirl hungry for knowledge.

The sentry winked at the girl sitting beside him, inviting her to share his opinion of the questioner. Frieda did not respond, but Shoshana's eyes froze for a moment on the face of her rival.

Paula, like a hostess who has suddenly realized that she has not succeeded in inviting to her salon the pick of humanity— "but the show must go on"—sliced what was left of the challah into tiny strips and gathered up the crumbs with the balls of her fingers. A thick wedding ring clamped her finger, beneath it an engagement ring.

The sentry was now explaining to Frieda, to Frieda alone, that only in Italy was it possible to learn the true art of eating.

"In Italy," snorted Paula contemptuously, "the worm sat down on the horseradish and thought it the sweetest thing in the world. What do you know about French cuisine?"

Her eyes—like two casseroles full of the delights of French cuisine.

Shoshana said something about *cholent*. He heard the sentry's voice, complaining to Frieda about "these Jews of ours, who can't even stuff themselves properly without some religious pretext."

"Because he studied in Italy they call him '*Duce*'!" Shoshana murmured to Dov, in an attempt at regaining her dignity. "All the gang call him '*Duce*'!"

"*Basta Duce!*" replied the sentry, injecting a fresh infusion of gaiety into her veins (in spite of everything, he was listening to what she said). "Now, a poor, fucked-up sentry who spends his evenings in orphanages."

"But they still call him '*Duce*,' "said Shoshana, obstinately.

Dov felt, suddenly, as if three generations stood between him and Shoshana and this *"Duce,"* a rift made wider by his inability to take pleasure in trivialities.

"In another year he'd have got his diploma," added Shoshana. "A veterinarian!"

"And that's why the cows are in love with him," said Paula.

"I specialized, basically, in the morphology of the udder," said the sentry easily, and for a moment his eyes lingered on her enormous breasts. The girls choked and stifled their laughter. Suddenly Dov was full of pity for her, perhaps because of the two rings that pinched her finger so tightly.

"Interesting," he turned to the guest with a friendly expression. "What did they think of Mussolini when you were in Italy, those people with the tradition of . . ."

"Garibaldi, Matteoti, strikes at Fiat," the sentry filled in after him provocatively, hissing beneath his moustache, between his teeth, and he grimaced at Frieda—who had turned into a kind of medium for all of them—with a look that implied "that which I most feared has come upon me." But when he saw the girl's eyes, which were also expectant, he turned his chin sidelong and whispered mysteriously, in Italian, *"Dolcé far nienté!"*

"The bread rose more than usual today," said Paula in Polish, a sign that the conversation of the others did not interest her, "and I was sure that the yeast wouldn't be enough. Those little hooligans of yours, Frieda, begging your pardon, stole my yeast this week. They think it's halva!"

The sentry interrupted her in a weak voice, a tone suggesting conscious awareness of the superior quality of his humor:

"Pani-Paulichka, *Proshechka*! Perhaps a little more of this cats' stink, eh?" He waggled his little finger over the sausage dish, where all that was left were a few rings of peel.

"Alas, truly, the best child is always forgotten," the cook growled over her gizzard, not moving from her place. "Go eat yourself!"

"But even so, Yosef," asked Frieda, clinging to his previous words (Dov noticed that she didn't use his nickname), "I can't believe that people there in Italy didn't care . . . and the war . . ."

"In every period there are a few lunatics," said the sentry without interest, "who invent theories for themselves, perpetuate them in books—a fake passport to future generations. And the future generations view their inventions as proof of the validity of the same lunacies . . . reality proves one thing . . ."

"*Dolcé far nienté!*" hooted Shoshana.

"You stick to shining your knitting needles!" he snapped, with a look that cut off her tongue. "War is the pressing need to copulate after a prolonged period of impotence, eh? What you people are suggesting is a world of hypocritical monks, cannibals on the quiet . . ."

Dov saw how the blush spread over Frieda's face, covering her neck and reaching the collar of her embroidered blouse, and how the sentry was out to conquer her mind by means of other advantages.

"But reality isn't a line of shop windows that a man goes and smashes one after the other," she said suddenly.

The sentry raised his hands, stretched his back until his vertebrae popped, yawned and declaimed: "Oh, the slogans! *Bambini*! Walk very quietly beside those windows. If you break them, you'll bleed, phew!" As he spoke he leaned over toward Frieda's mouth, as if to kiss her, then recoiled at her cry of protest.

"Otherwise it would be impossible to live."

"Correct, *bellissima*, correct! 'The lion shall eat straw like the ox,' " he recited, like a nervous girl on a school platform. "They shall all eat straw, carnivorous and toothless! What a charming manger! But the war! The ideal opportunity for all your straw-eaters, all the lean and brutish cattle hitched to the stalls of humanism, to the troughs of 'reward and punishment' . . ."

"He's also more comfortable bombarding from behind a stockade of slogans!" cried Dov.

The sentry, like a child absorbed in a game, jammed a piece of cheese between his teeth and carried on with mouth full:

"War is shit. But only in war does every stupid nonentity achieve the peak of his genius. Only there does he squeeze all the juice out of his glands and reveal his unique, true personality. And only after it is he sure that he's done something great, greater than himself, that he's caught Allah by the . . ."

"Stop babbling!" said Dov, feeling an urge to smash the pretty face. "I've known men more driven than Mr. *Duce*, who, in contradiction to your Al Capone theories . . ."

"*Santa Maria*!! Afterwards they suddenly got sick of it, it's a bit unpleasant, eh? Suddenly it isn't moral, is that it? The morality of a man who's fed up with the nymphomaniac who's been clinging to his body for years until . . . boo-hoo-hoo," he said with a shudder. "Afterwards they sit down and write pacifist songs."

"Listen, listen to this preacher! The way he chatters you'd think he'd spent ten years in jail!" sneered Paula, not understanding.

A few minutes passed without either of the men hearing the other's voice, as the young women rose from their seats and shouted at the tops of their voices in an effort to calm the protagonists. In the middle of all this the sentry picked up the hat, and when he turned back from the window his face was calm.

"The Communists have different remedies for the human tumor," he said to Frieda. "They have strikes, street battles, demonstrations, and afterwards differences of view, betrayals, purges, executions."

"Open the arsenals," cried Paula, without looking up from her game of "solitaire." "Generals! Open the arsenals!"

Suddenly he understood that everything had been said just for the sake of conversation and provocation, and that it was within the sentry's power to put a stop to all this at any moment. For this reason he felt a sense of exhausting emptiness, exasperation at the way the whole evening had been wasted.

"Haven't you had enough?" yelled Shoshana.

The sentry stepped forward, a little shorter than Dov, and stealthily approached Paula, who recoiled with fear, then turned away and tried to lay his hand on Dov's shoulder. Involuntarily he drew back.

"The trouble with your people, Markovski . . ."

"You're at it again!" cried Shoshana impatiently. "You've ruined the evening, the pair of you!" She began striding deliberately toward the door.

The sentry was already outside the range of the conflict, standing beside the table and picking up the crumbs. Shoshana changed her mind and returned to him, stood on tiptoe and snatched the hat from his head, and slapped it over her temples with a graceful movement intended to amuse him. Then she wrapped her arm around his waist, her hand playing with the butt of the revolver, which Dov noticed now for the first time.

The *Duce* freed himself from her embrace with a light shrug of the hips, removed his hat from her head, as if it were a hat rack, waved it toward Frieda, and shouted a farewell to Paula. When she did not respond he winked again at Frieda, mocking the "mood" of the old woman, and went out of the room. Shoshana hurried in his wake, swinging her embroidered knitting bag.

Markovski waved a hand toward the door, turned to Frieda, and chuckled silently.

"Do you have a sedative, Frieda?" Paula rose slowly from her seat, carefully stacking the cards. "I'm going to put myself to sleep! The evening has been very stimulating." Her manner was resentful, the resentment of an actress who has been presented as a prop.

"In the children's first-aid box," replied Frieda softly, turning to the table to gather up the dishes. Paula swept past and left the room without speaking, her chin in the air. Her small role had been played out today, but she could still make a dramatic exit.

For a few moments more they heard her footsteps and her rummaging in the box in the next room.

Now the room seemed bigger.

Dov watched the girl as she shuffled quietly beside the table and collected the plates, fitting saucer into saucer. It seemed to him that the evening's ridiculous storm had driven them closer together. Without knowing what to do, he tried to help her; she motioned to him to stop.

"A normal young man," said Frieda suddenly, without looking up from the crockery. He didn't know if she was being ironical. "I've always admired normal men," she added.

Dov felt scared. "Nor–mal?" he said as he followed her precise, too elegant movements, her body moving among the shadows, and her hair, which for a moment as she stood above the lamplight, was as red as brass.

Two years ago Bat-Sheva Greenspun-Tamarin had been a vessel filled to the brim with fears and a powerful sense of deprivation, but her luck certainly changed for the better when she was sent to the hostel from the house of Officer Tamarin in a police squad car.

On the very first Sabbath eve the new inmate appeared at supper wearing a dazzling white silk dress with checkered embroidery across the bosom, which immediately provoked gasps of envy and a hunching of the shoulders from the girls who sat watching her from their places, and from the boys a look of surprise and a murmur of admiration. Quickly the rumor spread that the new girl had brought with her two "made to measure" dresses, exercise shoes, biblical sandals (the ineradicable dream of children of the hostel since time immemorial), also rubber boots with soft white linings, buckskin winter shoes, fine underwear with the manufacturer's label, and a voluminous blue raincape (the one that she had refused to wear in the Tamarin household because she had inherited it from her cousin).

The Tamarin family, being "conscientious" and concerned for its offspring, took care not to throw the foundling from its home without first providing her with the full range of a girl's clothing and a girl's possessions.

Bat-Sheva Greenspun-Tamarin brought with her another painful world in the shape of a schoolbag with two locks and a key, which she hung cheerfully around her neck, and leather pencil cases containing row upon row of colored crayons, sharpeners, and high quality architects' erasers.

A superficial finger would have pointed at this as the source of the change in Bat-Sheva, an aristocratic young lady among the blighted and poverty-stricken, who carry their books in cloth bags stitched from faded women's clothing (which in the course of time come to be held together with string or bits of wire), borrowing one another's pencils and going about in hastily adjusted cast-off clothing.

Undoubtedly the girl, smeared with butter front and back, realized as soon as she arrived how dry were the rusks of the others, but the source of the change was different; it came not from the range of her possessions but from another process, more sensitive and deliberate.

On Bat-Sheva's first day she was asked the question that is always put to the new "victims" in prisons, hospitals, and institutions for abandoned children: "Why?" Meaning: "What was the storm that washed you up on this desolate shore?" She replied at once: "My father was killed in the riots."

It is easy to suppose that Bat-Sheva was then aware of the shock wave that swept toward her from her audience. It was bemused jealousy.

"He was killed!" and at once, in the same breath: "He was a

taxi driver. He was killed in 1936 on the Jerusalem road, and then they sent me to live with my uncle, Officer Tamarin from Kefar Saba. Haven't you heard of him? He's the one who . . . I caused them a lot of trouble, and they couldn't stand me, especially my cousins. My mother got a job in this neighborhood, in the big Pension on the hill, and then they decided to send me here and . . ."

Her father had been killed! But for that, she'd be riding on his shoulders to this day and she'd have had no contact with this place, with children of no-fixed-abode who can't be sure if their names are their own or invented, whose origins are shrouded in dark guesswork, confused and ludicrous, destitute orphans and bastards. And suddenly, here is wholeness, certainty, cleanness—the essence of purity!

Not treasure and not clothing, but one quality that she has, a quality with the power to destroy, humiliate, and perplex: the quality of purity. The purity of priests licensed to eat of the wave offering.

With the subsidence of the natural feelings of affection that she aroused, the girls (especially the girls!) began to interpret the coming of Bat-Sheva Tamarin (she had the wisdom to adopt the officer's name) as a new revelation of their worth. This must be the sign of some marginal change in their fortunes, a sign of that other world, hidden from their eyes, its virtue concentrated behind family nameplates, that had sent its angel to them to deliver them from the pit.

Unaware of their motives, the girls began lavishing affection on her. When they sat with her at the table they would watch how she—she too!—swallowed the insipid porridges, or they noticed how the stench of the dormitory absorbed the noble fragrance of her breathing and became a new, more bearable blend of aromas.

At the local public school they hung about her and publicized her merits: "Look! Eat your hearts out! She's ours! Ours! Someone like this—and one of us!"

Their despised and decrepit group, tacitly forbidden to associate with the rest, received an intoxicating, unexpected stimulus with her arrival at the school, and they were anxious that her brilliance should not be dimmed, helping her secretly in her studies and in her confrontations with the "decent" girls, all those children of "good" parents, householders, inspectors, and slaughterers, the apples of their eyes.

She was the eye-catching representative of a poor kingdom, demanding the recognition of the world. They were proud of her, as a tuber in the ground is proud of the red anemone that rises from it into the open world of the flowers.

This was, apparently, the beginning, and like every beginning it was sweet.

Bat-Sheva, her head anointed with the sacramental oil, took these new manifestations to herself with a sense of relief, but she was careful not to tread impetuously the field of wonders that was spread out before her. She was entirely a creation of the inflamed imagination of the girls, an image that they had created for their own needs, and they were bound to her with brightly colored threads of comradeship, exterior bonhomie, fascination, graceful airs, and little reciprocal acts of kindness. Until the gentle anointee made haste to break out from her chrysalis. Suddenly the treetop thickened and dimmed the eye of the sun. The constant and recurring process by which legitimacy is conferred upon domination with its thousand faces—the power that burgeons in light-heartedness—was gathered in from the extremities and then imposed on them again from the center outward.

In a long-lasting process invisible to the eye, within the soft loam of delicacy and ingratiation and admiration, there crystallized inside the girl the pearl of awareness that her own special qualities were the ones that endowed her with her nobility and strength. In the course of one year Bat-Sheva was transformed into the omniscient one "who giveth and taketh away." A temporary prohibition became permanent prohibition, every passing request fulfilled was sealed and became an etching on the face of experience, every stratagem a conquest, every word a new idiom.

The wine of authority became the essence of her blood, moved her body and lent a new tone to her voice. Boredom began to show its signs in her. Before it had been as if she sought to adjust her surroundings to the temperature of her body, and now, as they had compromised and she was no longer required to struggle, she looked around for new drugs, new stimuli for the alternations of heat and cold, the insufficiency of which was the cause of her sudden combustion into weird flame that aroused the dread of destruction in the hearts of her captive subjects.

All these years the mill of the Wolfson woman did not cease grinding, swallowing, and spewing, absorbing and expelling. She was still lying in wait in the doorway of the cellar of society, releasing new divorcees from the burden of the last link that ties them together, picking up the seeds sown in excessive cold or excessive heat, the children of mishap or the children of those resentful of their fate, creations of a civilization that is incapable of controlling the results of its creations, embryos inefficiently aborted, the backward fruits of modern sex lives, and—if you wish—the child of a woman set free for an hour, who does not wish to become a permanent drudge, and the son of one whose business is the correction of the universe but who has no interest in the effort of supporting his little molecule. Older children going off secretly to a new "institution," a new "father," a new fate, and newcomers arriving wide-eyed, each new arrival bringing a natural awe for the power of the veterans, for the confidence of an old existence, the advantages of precedence in time, of belonging to an elite.

The enviable privilege of being counted among the close acquaintances of Bat-Sheva was at first denied to every recent arrival, and to shut her out they gave their adored one full authority to be harsh to her, the new invader, while they stood around to protect the queen of the hive.

And as the older ones, those who had exalted Bat-Sheva for their own purposes, became fewer, and the new ones multiplied, so her authority flourished.

When Maya arrived at the hostel there no longer was a single veteran of the first generation—the bedrock; they all belonged to the second or third stratum of those who accepted her dominance from the tradition. The power of Bat-Sheva, simple and innocent in its origins, was now legendary, mysterious, a dim divine fact, and nothing could now be restored to its beginning.

10
A MODEL
OF STABILITY

When the smell of cheesecake wafts through the rooms of the hostel, it is a sign: the legendary father is paying a visit to his offspring.

Already, over the steam of the lunchtime soup, the staff had chattered in their Polish-Russian-Yiddish. About whom? One guess: "An ideal father!" "A heart of fourteen-karat gold!" Even Pani-Paula was for once in agreement with Shoshana: "A diamond!" Markovski could not resist adding between spoonfuls: "He's a diamond alright, you could cut glass with him!" And Shoshana stole a warning glance toward Modi.

He's jealous, thought Maya. Boria can't bear the sight of the women putting on clean aprons and hanging cheap trinkets on themselves in honor of *his* coming.

Although this was one of those sweet days of mud and leakage — a day when the lucky ones are sincerely thankful in the morning that Social Aid has stopped sending shoes and turn warm buttocks to the blanket—Modi's celebrated father was not missing out on his visit. He's never late and he's never early. That's what it means to be "fourteen-karat gold."

Still wearing his hat and his fine winter overcoat, raindrops hanging on its fur like a string of pearls, Mr. Glick untied the string knots that bound one of the three parcels, and then the smell wafted out, mild, sweet, and rancid, and drowned all other smells.

Modi and Yitzhakele—who had waited patiently for their father in the entrance, behind the curtain of rain—now sat on the older boy's bed in the "Invalids' Home," the cardboard box open between them, sharing, with heart-rending courtesy, the squares of chocolate that the cold had crusted with a film of white.

Only now, with the fulfillment of the first demand that children are apt to make of an ideal father who has come for a visit, did Mr. Glick allow himself to be divested of his coat, slap his hat on his knee, sink back on the bed, and fix on his offspring the eyes of a priest who has offered incense to idols and now waits for a sign.

When his scarf was removed, the rain-dimmed light revealed one of the distinguishing marks of the Glick household, the accordion-shaped neck of a lizard, screwed between the shoulders into the chest. This revelation inspired in Maya an agreeable sense of revulsion, a kind of malice.

"Pigs!" snorted Salomon through dilated nostrils, his elbows nudging and barging aside stomachs and ribs and midriffs. "Rotten pigs!"

The convoy of inmates, which had dropped anchor around the fragrant pier on which Glick Brothers, Ltd., were dividing the bounty, with intelligence and awareness of the importance of the occasion, began maneuvering gracefully toward the open sea, but against its will, its telescopes were still trained on the enticing port.

The more sophisticated had the wisdom to fix curious eyes on

the plaster faces on the ceiling. Only Stinking Rafi found forgetfulness and redemption through discovering the treasures stored
in his nostrils. For a long time his fingers were busy rolling his
spoil into little balls, and his inflamed rabbit-eyes glazed with
satisfaction at the sight of the accumulated mass, speckled with
purple and green.

At long last it was impossible for Glick not to notice the scene
unfolding around him. With surprise and a look of gracious condescension—purring cats nestling in his eyes—he turned his
healthy, well-shaven features to the children of strangers.

"Ah! Hello! Hello, friends!" And immediately he added with
jocular respect those obligatory sentences, repeated with every one
of his visits: "Real young men!" "I'd have hardly recognized you."
"Soon you'll all be old enough to run off and join the army."

"You people want some too?" asked Modi.

The well-known benefactor earned, as a token of esteem, a
whiplash glance from the baleful eye of his progenitor.

The children of strangers came a little closer and waited patiently for the Glick family to solve, within itself, the crisis of
wills into which it had fallen, waiting for a hint. They waited in
vain.

"We aren't hungry!" Salomon replied at last, but taking care
to pronounce a guttural "r," as is usual in displays of pride.

"We only just finished lunch!" said Modi with a kind of malicious joy, thrusting thumb and forefinger into the oil-soaked
carton.

"Sure!" Ketzele slapped his stomach. "A healthy lunch! Bean
soup! Every dish a Molotov cocktail!"

"Maybe, all the same you . . . ," Modi hesitated.

But Papa Glick had the ears of Haman. "And now, dear children . . ." He gestured with his chin toward the door. The crease
at the base of his neck opened and closed.

"In Jerusalem, near the House of Steps," wheedled Yaffa, "my
Dad bought me cake like that once." A crust of moldering, long-

remembered insult sprawled on her face. "Cake with lots of cream, lots . . ."

"Very nice, little girl, very nice . . . and now, children, if you don't mind . . ." Glick smiled toward the door, tigers roaring in his pupils. "Well, really, there are limits to everything!"

Modi Glick's face turned silver. You could see his blood freeze as clearly as if it was in a transparent test tube.

Because of the rain Papa Glick had made a serious mistake this time, making the gift ceremony so public. He usually hands over the ritual oblations to his sons in modest secrecy, outside the hostel or in the garden of the nearby yeshiva.

"This is my daddy," said Yitzhakele suddenly, his mouth full.

"Yes, my chick!" Glick drew him to his side with fatherly compassion. "Yours and Modinka's!"

"Only *my* daddy!" said the chick, shaking his beak this way and that with victorious pride.

"Friends, hey, what is this?" Papa Glick tried another tactic. "Don't you play games after lunch?"

"It's raining outside, isn't it?" asked Modinka in a pained, sickly voice.

The laws of nature bowed Glick's defeated head toward his little son.

"Well, Yitzhakele, are you glad your Daddy's come?"

"More chocolate!" said Yitzhakele, his eyes scouring the box.

"More?" asked Glick defensively. "There is none! All gone, Yitzhakele! All gone! In another month Daddy will bring lots and lots of chocolate, and now Yitzi will eat another cake!"

"Another helping of chocolate!" insisted the child. Glick smiled for a moment, taken aback by his boldness, and then turned his gaze to his first fruit.

"Modinka, you're . . . somehow . . . you don't look so . . . ay, ay, ay . . . like a citron after Sukkot, ha ha!"

The malicious smiles went round and round.

"How's the food?" continued Glick, paying no heed to the assembled company. "Good? The time before . . . somehow . . ."

"Good, good," snapped Modi, to silence him, nervous, his eyes fluttering as if a fan were blowing in his face. His fingers wandered to the box and withdrew.

"Look at this, look! His father only taught him to speak, and already he's teaching his father to shut up! Well, no matter, no matter. Eat, eat . . . even appetite he doesn't have."

He drew a bone comb from his pocket and carefully passed it through the boy's slanting locks, the fingers of his other hand searching for dirt or lice eggs.

"I see they've given you the paraffin treatment," said Glick calmly. Modi slumped, angry and embarrassed, while his father asked if they scrubbed hair with shampoo or just with soap.

"Ordinary soap causes dandruff, and the hair falls out . . . you'll end up defoliated, like your father . . . that's right! How unjust it is!" He laughed. "Your grandfather, may he rest in peace, had a head like Absalom's, but he didn't need it—he always covered it with a *shtreimel*—ha ha!"

Modi's head fell into the box.

"Of course there's shampoo," said Ketzele happily. "Every Friday a full shampoo bottle goes. Every bottle, a cup of health." Immediately imagination conjured up the sight of young Ketzele standing in the bath, his head turbaned with a fantastic froth of shampoo bubbles.

"Is there?" Glick asked his son, disallowing the testimony of the stranger. "If not, don't be afraid to tell me! Just tell me! Your father, thank God . . . just tell me and I'll send some to Frieda so she can scrub the pair of you. It's a very natural thing . . ." And his eyes made it plain to his son that, unlike all these flotsam and jetsam . . .

"There is!" they all replied in chorus. "Of course there is!"

Glick ignored them completely. There are limits to everything. His eyes demanded a reply from his son.

"They've told you!" Modi replied in a weak voice, between the crumbs of cheese.

"Today you're not in my good books at all," said the father, rising and smoothing down his jacket. He wrapped a scarf around his accordion-neck and told his elder son to tie up the parcels well and shut them away in a locker. "It isn't healthy to have everything at once! Everything in moderation!" Then he carefully wiped with his handkerchief the mouth of the little one and the elusive lips of Modi.

In the "Invalids' Home" there remained a bittersweet and disturbing smell, like the smell of disinfectant that stays behind when the school nurse has left the classroom and all must return to their books.

Modinka-Podinka was not orphaned of his mother, as he pretended to be. He had two whole parents. It would have been enough for any one of the children to hear just once the words of Glick to Frieda: "Only a woman is capable of thus abandoning everything—children, family, respect—and running off with a foreigner. Now she's living off milk and honey, over there under Hitler. How is it possible to demand of a husband that he just adore and adore thirty hours in a day? To all things there are limits."

On Stinking Rafi's blanket a moist stain darkened. A memento of the wet raincoat of Papa Glick, who had decided to go with his sons to the room of one of the staff members, far from the eyes of strangers.

Outside the storm groaned and wailed in turns, as if having difficulty deciding which was the more stormy sound, but when Mr. Glick speaks all other voices melt away, even those of the youths. In the dining room his voice rang out so clearly that even he himself was trapped momentarily by a kind of embarrassment amid the tense and polite attention of the others, or because of Frieda's gimlet eyes, which were fixed on his mouth, assessing the extent of his power.

Dov Markovski settled against the back of the chair, his eyes wandering over the newspaper that was spread surreptitiously in his lap, but between his spectacles and his chin, pressed hard into his chest, a coil of scorn was stretched tight. Thus he appeared to Maya wonderfully likeable and sympathetic, while Glick spoke of his spare parts business and the current state of the market.

"Won't you tell us, Mr. Glick," Pani-Paula interrupted him with a genial smile. "Tell us, you have two sons and yet you treat each one as if he were an only son." She spoke, characteristically, with contemptuous disregard for the presence of the other "imbeciles."

"Well, yes, certainly," replied Glick, without concealing his pride, and he turned his smile to his elder son who sat opposite him. "If I had ten such as these, let's say, then Madam could be right."

Mr. Glick is a model of stability in this amorphous world, and he has nothing in common with all those fools whom he derides, confused shooting stars sowing meteors on all the winds, arriving here suddenly at some point on their erratic trajectory, clumsily stroking the head of some tongue-tied boy, their eyes seeking contact, and then flying off, never to return.

Glick never forgets to bring with him some small gift for the women—a bottle of genuine "Maria Farina" or a collar of Swiss lace—and Frieda is the only one who does not respond. She always pushes away the parcel with her hand, intoning, in Polish, a few phrases of refusal, which always gives the situation the appearance of a small and intimate family scene, and always, finally, one of the other two accepts it as a bonus.

Mr. Glick commended the bread pudding offered for dessert. This evening they had sweetened it with sugar, that and the tea. "Oh, no, no," said Paula. "This time, really, it isn't so . . ."

"In that case, I'm trying to imagine, Madam, how it tastes when it *is* so . . . ha, ha." Glick laughed, eyeing her appreciatively as if she were the last representative of womanhood on the face of the earth.

"Mr. Glick . . . surely he's a man from another world . . . surely . . . a type who goes and hides himself from this mad world . . . only in books, good books, in poems . . ."

Bitter compassion flowed into Maya's heart for the cook, who was thus forced to surpass her own limits.

"In poems?" laughed Glick. "Oh, Madam, oh, oh, you don't know me, Madam. Mind your step, Madam! I'm a man who's been written about in only one poem: 'Mammon is the Rock of My Salvation'!"

The cook protested loudly and laughed, and with her Shoshana, who never stopped sniffing at her wrist, perfumed with genuine "Maria Farina."

Maya noticed Frieda's eyes searching for a gleam in Dov Markovski's spectacles.

"He's the only father," Paula continued with her game, her voice thick with emotion, "the on–ly one! An idealist!"

"Well, well!" said Glick soothingly. "What a word, Madam, what a word!" His eyes moved to Markovski, who gave the impression of ignoring the entire conversation. "In these times of ours that isn't a compliment. Look, only this week, this very week, I had a visitor at my shop, an old friend from the kibbutz, straight off the train to me! We ate together on boxes and drank from a clay jar—the Arabs call it a *jarah*. I'm sure you, Madam, don't know what a *jarah* is. *Jarah* is the first chapter in history; all history begins with *jarahs*. 'Well, we must drink a toast,' I say to him. 'I read in the paper about the new well that you dug. I always insisted that there was underground water in that region and you all laughed.' And what does he reply? 'Stashik, I want you to help me get started in business.' Can you imagine, in business! No well, no underground water! To establish oneself! This is the new cry for deliverance of a revolutionary generation. To find room at the table—and snatch! That's idealists for you!"

"And Stashik is helping," Paula prompted him pleasantly.

"Helping! Oh! As they say, 'There's no dead man who can bury himself.' Ow-wow-ow!" he replied to their laughter, mimicking the storm.

Several times the women had asked themselves why this dealer in tires and automobile spare parts chose to keep his children in this "cave of gypsies" of all places, until he himself explained— with characteristic candor—that in another place, in some large and prestigious institution, they would be as nothing, two out of a thousand, equal in rights, whereas in a kibbutz they would suffer from feelings of inferiority and deprivation. Only here, here of all places, could he be sure that they would be treated as they deserved and would never feel themselves inferior. On the contrary . . .

Indeed, everyone knows that the cook is fattening up the Glick brothers on the quiet. After lunch she locks the sleeping infants' room behind them and stuffs them with soft-boiled eggs and cream, paying no heed to their protests.

"Well, Modinka and Yitzhakele, time for bed!" said Glick, as he used to say to them in their own home.

The children all leaped up from their places smartly.

Before entering the dormitory Maya caught a fragment of conversation between Markovski and the cook, who were wrangling uninhibitedly on the darkened staircase.

". . . Madam's tongue has become light and very sharp lately," said Boria, "but she still gives off a strong smell of ass."

"Some day, sweet Lord, some day someone will find a big cork," replied Paula, her fury overflowing, "and then you'll stop barking through your asshole and polluting the air. You have no feelings at all, you have no human warmth—Bolshevik, poo!"

Pani-Paula always has enough in her pocket to pay back with interest. Dov laughed briefly, amused.

The jackals of the wind rushed between the fences. Maya entered the "Casino," the room of the privileged boys. It was Salomon who named it after the ornate refuge of his childhood, the "Casino" of Haifa; whereas the room of the more lowly of status was simply called the "Invalids' Home." Markovski had gone to the city and the women were entertaining themselves downstairs with Glick. The boys had folded their limbs beneath the blankets and she imagined the tips of their noses sniffing at their scarred knees. They were listening, as she was, to the crashing of the treetops and to the tubs rolling against the rails of the balconies, intent on escape. She loved to linger alone with them in the "Casino."

A melting peace descended on her, a gladness-to-be-alive untinged by fear. She felt this was a place free from resentments and petty-mindedness, its occupants united by a lively and straightforward sense of brotherhood.

In the dancing light of the lamp, casting discs of light onto the ceiling, she saw Ketzele in his underwear, shivering in the cold and tearing pages out of a notebook, stuffing them into his shoes. The nightly smell, a smell both fearful and pleasant, familiar and slightly repellent, when it belongs to others: the rancid stink of blankets, the smell of stale urine, the smell of dust overtaken by the aroma of sweaty feet; but above all else, the most delicate of hints, another smell, rich with promise: the aroma of cheesecake.

"Use rags," said Abie, close to his elbow, his entranced eyes wandering among the discs of light as if seeking inspiration for a poem. Abie's lovely eyes filled her heart with longing, this boy always so overburdened with the world.

"Rags!" replied Ketzele. "What do you think I am? A refugee? Rags are alright for refugees . . . writing paper—it's smooth and it doesn't absorb." He was right. With paper it's possible to arrive at school almost dry, but rags soak up the water straightaway.

Ketzele threaded grimy feet into the padded shoes and stamped on the floor. "Not too big now either," he said. "The important thing is that there's a bit of sole left around the holes."

He always knows how to satisfy his own will. Now he kicked

off his shoes and leaped onto his bed with a precise *salto mortale*. The bed responded to him joyfully, with a loud chime of springs.

"Why don't you put out the light, imbeciles," his voice grumbled from under the blanket. "Some of us here want to sleep!" Somebody laughed and went to blow out the lamp. A cloud of soot rose for a moment and subsided. The void of the "Casino" suddenly intensified before the half-closed eyes of the visitor, sinking and rising in turns, and a dull apprehension stretched her guts. The moment for which she had been sent was approaching, and she was afraid to break the sudden silence with her voice. Only the rustle of straw pillows testified to the presence of living bodies, which had not yet deposited their souls in the heavenly soul-bank of the night. She remembered her provocative question in the classroom: "What does the soul do at night up there in Heaven if the body below wants to go to the toilet?"

She could remember only the righteous long face put on by the teacher, and the scandalized murmur of the other girls, all of them destined to be the brides of rabbis, and her own indignation that not a single voice joined in her laughter. This was a skill that she would never master: to educate the tongue to roll out material appropriate to her surroundings, to subjugate it to the requirements of the occasion. And Bat-Sheva had sent *her* of all people . . .

A figure appeared in the doorway, wrapped in a long sheet, sending a thrill of foreboding through her heart, but she felt that it matched the fear inside her and it somehow soothed her.

"He's snoring already!" said the figure in the gloom that had been softened by the opening of the door. This was the hoarse voice of Salomon. (Yesterday he had been transferred to the "Invalids' Home." The cheerful atmosphere in the "Casino" was too bold for the taste of the staff, and Salomon was convinced to go by the only means capable of convincing him—his love affair with his stomach.)

They'll hate me for this, she thought defensively. They'll hate me, and all this goodwill, it'll be lost. How was she to say: "We, we want"—oh yes, they'll respect that! "We"—but who? Yaffa? The Quiet Loony? Hedva? Some formidable gang that is! Should I say it's what *I* want?

I, I want! Even her unwillingness had been taken out of her hands! For a moment she felt grateful to the Queen for bestowing on her the power of command, like a seal ring.

Salomon noticed her, bent down, and said "boo!" into her face, to scare her; but in this "boo!" she caught a hint of hidden affection and she didn't want to destroy it.

"Bat-Sheva told me to say . . . ," she said to Salomon.

"Yes, yes. What did she tell you to say?" There was a tone of defiance in his voice.

She trembled when the edge of his sheet touched her. "She told me to say 'fifty-fifty.' *She* said (so you'll know I'm only the mouthpiece of that one who can climb the ladder without looking down!) she remembers exactly who it was who raided the neighbor's beehives."

From the beds arose masculine grunts of scorn. This was the first time that the Queen had dared extend the range of her authority over the free-spirited boys. Maya felt that this liberty of theirs was based on a wonderful balance of strength—a sort of equilateral triangle: it would never be possible for Ketzele, the daring and light-hearted adventurer, to master the experienced casino-cunning of his comrade, and the pair of them together could never aspire to the sensitive and detached humanity, the mature judgment of Abie. The rest always chose to attach themselves to one or the other of the trio, for protection against the bites of the others.

"Dear Miss Shitface," Ketzele declaimed into the darkness from his bed, "be so good as to tell your Queen," he began to sing softly, scornfully: "Kiss me goodnight, sergeant-major . . ."

"Tell her to look for a crooked cop in Mister Tamarin's police force," said Abie.

Somebody began to curse. A kind of happiness climbed into her heart.

Come on, let's have some more, you bold spirits, lay it on! Now she would return to the girls' dormitory, put on a face of angry hurt, full of vengeful appeals, repeat their answers word for word and see how, for the first time, the Queen's nose came up against hard clay.

But in the darkness the voices were already losing their initial force. Midway through the defiant anthem of "Tell her, sneak to her grandma, croak it to the chickens," the discordancies already sounded false. That's the only dignified response they allow themselves, she thought.

They knew it would be enough for Bat-Sheva to chatter innocently in the ears of her mother, who lived in the neighborhood of the hostel.

"If we don't throw this at her, you'll get a kick up the ass. Oo—oops . . . ta boom—straight to the 'soup kitchen for the needy'," said Ketzele loudly.

She imagined the murderous look appearing in Abie's lovely eyes and felt offended on his behalf. If it had been Salomon, he wouldn't have hesitated to reply with something like: "Are you referring, perhaps, to the hotel in Hayarkon Street?" But Abie said nothing because he was Abie. He just hoards his experiences quietly and records them in his notebook.

A few weeks before, when she was sent to the town "to ask your father for a coat," Maya was wandering aimlessly in the street when suddenly she recognized her, the little, transparent woman. She was sitting on an open ground-floor balcony under a sign that read "Soup Kitchen for the Needy," apart from the others and trying to hide her face from them, waiting for the miday opening of the kitchen.

Maya retreated at once and hid, almost instinctively, behind the bulletin board, so the woman wouldn't notice her. Perhaps it was the horror aroused in her by the mystery of lonely poverty, or fear lest the woman tell her son of their meeting and he bear it as a grudge against her.

She often comes to visit him, the transparent woman, and then Abie treats her like a sickly child and goes out with her to stroll on the hill paths. He speaks with her for hours in their own language, and so they return, arm-in-arm, he talking and she grateful, her eyes brimming with emotion, hanging on his lips. He never mentions his mother in the presence of others. But the staff, to make up for this, are equipped with four wagging tongues. And so it has become known that this woman was a singer in Bucharest, where Abie was born, but unfortunately his father, a conductor in the opera, was the husband of another. Abie yelled beautifully, but his mother lost her voice. How does one lose a voice? Paula told Shoshana that this was one of those punishments sent by God to teach the rest of the fools, only it isn't the fools who learn . . . How could someone like Abie be a *punishment*? Then he and his mother were refugees, and he was given his mother's surname.

Maya suddenly realized that she had missed the end of the debate and was therefore unable to marshall her thoughts in accordance with it, and already she saw the shapes of the boys preparing for action and already they—and she with them—were close behind Salomon, who covered in three long strides the distance from the door of the "Casino" to the bank of lockers in the corridor. The only ones allowed close enough to touch were those equipped to help him with whispered advice. Here the natural division of labor, based on capability alone, was as elementary as breathing, as a game.

The little door was like the other little doors in the bank of lockers. Behind it in the dark would lie five gravel stones, corks from English beer bottles, razor blades, and a few shriveled cockroaches, but now added to all these was that thing from the infinite world, something whole, something on which expert and precise hands had labored—and only a few correct movements were needed to wrest it into their grasp, to flood them with the tastes of all conceivable possibilities.

Salomon probed the keyhole, the bent wire between his fingers.

Dissatisfaction mounted in her as she stood and watched him from a distance. Before, in the "Casino," it had seemed to her that everything would swarm with problems to be solved by concentrated, competitive activity of brain and nerves, and here it was as if the objective was blurred and only scratching was left. It was all too brief, too quick, too smooth.

Again the rain swallowed voices and breathing and brought with it fears of surprise. The voices of the women encircling the voice of Glick rose muffled from the ground floor.

The prodigious stature of Salomon, in his underwear only—despite the cold—the sheen of his calf muscles in the gloom, his professional assurance, the three years separating him from her, awakened in the girl some cautionary awareness that she should not linger in his company, that he was liable to probe with expertise and destroy the guts of anyone who let him scratch his insides; but she continued to watch him, a sweet longing tingling in her throat.

He stopped suddenly. In the soft darkness she saw the silhouette of his face glaring ferociously at the door that refused to respond, as he would glare at some doomed person who had insulted him. At this moment of frustration someone pulled the skeleton key from his hand and Salomon let it go. The other tried his strength, but the lock stuck out its tongue at him too.

Modinka-Podinka was now revealed to the eyes of all as a cunning and selfish creature. The darling of Papa Glick, the son in the coat-of-many-colors, had thwarted all their chiseled minds. Snoring there peacefully over his secret in the "Invalids' Home," there amid the foul stench of Stinking Rafi and the other weaklings, tomorrow he'll be able to buy himself friends at the cheapest price, at the cost of a portion of cheesecake.

With renewed courage, Salomon snatched the wire from the

hands of the other failure. The scratching rose now to an angry and ominous pitch, soon warm blood would stream from the heart of the lock. She waited in oppressive emptiness for the redeeming sound of the opening door. Nothing mattered now, only that sound, the one and only. Let it come at last! Salomon stepped back and in desperation aimed the battering ram of his shoulder against the door, but one of the "rabbits," some little pisser-against-the-wall, beat him to it, stood on tiptoes, stretched out his hand, and, as if inspired, pulled the handle. The lightest of clicks, and everything gaped open before their eyes. An Aladdin's Cave, endless store of delights! Splutters and repressed nasal laughter—everything lost its tension in the humor of relief—it had never been locked! The warm, flowing ecstasy of seizing the windfall . . . only the pure pleasure soon to ring out like electricity trapped in the filaments of the light bulb. The sweet, invigorating smell freed from its prison.

Salomon's hands stretched out, but again he was beaten to it. She was there already, casting in the darkness the lasso-eyes of the dog-catcher—Bat-Sheva.

Before they realized what was happening and had time to set in motion the tactics that were agreed on, apparently, beforehand in the "Casino"—which Maya had missed—the Queen was already pacing down the corridor in dance-time, bearing her spoil in both hands above her head. And four girls hurried behind her, carrying an invisible train, walking shoulder to shoulder for fear of lagging. The boys did not stir, pathetic Samsons shorn of their hair.

But only for a moment. And then somebody untied the string, and dozens, hundreds, thousands of hands collided over the one oil-soaked parcel that was left, and from the locker beer corks and polished gravel stones fell to the ground.

Some relief returned to her only when she remembered that the Queen had not explicitly instructed her to return. So at least she would not be forced to take part in the degrading divvying ritual now in progress in the girls' dormitories: a ritual of extortions and promises and sacrifices.

In the morning Pani-Paula seemed to be taking long and relaxing drafts of the unaccustomed peace that reigned in the dining room. Only Frieda's eyes sparkled as usual with uneasiness and with expectation of the words that would pass, pass away and have other things take their place. Modi's eyes wandered among the grains of rice, as if trying to work out what it was that made them stick together. He was not reckoned a fool. In school he was not overburdened with fat certificates, and he strove very hard to escape his "good boy" image, but his taste was different; they had cooked him from different ingredients—slow cooking in an electrified kitchen by chefs in white turbans, not in some seething cauldron over a campfire.

The others watched him out of the corners of their eyes with anxious expectation. He turned his gaze to the window opposite, to Frieda as she laid the teapot on the table. His eyes were empty of hatred, of vengefulness, of fear or disappointment. Just empty.

They were in no hurry to finish their rice porridge. Perhaps he had not yet discovered the other emptiness? Perhaps he was waiting until they had gone and would then run upstairs to grab a furtive slice? The thought infused in Maya a delicious sense of malice, and suddenly she felt the vibrant comradeship between herself and the others, the cunning identity in all their thoughts, wrapping themselves around him like the ropes that bound the Golem, the quivering pleasure of "we're all in this together." She imagined that if she smiled at Ketzele he would return her smile and they would both know why. If her eyes met Abie's, he'd look away at once, so she wouldn't think he was in love with her, just because last night they had stood together to one side and watched the others guzzling. And if she twisted her lips in a glance at the Queen, she would respond with the same grimace.

Now she looked at Bat-Sheva, who had pushed away her empty

plate and was spreading margarine on her last slice of bread, the one-for-the-road, then smearing on the margarine her portion of cocoa powder. The salty taste of the margarine, under the sweet flavoring, stuck to Maya's palate for a moment, making her regret that she had not done likewise and had wasted all of hers on the rice porridge.

Affection swelled up in her for Bat-Sheva too, for the artificial curl that lay on her forehead, for the long fingers working with such concentration on her slice of bread. She tried to catch her eye and play with her the understanding-game, but Bat-Sheva rose, leaning one hand on the table and clutching the bread in the other, and smiled at Modi, sitting opposite her, a smile of goodwill.

"You've got a bit of food there," she said, pointing with the concern of a sister.

He passed the tip of his tongue over the grains of cocoa that had stuck to the corner of his mouth. The grains disappeared.

"There's more, on the other side," Bat-Sheva smiled. The others looked on, perplexed at this sudden intimacy. The boy licked the other corner of his mouth and at once raised another spoonful to his mouth.

"You know what?" said Bat-Sheva. "My aunt puts a bit of lemon peel in it. With lemon peel it's awfully nice, improves it no end. That's what your cakes need."

You could have scraped the eyes of all of them from his face, like a mouse that has drunk gypsum and all are watching: what's going to happen? Modi stared at her lips, but his mouth went on munching the porridge and swallowing it down the accordion-neck of the Glick family.

Maya's eyes suddenly turned to Bat-Sheva's empty dish. On its base and sides were moist brown circles—this morning she had two portions of cocoa powder—one for the porridge and one for her bread. This was the first profit that she had grabbed from the sharing of the spoil in the girls' dormitories. Suddenly there returned to her that terrifying sense of loneliness, of trembling isolation, like being the single spectator in an empty movie theater. On the screen before her people moved, talked, there was even music to accompany their movements. But it was impossible to say anything to them, to stop them, change the pattern of their actions, make them say other things, draw their attention to you with a cry of alarm. Just watch them from the deserted auditorium, or close your eyes and wait until they open the doors.

11
A MOMENT'S
PLEASURE

In Regina's house Maya felt everything in her gut—the tension, the anger, the restraint, the jealousy, the loneliness. All these sensations in her gut—and she was always short of breath.

In her meetings with her natural mother her soul suddenly became as flat as stagnant water, and some light happiness fragmented within her into thousands of bright, leaping sparks. Then she felt everything in her chest, as if it was all springing upward, to the lungs, to the wind pipe, to the mouth, which would suddenly babble without restraint.

On those days that she and her mother had arranged for their meetings, it seemed that her heart was plucked from within her and hung on a high cord, to flutter in the wind.

She carefully locked the door of the bathroom, in which the

air was heavy with the pungent smell of baby muck. She cleaned the insides of her ears with a soaped finger and with her fingertips wiped off the dark circles of grime from under her chin, so that at least her mother wouldn't criticize her for being dirty. She took care to do all this secretly, so Regina wouldn't know the time of the meeting. But that woman had X-ray vision, and as Maya stood by the front door ready to leave she suddenly heard: "*Stoy! Stoy! Du!*" The woman approached her, breathless with anger, her teeth set and in her hand the bundle that Maya thought she had escaped. Regina threw down at her feet the bundle of clothes wrapped in a dirty sheet.

"You think you're going to sneak off like this, like a mouse? Your mother—that *grand dame* with the red manicure—and me a proletarian! Is that right? Is that socialism?" The distorted speech and the foaming Russian words maddened her more than the crudity and the hatred that she accepted as natural. Silently, submissively, she picked up the roughly tied bundle. These were her dirty clothes, which Regina had refused to wash since the baby was born. Maya was careful to close the door behind her quietly, so as not to give the woman a further excuse for attack, but still she followed her down the steps, her lips blazing.

A door opened up above, and she saw the head of the neighbor from the second floor peering curiously over the balcony rail and winking at her with gestures of questioning and sympathy. The girl pretended not to see the neighbor.

The bundle in her hand ruined the prospects of the meeting. With mounting fear she could already hear, ringing in her ears, her mother's response to the sight of the laundry, how she would flare up like a primus stove full of air. "So? And aren't you ashamed," her mother would chide her, "and you agreed to take it? Do you still not understand what you're doing? I didn't expect this of you, a girl in her eighth year . . ."

And then Maya would invent all kinds of terrible diseases that have afflicted the stepmother—she really does want to wash clothes but she's sick, some disease . . .

And she could hear her mother's voice again: "For her! Of course! For her you're sorry! Nobody's sorry for me! The woman who stole my house, you're sorry for her! Everything that was mine, she's stolen! She'll pay! She'll pay for all that she's done and I hope she breaks all her fingernails the way he broke me! And you! You have no character! Pushing rags into your hands, making you walk around like a tramp, and you accept it! No self-respect! And what's she ever done for you that you're so eager to defend her? Why are you so loyal to her? Take that home at once and tell her from me, from me, that she is . . . and she is . . ."

So she returned home with the laundry.

Desperately she racked her brains. She crept into one of the cool, well-tended gardens adjoining the avenue and waited until the man left the stairway, then hurried to the back garden and threw the bundle over the hibiscus bush beside the tap. She looked up at the house to see if her guilty deed had been observed. There was nobody at the windows. Maya went out into the street. All at once everything floated up to her lungs.

On the steps of the Habimah theater she felt for a moment like a captain on the bridge of a ship. Her hair, cropped efficiently and gracelessly in a boyish style, was tousled by the thin sea breeze rising up the avenue. Suddenly fear began to peck at her heart, fear that she might fail to recognize her mother. Then she narrowed her eyes toward every woman appearing in the range of her vision, concentrating herself with animated expectation, which flared up and abated with the approach of the figure. Perhaps it was the expectation that made her feel, suddenly, that she'd been standing there for hours, days, weeks without beginning. The dust of disappointment mounted in her throat and turned into a bitter lump. She hated her eyes for dimming, hated their readiness to weep, and to keep them from tears she descended the steps to the people walking about on the sidewalk below the theater and asked in a dull, indistinct voice, so the person asked wouldn't notice the lump in her throat: "What's the time?"

The time was later than that arranged for the meeting. Again her eyes dimmed and the lump was now so solid it was impossible to shift it. "I'm spoiled, I'm spoiled . . . a cry-baby," she told herself angrily, went down again slowly and asked the time again, trying to sound casual. Then she went down again and asked and went down again and asked. The fourth time, as she stood before the stranger who groped in his breast pocket with a fatherly smile, she suddenly saw, from afar but distinctly—there she is!—the figure of her mother. Without waiting for the man's reply she started to run. She remembered, turned her head, and saw the angry face of the man who thought she'd made a fool of him. But now it was too late to explain. Through the veil of her tears (the lump had burst suddenly and melted into flying tears) she saw the beautiful mother pacing toward her with an appraising smile, bending her head forward to see her better over the sunglasses.

As if she'd not been late at all, the mother asked suspiciously what that man wanted from her.

"Nothing! Nothing!" her chin quivering, and the wretched tears.

The mother asked if the man had insulted her, and if not, why the tears?

"It's just, just . . . I'm not crying," she answered hurriedly and wiped her streaming nose with the back of her hand, feeling exhausted.

The mother wiped the tears from her face with a fragrant handkerchief that she took from her bag, and she smiled. It was clear that the tears restored her peace of mind, as if she grasped their meaning.

The mother was young, clean, beautiful, eloquent of speech, and men turned their heads as she passed. As the two of them walked side by side in the street, Maya's heart swelled with pride. She wanted to shout in the ears of all the passersby: "Here, take a look! This! This is my real mother! Haven't I told you a thousand times, *she* isn't my mother!"

Even in their walking together there was a different aura. It was the mother who now looked from side to side, watching for cars. Maya put herself entirely in her mother's hands, freed from concern for herself, for her life. Now she was sure that by herself she was quite incapable of crossing that road, which only a short while before she had crossed at a run.

"You smell terrible! It's just impossible to cross the street with you," says the mother. To make the excuse that the bath was full of the baby's diapers—that would be shameful!

Now she knows where they are going. Walking down rustic little alleyways until they arrive at that three-story building. In the gloom of the stairwell hangs a smell of mold and of defensive sandbag emplacements.

The bell is mute, as usual. The mother knocks vigorously on the door. A woman's voice is heard and the sound of clattering heels. "Who's there?"

"It's us!" trills the mother. Only when faced with Maya is she nervous and agitated. The door opens and the three sisters swoop on them with cries of wonder. They are dressed, typically, in very domestic attire—flannel gowns without buttons over shabby corsets—a form of dress that they allow themselves in the confident knowledge that men will rarely visit their house.

The apartment is cramped, heaped with heavy old wooden furniture far too big for it, but everything in it seems to Maya gay and light. The warm smell of newly cut cotton fabrics, the hum of sewing machines, hundreds of pearl buttons sewn onto coils of rustling silver paper, magnetic scissors, and thousands upon thousands of pins stuck into giant cloth cushions that hang at the windows like bright little suns, and the new corsets scattered all over the room—pink, white, and black.

"Now, straight into the bath!" cries the plump woman, the oldest of the three, to Maya, who is playing a little game with magnetic scissors and pins.

The three of them rush forward to strip her.

Ha! With what pleasure she now takes in their hurried, eager chatter.

"She's got ribs like the whale bones in a corset!"

"Look, look what they're doing to this child! You can see every beat of her heart!"

She surrenders her body to their hands, staring like a new Pinocchio as they strip off the stiff and grimy khaki pants, the blue blouse with a button missing at the neck. She walks before them in her nakedness and feels no shame, happy and recoiling from them at the same time.

The mother puts on one of their gowns and starts scrubbing the girl's back with a brush. "You need a horse brush!" cries one of the sisters.

"Look at that dirty stain, it'll never come off! You need rubbing alcohol!"

And all the usual jokes about what you could plant in her ears and behind her knees. The women crowd together in the doorway, looking on with eager eyes and loudly critical of miserable roosters who neglect their chicks.

Eagerly she stretches out her ears, her neck, her knees, looking forward to a cleanness that she could never have achieved by herself. When her skin is all rosy from the painful scrubbing, the hot water lashes her body, is absorbed into her blood, bubbling in every cell and fiber and melting her limbs one by one. The three sisters hurry to wrap her in a big, hairy bathrobe, giving off a feminine smell. They rub her and crown her head with affection.

Again they are standing around her in the big room, exchanging opinions of their handiwork and looking at her and her mother, who is now dressing her in clean underwear that she's brought with her in her bag and a white organdy dress, specially prepared for their meeting.

"You're very lucky to have a mother like this!" says one. She looks in the oval wardrobe mirror and sees her reflection, freshly scrubbed in the bright dress and with the big butterfly ribbon fluttering on the top of her moist head, and suddenly she imagines herself a big cooking pot, polished inside and out, ready to accept a delicious pudding. Now that there's hardly any need to be ashamed of her in public (aside from her thinness, her "vitamin starvation" and her worn shoes, as the three sisters point out), they take their leave of her by the door, showering her with cries of wonder: "What a lovely smell! What a lovely smell!"

Those sights, which before she has taken at their face value, are now imbued with hidden intentions to brighten her heart. The leaves of the young trees quiver now to greet her, every tree with its own special vibration. The open doorways of grocery stores, whose smell always fires her imagination, now exude for her benefit smells of jellies, halva, marmalade, pickles, and colored crystal candies.

The signs over the entrances of shops are revealed to her suddenly, inviting her to read the names of secret and mysterious things, hiding for her sake their goodness for the future, when she grows up: "Ped–i–cure, gy–ne–col–ogist, con–fec–tion–ery, ad–vo–cate, Bar Monte Carlo," and anyone who knows their meaning just *has* to be wise, grown-up, and expert in the ways of the world.

"Garden Butcher," she reads. Why "garden"? Everyday she passes this place, but now, in her mother's company, she has the leisure and the desire to find out for herself. "Why 'garden'?" she wonders aloud in a pleasant reverie. "Maybe it's because the cows graze in a garden. But why let cows graze in a garden, wouldn't they wreck it? Are these special, privileged cows, or . . ." But the mother is standing at the next shop window, looking at shoes and replying distractedly, as if they are used to each other's company daily. "What's all this about a 'garden'," the mother replies, her eyes on the shoes: "It's 'Gordon'!"

What's this 'Gordon'? She feels sorry for the fine cattle who could have grazed among the tomatoes and lettuces had it not been for this "Gordon."

The mother detaches herself at last from the shoes.

"Ice cream!" Maya pleads, and regrets it at once. The mother talks and pays no heed to the ice cream girl, or she talks just *because* the ice cream girl is standing there.

"A moment's pleasure—and afterwards? Do you want to be sick with *her* around? Yes, yes, I know! *She*'ll look after you. *She*'ll run to the doctor, *she*'ll prepare you good food. You'll be lying there like a corpse and she won't so much as look at you."

The ice cream girl looks out into the street over the mother's head.

"I don't care! Let them all know who your father is! He'll sleep peacefully while you're sick, or send you to me! He'd thank God sincerely if He took you to Himself once and for all." (No! No! Maya cries inwardly, not knowing whether to believe what she's saying.) "What matters to him is always to have a fresh female in his bed!"

"Yes, yes, you may as well know exactly who your father is, the one you admire so much!" (Stop it! Stop it! Please stop!) "You're a woman!" (I'm not a woman! I don't want to be!) "You're growing up! Soon you'll have children of your own! Don't think that life is so long and sweet." (That won't be for ages yet, and everything will be different, completely different!) "You'll have children and then you'll understand what he's doing to me and to you! Oh yes! He makes very fine speeches about the education of the young—'Youth is the future of the world'! Don't you love hearing that, eh?" says the mother, turning to the ice cream girl as if she is a judge. "And she still loves him, sides with him! She always sides with him! She's as weak in character as he is! You could buy her with one soothing word! If I had a father like that I'd spit right in his face and say: 'Is this how a father behaves? Are you a father at all? What have you done to my mother? What have you done to me? Bringing home one harlot after another and then marrying the worst of the lot!' And you're still loyal to her, devoted. I've seen you out shopping for her! If it was me I'd buy her poison."

Maya tries not to listen any more. Everything is losing its luster. The inquisitive eyes of the ice cream girl turn away tactfully. Why doesn't she stop! Make her stop! Shut her up! Make her stop saying all these things, please!

The mother stops suddenly, and as if seeing the salesgirl for the first time in her true role, says: "Half a portion."

Maya grabs the ice cream, bending forward so she won't soil her festive dress.

The walk goes on until the moment comes that she has dreaded—her mother meets an acquaintance. He waves to her from across the street and advances to meet them through the traffic with a smile. Now they are both standing in the shade of a tree and talking. If this had not been a mother of meetings and walks, she would have tugged at her skirt and demanded: "Hey, come on," but this is now a mother of meetings and walks. Maya stands aside, licking the ice cream, shuffling her feet, and trying to turn her mother's eyes back to her. She hates the man and his smiles. Suddenly she remembers him. Her mother's lodging is a converted laundry shack in the backyard of a house. Eucalyptus trees surround the shack and Maya sometimes plays beneath them among their fallen fruit, waiting for her mother. This is the one and only place where she lets herself get totally absorbed in her games.

Once when she arrived, that man stood under the tree, in that same short leather jacket and the same embroidered Russian shirt. The mother came out into the yard wearing a long robe. When she saw the two of them under the trees she seemed embarrassed, which was not at all like her, and she said to the man: "Ah! The plumber! Good of you to come. Good afternoon, Mr. Plumber!"

Maya remembered the smile on the man's face as he replied, "Good afternoon, Madam. I've come to inspect your installation!"

They smiled at each other thinly. Then they sent her home, her pockets full of sweets.

Now the "plumber" is chatting with her mother under the tree. Maya knows that the walk is nearing its end. The sun has sunk behind the houses and the storekeepers are hurrying out to pull down the blackout screens over their windows.

"Well, how are you, gorgeous?" says the man, pinching her cheek. "What a pretty dress! Remember me?"

She moves out of his reach and replies innocently, exactly as they expect her to, "Of course I remember. You're the plumber!" She distorts the word deliberately, so they'll think she doesn't understand. They chuckle to each other, as she expected.

"A head of iron!" says the mother proudly in Yiddish and laughs again.

The man accompanies them to the three sisters' house and waits in the lobby. This time the women are busy with their sewing. One of them hastens to open the door and then returns to her machine.

The mother removes the butterfly ribbon from Maya's head, rolling it up and stuffing it into her bag, then waits while her daughter strips off the dress, putting on in its place the khaki pants—disgusting now in their filth—and fastening the safety pin at her throat.

"The king is no more, a beggar returns," the youngest sister laughs from her machine.

"I want her to go around like this for all to see," says the mother. "So the whole world will know how the great Kashka Hermoni cares for his daughter."

Now comes the "parting speech." The mother drums into her ears all the sharp and subtle words that she is to say to "the wretch" and then insists that the daughter repeat the words over and over again so she won't forget them. Maya repeats them mechanically until the mother fixes her with a hostile stare: "I'm making all this effort and she, of course, won't say a word to her. Not a word! Alright, alright, let it be so . . . better to give birth to wolves . . ."

The "plumber" emerges from behind the sandbag wall. "Don't you forget a single word," the mother says to her again. "Do you hear? And next time tell me everything!"

Maya grins a desolate grin to herself. To make herself forget the words, she whistles loudly in the street and jumps between the cracks in the pavement.

When she arrived at a run in the strange garden, the darkness already surrounded her, only a few panes on the upper stories glimmering in the dead moonlight. Holding her breath she began poking around in the humid darkness. No, not this bush, that one, she said to herself with hope ebbing away and yielding to an ominous thumping of the heart. It *has* to be this one! Angrily she parted the branches and was pricked by thorns. *That* bush didn't have thorns. In front of her she saw the frame of the fence. The bundle—it was as if it never existed.

For a long time she searched the garden, examining, choked with fear, every bush, every stone, every corner of the stairwell. Then she stood for a while in the dimly lit stairwell, leaning on the gleaming mailboxes and reading, almost unconsciously, the strange names, each name with its apartment upstairs, and the instructions of the Civil Defense on how to act in the event of alarm or attack from the air. She prayed for a sudden attack from the air. Then she sobbed briefly, silently. Suddenly an idea occurred to her, one of those ignoble ideas that hide themselves, intentionally, until the mind is close to distraction: she'd say she gave the laundry to her mother! As for the rest, she'd think that out later.

As she left the stairwell she breathed in the evening air rich with the fragrance of summer growth, the sickly sweet scent of climbing honeysuckle mingled with the scent of a freshly mowed and watered lawn.

The object that she saw on the paved path at her feet filled her now with a bitterness that clouded her happiness. There it was, clearly visible. She didn't need it now. She didn't want it any more! As she bent down toward the ground she could tell it was indeed the laundry bundle, lying on the path, right there on the path.

Again she walked slowly, dragging her feet, weighed down by the bundle. Now there'll be a scandal! Now everything will be turned around like in a mirror. Now we'll hear the counter-speech, the one about "the cuckoo who lays eggs in strange nests."

I don't want it! she wailed inwardly in helpless anger. I don't want this, don't want any of it!

As she stood beside her house with the bundle on her arm, at this hour when all are sealed away in their apartments and the only sound to be heard in the gloom of the open spaces is the air-raid warden's whistle and his angry shouts of "Put out that light!" she was suddenly swept by a powerful wave of self-pity, a feeling that she is now the only one in all the world standing thus in the darkness, and with the knowledge that this is not the end of her suffering.

On the stairs she heard loud voices from the apartment, the voices of men arguing among themselves.

They're waiting for me! she thought, scared. To see me with the laundry. But at the same time she knew what the voices were: a meeting, one of her father's meetings.

At once she recognized the voice of Boria Markovski, a voice drawn up from his warm depths and rising to a screaming pitch of ludicrous and tremulous fury.

Regina wasn't home. In a mood of fretful emptiness, Maya threw the laundry bundle into the corner of the bathroom and crept furtively between her sheets, weary, disappointed to death.

12
A BAD BARGAIN

The taxi driver lifted out three suitcases, one after the other, and the girls ran after each case from the door of the taxi to the workroom where Frieda sat, sorting and fingering with obvious delight the little muslin dresses and colored tunics that a whole regiment of aunts and grandmothers must have been busy preparing for the occasion, for the journey of the smooth and oval-faced girl, who peered at everyone with a look of sympathy and satisfaction.

After she had surrendered her body to the farewell embraces of her mother, she blew a kiss and turned at once to the girls, without another glance at the receding taxi.

The girls clustered like petals around her embroidered dress, which she lifted slightly to show off her pink silk petticoat, and before they had time to breathe she skipped happily and cried: "I've got an autograph book! Who wants to write in it?"

They all chased her up the steps, then flicked in awe through the fine quality pages. Droras and Zipporahs had written there one after the other:

Bim-bam-boom
Open the alboom.

Beauty is vanity, charm a lie,
A honest girl need never cry.

How lovely is the time of youth,
Like a glorious summer's day.
But all too soon this day is moot,
So enjoy it while you may.

My wish for you will not be said
In poetry or phrases fine,
In life's long war that lies ahead
May victory be always thine!

How they all must love her—this little Malkalé—all those who have written here, folding the pages in corners and writing their "secrets": *The one who's just opened this corner—is a fool.*

Someone called Hannah Leipschitz had written something quite spectacular:

Not in fine phrases or flowery tongue
Will I write in abstract glory.
Life is a titanic war
And I wish you victory!

Not in fine phrases! What style! It makes your mouth water. Flowery tongue! Life is a war, a battlefield without limits, clash of spears on chain mail, and the blood flowing in torrents, sticky red blood, full of literature and poetry! And finally it's all over—flags in the wind, trumpets! Medals! Victory! The little queen has triumphed!

Malkalé glances into the book. "Who? This one? Hannah Leip-schitz? The laziest girl in the class, but she's got lots of good autograph rhymes. She copies them from her big sister's book."

Hannah Leipschitz's big sister! What would Maya have given for the chance of reading that sister's autograph book, in which big girls, giving off the mature smell of almost-womanhood, have written from experience and from the top of the tower.

When they finished reading, they were eager to write. All man-kind's transgressions stem from imitation. Without pausing for breath, they snatched the olive-wood scented album one from another. Now, as they write again *"Bim-bam-boom / Open the alboom,"* they become a part of the beautiful world of Droras and Zipporahs from Tel Aviv, composing "secrets" in corners and trying, in vain, to match with their crude oil crayons the refined and multicolored handiwork of the Tel Aviv girls.

That's not the way to write, thinks Maya, the creative urge mounting in her. You need something different, something that's never been written before, something others can copy if they want. She took the album and wrote down the page the letters of the word

(M) *Matters it not from where you came,*
(A) *And from what rank or borough.*
(L) *Love dost drive away all shame,*
(K) *Kind sister, forget your sorrow.*
(A) *And be thou welcome to our home*
(H) *Here, now, and tomorrow.*

This was true happiness—to read it again and again, amazed at the rounded harmony, all her own work, and the murmurs of admiration above her head. The album passed from hand to hand, from astonished eyes to astonished eyes. When it came back to her, it came back a corpse. Now she understood the meaning of the words. They were ugly in their falseness, their foolish pretense. Everyone knew where Malkalé came from—and it mattered more than they would admit. And what's all this comradely welcome stuff—sister!—don't they all envy and hate her in their hearts? The sour taste of the blunder stayed in her mouth. But they were all excited, and Maya consoled herself with the thought that if all were exultant, it meant there was a reason for exulting.

Now Bat-Sheva wrote. When she finished there was an awkward silence for a moment, and a strange stupefaction enfolded Maya. Dizzy, she asked herself again and again if she really had written anything, and for a moment it seemed to her she'd written nothing. Bat-Sheva inscribed: *"Matters it not from where you came . . ."*

Now the fate of this "remembrance" was the same as the fate of all the others, all these words materializing from some obscure origin and trickling into the shallow sea of *"Bim-bam-boom."* They would never know whose brain invented it.

Bat-Sheva encircled the creation with red roses, with an air of unhurried calm, and thus claimed it for her own. "This is the most beautiful remembrance in the world," said Bat-Sheva.

Malkalé was quite unaware of the little drama that was unfolding here on her account. She took the autograph book, which still contained many blank pages fragrant with the smell of olive wood, and cried eagerly: "I know all the words of 'I like to whistle'! Who wants to hear it?" She sang: "Who——wants——to—— hear?" They all wanted to hear.

Malkalé jumped on a chair, pulled out her dress sideways with both hands, Shirley Temple style, and in a sweet and marvelously thin voice, with admirable pronunciation, she sang the whole song. When she finished they all crowded around her to inquire how the words should be pronounced: "It makes me mewwy" or "It makes me merry"? At long last there's someone who can explain the difference. Then the little queen sang more, and more. She sang "Singing-polly-wolly-doodle-all-the-day"! The girls feasted their eyes on her oval face, her pink underclothes, the hem-stitched embroidery of her dress, her rosy lips, the lacquered shoes with the little buttons. Bat-Sheva immediately invited her to move her bed next to hers.

Malkalé sang "Horsey-horsey"! This was more than could ever have been imagined! Ecstasy! She knows the words in Hebrew too and can dance to it! God Almighty!

She jumped down from the chair and her little shoes, the button shoes, began gracefully prancing forward, back, and sideways, with sudden twirls of the body:

Horsey-horsey,
Get into the mood
They dance this dance in Hollywood
Kick with your right foot, then with your left foot
It's easy to do and you feel so good!

"How do you do it? How?" They all swooped upon her, sweaty with excitement at the wonderful discovery that had fallen among them. All that day the ceilings of the ground floor resounded as the girls pranced about the corridors, singly or in pairs, kicking with the right foot and then with the left, pirouetting clumsily: "They dance this dance in Hollywood! Get into the mood! You feel so good! It's easy to do! They dance this dance!"

That night Malkalé told them about Tel Aviv. She lay beside Bat-Sheva and chattered happily: "These days all the top people are sending their children to be educated in the country. That's what my mother told my father. It's safest from bombs. All the kids in Tel Aviv have bronze Land Fund rings. I've got a silver one, because I contributed more. Those Australians just love to hug things, even electricity pylons. And they sing: 'We're going to hang out our washing on the Siegfried Line' " (she sang this in English). "But they throw money to the kids too. The kids run after them in the street shouting: 'Money, money!' The kids have little leather tags to hang round their necks—I've got one too— with a celluloid cover. They write your name and address on it, so if you're killed in an air raid, they'll know right away and tell your parents, so they won't think you're still alive and waste time searching. In the space where we play hide-and-seek at night there's a sign: 'Trespassers will be prosecuted.' All the kids think it's 'Tras-Pissers,' but that's something quite different. Anyway, there's lots of disgusting words that the kids use, the older ones who come to our neighborhood from a long way off, Herzl Street maybe. There's words that shouldn't be allowed. It's awfully frightening, sometimes you'd rather drop dead.

"Rudolf, that's the son of our neighbors from Czechoslovakia, he knows lots of words. His mother always makes them tea with milk and lemon inside. It's really disgusting, but they're the richest people in the house, they've got all these crystal chandeliers. I was there once and his father was sitting by the radio—a radio this big—and suddenly he began to cry. The Nazis were playing happy tunes with drums on the radio and he started crying his eyes out, like a baby. 'Hey, children, listen, they've taken Prague, our Prague!' Their mother broke three plates. Afterwards we picked up all the pieces. The plates had pretty roses on them. I took a piece—just in case they would change apartments in the meantime. Rudolf told me how they do everything. In the drugstore there's a sort of machine. A boy with no clothes on comes and stands on one side, and a girl with no clothes on stands on the other side, and they do something inside the machine and a baby comes out. We hide in the shelter too. It's not nice to tell, but that's where he says all these things to me. Suddenly you feel yourself tingling all over, sort of. Sometimes he strokes me like this. It makes you tingle all over and you don't want it to stop. The way he says his 'r's' is awfully sweet. Always when he comes to see us my mother says: 'Hello! here comes the cavalier!' It's awfully annoying. And it always makes him upset and he wants to go. I think this tooth's going to fall out . . .

"Is it true you're all terribly poor here, and not very pretty? Where do you go around here when you want to pee in the night? Aren't you scared to go by yourselves? Once when Mother and

Father weren't home I was too scared to go by myself and I did it in a potted plant. I thought it was going to wither, but it didn't. Best thing is to be in the Scouts! That's a lot of fun. An Arab came around one time, selling Indian candy, and all the kids ran after him, all the way to Allenby Street maybe. Suddenly I saw a procession of Scouts, with ribbons on their shoulders and sticks, and those big hats of theirs and trumpets. Lots of big boys and girls with fat bosoms. All the kids started chasing after them and me too. A button fell off my dress and I put it in my mouth. It was a nice one, blue-colored glass. Suddenly the button wasn't in my mouth. I was awfully scared and suddenly I felt it stuck in my throat. I went cah . . . cah . . . and I cried, but it didn't come out. I knew I was going to die and I was sorry, but in the end it did come out. I ran home straightaway and I cried, I couldn't stop. My mother . . ."

Malkalé fell asleep. Nearly all the others were asleep before her, and she was spared Bat-Sheva's Royal Welcome.

A week later they took Malkalé away in a taxi. Her father, who came for a visit, realized at once that here he had got a bad bargain.

13
HOW BATYA WOLFSON BECAME A PHILANTHROPIST

Her older acquaintances used to ask themselves, sometimes with an air of compassionate scorn, by what force Batya Wolfson, a homely and decidedly neglected woman, came to fall upon the magician's dagger box of philanthropy. Even she herself, by this time, was already tired and listless, like one bearing a yoke thrust upon her against her will, and in her conversations with people she would advise them, repeatedly, not to take public affairs upon themselves, for if they did so they would be like the foolish tortoise that bears a scorpion on his back to ferry him across the river. But in her heart she knew she could never rid herself of the yoke, like a mother who has given birth to a monster, a cripple whom she hates—sometimes even prays for his death—yet in spite of all this becomes excessively devoted to him, full of compassion and guilt.

Even more than this (which Batya Wolfson would never have dared admit to herself), by virtue of this activity she acquired for herself a new status in the eyes of others, a status that she had always needed in order to resolve the growing alienation between herself and the world.

For several months those close to Reb Yehiel Wolfson had been saying behind his back, with mutual glances of concern, that "he's pale under his ears," and, sure enough, one morning his secretary found the great, dark-bearded head slumped beside the telephone receiver. A doctor, called immediately, was able to determine that he possibly tried to summon aid and he possibly died very suddenly—"And that, Mrs. Wolfson, is the very easiest of deaths, one that we all may envy." This was also the coroner's verdict.

The funeral cortège left his house on time, one of the first large houses to be built in the city. Already posted on the bulletin boards were messages of condolence on behalf of the municipality, on behalf of the committee of the grand synagogue in which the deceased had occasionally listened to the chanting and the prayers, and also on behalf of certain establishments linked with the building trade. One morning newspaper printed a front-page obituary.

At the end of the *Shivah* period, all the mourners except Batya left the house. The son went off to settle his father's affairs, the daughter and the boy "going out with her" returned to Jerusalem, and the widow was left alone, wearing the same old gown in which she had received the news, a woman not yet old and still attractive, a well-stocked larder that had not yet aroused the appetite of disease.

Ashamed of the strange feeling of release that had invaded her heart, Batya Wolfson stood before the portraits of "his" people (the father-in-law and mother-in-law) that hung side by side on the west wall of the "salon," as if guarding the window half-open to the trees of the garden, and noticed in their eyes that look of eager expectation. The message that she read in their eyes was also the same: "Well, pretty little Polack! Come on, let's see how you manage your affairs without a living eye to supervise!" They always seemed to her, in their lifetimes, to be waiting for the bride, this excessively lovely girl whom their son brought to Odessa from Poland without consulting them, to break loose and cause some scandal that would justify their antipathy toward her, but she did nothing strange or extraordinary then, nor in the days following their deaths.

The guilty sense of liberation withered as quickly as it had blossomed. Batya Wolfson had worked hard all the years of her marriage to blur her own distinctive colors, to be woven and absorbed into the tightly knit family tapestry, to satisfy the will of all, and now it was too late to go back.

"Now there's nobody to whom I can say, 'Yehiel, *come eat*, Yehiel, *come sleep*,'" she said regretfully to a neighbor some two weeks after his death.

In the long hours of the night she would toss fretfully in her portion of the double bed, drowsily stretching out a probing hand to "his" side, then waking and recoiling instantly, not because of a flickering of memory but because for a brief moment it seemed to her he was there, restless, turning his back on her, groaning and sobbing in petulant and degrading insomnia.

Several times during the night she would switch on the bedside lamp. The light filtering gently through the silk shade revealed the empty portion of the bed, which night after night she left covered with the old (but still serviceable) embroidered quilt, and peeping beneath it the green taffeta bed ruffle (the one she'd brought with her, years ago, from the "*magasin*"), and then she heard the fluttering of her heart, in her ears, in the veins of her neck, and, driven by fear, she would get up slowly, murmuring to herself, and thus, in her long nightgown, wander through the darkened rooms, stumbling over the furniture, starting at her reflection appearing dimly, momentarily, in the depths of the mirrors, opening the refrigerator and standing there a long while, dazzled by its light, and then slamming the door without taking anything, not that there was much to take, only a few week-old tomatoes and a pan of milk, and what a waste of electricity! Then she would go out to the balcony that overhangs the desolate street and lean on the rail, shivering in the pre-dawn cold, breathing in the living air and following with her eyes some human shadow emerging from the gloomy nothingness.

There, there he is, a black shape moving between the buildings, approaching with ringing steps and separating from the chorus of echoes. The pale, moonlit street has become all his, the property of his anonymous body, a fleeting, eternal kingdom of sickly light. For a split-second his face appears—and already his back, his shoulder, and the fringes of his coat. The gloom of doorways holds its breath as he passes them, his fading shadows-of-shadows follow him softly, lying in wait for him and disintegrating around him, lengthening, shortening, rolling up at his feet and escaping, until he melts away and merges with the dark nothingness on the other side.

And she, Batya, unknowingly, tenses her face, strains her ears to hear a last faint echo in the street, the minute echo of a footfall fading into thin stillness. And already there's a new shadow, feeling its way from afar, on the pale sidewalk.

"Going, going. Going their way, going and coming . . ." The thought flashes through her mind. "Coming and going and not knowing and not feeling that someone is watching, looking down on them from above . . ." And then, frightened, she feels with her hand for the nape of her neck, untying the long braid and letting it fall on her breast, gathering it up again and letting go, and as she hears her own voice whispering weirdly into the street that is now empty of his form, she is alarmed and again finds her way through the darkened rooms to the refrigerator and stands in its light, facing the empty metal trays sheathed in ice.

Gradually her days were unstitched from the crowded tapestry of events, giving way to a listless scrutiny of her surroundings.

Feeble, sleepy thoughts, which do not hang together. In the mornings, after rising from her bed (on which she had slumped, exhausted, at daybreak), she would stand, brooding dejectedly, looking out through the kitchen window to the same street.

Now the street was bright, all its secrets exposed, its doors wide open, gaping full-mouthed, swallowing noisily, chewing, yawning, spewing out, puffing, arousing in her fear and revulsion greater than those of the night, but she would stand and watch it, drumming with her fingernails on the sill of the window or scratching in her ear with a long hairpin, the conversation of neighbors floating above her head. Thus she would stand and wait, unconsciously, for the bell. When it sounded she would lean forward and watch the girls streaming out from the gate of the school to the kiosk opposite, which until now had stood desolate, and laying siege to it with their shrill cries: "Mr. Greenberg! Got anything good? Anything good today?" Then they dispersed into noisy groups, opening and filling their mouths with wondrous, Day-of-Atonement eagerness, snatching from one another, chasing one another down the street, ignoring the curses and the blaring horns of the drivers, with hoarse cries of: "Greedy pig!"— "I'll get you for that!"—"Give me a bite!"—"You greedy pig!"

"How crude are these girls!" she would think bitterly. "How ill-mannered. It makes you weep to see them."

And yet she still waited, morning after morning, for the ring of the bell.

With the end of the year of mourning, on a day when the dust was so thick that electric lights burned in the shops, they all traveled to the cemetery in an old hired bus. Some of Yehiel's acquaintances were there, a few of them close friends and the rest—unknown, blurred faces and just one friend of hers. During the journey, and even at the cemetery gate, the men were chattering among themselves, trying to fill the time with matters of real importance. The women, whose feelings were more delicate, kerchiefs and hats on their heads, lowered their faces and their voices every time they caught her eye. The members of the family and a few close friends, unnecessarily silent and solemn—which meant they were probably enjoying themselves—crowded about her solicitously, supporting her when she sat and when she stood up and when she walked, as if they expected her to collapse at any moment.

When the tombstone was unveiled she stood by the grave—which had not yet settled down among its neighbors—and waited for sorrow to overcome her. She strove to summon up the image of the big, disintegrating body, the broad bones peeping out from the swarm of maggots, trying to shock herself into grief, but at the same time the thought flashed into her brain: did they bury him with his false teeth?

The cantor was trilling elegantly, his pompous voice swelling grandly, and all she could think of at that moment were their loud, invective arguments of the last years: whether to open the windows, whether to close them, and who left the light on in the bathroom. Amid these fleeting thoughts, her attention was drawn to those standing silent, bowed, around the grave and on the paths nearby. Studying their faces, their clothing, she saw how some had aged and withered, others grown up and grown beautiful.

Suddenly there came the first patter of the rain that they had feared since the morning. There was a diffident murmur of thunder, gathering its strength for a storm, but it abandoned the attempt and turned to thin drizzle. A whisper of alarm passed through the company, some of the women did not hesitate to open umbrellas. The rest turned up their collars and began peering around in search of shelter from the intense rain that was now lashing the cantor, who stopped chanting and raced through the service, garbling the words in his haste. Through the grey veil of water, like worn muslin, a party from a burial society was approaching, carrying a stretcher. As they passed by the next row of graves, she saw the outline of the stranger's corpse, long and rigid, ankles together, wrapped in a wet prayer shawl, and then she saw the two lonely old people, a man and a woman, trailing in silence behind the stretcher through the curtain of rain, their eyes on the ground. For a moment she felt she should join them, walk with head bowed behind the rain-soaked corpse. The others were increasingly restless, their hats dripping water, and she sensed in their eyes, turned toward her, that they were waiting for a signal, for permission to move from the graveside and seek shelter, but just as she was about to grant their wish, it seemed to her that there was a mistake in the inscription on the tombstone, and she stepped forward to take a closer look. The others, interpreting this as a new expression of her sorrow, stopped moving. Senya hurried forward at once to take her arm and she approached the grave and bent down, so that she saw clearly on the rain-swept stone, as she had thought: "Age 55." "Age 55?" she whispered to her son, her arm clasped around his waist. Senya looked down at her, puzzled, embarrassed. "Why age 55?" she whispered again. Resentment and anger suddenly erupted in her with unexpected violence—fury at the rain, at the people, the strange faces, herself, her indifference, the craftsman who had spoiled the tombstone inscription. "Why age 55?" she murmured again and again, as if uttering an oath, an incantation, and suddenly, from amidst all this, at long last something pleasurable emerged, like the tiny weak flickering of a dying lamp. And as long as she allowed herself to repeat these words between the damp arms of those supporting her, leading her from there to the shelter of the booth, her whole being was directed inward, devoted to that faint light of grief, which was slowly gaining strength, isolated, pure.

Because of the driving rain the funeral guests parted hurriedly beside the entrance, pausing only to shake hands. The widow was accompanied to her apartment by her son Senya, the young daughter who had come specially from Jerusalem, the boy who was "going out with her," and her own childhood friend Paula Berger, who had arrived in the country a few years before.

Paula had nursed an undefined grudge against Yehiel Wolfson since the time he took Batya away with him to Odessa, and she only came to visit her friend on rare occasions, when she was sure the man of the house was not at home. Paula never remarried, and she overcame this by appearing before herself and before others with the cynical worldly wisdom of a woman of affairs, someone to be taken at her word, someone from whom a rare compliment is no mere trifle—you may depend on that.

Paula Berger sat at the oval table in her black veil, red specks in the whites of her eyes, and her nose like yeast dough. From above her squashed double chin she watched with angry wonder the activities of the *"jugend,"* who after a brief period of silent lingering at the table had begun moving about the rooms, slamming the refrigerator door in the kitchen, and from time to time could be heard emitting suppressed, indecent chuckles in the adjoining rooms. Batya sat, limbs spread-eagled, head slumped, and a long lock of wet hair falling on her cheek.

"That's the way it is," Paula finally said to her companion, no longer able to restrain herself. "Once there were angels walking about on the earth; today even in Heaven there are none."

It was as if Batya Wolfson was awakened by these words. Until this moment she had been absorbed in her devotion to grief, which on her return from the cemetery had been supplemented by a vague sense of satisfaction. She herself looked distractedly at the actions of her children and found them neither good nor bad.

". . . And at Senya, in particular, I'm surprised," added Paula, raising her voice. "Isn't he already a respectable member of the community, a businessman?"

"Didn't you know? That's how it is with young people when they come back from the cemetery, death reminds them of life." Again Batya had the feeling that she was speaking of the death of a stranger, but when she met Paula's narrowed, red-tinged eyes, little clusters of wrinkles radiating from their corners, she said hastily, "Why did they write on the tombstone 'Age 55'? He was fifty-four years old!"

"They're all liars in this country, out of habit, even when there's no need," said Paula, squashing her double chin. "And as for him, it's all the same now, fifty-five or fifty-four . . . seeing life in Heaven, while we suffer below . . . lucky for you Reb Yehiel, that you dwell so high," she said with sudden spite.

"This year wasn't his," added Batya, this time to herself, as if doubting her friend's ability to understand the significance of this year. "Not mine either."

When the rain began to bubble in the gutters, the "*jugend*" put on their fine coats and planted dutiful kisses on the cheeks of their mother, who said "Already?" in a tone of practiced resignation. As they stood by the door in a close-knit, robust group, they promised to "drop in" again that evening.

"Extraordinary!" trumpeted Paula Berger after them.

"No, they aren't like that," Batya said hurriedly as the door closed. But her face said: They are like that.

The two of them were left sitting silently by the oval table, their black veils glinting in the light from the crystal chandelier.

"It all depends on the example set by the father," Paula said at last. "Go and pick an apple from a fir tree."

"Eh, what? Why? I tell you, Senichka's been very good . . . behaved very well," Batya protested lethargically. "He said *Kaddish*, even grew a beard for a whole month . . ."

"For good business, they'll even put a *mezuzah* in the dining room of a kibbutz!"

"No, no, he's not like that . . . he's really devoted, very . . . how well he managed the office . . . no one would have believed it . . . he even left the Working Youth Movement."

"From a rotten potato you always get the best pancake," grumbled Paula shamelessly.

The implication of these words provoked Batya.

Look, he sent me a Yemenite girl to clean, respectable she was, and quiet, but I sent her back once she'd cleaned the panels, which really were neglected, and I can't bend down . . . but to have a stranger in the house? And what am I to do? Sit and read *Der Amerikaner* all day and give orders? And what else can I do except clean the house? The only pleasure I have left is to open a closet and find no moths, and to see the sheets folded like in the shop."

"Yes, yes," said Paula impatiently, as if she had not expected the conversation to descend to this level. "The world is big, and always there's someone who messes it up and someone who has to clean."

But Batya was one of those who once drawn into a conversation cannot stop themselves; she needed to cling to speech—the servant of those deprived of activity. "But now there's nobody to . . . to clean for, to cook for. Am I going to stand up now and fry myself schnitzels? All year I've been asking neighbors for cake recipes, as if I mean to bake, but all year I haven't baked a single cake, and if a guest ever comes, well, he knows, he understands, in my position it's impossible . . . and all I need is a few tomatoes, a bit of air and a glass of milk . . . Now if Senichka was to set up a home, a family . . . and that idle daughter—not idle, she wants to 'study' . . . all the young women are asking for equal rights. Of course you know, even in our day . . . but the truth is they're just spoiled kittens. Even my daughter . . . skimming the cream off the milk. That's the way it is today—they want a good time, but soil their fingers cleaning a pot? Equal rights! Look, every week some different kitten is stalking after Senichka, in pants. Once, just imagine, a girl came to my house barefoot—com–plete–ly! Does it make you feel sorry for the poor girl, who can't afford to buy shoes? It wasn't like that . . . she had nice feet, she thought, so she ran about the streets without shoes. Equal rights! And this barefoot girl, she turns his head, wailing, making up her eyes and nails, and everything—in front of me! And 'Mother' she called me—I didn't even know her name—and after two days and nights—*pista*, she's gone! Crept off to some other bowl of milk . . . And where did all these spring up from? Equal rights! How different we were, Paula, oh, how different . . ."

"And oh how stupid!" The other sighed, and as she adjusted the veil on her head she turned it this way and that with a slow gesture toward the portraits of the father-in-law and mother-in-law.

"No, not stupid!" Batya flared up, deeply offended, grasping exactly what her friend meant. "A decent man he was, learned, a talented man . . . and how he studied German, sat up whole nights learning German from magazines . . . and when the *yekkes* began to arrive he knew exactly the way to talk to them . . . And why did they all come running to him, to him and not to Pudim, who's an engineer after all, and not to Weinstein, but only to 'Herr Wolfson'—God first and then Herr Wolfson . . . And this morning you saw for yourself how people . . . And this house in Montefiore Street, who designed it ten years ago? Even Pudim the engineer said to him when he inspected the house, 'Reb Yehiel, I hand you all my diplomas.' With my own ears I heard . . . and to this day they come to this house, all the *grosse Professoren*, to see how you do a really finished piece of work."

Paula looked at her from over her double chin with an expression of scorn, as if saying: go on, go on. And Batya went on:

"And what a family man he was! How he insisted on sending Senichka to the Herzliya High School even though the boy didn't then want to be a bourgeois. And the boy studied, and Vera he sent to the seminary in Jerusalem. 'My only daughter isn't going to pack oranges,' he said, and . . ."

Paula gripped Batya's right arm with four gentle, well-meaning fingers, as if seeking to concentrate her attention. "And for you?" she said, almost in a whisper. "For you what did he do?"

"For me?" cried Batya. "What should he? Was there no bread to eat? Look, he bought me a refrigerator when nobody in this country even knew of such things."

"I'm not your neighbor, Batya, you don't need to throw sand in my eyes. I'm willing to swear he didn't leave you a cent of your own. What did he write in the will?"

"What are you talking about, Paula? What has entered into your head?" She waved her arms in an angry gesture that took in the entire apartment. "What strange ideas you have! And, anyway, he didn't have time to write a will . . . he died young . . ."

Suddenly she regretted her inability to confirm that indeed he had put the house in her name.

"And why did he have to die now? Didn't I tell him, warn him . . . I would have cared for him now, kept him . . . he should have taken care, avoided stress . . . we could have lived out our old age together . . . sat together on the balcony playing cards . . . sat together here, at the table, playing cards . . . Now everything would have sorted itself out . . . and the grandchildren . . ."

As she spoke Batya felt that helpless fear returning to her, the fear of emptiness and uncertainty that had sprung up in her from the time of their arrival in the country, from the terrible speed with which Yehiel became distant from her, his enthusiastic assimilation among new people whom she didn't know, his command of the language, and how he mocked her opinions, and how he cut her off in mid-sentence, in the presence of other people . . . "Why has God done this to me? Why has He done this? Lonely in grief and weariness . . ."

"You shouldn't blame your problems on God," said Paula. "He'll say: 'You want to know the reason—come to me!' " But at once she smiled at the tears rolling into her friend's black handkerchief.

"Enough, enough! That's our tragedy, we women, to knead our brains and make tears out of them. What's this grief that you're complaining about? You should be glad! A beast in a golden cage, that's what you were, picking up crumbs . . . couldn't even move a muscle without special permission from the 'commissar.' And as for him . . . for you he scrimped and saved! For you he went into business, built houses! Of course! Haven't you told me yourself he used to pick up bits of rope in the street, your hero, untwine the strands and give them to you as 'straw' to clean the dishes . . . even 'straw' he wouldn't let you buy!"

"Straw? What about straw?" said Batya in a choking voice, as if remembering from this description her husband, as he was in his life. "You don't know anything. Any–thing!"

"You know! You're the one who knows it all!" cried Paula. "Before you he knelt down and confessed! And how he dressed you! Just look at yourself, what do you look like? A neglected old woman! But to give a statue to the museum as a gift—oh yes! A real benefactor, this rope-splitter . . . some modernist lump of shit, pardon me, that they were actually ashamed to put on show . . ."

"What statue?" wailed Batya. "What *are* you talking about?"

"What statue? Poor woman! A year after his death and you don't know? No, no. I'm not one to let sleeping dogs lie. You must wake up! Cold water! Wake up!" And here her voice softened. "I just remember how he was then when he saw you, at our house . . . how he fell at your feet, this peasant. *That* was a statue! He made an 'idol' out of you to worship, this peasant, this hewer of wood . . ."

"What are you saying?" Batya whispered in shocked bewilderment, her eyes fixed on her companion's mouth.

"Yes, yes. He knew well enough what was the bargain in this business."

Batya made a movement, as if she could bear to hear no more, but the other continued relentlessly, with a kind of obsessive malice. "You see, he acquired for himself this idol, and at once began to break it, destroy it. . . . and then came this sculptress!"

"Shut up, shut up!" yelled Batya, her whole body trembling, but in an instant everything was tied together! All the little details, the suspicions, the hints, his sudden interest in art. In truth she already knew, had sensed it long ago, but had resigned herself to deliberate ignorance, as if when knowledge is admitted it turns into reality.

"Why? Why should I keep quiet?" Paula went on with her cruel words, paying no heed to the convulsions that they caused her companion. "And who is more dear to me than you? Don't I know what you've been feeling all this time in silence? Why didn't you go out and meet people? I can well understand the paralysis that takes over the heart of a beautiful, blossoming woman, when some little vampire in glasses . . . some little shit molder . . . is preferred to her . . . how she feels she's lost all value, in her own eyes, in the eyes of others. Don't I know the psychology of a woman who's a symbol of beauty, goodness, devotion—and then, suddenly . . . What greater proof than that of her inferior worth, her degradation? And this is how it all starts—she shuts herself away at home, talks to the chicken in the pan . . . suspects that everybody, every friend, despises her in his heart for her decline."

The rain began plucking again at the shutters. The electric light went out for a moment and came on again.

"It's a lie! You've told a great lie, Paula! I'll never forgive you for this!"

"Please yourself—call it a lie! The statue is a great lie! It's a lie that one woman, for the sake of Yehiel Wolfson . . . a great man! It's too provincial, too bourgeois! And the slut from the Bohemia Cafe—a lie! I've seen this lie with my own eyes, Batya, in the Workers' Kitchen! An ugly lie! A bat in glasses!"

Batya went on listening to her friend's words, her vindictive appraisal of this woman, whom she'd been afraid of all these last years. She had always imagined that the moment the truth of these things was revealed to her—and *she* knew that the moment would come—everything in her would be blown apart. And yet here she was, sitting tense, trembling indeed, angry on the outside, but inwardly dominated by a strange calm, almost indifferent, as if all these words lost their meaning once they had come to her companion's lips. And she even felt that as long as Paula went on talking, the strange calm would continue to strengthen its grip.

Suddenly she asked in a tone of utter exhaustion:

"And she, was she there, at the funeral? And this morning?"

"What a fool you are, my dear Batya," sighed Paula. "Of course she wasn't! Why should she come? Shrouds have no pockets! Now listen to me, Batya, only to me! The time has come to dip your pen in ink and cross out the past! Now you're a lady in your own right! Madam Wolfson! It's lucky for you he died without a will, and left everything to you."

And now she stood up and smiled gently, as if she had successfully completed a necessary operation. "And now, dear Batya, we've finished with all this." She pointed again to the father-in-law and mother-in-law: "Let's go to the kitchen and make ourselves a nice cup of tea."

After this conversation the friendship between the two women was renewed and strengthened, Paula Berger being the telescope that brought Batya Wolfson into closer contact with the outside, with the street, which had always frightened her.

In the afternoons, when Paula was released from her chores in the Workers' Kitchen, where she was a cook, the two of them would meet in the avenue or in a small café, and there they would converse in Polish, always a treat for Batya. They went out shopping together and sometimes even to the movies. Paula had no family and was almost alone in the world, but her workplace constantly provided her with new acquaintances and the opportunity for gossip about the bourgeois tendencies behind the working-class facade, seeing that all, including even the nation's leaders, chose to dine in those days in the Workers' Kitchen.

About two weeks after the unveiling of the tombstone, Paula

Berger brought with her a suggestion. First she spoke of it only in a general way. Friends of hers, a Jewish couple from Warsaw who emigrated to Belgium and made a fortune in the diamond trade, were now in Palestine and would stay another two or three weeks, until they found a suitable place, a suitable person, and some minor local contributors.

What was in question was a modern institution for abandoned children, similar to ones they had seen in Belgium, in memory of their son who had died of tuberculosis. A group of trained teachers, refugees from Austria, was already waiting in Brussels for a sign from them. The funds for the project they had already brought with them, and the continuing upkeep of the home would be financed by regular transfers of money from the Belgian capital. All they needed now was a man or a woman, free of personal commitments, someone not too old, who was capable of taking charge of the administration of the enterprise. This work consisted simply of long-range supervision of the home with only occasional visits—no more. There would be some decision-making on the acceptance of new pupils, a little attention to the procurement of funds, and the rest the secretariat would do. To improve the status of the institution, there would also be places for children who were not "social cases," on a progressive scale of fees. Everything would be worked out in detail from the start.

"A dining room and a modern kitchen!" exclaimed Paula. "A healthy site on the top of a hill!"

Paula herself had already been offered the post of "inventory and estate manageress."

Senya Wolfson immediately opposed the idea, which she put before him after much hesitation. That Paula Berger—all her busybodying was not to his liking—where was she before his father died? He caught a whiff of gold-digging. He would not allow any newly arrived, so-called "friend," some pauper, to "take care of" his mother's inheritance. Yes, yes! He could already see her baring her Polish claws. Instead, he advised Batya to invest her share of the inheritance in the building trade and watch it grow, seeing that the flow of refugees from central Europe was increasing, and many of them had money and were searching for a roof over their heads.

" . . And I'm to sit at home, drink tea with strawberry preserves, and read *Der Amerikaner* until my eyes grow dim, until you and your sister condescend to visit me!" replied Batya sharply, and she almost flung his father's misdeeds in his face. "I'm a grown woman, and I've a few years yet to see the world before they wrap me in a shroud!"

Senya summoned his sister from Jerusalem to try and avert "this attack that Mother's had," but it was their very opposition that convinced her—she'd had enough of their father's misdeeds and the golden cage!

That same week she had her first meeting with the diamond merchants from Belgium, and in her own apartment! Thus Batya Wolfson returned to the life of contact and dealings with people that she had abandoned with her departure from the *"magasin."*

At the inauguration of the home in Kiryat Shkak, Mrs. Wolfson cut the ribbon at the door, and the photograph was sent to the diamond merchants in Brussels. And Paula Berger, after a last drink of tea with the girls in the Workers' Kitchen, moved to the hilltop and took over her catering responsibilities with great energy and ability.

At first Mrs. Wolfson was hesitant in her contacts with her subordinates, treating them with much apprehension and with deference to their dignity, for they were recognized scholars, graduates of universities and special courses, and she avoided any display of seniority over them. In her visits she would give them instructions as if apologizing for the inconvenience caused them on her account. But these people sensed her weakness and hesitancy at once and it was not long before they became insolent toward her, accusing her behind her back of embezzling money into her own pockets and the pockets of her son, and at the same time putting to her demands that she could not possibly fulfill! Gradually there was a change in her dealings with them; she stopped inviting them to her house and guarded herself against intimacy. Because of her soft and nervous nature, and not being trained in social graces and the art of forging friendships, she put on a stern face toward them, until this became the norm, and when she dismissed a worker for negligence in his duties she earned their respect and hostility—eventually even the hostility of Paula Berger.

By this time she had been drawn, as if in spite of herself, into a world of frantic errands, unremitting effort, concern for the provision of equipment, contacts with womens' and other aid organizations, and she even extended her patronage over other similar institutions. Then the war broke out and the sources in Belgium were cut off.

Now Batya found herself securely trapped in the magic box of philanthropy, knives and daggers piercing its sides, but there was no spell to release her from it.

When the moisture dries up from the walls of the nostrils and the black asphalt becomes sticky, like a strip of licorice stretching away into infinity—the air is packed tightly in a strong box and the white-hot ground sends out probing rays to seek an outlet from the grey, oppressive cover— they pause on their way home from school to rest on the stone seat.

The cool binds them for a long while to the bench, which some enterprising builder erected in the narrow noonday shade of his house, filtering pleasantly through their buttocks and the backs of their knees. Then they drop their leather and cloth satchels on the limestone earth, rubbing their backs against the wall of the cellar. Lumps of dried mud and split leather irritate the soles of their feet, the shoes fall off of their own accord and eight bare feet kick in the cool, dead sand.

They talk of matters of the moment. Wide-ranging conversation, pleasant and superficial, matching the movement of their feet and the probing of their toes among the grains of limestone and the withered kernels of summer fruits. From time to time these languid bodies are troubled by the awareness that soon they must rise and ascend the sticky licorice path, but this only increases the pleasure of delaying.

"It's an awful pity," muses Hedva, her tongue wagging hurriedly against the swelling of her lip, "an awful pity there isn't a soda tap here." And Yaffa at once points to the place with her finger: "Here, here!"

"When I'm married," announces Bat-Sheva, "I'll have one of those taps in my kitchen."

"Oh, absolutely!" cries Hedva.

"You should have a tap for pomegranate juice and tamarind as well," Maya says.

"Why not rose water too, and honey syrup?" adds Hedva.

Always to find *her* in the crystal ball of the future. Whenever they peered into the ball, sidelong, with disbelief, distorted arachnoid images were sent forth, converging and fleeing. The future of a young person is the reflection of his past, direct or inverted, but the blurred mind sees blurred images. Only looking into her future, the Queen's, focused their desires and created picture and story.

"The best thing is if there's just one tap," says Maya. "But a magic tap. You touch it with your wedding ring and say: 'Tap of wonders, wonder-tap, fill with soda O my cup'!"

"That's exactly what I'll have," the Queen confirms without surprise, a hint that she herself has already thought of this, by herself.

Yaffa, who will never learn to dampen her jealousy, looks

nervously, tentatively, into the eyes of the Queen. "And what about us?" she asks. "When we come to visit . . . then . . . do . . . do we get the same thing?" Thus she fastens to herself with a safety pin those who seek to float to a freer status in the royal hierarchy.

Pretty flowers open in the eyes of the Queen.

"Of course . . . you'll come every Sabbath. And you'll get whatever you want: Tap of wonder, wonder-tap, give me a belly full of soda (rhyming or not—it's all the same). And you'll get the lot. All day we'll guzzle and lead a crazy life. Me and Hedva, and you, Maya . . ." She calmly studies the effect of the list of names on the lengthening face and the mouth chewing to overcome its affront. And once she's satisfied, she shoots another arrow at the dejected one: "Do you know, Yaffa, what a silly fool you are? This is the only wisdom you have! You really don't know why you won't be coming."

"Y–yes . . ."

"Yes, what? You won't, anyway, because you won't. Because you'll live with us!"

"W–hat m–m–me?" A quivering ray of hope.

The others wait, all their reactions suspended. The Queen lifts two scoops of sand with her toes and drops them in Yaffa's cloth bag.

"And you don't know what you'll be doing at our house?" Her head inclined, her hook baited.

"Y–yes. Don't know . . ." The ray quivers.

"Because you'll live with us—you'll be the servant!"

"The servant!" cries Hedva with surprised relief.

The ray wriggles like a worm.

"And you know what else she'll be?" breathes Maya, accepting the signal to be cruel. "She'll do tricks. She'll be a sort of pet monkey—she'll do tricks in a cage and they'll give her bananas. And they'll call her 'Little Monkey'!"

"Little Monkey!" shrieks Hedva.

The Queen looks with affection at her newly qualified protégée. She loves to see them squirming comically in the traps that they set for one another. Yaffa won't rebel—lack of grace is worse than humiliation, and in the name "Little Monkey" there is even a hint of patronage.

"And she'll be the cleverest monkey of them all," says Hedva. "She'll understand everything!" In her delight she momentarily forgets the Day of Judgment.

"And she'll sit there, like this, and hunt for tidbits! Yum! Yum! Spiders, yum, yum!"

Propelled by the Queen's playful mood, they sail between dangerous rocks. Oh, how Little Monkey looks in a little mirror and searches for the other monkey, and how she swings in the air on a trapeze . . . oh, I'm dying! A red ribbon and a bell and a turban, and how lucky she won't need to dress up at Purim, and they'll take pictures, and Bat-Sheva will stick the pictures in her new album.

The encouragement and esteem that the Queen infuses into their hearts amid this flood of imagination works intoxicating wonders on them. Thus, always, they forage obstinately through the garbage of insults, searching for this drop, this droplet, this molecule of complicity. Besmirching themselves and others so that just once perhaps, just once, they'll acquire—each one for herself—a full bottle of this niggardly elixir of life.

The newly appointed servant doesn't protest and doesn't shriek with joy. All pretenses will be interpreted—always—this way or that as the Queen wills. She slides slowly from the bench, coming to rest on her satchel, crushing yellowing scraps of paper and dried stalks between her fingers, but it's clear to them that, for all her display of indifference, her ears are tensed with dread.

She grew up in Jerusalem at the house of Grandpa and Grandma Matosevitch, both of them religious and active in public affairs. Grandma goes out every morning, a big purse in her hand, "to do *mitzvot.*" In the purse there's always charity money that she's collected to distribute to the poor, to couples who can't afford to marry, and to orphanages. At midday she returns home, breathing heavily, and at once lights the stove. Yaffa, arriving early from school, always eats her lunch half-raw and the pudding is watery, which fills her heart with a sense of deprivation and resentment since the other members of the household eat their fill at a later hour, their meals properly cooked. Only Grandma never eats, or so it seems, seeing that all afternoon she runs back and forth between the oven and the dining room to serve her young sons and her husband, who come in one by one and at times that suit them.

Grandpa is always raising his voice, and Grandma hastens to close the windows so the neighbors won't hear him. "Busy with *mitzvot! Mitzvot!*" yells Grandpa Matosevitch, who always needs an outlet for his anger. "It isn't *mitzvot* we need, but buttons on our shirts!"

So it went on—until Grandma aged suddenly and they moved Yaffa Matosevitch to the hostel in Kiryat Shkak.

Her first cry was the signal for her parents' divorce. Her mother lived in her consciousness only by virtue of the knowledge that every child must have been born, while as for "he that begat her," a clerk in Jerusalem, in the office of the Jewish National Fund, her powers of imagination were too weak to carve an image of him, or to boast of him in times of need—until one day he arrived. The man, his complexion a sickly green, said, when he suddenly came, that he was looking for "the Matosevitch girl."

Oy vey! The Matosevitch girl! How she clung to him then without any doubt of his identity, to kill the doubts of the others, and how she led him through the house, her gaze—full of pride and pain—fixed on that cleft and bilious face as she chattered to him with eager intimacy and suddenly pointed to the startled Bat-Sheva and said: "This is my friend, my best friend!"

And at once, to prove it to him, she asked the Queen, quite

fearlessly, to lend her (sentence of death!) her silk dress "for a walk in the village," and then, miraculously, her request was granted.

Oy vey! Sheina-Sheindel Matosevitch! How she sacrificed to him all the spoils of victory in her eyes, to this bitter clerk! And when she went out to put on the regal attire, he said suddenly to the girls who surrounded him: "She, my daughter, has very good friends!" And in his voice there was the same contrived submissiveness.

Vey, vey, poor Matosevitch! When she returned with him from the walk—eat your hearts out all of you!—there was something wrapped inside the silk dress that she gave back to the boss!

"Little Monkey! Come on then, let's go home!" said Bat-Sheva, standing up and handing both of their satchels to Yaffa.

15
WHAT WILL
HAPPEN NEXT?

On Sabbath eves, when the sky is painted with layer upon layer of marmalade colors, the children tend to abandon themselves to the pleasures of contemplation. Most stand in the yard while a few of them rain down shouts from the balconies above, shouts that blend into the clear, balmy evening air hovering around ears scrubbed clean for the occasion.

Already they have gobbled like colts the delicious preparations of Sabbath eve—bathing in hot water, underwear smelling of soap, the tiled floors of the dormitories scrubbed, their seams dark with moisture—and there still remains, at the bottom, the sweet expectation of a further blessing to be bestowed on them, Sabbath eve supper. To shorten the interval of expectation, they busy themselves with contemplation, for its own sake, of the world that is slipping into the Sabbath as into a sparkling shell.

In the dining room, where the daylight still lingers, it is pleasantly cool and the window open to the north admits the sweet smells of mint and moss, which grow in profusion beside the streams of the open drain. Maya listens to the voices of the children, enviously guessing at what's happening out there and glancing now and then at the window and at the dust track beyond it. In the shadow of the short avenue of mulberry trees, still clad in defiant greenery, there appears, as on every Sabbath eve, a last group returning from the bathhouse. A few children of the pious, in their flat hats and black kneesocks, stride in the footsteps of their fathers. This repugnant familialness arouses in Maya a vague sense of bitterness. At once she cherishes the notion that a smell of old age emanates from these children—even the structure of their faces is different, as if incompletely sculpted, or perhaps it's not the structure so much as a different range of expressions, a different twist to the corners of the mouth, a different contraction at the root of the nose. As they pass by the hostel, the wind carries fragments of their conversation in that nasalized Yiddish that arouses in her a feeling of degeneracy and the shabby relations between man and man, a vexatious failure to distinguish between the ugly and the beautiful.

Now great flocks of silhouetted starlings cruise idly between the horizon and the house, a hidden desire guiding their flight, in which there is no logic other than to fly in formation in the shape of a cloud.

The children in the yard, like Maya watching the birds, stare at them in passive self-oblivion, frail mouths hanging open and eyes narrowed toward the sky.

Up there, on the roof, as usual at this hour, stands the Old Man Slonim, his thin, transparent limbs vibrating as he looks toward the West and sets his Sabbath watch.

"Even when I was a girl, they all knew I'd have beautiful legs. I remember like it was today. Once I was lying on my bed and reading something. I was just ten years old. You can imagine how I was lying. Like this, on my stomach, with my legs in the air." It was Shoshana's voice that brought Maya back to the dining room. "I lay there reading something. Suddenly a neighbor comes in and she says to my mother in a loud voice: 'This girl's going to have legs that will drive the world crazy!' My mother said: 'Shush . . . shush!' But since then, ever since then, I got the idea in my head that I'd have legs like these, no worse than Grable's."

"That's interesting!" says Pani-Paula. "Legs have never given me ideas."

The women move around the table and cover it with yellowing sheets. Maya waits by the window, the tray of forks in her hand. In the middle of the sheet, where the dirty color of the oilcloth shows through the tear, Pani-Paula lays a bundle of anemones in a washed out yogurt jar. "We must have a proper *Shabbes*," she says.

"Their breath will be enough to knock that over," grumbles Shoshana as she lays out the enamel plates on the table with an expression of disgust. "Maya, do you mind telling us what you're dreaming about? Get on with it! What were we talking about before? Legs. Oh, I was going out once with quite a nice boy, we even thought about marriage, and he wanted his mother to get to know me and he didn't know how. Then the opportunity came. We went together to a Hanukkah party in Petah Tikvah. His mother was one of the organizers—ORT-Shmort—and then something funny happened. His mother didn't know anything about me because I wasn't standing with him. And I was wearing a really short dress, the kind that only I can allow myself . . . Suddenly I hear his mother: 'Who's that girl over there, showing off all her thighs?' You see? *She* noticed my legs, the bitch . . . Maya, you're forgetting what you're supposed to be doing here!" Pani-Paula squashes her double chin in polite attention. "So that's how she got to know you," she says.

"Yes!" replies Shoshana happily. "But in the end I changed

my mind about him. A well-launched young man and all that, but he wasn't manly enough . . . well, you know . . . when I walk around in a swimsuit and high heels, you won't find one man on the beach who doesn't want to show that he's a man. And that boy, him of all people, was the only one who never lost his cool."

From outside come the voices of the children, who are already crowding around the locked door. The darkness, wiping the colors from the sky with a damp sponge, has driven them toward the house.

"The challah's falling apart today, like a corpse," declares the cook.

Somebody is knocking hard and persistently on the back door of the kitchen. Pani-Paula grumbles and goes into the kitchen to yell at whoever it is.

The nursery attendant sinks heavily onto one of the small chairs, folds her hands behind her head, and glances casually toward Maya, who is silently doling out the cutlery, then closes her eyes wearily.

"There's chicken today!" cries a voice from outside, the voice of Handsome Rafael.

"There's been an epidemic in Feigenbaum's poultry farm," replies another voice, the knowing voice of Abie.

"Chicken!" says Shoshana, opening her tired eyes. "Dead cockerels at a quarter the price with a special kosher seal from the slaughterer! Ah, and here comes another cockerel," she says to Markovski, who appears from the kitchen with the cook, his damp hair pressed into a net.

"My queen, the hungry masses may break in at any moment," he says to Paula. Then, in response to the words of the girl, he raises his fingers to his head and bows a courtly bow. "Ha! Good evening, my Lily of the Valleys!" (He has called her this ever since that lunch when she attempted to dissect his character in the hearing of all.)

"Won't *Duce* be coming this evening to his garden that is so 'blasted by the storm, her leaves are withering'?"

"Withering-shmithering," replies Shoshana. "One look at you, the Immortal One Himself would wither."

"You'd look more intelligent and handsome if you took that thing off your head. Frieda will be down soon," says Paula, gesturing with her eyes toward Shoshana, who is still sitting there, and angrily thrusting into her hands the dish of cold kidney-bean salad, garnished with onion.

Markovski advances toward the table, to the girl, as if singling her out from the rest.

"Well, little duty-girl, how are we settling down?" He jangles her cutlery and tickles her nose. "What do you reckon—everything will be alright, eh?"

Maya cautiously moves her face aside. She doesn't want his affection, this man whom the women dislike for some reason.

"There you are—another one!" He turns away from her with scorn. In spite of her aversion, she feels a pang of something, compassion or regret.

"Why are we standing here like Cerberus at the gates of Hell?" He raises his voice again, with renewed and lively self-assurance. "Let's open up to them!"

The thumping of the children's bodies against the door intensifies.

"Of course nobody understands your philosophies!" says Paula in Yiddish. "You'd better stop preaching and start doling out the challah."

It's going to be chicken, thinks Maya happily.

"Oh, how I love this woman!" cries Dov to Pani-Paula, stretching out his arms as if to embrace her. "Venus of Willendorf! The very highest ideal of womanhood, renouncing everything that our desiccated world calls by the name of culture! The only woman in the world whose utterances I can trust!"

"Which Venus?" asks Shoshana, a little spark of curiosity in her eyes.

"Venus of Willendorf, discovered in 1908 in the region of Willendorf on the Danube by Professor Abermayer," he cheerfully declaims. "Characterizes the ideal of feminine beauty of the race that lived in that area in the Stone Age and also my ideal in the Age of the Stone Heart. A healthy, fleshy body, with drooping belly and bosom. Eternal proof of the continuance of life."

"Idiot," says Shoshana, with a knowing wink toward Paula, inviting her complicity.

"Strange. And I thought simple-minded folk were the kind you like."

Why does everyone around here have to be so nasty to one another? Maya wonders.

Paula drags her heavy legs toward the door. She scratches around for a moment with the key, then steps back with surprising agility, which could be interpreted as a gesture of respect to those entering but is in fact a protective movement learned from experience. As if shot from a mighty bow, the girls and boys swoop upon the table, each body with its own trajectory, colliding with the chairs and at once overturning the vase of anemones. Enamel plates tumble to the floor as, still standing, the children reach for the brittle slice of challah that lies beside each dish. It is Frieda who has always demanded this token reverence on Sabbath eve.

A moment later Frieda comes hurrying in, wearing that big blouse with the voluminous sleeves that barely reach her elbows, over her heart the foreign monogram that makes it appear she has only one breast, her hair drawn back from her forehead and clamped to her temples in a gold crown, a work of craftsmanship that the girls are always eager to imitate.

With Frieda's entrance there is a feeling that the essential has arrived—all is complete—but the thin angry wrinkles between her brows spoil the dignity of her smile. She's coming to something that's already ruined, thinks Maya, observing the scene through Frieda's eyes—to the noise and to those challah loaves that she's obtained from the Wolfson woman after so much bargaining, already gobbled up between the pulling out of the chair and the parking of the behind.

"Stop all that racket immediately! Shlomo! I'm talking to you! You look very tasty today!" She points to his greased hair. "Where did you get all that margarine from?" She cuts short the outburst of laughter. Now she stands at the head of the table, her beautiful face contorted with pain. "Now listen!" she says quietly. "Anyone who makes one more sound gets no chicken."

Everything is suddenly sealed under a giant glass bell that blots out the voices and the whispers. Frieda seems to be expecting further noise, so she can give her anger free rein, but no noise comes. "So. That's the language you understand! Nothing to do with reverence or enjoying a festive occasion! Guzzling! Just tell them there'll be less guzzling in their bellies!" Now she seems irritated by the glazed eyes, fixed on her mouth, blinking in response to her attacks with drowsy patience. Markovski can't comprehend the nature of the pressures that drive her to castigate them thus from time to time. He hates her at this moment. Finally she twists this last sentence into a comprehensive moral lecture, bristling with intimidation, but you can sense in her words the first signs of conciliation.

When the signal is given, the eyes come back to life and dozens of plates are held out to Shoshana, who wearily distributes the kidney-bean salad garnished with onion.

"Children!" commands Frieda as they start handing out the chicken. "Chew the bones as well! There's lots of lime in them!"

"Lime!" Salomon mimics her voice as he carefully removes his cufflinks, reserved for special occasions, and rolls up his sleeves.

"Good appetite!" he calls to Frieda. "In the backyard there's a pit full of lime," he adds softly.

"What a small piece I've got!" complains Bat-Sheva to Maya,

who's distributing the portions, but she won't allow it to be exchanged for another and chews the meat as if resigned to her fate. The festive flower that has blossomed for a moment in Maya's heart is crushed.

"The French chef at the Casino would've thrown this stone straight into the sea!" Shlomo shouts to Pani-Paula, to provoke her.

"Tie it around your dirty neck," snaps the cook with disgust, "then go ahead and throw it!"

Yaffa, who until now has been carefully peeling the covering of skin from the chicken leg that has unexpectedly fallen to her lot, suddenly bends down under the table and keeps her head down for some time. Maya waits to see what will happen next. The girl sits up again, her face flushed and her freckles hot. Her glance meets Bat-Sheva's scornful eyes, which immediately glide to Yaffa's emptied plate; it is Yaffa who has attempted to circumvent her. This look of the Queen is enough to throw the three girls sitting closest to her—Nira, Hedva, and maybe also the Quiet Loony—into a whirlpool of conflicting physical and spiritual interests. Maya knows what's happened now.

"I, I dunno," says Nira. "I've got a sudden tummyache, sort of. I can't even go on lookin' at this chicken. Not 'ungry." She always talks like an immigrant.

"You're leaving your chicken?" asks Bat-Sheva in amazement, as if discovering some flaw in her.

"Yis," whispers Nira, "I'm leavin' it." An emphatic whisper meant to indicate that tummyache *isn't* the cause.

"You see this loony?!" cries the Queen. "She's leaving her chicken!" And Yaffa giggles at her foolishly.

"Am I to blame for my tummyache?" Nira protests, squirming in delicate embarrassment.

With apparent reluctance, Bat-Sheva holds out her plate. The little wing glides into it gladly, among the chewed bones.

"Dear, dear, what a lot of skin!" she says. The gift is accepted.

To her right sits Hedva, her housewifely face tensed with anxiety. With her short fingers she sticks her fork into the gizzard and shakes it onto the plate of the one sitting to her left. "There's no skin on this," she says. Bat-Sheva is dignified! She doesn't even look at Hedva, not wanting to embarrass her, and immediately cuts into the gizzard, as if it has been on her plate from the start.

Yaffa pales suddenly. Now she realizes the gravity of her mistake! This is like a line waiting for injections, growing smaller in front of her. Maya's turn is approaching. To flee—impossible. Before sitting down in the place that awaits her, Maya takes her plate and empties it without a second thought onto that of the Queen.

"What's this?"

"This? It's the chicken that was mine," replies Maya, choosing her words carefully and avoiding the other's eye.

"What do you think I am, a public trash can?"

"I thought . . ."

"That I'm a trash can! Take it back, hypocrite!"

She just can't get through to Bat-Sheva. And still this vague desire of hers to possess her for herself, herself alone, this power of patronage, this egotism.

As if through a mist, she takes in the reassuring voices of the boys, which prove that other worlds still exist. They are talking about the theft of a football from the Betar youth hut by members of the Sefardi team.

"It's the new ball," says Handsome Rafael, his red hair sticking up from his scalp and a strange angry flush on his rosy cheeks.

The boys stop chewing.

"Stole it!" cries Ketzele scornfully. "They shifted a couple of screws in the lock that were hanging out anyway like—like your father's whatsit. That isn't even breaking in."

"Not breaking in?" yells Salomon, who has recently become a supporter of Betar, spluttering over his "r's" as he usually does in moments of forgetfulness. "You're all so dumb, they could use your heads for balls, enough for the whole of League B."

"What about the other lot?" says Ketzele contemptuously. "When your Betarniks catch them, you know what'll happen?"

"There'll be blood!" says Salomon thickly, putting his fingers to his waist as if pulling a gun.

They're obsessed with the outdoors. Always the outdoors.

"Stop that noise immediately!" cries Shoshana.

She too has become severe lately. Noise! What is it with the staff? They're always so afraid of silence you'd think it was a vacuum, trying so hard to fill it with all kinds of nonsense, yet where we're concerned they squash real conversation. Why do they hate the children's voices?

"Next time *I'll* give you mine right away," Yaffa whispers to Bat-Sheva.

"I'll never take anything from you, ever," says Bat-Sheva, "Little Monkey!"

Maya chews her food anxiously, the saliva refusing to slide down her throat. Suddenly she finds the Queen smiling into her face.

"Next time, if you don't want your chicken, then *you* can be the first to give it to me," she says calmly, with a look that seems to caress her cheeks.

Maya raises veiled eyes to the new light bulb and sees in it a rainbow of colors.

16
THE PRINCIPESSA
OF TEL AVIV

Since the nature of women is such that it does not allow them to live, even for a moment, without love or its opposite, there suddenly sprang up and flourished among the three women of the staff a new camaraderie, a sort of trench solidarity.

All this on account of Berta.

They immediately sensed in her, in Berta, that she was involved in, aside from her domestic duties, certain activities that demanded investigation. Exchange of hints, and guessing of guesses, until enlightenment descended and her weakness was revealed— this from the gossiping of the children.

Berta came to the hostel with the first heat waves of the spring. Carrying only a small bundle, she entered the office. Sitting at the desk over notes for his new article, Dov recognized her immediately, with astonishment—it was that Carmen herself, the "seed-splitter." She recognized him too and smiled with great relief, believing this an omen.

"Ah! So this is the place you were looking for that time, Sir!" she said.

"Yes, yes," he replied, as if finding something lost. For a moment he marveled at the happiness that she awoke in him—she still belonged to the no-man's-land between him and the others.

"I saw your advertisement in the kiosk near the factory," she added hesitantly, as if she expected rejection.

"Ah, very good, very good!" he said to encourage her, feeling like a bureaucrat behind the desk. "I see you've brought your things with you, a girl with initiative!" He felt he should be speaking with more emphatic friendliness, but his happiness was something quite real, as if she was just what he had been missing. "We've at last received a grant to employ a cleaner," he added, biting his tongue. The boss hiring a servant. Feeling the need to seek assistance from outside; he left the girl standing by the desk and went out to find Frieda, to lay on her shoulders the disagreeable task.

Frieda came with him and smiled at the new worker, as if appraising her from a distance, in her hands a long pair of tongs.

The first of the boys and girls returning from school saw the vigorous rump of the new "staff" waving at the ceiling of the staircase, moving downward in time to the clattering of her clogs: a clonk, and one buttock sinks to the left; a thump, and the other sinks to the right, her hands clutching a rag, probing and gathering up the accumulated grime of weeks from the joints of the stairs. When she turned her head toward them over her shoulder, and then without a word let them pass her and spread fresh dirt on the clean floor, they saw the pearls of sweat glistening on the skin of her cheeks and chin. As they passed she straightened up, the rag in her hands, the fringes of her dress tucked into her belt, and smiled an affectionate smile at them, like a welcome to long-awaited friends. Every time they paused on the stairs and turned back to look at her, their eyes met the same smile.

Fate endowed Berta with a rare privilege. The inmates were well disposed toward her from her first day, perhaps because she was just three or four years older than the oldest of them, perhaps because she did not look at them with either pity or revulsion in her eyes, but with undisguised familiarity, as if saying to them again and again: "What is there about you that should shock me? Your waists tied around with string? Your trailing baggy pants? Those knees, so thick they make your thighs look like boiler pipes? Your lips, split at the edges from malnutrition? All of it—it doesn't surprise me a bit—it's all like a song I know very well but whose meaning has been forgotten, a song that's always on my lips and always demanding to be sung: 'Na, na, na, na . . . Argentina . . . Na, na, na, na . . . Argentina.' "

All the days of the week Berta would walk about in her wooden clogs, dragging and clattering, as if trying to split the floor. Often Maya would stop to listen to the clogs and derive pleasure from them.

Coughing, coughing, striving toward the summit of coughing and not reaching it, like the cough of the Old Man Slonim. They are a pair of blacksmiths, like the ones in the street of the village, who stand glowing in the fire light and hammer in turns at the iron ingot; but Maya is troubled by the thought that one is hampered by a sense of inferiority, trailing behind and answering a weak "amen" to the hymns of his stronger companion. Listen . . . they've stopped, pausing for a moment, searching for something new to say, racking their brains, until this one, the stronger, breaks the silence and then they are swept back into their old conversation, one vigorous and the other hesitant.

"What a cacophony!" yelled Paula from the start, bowing her head in a display of unbearable suffering, screwing up her eyes and squeezing their corners between finger and thumb. "A ca-cophony!" And this before the really discordant things became known.

In the course of time the curiosity of the boys regarding Berta cooled and that of the girls grew warmer, perhaps because Berta was careful to sustain it, and within a short time she forged with some of them special bonds of friendship and trust, giving them a surreptitious taste of the things she brought in her bag on her return from secret visits to the town, setting their hair in a style similar to her own coiffure, letting them preen themselves with her cosmetics or sending them on her behalf to the one and only "perfumery" of Kiryat Shkak. There they would stand on tiptoe before the counter, their nostrils wide open to the fragrant smells and their eyes feasting on the pictures of elegant women, smiling from the walls their smiles of permanent happiness, glittering to the point of painful self-pity.

For the first three weeks Berta did not once leave the house. After Frieda had attended to extinguishing the lights and with-drawn from the girls' dormitories to the tasteless concerns of a grown-up woman, who greets with a sigh of relief the brief span of freedom allotted her until morning, Berta would creep stealthily into one of the dormitories and there, silently, amid the foul stench, would sink down on one of the beds. The girls gathered around her in the darkness while Berta told them startling facts about life, things that the others, in their grown-up stupidity, seemed determined to hide from them. She would join with them in warm-hearted abuse of everyone who deserved abuse, carving out their futures and attributing praise and blame to each and every one of them to her face, and, finally, would reveal to them her secrets, woman to woman. And the more she revealed, the more she veiled herself.

By the end of the three weeks the girls know she can no longer bear to stay in this place. Her peace is gone. She lies awake at night, listening to the sounds of the house, which rapidly fade until she is left with the beating of her heart. In her house there were always voices—her old man and old woman. The old woman has just returned from the maternity ward, not a drop of strength in her, and the old man already on top of her. Like figs from the tree, a little shaking, and children fall down.

There were always sounds in the night. Now Maya can almost hear the sound of the girl's big heart. Suddenly they have imprisoned Berta on the top of a dark hill, while in Tel Aviv there are speeding headlights dimmed with blue shades, the mysterious, almost underground tumult of blackout nights, cafés packed with all the noise and commotion of the city. Berta needs the eyes of men so she can flourish and bloom before them, eyes that will follow her down the street and be maddened by her charms.

"There's no men around here!" Berta complains in the darkness. "No shop windows that you can look in and see yourself! Markovski, eh? He's only interested in what comes from the mouth. Always talking, talking, talking, as if he's got to fill a million and a half holes with words! And how he enjoys words, how his nostrils flare as if he sniffed 'soir de Paris.' He hasn't even got time to kiss anyone, he'd lose too many words!"

Berta talks a lot about Markovski with a strange kind of grudge. This doesn't please Maya. She herself has an obscure grudge against him and doesn't like the idea of sharing it with Berta. Maya knows that she doesn't like Berta, perhaps because she gives away so many of her secrets, but she is drawn toward her as if to a nightmare vision. Berta knows this too, and she's always careful to isolate Maya from the rest, or to attack her with childish displays of friendship.

"No men in the place!" Bat-Sheva, Nira, Yaffa, Hedva, and the Quiet Loony agree with Berta.

After three weeks Berta began going out to the city in the evenings.

Another fascinating thing about Berta—her transformation before going down to the city.

Berta finishes burning the new generation of bedbugs and, bestowing a momentary freshness on the floors, hides herself away for a long while in the bathroom, washing in the first hot water from the boiler and scrubbing her inky-black heels, then stands in the door of the workroom, all pink and steaming, one thigh sheltered beneath the bathrobe and the other projecting sideways through the flap, a loose red sash around her waist and her head wrapped in a high towel-turban, one hand resting lasciviously on her hip and the other clicking its fingers in the air, and she calls to the girls, already waiting for her in the big room: "Carmen Miranda! Carmen!"

Then she starts to move toward them, cooing softly, tossing her hips, until they're all pressed so close to her that they could wipe their noses on her gown. She threads her way between them, taking an oval mirror from a special case, breathing on it and polishing it carefully with the sleeve of her gown, from the wrist to the elbow, breathing on it again and bringing a shine to the mirror and the reflection of her teeth. Now she puts the mirror on the big worktable, raises her arms, and rolls up her sleeves with a ceremonious air.

When she sits the girls compete to grab the chair to her right— the one to her left is permanently reserved for Bat-Sheva—giving her an unhindered view of Berta's face from the side. For happy is the eye that has seen Berta at the hour of her Sabbath eve toilet.

With all the conceit of a master craftsman, Berta takes a little pair of tweezers from a tiny case ("Isn't that cute! Cute!" prattle the girls), leans her face toward the mirror with a look of surprise, ponders for a moment, then carefully plucks from under her brow the tiniest of tiny hairs, breathing in through her teeth as she does so, plucks a hair from the root of her nose with another whistling intake of air. Once her brows have been changed into smooth lizard's tails, she turns her weapons on her soft little moustache. Now she plucks, whistles, sighs, plucks, whistles, sighs, enough to make you cry, and the girls, anticipating the end of their childhood, gaze at her with faces awash with fascination, oblivious of themselves.

Only on Bat-Sheva's face is there a flickering grin of cynical encouragement to disguise her envy.

When Berta has finished removing the traces of masculinity from her face, she shakes her head and peels off the tall turban. Her wet hair stands up like the finest of raw materials. Now they wait with motionless eyes for that miracle, repeating itself week by week and turning the field of riots into a Parisian barricade— this new hairstyle that has wondrously penetrated the enemy lines and filtered through to us.

Always, at this very time, Bat-Sheva bends Berta to her will, with some innocent conversational opening such as: "Bertola, did you know Sima from the drugstore already has a French *coiffure?*" She is all goodwill, seeking to gladden Berta's heart by comparing her with this Sima. Amazing, but Berta always falls into the trap.

"Sima-Harima! Always with Sima! Two-and-a-half hairs on her head—and still talking! *Her* with a French *coiffure!* Of course! Her too—she just sees me in the Oasis with the English—you see her guts on fire. So what? This is her style!" Berta is never hurt by the thought that somewhere around there's a girl with more beauty and sex appeal than she has.

Grumbling, she draws toward her temples the tendrils from her nape that have fallen from the heap of curls, a bundle of hairpins in her mouth, and Bat-Sheva radiates smiles toward the girls, who don't know whose victory they should be hoping for.

"Sima!" Berta goes on chewing the bait, her voice blurred by the pins. "I could tell you another million-and-a-half shocking things about this drugstore bottle. Sure, they all think she's dying to have a Tommy—not one of those rough guys."

Now it's time for the most important question of them all. "Tell us, Bertola, truly, why do *all* the girls want Tommies?" Bat-Sheva asks, her innocent eyes glazed.

"Why? Because they're English, that's why!"

"Why, why?"

"Because they speak English."

"Abie says they speak to you in Prickish."

"Sure! It's very important in life to know languages," declares Berta distractedly. They giggle softly.

"Then why don't you make friends with Pani-Paula?" Bat-Sheva makes the lightest of light tugs on the line. "She speaks beautiful Polish!"

"Polish!" Berta flares up, pulling the pins from her mouth. "Are you trying to tell me that's a language for human beings? A language of snakes, pish . . . pish . . . some language that is!"

Her eyes light up. "Hey, I've had a great idea. I'll take your Polish friend to the Oasis! If the manager sees her just once, he'll take her on as a regular dancer!" She stands up quickly, squawking, tucking her chin into her chest. For a moment the girls see before their eyes the cook shaking her thick puddinglike buttocks, which twitch to the rhythm of the rhumba. Every now and then she adjusts the girdle on her behind, stepping carefully so as not to trample her imaginary partner. Another moment and their bodies, racked with laughter, are leaning on the table or seeking support on the walls. They clutch their stomachs, shrieking "*Mamale, Mamale!*," but their eyes are on Berta, not wanting her to stop. Now it's enough for the girl to say "Pish . . . pish . . . pish . . .," and they're caught up again by the glorious spasm, crying out for help, groaning dreadfully, looking tearfully at one another, until the wells of laughter dry up and they return to their places, still croaking feebly, and their eyes wide with admiration fixed on Berta, who's already sitting there quite at ease, adjusting her loosened hair.

Only Bat-Sheva doesn't give up: "Come on, tell us the real truth! Berta!"

"I've told you!" she replies calmly, but at once she drops her mask of pedagogic dignity. "Why? Because they know what it's all about! What a girl is, what a good time is, what it is not to treat a woman like an Arab. Jimmy, what do you think, you reckon he's really my type? You'll be surprised—he's too old for me! But he knows what it's all about!"

"And our guys?" asks Hedva.

"Our guys! You'll find out soon enough they don't even know the word 'gentleman,' and straightaway they say the cheapest words and put their hands in the most expensive places. What do they know about? Motorcycles—Hadassah Gardens—the beach! And what does a girl have to look forward to in her life before she falls into the trap? To have fun, dress up, see things—a little drink, a little 'swing'! Without that you might as well die—today!"

"I'll never go out with Tommies," says Nira.

"Don't worry, sugar, not one of them will even look at you," replies Berta scornfully, taking between her fingertips a lock of Nira's greasy, lank hair.

Bat-Sheva slings fresh bait on her hook.

A few days before, certain people were distributing leaflets among the girls in the school and in the streets. She takes the leaflet from her pocket and reads:

Warning to the daughters of Israel! In the light of the fact that in recent days young girls have been trailing after foreign soldiers, we turn to these girls with a warning and give them the opportunity to mend their ways before their names, their addresses, and pictures are published and exposed to public shame. These words of ours are directed especially at students and young girls, whose activities are not to the credit of our people and our country. YOUNG DAUGHTER OF ISRAEL! Do not bring shame upon your people! Mend your ways while there is still time! This is our first warning to you, do not force us to take action against you. Remember! You are destroying your own future with these acts. And if our words do not touch your heart and you continue in this manner, we shall expose you to public shame and disgrace.

Sons of Pinhas

"Be careful, Bertola," says Bat-Sheva, "One of these days they'll give you a haircut like that one from the orchard." Kiryat Shkak is still buzzing with rumors about the daughter of the Hasidic rabbi whose head was shaved in the orchard by the zealots of the Sons of Pinhas.

"They'll tie you to a post. They'll do things to you."

"Things, eh? What good people they must be to do things to Berta! Now I've nothing more to say." She turns back to the mirror with a look of aloof concentration and is silent. With the knowledge of experience, the girls wait in silence for the seething wave of her fury to break through the opaque crust. Here, here it comes . . .

"She compares *her* with me? You should be ashamed to say such things! Have you any idea what *she* was? What do you know about life, eh? Always clucking, clucking, and not a single egg to show for it! That one from the orchard!" She mutters to herself angrily, but at the same time she meticulously smears three blobs of rouge onto each cheekbone, rubbing with her fingertips until the color reaches her temples. "What do you think, eh?" she cries with renewed heat, as if remembering something conclusive. "You think Jimmy's some miserable corporal? You think he'd be stupid enough to waste his time on me if I wasn't worth it? There's enough tarts parading about on the beach. Two a penny! I'm not one of those who makes a profit on the staircase! If Berta goes out . . ."

"Then it's only with one!" they all chime in triumphantly with the chorus that they know so well.

"That's right!" she snaps. "I'll never go behind his back. All Jimmy's buddies know they mustn't even breathe on me!"

They listen in fascinated silence, eager to catch every nuance. Only Bat-Sheva murmurs feebly that she doesn't really want them to make her, Bertola, bald, because she wouldn't look right without that French barricade.

Berta is appeased at once and ready to grant their request, needing the display of their affection as much as they need her.

See, now she's going to explain what it's all about! On Saturday night a week ago they went out to the Oasis—she, Jimmy, his captain, and a few other officers and girls from the town. There were tables outside, in the dark, under the trees—palm-trees like in a movie—dance music, and real waiters with napkins on their arms.

Berta wore her white dress, the one the girls love. Suddenly they heard the Master of Ceremonies announce, in Hebrew and English: "Ladies and gentlemen, talent com–pe–ti–tion! The winner of the competition gets a double gin!"

Onto the stage climb all kinds of good-time girls, like Sima-Harima, striking poses and squealing: "Oh! Oh! Oh!" God only knows what they think they're doing. Jimmy and the officers join in the laughter. Then they exchange whispers and suddenly, before she knows what's happening, they've grabbed Berta, picking her up in their arms like this—would you be–lieve it?—and carrying her straight to the microphone! She yells "No! No!" and kicks out with her legs. But she's enjoying it really, so is the crowd. She clutches the microphone in her hand, like Alice Fay in "Flying Down to Rio," lifts her skirt a little, just to please the audience. All around her there are shouts and whistles, but if Berta's nervous, she'd better not show it—that would be the end of everything! Then she swallows her saliva and says in English that she's going to sing "Yes My Darling Daughter." What a treat! The English stand around the stage shouting "Berta! Berta!" And the crowd is shouting "Berta!" Just as she opens her mouth, a noise interrupts her. She looks around angrily, and suddenly realizes it's the orchestra. A real one, like in a movie—it's just a pity the lamps are blue for the blackout. She pauses, sees the conductor waving the white baton, signaling to her with his hand not to start yet. The orchestra plays. She taps out the rhythm with her foot—she's got the rhythm and she's got the mood! The conductor gives the signal, and at first she feels the microphone dancing in her hand, but suddenly she isn't frightened of anything anymore, and she sings, "Yes My Darling Daughter" without one mistake, from beginning to end!

"And who got the gin?" asks Hedva.

"What? Who? Sima-Harima maybe? I tell you, even those rich types from Ramat Gan, who always have tables reserved for them, and the elegant ladies with pearl necklaces, they clapped their hands and thumped the tables when Berta walked past." The gin was real gin. Now she'll tell them straight just why Berta got the prize.

"Because she's pretty," says Yaffa diffidently.

"Because she's got the rhythm and she's got the mood!" guesses Hedva.

"Because she goes out with Tommies!" says Maya.

Berta asks if they're stupid or what, the light of the great moral lesson sparkling in her eyes. "Because I could sing the whole song from beginning to end without mistakes. It's the most important thing in life to know languages!"

"Teach me the words too," begs Hedva.

"I've got the words in Hebrew letters that my friend gave me," says Berta.

Captivated utterly, the girls crowd around the table, staring devotedly at Berta, who becomes ever more beautiful, ever changing the expression on her face, assured of her limitless power.

"No matter!" she says in a low, emotional voice, her lips puckering under the layer of rouge. "Berta won't be staying long in this hole. Pani-Paula will have a fit when she sees me in the most elegant places in Tel Aviv."

In their eyes there's already the sadness of parting, but she puckers her lips together to settle the color, and at once she enfolds them in a look that declares she'll never desert them. All of them she'll take along to the most elegant places in Tel Aviv.

Afterwards they go out with her to the gate and follow with their eyes the new manifestation of Bertola, stomping down the hill on her high heels, wrapped in a bright spring dress, flawless, her hands bejeweled and all of her in love with herself and with the world.

"The girl must be saved," Markovski repeats in the ears of the women. "Somebody must talk to her." But this statement always elicits their bitchiest, most irritable responses.

"It's blood! You can't change blood!" declares Shoshana authoritatively.

"Blood! My ass!" sneers Yosef, who happens to be passing and gets drawn into the argument. "A man! You need a man around here, someone who'll slap that 'Principessa of Tel Aviv' so hard she'll forget the place where they do these things."

"And you, of course, are the man!" exclaims Paula.

"Talk to her, save her!" Dov repeats like an oath.

"Alright, go on! Talk, talk! Save her!" growls the cook. "She's just waiting, standing and waiting like a *mezuzah* for the kisses of the faithful."

Maya can't bear the sight of Dov Markovski. In her eyes he's like a sealed book, hoarding within it the secrets of her life. His concern for her seems to her vaguely like a plea for forgiveness, his inquiries after her health an attempt to erase something that troubles him.

It's funny, in her father's house there's a cut-out photograph showing a youthful, smooth-faced Boria, wearing a beret and without glasses; to his left, baby Maya in a perambulator, and her father to Boria's right. The picture has been cut roughly, removing the figure of her mother; this she knows because her mother has a copy of the same picture, but this time with her father's figure cut out of it. Boria and Maya remain in both pictures.

Even on the second night after that meeting "with the loud shouting," Boria Markovski stayed in their house. He was always disappearing for a while and suddenly returning, always with something for her in the pocket of his coat—an ancient rolled-up children's newspaper from a period when she was too young to read, or a collection of incomprehensible but very vigorous poems, published in Warsaw or Odessa, in strange type and with dog-eared bindings—and on the First of May he would take her with him to children's matinees. Yet in his conversations with her father he always spoke with stubborn and impassioned ferocity, as if there was deep hostility between them.

Even on the second night they were yelling at each other, and their voices were like the sounds of vessels filling with water, dim at first, gurgling, and gradually, as if climbing a ladder, rising, speeding up, thinning, as if yearning for something, and, suddenly, breaking off just short of their target and sinking back into dimness.

She made an effort then to listen intently, because it seemed they were talking of her. She always imagined they were talking of her, but this time there was no doubt—she heard her name plainly.

The pair of them suddenly came into the bedroom. She pulled the sheet over her head. Yes, they were talking about her. The two grown men, in the middle of the night.

"It isn't the place for her," said Boria in Russian, agitated.

"Hush . . . she isn't asleep," her father whispered.

"There's the Ben-Shemen children's village, there are kibbutzim . . . a different *niveau* altogether!"

"And who will pay?" her father protested. "And there . . . you'll be with her."

"Yes, I will," replied Boria's voice. "That at least will be some justice for you."

When her father went out she removed the sheet from over her head without fear and saw Boria pacing about the room in a sort of aimless dejection. He lit a cigarette and stood still, his eyes on the ceiling. (He didn't care about smoking in a room where a baby was asleep, the grateful thought occurred to her.) For a long while he stood thus, absorbed in his smoking, and then he took off his glasses.

"Boria, what's a '*niveau*'?" she asked suddenly.

He jumped, startled, and moved closer to her bed, bent down and looked into her open eyes.

"Hush . . . go to sleep!" he scolded her, absently.

One evening soon after, as she stood and watched her father shaving, as was her habit, she found above the sink a little piece of straw.

"What's this?" she cried excitedly. "I've found some straw!"

Her father's eyes, peering over the soft foam, looked for a moment at the straw and were trapped by it, as if something was ripening in his brain. Suddenly he smiled.

"You see? Father promises and father delivers," he boasted. "You wanted a straw—and look, he's brought it."

She was amazed that he had remembered to bring her "such an idiotic object," as he had described it.

The season of bubble-blowing was at its height. All the children were blowing soap-water bubbles on the balconies and she wanted to do the same, but she didn't have one of those paper tubes wrapped in wax. Her imagination revolved around a cup of red and frothy, nostril-tickling juice that she could suck through a straw, leaning on the counter of a kiosk, until all the last bubbles had been inhaled—the air spluttering with angry sounds—and then she'd be left with the "straw" wrapped in wax, and she could take it with her and blow bubbles on the balcony in full view of all those other children.

Once she ventured to mention this desire to her father. At once he looked at her with surprise, at his daughter so obsessed with trivia while his own brain bubbled night and day with concern for bread and for the greater destiny of the world. And then he made the remark about the "idiotic object."

After that she was careful not to speak of "straw," waiting instead for some child to decide he could spare one of his and she could cut off the ends soft with spit and soap and make it her own.

And now her father had surprised her—he himself—with a stalk of straw, all hollow and thick, with the genuine smell of the field, smooth and pliable and infinitely better than a "straw" wrapped in wax.

She must frame her questions carefully.

"I picked it in the field, in a village," replied Katriel Hermoni, still tugging at the skin of his cheek with the fingers of his left hand and shaving it with his right. She sensed that he was hesitant and tongue-tied.

"Is there more?"

"Lots, lots," he replied gladly.

A field of straw stretching and meandering from horizon to horizon. You could walk and walk and pick straw and more straw, lose yourself in the flying bubbles of froth.

At once she demanded to see it with her own eyes.

"If you want, you can even live there, right beside that field. Is that what you want?"

Here it comes—the big change.

He lowered his voice to a tone of solemn sweetness: "There's a love–ly house there and lots and lots of nice children and nice teachers."

The thought that he'd already been there, without her, in this field of wonders with all those nice children, brought upon her a vague sense of envy.

"Well, would you like to go and live there?" He moved the razor from his cheek and his hand was suspended in the air, waiting tensely.

"Yes, yes!" she cried, with no attempt to restrain her flooding joy.

"Without your father?" He studied her face. Fear mounted in her.

"Sure!" she said happily, but then again she didn't know . . .

Now he looked thoroughly insulted. He sat on the edge of the bath and, with one cheek still covered in lather, he pulled her between his knees and held her chin.

"Look, Mayaka. We're not throwing you out, eh? We love you, and this will al–ways be your home, eh?" (We!) "I always wanted us to live together, all of us. I married her because I wanted you to have a mother, somebody to treat you nicely. But life is hard, all those sucking parasites, sucking . . . A father must leave home to work." (Just listen to him talk, him too!) "Regina is busy. She's worn out with hard work. You don't know how much she wants to keep you with us. She feels close to you, she loves you," he said in a lilting voice, like a grandmother telling fairytales.

Any moment now he'd say: "When you grow up, you'll understand."

"When will I go there?" she said to forestall him.

He understood, but opened his lips wide to continue the game and blew air through them as if sunk in thought.

"I reckon another week, about, so you can be there for the start of the school year." (It had all been arranged from the beginning!) "We still have to sort out clothes, shoes . . . money! Money! Money!" he said anxiously, so she'd know how many sacrifices had to be made, even for the sake of removing her from the house.

"Well," he rose from his seat, looking relieved, and said generously, and again with the lilting tone of a storyteller: "And your father will come to visit you! And you'll come to visit your father, you'll learn, you'll play . . . and maybe, maybe there'll be somebody there you know." He smiled as if hiding a sweet from her.

"Boria Markovski!" she said stiffly, provocatively.

He looked at her like an animal that's fallen into a trap and fearfully awaits the arrival of the hunter. But she was playing with the toothbrushes above the wash basin. When they came out, Regina was standing by the bathroom door. You could tell she'd had a good listen.

"And now she'll learn respect!" she rattled away in rapid, angry Yiddish, her eyes fixed on the girl. "There they'll teach her to respect and value what people do for her! She won't get away with her insolence there!" And at once she began sawing in her Russian, sawing, sawing—any minute the walls would collapse and the furniture disintegrate!

"Enough! That's enough!" snapped the father and collapsed on the sofa, to the newspaper awaiting him on the cushion.

Maya felt a sting on her arm. It was Regina pinching her in impotent rage. She felt sorry for this woman, to be left here with her father to saw the whole house apart.

She prodded the girl into the kitchen. On the table lay a neatly piled heap of clean clothes.

"Madam, kindly embroider your name," she whined like an excited bitch.

"Why embroider my name?" Maya imitated her voice and laughed, for the first time, free from deep-seated pressure and bitterness.

"You! Uh! Uh!" croaked Regina.

"I'm driving her mad," she thought and put on a foolish expression, as if she didn't know that it was her task to weave the certificate of her liberation on the clothes.

Untypically, Berta woke up one Sabbath morning at a dewy hour and at once hastened in all her warmth to the girls' dormitories, dragging them from their beds still in their underwear. And into the face of Bat-Sheva, bleary from sleep, she tossed a big paper parcel, crying eagerly: "Quick! Take this, quick! To the big balcony! You've never seen anything like it! Never had such a treat!" With busy hands she prodded the girls, dizzy from the sudden awakening. "All night I haven't slept," she said breathlessly, clattering after them. "From the moment I arrived I've been wondering how to show you this. You'll go crazy!"

Shaking the door to the balcony, which as usual refused to open, Berta yelled impatiently, "When will they repair this damn door?" The boys, drawn to an invigorating dawn encounter, also began pressing onto the balcony, sunken-cheeked and smelling of sour bed linen.

Berta snatched the parcel from Bat-Sheva's hands. She thrust a hand into it, then changed her mind and paused, closing one eye with a tantalizing air. "What's in the parcel, eh?" But as the mouths opened to guess, she wouldn't let them. "No! Don't tell me! Whatever you'd say is nothing compared to this! In all your miserable, stinking lives . . ." And as she spoke, as if revealing the innermost secret of life, she drew her hand very slowly from the wrapping with a sigh. Into the air was borne something airy and reddish, a blooming fabric. Without a word she put one of its wings in Yaffa's hands, the other in Maya's, and pushed them apart forcibly.

"What's the matter with you?" she cried, seeing before her a pair of gaping dummies. "Move! Move apart! Stretch it!"

The fabric was drawn out and unraveled between the two girls, and Berta inspected it this way and that with the eyes of an artist. "More! More! What are you trying to tell me, you think it's that small?"

The flowery sail was stretched taut between the two, standing right at the ends of the long balcony. The shape and the pattern were revealed to their bemused eyes.

"Did you ever dream?!" cries Berta, scouring all their faces with her eyes, clattering over to the fabric and tapping it with a finger to test the tension. "Did you ever dream of such a skirt? Not even on hashish! The biggest Parisian *cloche* in the Middle East! A perfect circle—one piece!"

The boys stared for a moment at the *"cloche,"* heart-grating sneers on their faces. Somebody shouted: "Look at the size of that!" And another: "Just like Jimmy's!" But Berta paid no attention to their crudities. Her moist eyes, fixed on her protégées, said clearly: only Berta is capable of treating you to such excitements.

Maya gazed at this Goliath of skirts, at the ripples stirred by the morning breeze in its great flowers, and knew she was expected to express wonder and emotion, but she found nothing here to moisten her eyes. Suddenly she saw Frieda, who had been summoned to the place by the fear of commotion. She felt herself trapped in a ridiculous pose. Frieda paused in the doorway, looking from one wing of fabric to the other and at the faces of the girls holding them. Then she propped her chin and one cheek in the hollow of her hand, her elbow resting on the other hand, with an absurd air of contemplation.

Only now, with her appearance on the scene, were the girls impelled by some obscure force to finger the garment, and at once they began to sing its praises. The balcony was filled with twittering, with sighs of envy and wonder. Frieda smiled the restrained smile of a delicate soul, the smile that before Berta's coming had been enough to move the girls to appease her with the tasks that she allotted them. Now Frieda was an artist whose tools were obsolete. She froze every sinew in her face, leaving only that fixed smile. After a moment she disappeared from the doorway.

Dov changed his trousers but stayed in the pajama top, and as he fastened the buttons he turned the handle of his door. Standing on the threshold, Frieda said that she couldn't bear this any longer, a note of hysteria breaking through her usual restraint. He knew at once what it was that she couldn't bear any longer. A kind of sweetness was sprinkled in his heart, as it did each time that he served as a lightning rod for her emotions, and for this he was almost grateful to Berta.

He took her hand graciously, drew her after him into the room, and at once pushed a chair beneath her, as if supporting an invalid. When she sat down he dropped her hand sadly and stood blinking in silence, as if concerned for her health.

"The ludicrous part of the business is that this house is now run by . . . ," said Frieda with that restrained agitation, her voice grating slightly, as if ignoring the calm that the man was trying to create about her, "and you're the one who sets yourself up as her protector."

His glance lingered on her ash blond braid and nervous lips, and he longed to touch her and talk of something else. He told her he knew how much this place meant to her, and how she could devote herself to things, but . . .

"But—I'm exaggerating?" she interrupted him morosely. "The moral damage that she's doing to them on the very verge of adolescence! God Almighty! When I just think of the expressions that they're picking up from her . . ."

These words of Frieda's—a direct continuation of other conversations on this subject since Berta came—aroused in Dov a vague suspicion that with them she was allaying a different tension.

From day to day she sees how they are falling from her hands into the hands of someone who rejoices in her weaknesses, who shirks all effort by adopting the guise of shortsightedness and stupidity . . . how they check themselves before her, as if conspiring . . .

"What's the matter, Frieda?" He couldn't believe it was this that was embittering her life.

"Comrade Secretary!" she said suddenly. "I have the honor to inform you at this moment . . ."

He grinned inwardly. Ultimatum!

"And her laughter!" she said. "This laughter! The smell of the whole British army rises from her! It's a joke."

"Pleasant or unpleasant?" He knotted his brow in a clownish gesture so that she herself would be aware of her exaggerations.

"You win!" She stood up from her seat, her face like the face of a corpse. "Long live the male perspective!"

What was it that so troubled her that she could not let herself be amused? Dov hastily clutched her arm (the game permitted this now). "Throw her out, then! Throw her out! We'll throw her out! Tell me, where to?"

"To the same place she sprang up from!" she said maliciously. "The way a person wants to walk, lead her!"

"Be careful, Frieda, don't convince me this is what you really think!"

"I have no philosopher's stone to turn garbage into gold!" She released her arm from his grip and turned to the door. "I'm going to put a stop to all this business!"

He hurried to prevent her. He had realized long ago that Frieda served, unknowingly, as a kind of emotional barometer for the other two women.

"Fate has been kind to you!" he cried, as her hand was on the doorknob. "It's your luck that your father is dead!" She froze. Why did everything always seem to him like a game?

"Yes, exactly!" He shortened the rope (all this posing, in pajamas, oh God!). "Your father died of a heart attack in the prime of his life!"

"Yes?" She set her teeth at him, her characteristic gesture at times of deep concentration, or when her innermost self was being invaded.

"Because he was dragging up the hill a burden too heavy for him, so that Yosele and Gitele and Friedichka and Hayimka— all four of them!—all of them should be provided for, should go to high school, because it was impossible otherwise. It couldn't be otherwise! Isn't that so? Twice a year he went with Yosele and Friedichka and Gitele and Hayimka to the shops to buy shoes, stockings, dresses, coats—on credit if necessary because it was impossible otherwise! In the house the high school darlings used to gather in the evenings because Mama Auerbach was serving tea, sitting them all around the table, her eyes streaming like fountains while her scholars discussed Slovatski and Julian Tuvim."

He fixed his eyes on hers so she would understand him perfectly, until in their depths he felt her cold silence. She stepped back into the room and spoke derisively.

"Alright, go on! Now talk about her! A cursed infancy no doubt, a miserable childhood! Ignorance, poverty, disease, superstition, a cruel patriarchy! Everyone has excuses! Everyone has written and sealed motives! Don't say a word—take a spade and dig down to the foundations and write a thesis! And maybe sometime you'll admit the truth—that it's nice, nice for you to see her here, this theory of yours that's put on skin and sinews, to dissect, analyze, amuse yourself with . . ."

Her words seemed to remind him of the style of another, as if she were repeating the words of another.

Suddenly she waved her hand, as if it was all the same to her, as if angry that she'd been tempted into hearing his words. "You can do just as you please!" she cried suddenly. "Go ahead, get out of her head the dreams of silk underwear, the tarty hairdo and the American songs, teach her Rosa Luxemburg and Bernard Shaw's *Intelligent Woman's Guide!*" (This was a book Dov had lent Frieda.) "Go on! Right now! She's waiting for you there on the balcony, in a new harlot's costume, a red one! Take her to your clubs! Put her at the front of a demonstration with a banner: 'Fair Pay for Prostitutes'!"

She had never before revealed herself like this. Her eyes wandered among the objects in the room, as if detesting them in turn, but at the same time it seemed to him she was enjoying the anger itself, the untempered words, the opportunity to shout.

"You know quite well that I don't go to clubs anymore," he smiled at one who wasn't listening. "*I* will talk to her," he said confidently. "*I* will know how . . ."

"Words!" she spat. "Juggler of words!"

As much as Dov was pedantic toward men, discovering and exposing in them every crack, every hint of a bad smell, every flaw, belaboring them unrestrainedly with the goad of his tongue, so he experienced total anosmia in relations with women, and his misfortune was that he recognized this. There was no man, living or working in his proximity, with whom he did not enter into argument, argument that rapidly was reduced to personal insults. A whole regiment of men was already ranged against him in the category of "When he sees me, he crosses to the other side of the street, ha ha!" Not so with women. In their words he found double meanings, ancient wisdom, hints of perception, signals of under-standing, and in their company he was always assailed by a pow-erful sense of wonderment, which made him wary and embar-rassed at the same time. And, above all of them, Frieda, ever since the evening he saw her listening to the foolish argument between him and the sentry.

All that Sabbath morning Dov stayed in his room working on his article, but in his heart was a strong desire—to prove! All the time he wrote he was imagining to himself the moment when she would smile at him weakly and say she was mistaken, that *she* had been at fault, and at that moment what she had ripped so impetuously would be stitched together. And all this amid a scornful amazement at himself, that he had been roasted for her sake on the coals of his heart.

In the afternoon he went out to look for Berta. The boys were in the yard immersed in a new seasonal game, and every knock of the bat on the wooden ball sounded clearly with their cries.

Suddenly, before he had weighed what to say, his eyes en-countered her. She sat at ease at the worktable, bathed in the dim afternoon light from the east window, stretching out her fingers before her eyes and smoothing the nails with a long file. For a moment he stared at her upper lip, projected forward and resting casually on the lower, like the lips of a baby intent on his business. It was obvious she sensed his presence, but she was too lazy to look up. Why should she?

Beside the table the thought occurred to him, amusing in its simplicity, that although he had "set himself up as her protector," in conversation with Berta he had never gone beyond the dis-cussion of household chores. And she aroused in him no inclination to do so, rather the opposite, as if this was an intentional but distasteful deviation from the source. He cleared his throat briefly at the head garlanded with curlers.

"What is it!" At last she looked at him with the face of a contented cat, as if she'd been offered a dead mouse.

A foul and greasy taste in his mouth when he said he had "something important to say," and then an impulse to retreat immediately.

"Then say it!" she said to her nails.

"No, not like this," he said, forcing himself to smile paternally. "There isn't time just now. Later maybe?"

"You can't fool me, I know all these tricks." He hadn't come to the right address. Most of all, he wasn't the type!

"After supper, eh?" he tried again and smiled affectionately.

"Sorry! I have a rendezvous," she replied with the indifference of a *femme du monde*. One earring wobbled on the lobe of her ear.

"Rendezvous! A woman of sixteen going to a rendezvous!" Never in his life had he met a woman going to a "rendezvous."

"Could we do it tomorrow evening?" Again the greasy taste in his mouth.

"*You're* not going to do anything! Get that idea out of your head!" Her eyes pierced through his spectacles and into the retina, the repository of the weakness of the stronger sex. "You won't believe it, but tomorrow I'm also going out to have fun." As if she were saying: "You won't believe it, but tomorrow I'm going out to conquer Berlin."

"Alright, alright, just as you please, Madam. Go out by all means . . . and have fun." The patient pedagogue. Even the words "have fun" arouse aversion in him, as if stinging his palate. So there's an alternative way of interpreting actions—to have fun!

"Oh!" she replied with a strong Anglo-Saxon inflection. "How very kind of you to permit me!"

A fog dulled his brain: mounds upon mounds of words, all of

them useless. He'd been afraid lest he be forced to descend to her level, and here he was climbing a slippery glass mountain. Suddenly Berta spoke.

"What is it?" she said calmly. "Something they don't like, eh?"

She stood up, gathering up with a swift regal movement the train of the red flowery robe, the one that had been spoken of, apparently, declaring that she knew everything, everything that they thought of her, and it interested her "exactly this much." She held up before his eyes a severed piece of fingernail. Until this moment she hadn't dared tell any member of the staff her opinion of them. And, of course, it had to be to him. His idle desire for intimacy, his hesitant probing with the end of the rod, and there you are. Every man is for her a bargaining object, he told himself. Still a girl, and, already accustomed to one-dimensional relationships with men, she knows no way of negotiating with them other than a process of classification.

He lowered his eyes and looked at the leg of the table, at her leg, and at his leg.

Berta came sooner than he had expected.

As early as that Sunday evening she knocked at his door. Instead of "going out to have fun," she had been seized by the impulse to talk about herself.

Markovski was unable to conceal his excitement, which was out of all proportion to the event. With extravagant gestures of welcome he guided her to the folding chair, the same one that Frieda had occupied the morning before. Berta obeyed, like a patient coming willingly to the dentist. With modest grace she gathered in the folds of her dress. He himself sat on the end of his bed at a respectable distance, to dispel suspicion.

"Cigarette?"

She was weighing something in her mind when she encountered the cheap pack, then she drew out a crumpled cigarette, puffed at it briefly, but immediately stubbed it out with disgust on the lid of the tin box between them. Perhaps to show him that other men treated her better.

Now she lifted an eye to him, a well of innocence, until all the sentences ranged on his lips were swallowed up. Had some terrible mistake occurred, he wondered for a moment. Was it just the delusions of boredom that had brought them together? And he—perhaps he had set out to blunt and was sharpening instead, to uproot and found himself scattering seed?

"I'm sure you have friends, Berta?" he asks, always one to test things from their essence, without preconceptions.

"No, I haven't," she replies calmly. "I'm waiting for my old father to marry me off to a boy from a good family."

He smiles, so she'll know how much he appreciates humor. Why does Berta (he says, with the smile of one prepared to be a co-conspirator) keep so aloof from the members of the staff? After all, it's a pleasure to watch her with the children. "You know you have educational talents."

"Educational talents!" she repeats after him, conscious of his flattery, pronouncing these words for the first time in her life: "Educational! I tell them about life, and this excites them. It's . . . educational!" But she also enjoys uttering bold words like these.

"But," he unfolds before her a hand full of reassuring fingers, "try just once to be friendly. I don't mean with Pani-Paula—we all know—but with Shoshana or Frieda. If you were to find the way to her . . ."

"You find the way to her, and I'll be right behind you!"

He smiled, and restrained himself.

"That's a woman who's never known what it is to be alive."

"Has she ever said anything to you about . . ."

"I can hear all the buzzing in your heads . . . like bees on sugar."

"We're going around in circles, and this isn't . . . the main thing is what you . . . if you're really whole with yourself."

"If I'm a virgin?"

"Well, really," he said plaintively.

"I understand you perfectly. Everything in my brain runs on the best fuel," she replied sagely and helped herself to a cigarette. "They all know Berta's a lively girl who's good company. Ask anyone, ask Jimmy, it's only with you people that . . ."

Now it was she who was launching the boat and he who was hurrying to jump aboard, not to miss it.

"I know . . ."

She looked at him. "I'm not hiding anything! Jimmy's a decent human being, it's only with you people . . ."

"In my eyes all are equal," he declared, "Englishmen, Jews, or Martians."

"Not in my eyes! I don't know about Martians, but Jews don't know how to behave with a girl."

"We all misjudge the foreigner. We think he's got something different from us. Generally this arises from lack of confidence in ourselves, from contempt for ourselves."

"You don't need to tell me that! But if I was going out with a Jew, you'd send an orchestra to serenade us!"

"That isn't the . . ."

"What am I doing different from Shoshana with her precious sentry? What are they doing in her room—trying on clothes? I'm a modern girl no less than she is. No less and no more! And Jimmy's more of a human being than all of you! He's made me *something*. I, I don't give a damn what you think!"

"Berta!"

"Berta, Berta! Jimmy's different. He says to me: 'Girl, you are wonderful.' He'll never be cross with me if I put on powder or high heels or earrings because he's been brought up to respect people, to respect women. He looks at my shoes and says, 'I've seen just the shoes for you in a shop window.' A Jewish boy would say, 'What crappy shoes you're wearing!' But Jimmy—he'll run off to buy me things even if he has to borrow the money."

"How did you get to know a British officer?"

"A British officer! A British officer!" She snorted impatiently. "I sent a message to the High Commissioner and told him I loved British officers! He sent me a dozen, and I chose Jimmy! At first they all looked at me as if I wasn't there. Laugh, go on, laugh! That suits you better! Especially the girls, out of jealousy. There are other girls who go with Tommies, Ashkenazis that is. He told me right away I danced nicely. I understood right away. I'm good at languages. A local boy would never tell me I danced nicely, he'd never tell me I was anything at all. He'd be afraid I'd think I was worth something. Anyone who isn't a real man is always afraid a woman will ride on him. Avram guarded me as if I was his private property. We went out together, because he's my cousin and the only one I was allowed out with, but there were friends I went out with before. I went with Avram to the new bar they opened on the sea front. Some English officer came up to me. At first I was scared, but he asked Avram's permission to invite me to dance. Avram makes all kinds of faces. What is this? He wants to show them all how anti-British he is. But you won't catch him joining the underground! Suddenly I wanted to show him. I went with the officer to the dance floor. Before I went Avram pinched me and said: 'You'll be hearing from me.' Of course there was shouting at home! My father wanted to kill me— sure, he can always make more daughters, it's cheaper than rubber! How *can* I get home at nine o'clock when Jimmy only *comes* at nine. At the factory they started on me too. That foreman, a Polak, waiting for me every morning with a watch in his hand, as if I'm BBC Radio. I thought I'd be better off working here and not living at home. I even gave up seeing Jimmy for a while. How can I get there at night? He's not like your young men, to let me come home in the dark alone. He takes me in a jeep— his camp isn't far away—and he puts me down on the tarmac. He'd like to bring me right here, but I don't need all of you opening your camel-mouths at him. He never counts up on his fingers and toes. He can blow all his pay at once! Would I look like this going out with one of your skinflints? I might just as well run naked in the streets, and not like your Frieda with the old geezer from Warsaw."

Markovski rolled a piece of paper between his fingers.

"When we walk to the jeep at night," she laughed softly, remembering, "he leans on me. Everyone's already asleep, just us in the street. Jimmy sings songs in English, in a sad voice. Suddenly he weeps quietly, an English kind of weeping. He's so sweet like that," she said with a sort of wonder, as if searching for a meaning.

Berta doesn't know what dams she is tearing down. A life whose reality he has never perceived is suddenly swirling about him, impetuous, aimless, a life that sees no need to make formulations, instant decisions, or determine which way the world is going.

"And the end, Berta?" he said softly, his curiosity inflamed. "Little Berta will fly away to the great misty island, to England?"

"England? What do you think I'm supposed to do in England?" she cried, suddenly furious. "Are you completely stupid, or what? What do you think he is, a kid of nineteen? You think he doesn't tell me what he does? What he thinks? He's the most honest man I've ever met! And he's got a wife there! A wife!" she cried triumphantly, as if doing her best to hurt him. "He's got a son too! Do you think he's like you people? He's honest, reasonable, clean! Do you think he hasn't shown me their pictures? And what a lovely wife he has, a thousand times prettier than me!"

"And what . . . what is his relationship with . . . with this woman?" Dov murmured cautiously, an awkward fool.

"What? She's his wife, isn't she?" she cried as if defending everything that belonged to him, this Jimmy. "And what long letters he writes to her, pages and pages! And the letters she writes him! He reads them to me aloud and weeps! And how mad he gets when he hears about the bombing in London."

Dov doesn't know whether to pity or admire her.

"I don't understand," he murmured.

"Understand! Understand! Maybe you want him to send her a divorce, eh? In England people don't separate that easily; there they respect the woman and marriage!" she railed at him, as if he had the malice to suggest such a thing. "I'm good to him— and he's good to me! There's a war on! It's the same everywhere! These aren't Victorian times."

"And are you happy?" he asked cautiously, expecting a negative reply.

"Happy? These are the best times I've had since the day I was made!"

He in her place would be simply biting his flesh day by day.

"And what will you do afterwards? Let's suppose the war ends, one way or the other. Jimmy says goodbye and sails away. What will you do?"

"What will I do? I'll spend the rest of my life sitting looking at his picture! What about you? What will you be doing a year, two years from now, eh? What will Shoshana do when she's tired of her sentry?"

Life suddenly seems to him frail and brittle, frightening, demanding strength.

"Life is like vessels!" he heard himself preaching. "It must be filled while we're still capable of being poured from one vessel to another, while we're soft, before disillusionment makes us hard. It's bad, very bad, Berta, to live with your vessels empty! Tomorrow, Berta . . ."

She stamped her foot, waving two impatient fingers at him.

"Tomorrow! Tomorrow! Only to children is tomorrow important, because they want to grow up! Tomorrow's already here! Now is tomorrow! You think tomorrow morning will be better for you than now, tonight? You'd tell the undertaker, 'Leave me alone—tomorrow!' "

Dov took a deep breath, lowered his eyes to stare closely at a crack in the bedside table, a crack so deep the whole table could fall apart with the first careless movement. Amicably he asked how old she was.

"Seventeen years and *that's all!*" Berta answered, almost with a shout.

In her eyes he saw a tremulous gleam. She began panting morosely, as if carrying something on her lungs.

"You're right, all of you! Fat Paula is right! Precious Shoshana! Saintly Frieda! I'm bad, bad, bad! I've no morals! I'm a whore! That's what you wanted to hear, isn't it? You've got it! I sell myself for silk stockings!

"Okay, okay, I'll do what you want!" she said suddenly, lowering her voice as if in a nervous seizure. "I'll be a good girl! In the evening Berta will finish cleaning the black pans and go straight to bed. In the morning she'll scrub floors. In the evening Berta will clean the pans again and go to bed with the little bugs. That way Berta will be a reasonable human being! A sweet girl! A doll of a girl!" she yelled into his face. "She'll sleep with the little bugs and wait for a big bug!"

She talked, and still he could find nothing real to say. He clutched her hand and she pulled it from him angrily. Life was before her, he said softly, paternally, she could still learn something, "some nice profession." She would still find somebody to love her, to be interested in her forever.

"Forever!" she laughed, irritated by his refusal to understand. "Forever! Who takes anyone forever? Are you a kid or what? How old are you, eh? Nobody takes anyone forever! Even your affairs won't last forever! After a year or two you'll remember all the million women she's deprived you of!" Somebody to love her? Some gutless Avram who'll knock her up and turn to prostitutes? Then she'll be in her place, right? The proper place for one such as her, right? They don't like to see this *'principessa'* going out with an intelligent man who has power over them! A nice profession, eh? To look after bastards, like Frieda! It takes a saint to spend her life clearing up filth. She's had enough of filth! Not for this was Berta born into the world! And him! Him! What's *he* doing that makes him better than her? How's his life better than hers? Books, books! He takes books to bed with him, even a simple woman from a hotel he doesn't have. Walking around puffed up, as if any moment he might explode! Instead of the books, he should find a woman to sleep with! Then suddenly he'll see and he'll stop worrying how other people ought to live. At first she thought: Who knows? A great man! He's miserable, miserable like all the rest of them!"

He sees before his eyes a bubbling swamp, full of acrid water. He consoles himself that she's not equipped with the right antennae to tune into his personality. Again he hears her voice, intoxicated with itself.

"Reasonable!" she cries. "All the fools in the world don't know how you hide away at night and guzzle the children's sausages! But what does it matter? You deserve it, of course! Why not?"

Her cheeks are aflame. She knows she's touched an exposed nerve.

Long ago he decided that once he settled into the place he would persuade the women to give up these midnight feasts.

"That is a real mistake, Berta, a serious mistake. You see? There's always something to put right."

"A mistake? Why a mistake? This is your 'good time'! You won't stop guzzling sausages—you'd go mad with boredom! This is your 'good time'—and I have my 'good time'!"

She's already threading the strap of her handbag over her arm, pointing her elegant pinky. "Look at your navel . . . it's round and tied like all the rest of them!" declares the goddess of victory, her foot on his chest. "Now goodbye! Thanks to you I'll be late for the bus!"

Now there's a look of triumphant glee radiating from Frieda's face when she meets Dov, as if demanding: "Well? Did you succeed in making the vinegar catch fire?" But she doesn't insist and doesn't press him with questions.

As for Berta, from now on she seems to stride with greater vigor on her way down the hill, as if charged with fresh fuel.

One twilight hour, when the girls came out to see Berta in her fine manifestation, showering her head with best wishes to Jimmy and requests for chewing gum, Markovski and Frieda stood there.

Dov responded with a pleasant smile to the flash of Berta's white teeth, which was directed emphatically at him, and followed her with his eyes as she ground the limestone of the path with her white stiletto heels.

"She's still suspicious, Frieda," he said as if apologizing. "This isn't an automatic process."

"Once you tried to impress on me that it was," she replied scornfully, with a pretense of deep sorrow.

"You should try treating her with respect," he said. "She spoke with me quite openly."

"Respect! You've treated her with great respect. You can tell by looking at her! That's the problem, the moment *they* hear your heroic literary language, they despise you in their hearts."

"Tell me, Frieda. Does it really make you happy, saying things like that?"

"Happy? Dov Markovski—an institution for the supply of happiness, retail and wholesale!"

"You don't understand. If she's thrown out into the street, the force of the impact will unbalance her completely. When you meet her like that in the street, you won't be able to avoid responsibility."

"Yes, yes," she said softly, her eyes closed like the eyes of a Modigliani figure. "To look into your tortured face—it's a spiritual experience! I don't know why, but again and again you remind me of the women of Mad Stephen." She laughed bitterly at his astonishment. "Saint Stephen used to wander about in our marketplace, the spittle running down his beard and the pious peasant women running after him with dishes of food in their hands: 'Stephen, Stephen, eat! Bless us, bless us, Stephenosh! Look kindly on us!' But Saint Stephenosh refused to eat. He preferred the scraps that he found on the garbage heaps. He used to strike them, the pious Gentile women, tipping the dishes of food over their heads, cursing and dribbling. But the pious Gentile women were happy. 'Stephen *spoke* to me!' And they still go on running after him: 'Stephenosh!'— 'The Devil take you!' And they kneel in the marketplace, kissing his dirty toes, and he kicks their faces."

At last the women were forced to act, when the Wolfson-woman came for a visit. She was outraged, as if she had never imagined "stories" like these. She was especially annoyed at the "conspiracy of silence" that had surrounded the "nasty little thing" until that day.

"Don't you realize," she asked, "that it only needs somebody to hear and that's the end of our donations?"

At the risk of endangering himself, Dov sprang to the defense of the "nasty little thing," trying to convince Batya that *she, she* of all people, must know how a person can be rescued from degeneracy. His words had the effect that the Wolfson-woman at once looked at him with suspicion and shot a questioning glance at Pani-Paula.

At lunch time, when the "nasty little thing" was revealed to her, in her unprepared splendor, in curlers and clogs and with sharp, downcast eyes, she sentenced her to instant dismissal.

All that now remained for Dov was to announce his own resignation before Berta's dismissal. Any other form of protest would be base opportunism. Not doing so, he would be untrue to himself. Doing so, he would expose himself to absurd suspicions. In a sudden blinding flash, he realized that in leaving he removed himself from the presence of Frieda.

He must find a way to strike, and he racks his brains for a way to soften the blow. One careless pull at the oar, and he's swept overboard. And certainly at this time he has no desire to play with his own fate. If he acts temporarily as Berta's guardian, she won't thank him for it. But he can't allow himself to shirk responsibility. Anyway, he took it on himself to make the parting speech to Berta, and deep in his heart he expected a miracle that would save her and relieve his conscience.

We're walking about with bare hands, he thought bitterly, scratching impatiently at the upper stratum of the earth, and in our anger we cover with dust the fruits of the isolated few, the happy.

He found her alone in the kitchen, the cloth under her bare feet, dragging it hastily over the wet floor, strewn with scraps of food. This is the worst moment for passing sentence, when she's like this—shabby, hardworking, conscientious. He wished he could retrace his steps.

"Madam didn't like me, is that it?" she said provocatively, without pausing from her work. There was a sort of obsolete friendliness in her voice.

He advanced to the middle of the kitchen and leaned his hands on the stove. It was still lukewarm. The cooking pots were already laid out on the wooden shelves.

"Would you mind moving from the stove?" she complained. "Can't you see that . . ."

"Oh, I beg your pardon!" Rebuked, he side-stepped on tiptoe to find a dry place.

"Would you mind standing in the door? Around here nobody ever gets a chance to . . ."

She picked up the rag with her toes and dipped it in the grimy water in the bucket, then flung it with her toes over the floor. Drops of water splashed on the shelf and fizzled on the stove.

"They think I'll always be too weak to stand up to them!"

Dov took a chair from the dining room and sat in the kitchen doorway.

"Like in the cinema, eh?" She paused for a moment, dropping the rag.

"Look, Berta, none of us is an angel."

"You—you're an angel!" she said mockingly.

"Berta, even I, to this day I stop dead in the street and I can't go on walking . . . shame stops me."

"I've got nothing to be ashamed of," she said.

"Things happen to everybody."

"Nothing's ever happened to you," she said, "and nothing ever will! You only do good deeds!"

"I've never yet done anything good in my life," he said. "I'm preparing myself to do good. Always preparing, intending. But I haven't yet done anything good in my life."

She waited for him to continue, as if laying an ambush.

"Berta, you're a young, sweet girl . . . This human race of ours has a tendency to sink, to wallow in mud, in dirt . . ." He caught himself sloganeering. "We have a duty to help one another to drag ourselves out of the mud . . . to grab the hair and pull, even if it hurts."

"Don't you worry, they'll never pull *you* by the hair," she said. "You'll never fall in the mud!"

"No, Berta, no. Believe me . . . I've never told this to anyone before," he mumbled. "I wanted to wipe it all out, forget it, but just so you'll see . . . I did something wrong. It even went on for several months . . . some stupid weakness, and she was the wife of my friend, a woman that I didn't love. To this day I can't go on walking in the street, when I remember. Shame stops me."

At once he understood from her face that he was talking nonsense. She had an air of calm satisfaction. All his attempts suddenly seemed to him paltry and futile.

"Really? That's quite charming, it makes you more . . .," said Berta. "But are you telling me this so I'll think you're like all the rest? That won't help you where I'm concerned! Where you're concerned, being like the rest of them is like an old woman who's scared of the mirror!"

He felt a blockage in his throat. "Berta!" he cried as if pleading for her mercy. "Mrs. Wolfson came here to . . ."

She tensed backwards, as if he'd punched her on the chin, and her eyes were like frightened birds. There was real fear in her voice.

"What? What have I done to her, eh? What have I done to her?"

"*They* say it's harmful to the children. *They* say it isn't a good example to children in their situation." (Not hurting, not crushing, hinting that there was some sympathy in him.)

In her stare he found despair, incomprehension, sincere astonishment, as if only now did she see the abyss before her, as if before she had only been playing—isn't this game also a part of the process called fate? Her eyes were fixed on his, as if telling him that really she had trusted him in a twisted fashion and look— he'd betrayed her.

"That's the situation, Berta," he said in a weak voice.

"You won't throw me out into the street," she said. "You aren't the kind of people who throw somebody into the street . . . *you*, you're not going to throw me out like that . . ."

He must search, grope, discover some life line that he can throw to her.

"It's my dirty blood! Is that it?" she cried with a sort of jubilation. "You want to see how this dirty blood works, eh? All the sheets of that darling of yours have the sentry's stink on them!" Suddenly she began crowing defiantly:

"But I won't allow you that satisfaction! Not me! Not Berta! It'll be good for all of you! For Jimmy, for you! For me, for all this dirty world of yours!"

"Berta!"

Strike! Hammer away to open some way through to her.

"All this dirty world!"

"If I were you, I'd already be on my knees."

He was startled. This was Frieda's voice, smooth as a fingernail. She came up behind him, from the dark dining room. She had been eavesdropping, no doubt! He smarted with pain that she had demeaned herself thus, and with shame at his failure, which she had witnessed.

Frieda pushed her hips between his chair and the doorpost and advanced into the kitchen. The pupils of Berta's eyes froze for a moment, mesmerized.

"Frieda," he whispered, pleading to her back. "This isn't the way . . ."

He didn't want to restrain her forcibly, to degrade her before Berta.

"Not the way? And what is the way? Pull out the soul," she said, her back to him. "Pull out the soul and paint it with your favorite colors?"

"It's a failure, it's a failure," he pleaded to her back.

"I take full responsibility on myself," she said. "I'll wield the surgeon's knife! *Finito!*"

"You . . . you . . ." He wanted to strangle her, but at the same time he felt nervous admiration for the decisiveness of her attack.

From then on Berta behaved as if nothing had happened, as if she sought to make herself forget through immersion in the day-to-day routine, as if time had frozen. The women moved about her with an air of limp indifference, as if she were an invalid whose days were numbered and everyone had got used to the idea. And Paula smiled at her once when she handed her a dish of lentils to put on the table. All that remained was to make sure that on Thursday she should draw her wages and leave a substantial space behind her. The rest was of no interest, thank God. The pungent excitement subsided, giving way to a tranquil expectation.

On Wednesday morning Paula stood in the kitchen, before a

tower of supper plates that Berta hadn't washed, and allowed herself a certain degree of bitterness, though with no hint of malice. Finally she said to Frieda, with surprising lightness: "I'd have behaved just the same myself."

"Perhaps she left in the night," said Frieda, but added at once: "Without her wages?"

Paula read the signs of concern in her eyes. At once she hurried toward the stairs. Two girls who had come out for their morning coiffure in the corridor saw her ungainly running, making the banister shake. Two others joined them, exchanging glances at the sound of the rhythmic thumping and the yells of the cook.

"That's Bertola's door," said Nira, "now there's going to be fun."

Dov came out of his room, threading his way through the herd of children crowding the corridor. He remembered the groans that he'd heard in his sleep.

"Why are you standing there like a kosher cow?" grated Paula, her eyes accusing. "Don't you understand? The key's on the inside! Do something! Do it!"

"She's done something terrible!" he said. "Something terrible!" And a strange calm descended on him, as if his wishes had been fulfilled.

The running feet of the children on the stairs made the house shake.

"Then break in! Break in, damn you!" At the children she shouted: "What are you doing here? Out! Out of here!"

Eagerly the children moved toward Markovski, who was attacking the door.

"What has she done? What has she done, the wild beast? Mad fool! Snake!" cried Paula. "And what a good worker she was!"

When the panel of the door was broken, Markovski put in his hand and found the key. Through the breach they saw Berta curled up on the bed in the white stiletto heels and the white summer dress.

"Out! Out of here!" Paula pushed away the children who were

held as if by strings of magic. "Where's Markovski? Where's he disappeared to? Where's that so-called genius of yours?" she howled at Frieda, who had arrived on the scene looking green in the face and the dimple of her chin bouncing like a faulty pump.

"Tell him to go fetch the doctor! Doctor! Doctor!" She approached Berta, not sure whether to touch her, fear and disgust in her face.

"He's already gone," said Frieda weakly, as if she too was about to collapse on the bed.

"I knew she'd do this!" fumed Paula. "She's capable of anything . . . no consideration! No self-respect! I've been in some situations . . . and never, not once, never!"

Hedva approached and looked with a smile at Berta, at her hand flung lazily above her head and the black, closed lids.

"Don't touch! Don't touch!" the cook writhed. "What are you laughing at, wild beast?" She groaned at the smiling girl, as if at last she'd found the real culprit, and she seized her arm to eject her from the place. "Berta is dead," answered Hedva as she laughed.

The local German doctor came in, still buttoning his trousers (a sign of the seriousness and urgency of the case). He snapped open his solid medical case and spoke angrily to Frieda, whose customary efficiency had deserted her. "Vot's zis? Get ze liddle jildren out! Get zem out!" He himself began pushing them toward the door with a scornful glance at the helpless young woman.

Only then—as if she wasn't the main issue—did he turn to Berta.

The children stood in the corridor, their ears sucking in the voices escaping from behind Frieda's body, which blocked the opening in the door, then watching with eager eyes as the staff carried Berta to the washroom and closed the door behind them. They crowded together outside the washroom. Their prerogative had been stolen and they were determined to retrieve it, but Paula stationed her body against the door, a massive cruciform shape.

"Joy! How happy they must be! Shit! What a treat for them!

Licking their fingers! Killers! Murderers! You'll all go to jail! For ten years not one of you will see the sun!"

"Ze enema vater is already clean," said the doctor to Pani-Paula, his eyes on the ceiling, as if trying to ignore all the rest. "No need for ze hospital. Zome coffee pliss. Now to make sure she don't zleep, talk wiz her, keep ze room all ze time varm, aftervards let her zleep, get vell. Fools! Now be taking her back to ze room."

All was lost—the grief, the weeping, the funeral crowd, the pondering on the nature of death, the ceremonies, the burial— all gave way to emptiness, to disappointment.

Determined that something must be salvaged from their cheated expectations, the boys and girls stood all that day on the staircase— school was forgotten—chattering vividly about what had happened, exaggerating and secretly hoping that there was still some faint possibility of death.

"He slapped her face ten times."

"He didn't! It was Pani-Paula."

"They beat her with a towel . . . shouted at her."

Thus until they had familiarized themselves with the picture, without the awe that accompanied it.

For several days the German doctor comes to see the sleeping beauty. Every day the regular visit of the doctor. The routine dispels the death of Berta, but they still peep in to see "how is it?"

One by one they carefully move the sheet that covers the breach in the door and peer furtively at Pani-Paula or at Frieda, sitting by the bed, reading or mending clothes, and the really lucky child sees Berta sitting up among the blankets in a nightie that isn't hers, retching, shivering, mumbling, drinking something from the hand of the sitter and sinking back again.

On the third day, at noon, Berta suddenly got out of bed. The peepers saw her crumpled face, her wild eyes. Berta stood up and swayed, groping about her for support, asked in a puzzled voice, "Whose nightie is this?" and at once tried to strip it off.

Shoshana, who had returned that day from her vacation and at once volunteered to sit with her, armed with a strong and vibrant sense of sacrifice and caring zeal, very similar to happiness, grabbed at Berta's hands to prevent her. Berta turned eyes burning with recrimination at Markovski, whom the children had summoned, thinking he was the right one to help Berta.

"You can stay until . . .," he said to Berta softly, supporting her by the elbows.

"I want to go!" she growled, leaning against him weakly and her eyes on the rumpled bed. "I want to go!"

"You're not to let her go," said Dov to Shoshana. "Don't let her go!"

"What do you think I am, the sheriff?" she replied.

"Berta's got up!" the children cried to Frieda, who had also been summoned. Markovski went out, to let her get dressed.

"What a lot of dreams you can satisfy in four days," said one of the girls.

The door opened and Berta stood on the threshold in the crumpled spring dress.

The girls cried "Berta! Berta!" as if witnessing her resurrection. But she didn't look at them.

Shoshana closed her fingers on Berta's hand, which held the handle of the suitcase.

"Move!" Berta shook the case to get herself free, but it was as if she was waiting for Shoshana's second touch.

"You can't go like this, Berta!" said Shoshana. "Do you understand?" She moved closer to look into her face. Berta butted her in the forehead and started down the stairs, as if to order, her legs quaking and her whole air that of a princess determined to walk with dignity to the scaffold.

Apprehensively they all followed her to the ground floor. Markovski stood in the doorway and took the suitcase from her hand.

"Didn't I tell you not to go?" He peered into her eyes. "Come on, honey, come to the dining room."

With a force not her own, she snatched the suitcase from him and spat out her cries in a strange, grating voice, as if it too had changed in the past few days.

"You thought I'd be dying to sleep with you. Right? What does it matter! I'll make you all pay! I'll show you up in all the papers. You thought you could kick me out and I'd come and plead with you, right? You're all whores, every one of you!"

A mighty tank came thundering down the stairs. "Out! Out! Get rid of her!" Paula rammed Berta with her stomach, pushing her into the yard and from there to the gate. "This, this is your thanks! You should have kissed his feet, scum!"

At the gate Berta gathered strength—from where, God knows—and repelled the attack. Without retreating, she flung the suitcase down on the limestone and lunged at Markovski, as if meaning to crush his face to the bone.

"Ah! Kiss his feet! What is he? Your saint! The most righteous man in the world! Teaching people how to live! This good man, this wonderful human being, he slept with a married woman! You don't believe me?" cried Berta. "Ask him! He'll tell you himself!"

"With my mother!" thought Maya suddenly, with a flash of strange, heart-stopping revelation, and not knowing why. "With my mother!"

"Wallowing in the mud, eh, so all the world will hear, so God will hear, so the Devil will hear? Wallowing in the mud!" She shouted at the deputation of wolves that gathered about her and growled in agreement, those head-scarved neighbors summoned from their nearby burrows, their eyes ablaze with hatred for this abomination, this house of ill repute.

"He's the great man! He's the saint! Why don't you leave me alone, you fat tick!" she screamed at the cook and aimed her heel at her knee.

"I'm going! I'm going! No need to worry about me! Can't you see how glad I am I won't see your ass-face any longer?"

The righteous she-wolves made way for her, some of them even protecting her with their bodies and keeping Paula away. *"Richtig!"* Voices were heard. "That's what they deserve, at last!"

"Berta!" cried Dov as if from a high stormy sea. "Berta! Come back! Come back! Let's talk! Let's talk first . . ."

The wolves bared their teeth as they watched Markovski chasing Berta down the hill, she shrugging off his desperate appeals.

"How did we ever keep a thing like that here?" fumed Paula, when everything had subsided and the head-scarved wolves had scampered away to convey the news to their neighbors who had missed the spectacle.

She anxiously rolled up the hem of her dress, to examine her bruised knee, and then, as if remembering, fixed her eyes on Markovski, who was slowly returning.

"Hoorah! The missionary team is back!" she sneered. "You, you're the one who took her in!" She inhaled between her clenched teeth. "You accepted her. Just the perfume that we needed in this public shithouse!" She bent down to rub the bruise on her knee. "A fine pair—she opening her legs the way he opens his mouth!"

Dov felt she was trying to squeeze the last drop of honey from the hive.

Frieda glanced at him sidelong. There was no provocation in her face, just calm and sincere sympathy, like a promise at the end of a journey full of disappointments.

The German doctor arrived, staring with angry bewilderment at the idlers chatting by the gate.

"I chust zaw your girl on ze vay. Haf you zent her already shopping? Is zere no time? Ven she come back . . ."

"She isn't coming back!" said Shoshana, sounding indignant, as if he was poking his nose into somebody else's chamber pot.

"Pliss!" he exclaimed angrily. "Zoon as she came back, zend her to me, zis is great irresponsibility!"

"I told you, she won't be around any more!" said Shoshana.

"Vot? Vot? Ach! She von't die! Zilly girl! She took only small dose of feronal! Pliss zend her to me, fools, for general examination!"

He turned on his heel and strode away at once, to show that he wanted no contact with them, except in his professional capacity.

19
THE GOLDEN BIRDS
OF THE IMAGINATION

Frieda felt for a moment in the tin box and changed a needle without fumbling. Then she lit the candle in the candlestick and put it on the night table. When she breathed on the flame the room changed its colors, as if bathed in a new solution. This was her fixed routine before playing Beethoven, and Dov silently admired the wholeness of her practiced movements, which had been perfected before she broke into his territory.

He slowly moved the handle, stirring the entrails of the old phonograph that lay before him on a wooden chair, and felt his own tension grow with the tightening spring. His eyes on Frieda, who stood facing him, carefully drawing the record from its grey, dog-eared sleeve and studying it closely. For a moment he caught a glimpse of the eyes of the Botticelli Venus, staring at him over the girl's shoulder in the dancing light.

"It's a pity the first record's broken," said Frieda softly. "That's where the drums are." She had said this the last time too, a week ago perhaps, as she fumbled with the record on the turntable to find the center pin.

The voice of the violin dropped suddenly, like a bird from that hidden roof. The secondhand phonograph, she told him the last time, she bought on her way to the country with the last of her money, along with this violin concerto. A phonograph with the smell of a little harbor on the Mediterranean. One of those junk shops, with colored beads ringing in the doorway, and always, when the *pizzicato* comes, there rises to her ears the sound of the beads—a world that has sunk into the sea and disappeared.

How he comes to be sitting in her room in the flickering light of the candle is not quite clear to him. A process like other natural processes. She began coming to his room, apparently to borrow a book, and stayed because she needed a dose of human conversation above the daily tedium. Then they began eagerly comparing their tastes, their sensitivities, the sweetness of understanding implicitly shared, the wondrous self-realization of spiritual twins. But only after their confrontation in the Berta episode did she open her door to him, as to one elected to the academy of the immortals. And that night it seemed to him that all had changed the calendar in their homes.

The first few times he pretended. Putting his head heavily between his hands, as if accustomed to listening to music, so he wouldn't lose grace in her eyes, he made an effort to sink and rise in those waves, to float on the surface of those whirlpools without beginning and without end, and to find in them Frieda and again Frieda, out of self-torment for its own sake, or perhaps because Frieda said that indifference to music was the worst of disabilities. On the days that followed he would wander about the house, and amid the pale everyday drabness he found himself surrounded by the sprinkling fragments of those intermingled melodies, fragments that he tried to stitch together in his mind and with his lips, like a jigsaw puzzle, and suddenly his eyes would encounter the everyday Frieda, in her heavy work shoes and with her curt instructions to the children.

This evening he felt himself opened up, his insides smiling in expectation and his head anointed with oil, smooth, mysterious, vibrant. She forbade him to speak whenever the music played. Only the record was allowed to draw up words from the deepest depths of time. Even in the intermissions she insisted on silence. It was his duty to turn the handle, to hold his breath and wait until she had laid down the needle on the record and the sound vaporized again.

In the room hung a warmth without movement. The girl closed the shutters and the windows so not a sound would creep outside. She couldn't bear the thought that her Holy of Holies might grate on the ears of Pani-Paula.

"This place—now," she whispered as she stood facing him, like a goddess bestowing favors on her chosen one. Her manner of speech at such times always imparted to things a sense of impending doom or of a time that is the very perfection of existence and must not be missed.

Frieda stands and does not stir. She has turned into a creature that is not of this place—bewildered, uprooted, shedding a silent tear, when the heart can no longer bear the pain of beauty. This Frieda of the late night hours, with the violin of Kreisler, is revealed just to him. Nobody else knows this Frieda, only the energetic one who does her work in silence, with patience, with bitterness, as if waiting for a miracle. Frieda sighs softly. He should lean forward and touch her hand, but dares not. Suddenly, as if reading his thoughts, she breaks her own rules and comes to sit beside him, and while the music plays she tells him in a whisper what she saw at a concert, one of the first that she heard.

As the music rose to a crescendo, one of the strings of the soloist's Stradivarius suddenly snapped. As if in a panic he turned to the orchestra, held out the damaged violin to the first violinist, snatched the latter's instrument from his hand, and at once, desperate to stitch together the broken melody, he resumed the theme, but then gave up, paused, signaled to the conductor, conferred with him briefly, and the concerto started again from the beginning, with the first violinist's instrument. Suddenly it seemed to her that this was a completely different music, as if an act of rape had been committed before her eyes, a lord had allowed himself, in a moment of lust, to snatch the wife of his serf. The serf continued to play, clutching with his chin and his arm the violin of the international soloist. Was the first violinist proud of what had fallen into his hands, or full of bitterness and a sense of worthlessness? Was he jealous for a moment? Did he think of his own violin, which had earned at last, if only once, redemption and deliverance from inhibition, soaring to ecstatic heights under the fingers of the virtuoso? Never, it seemed, would the little violin be able to forget the night of the virtuoso, never obey its master with the same submissiveness. Was the little violin happy then, or miserable?

"Come," he whispered suddenly. She started, as if only now becoming aware of his physical presence. The flickering light lit up her high cheekbones. Her arm was stiff. Above her elbow he felt the roughness of blisters. Her arm was motionless in his hand. The needle began to grate around the center of the record, which was emptied of its music, as if all was neglected, forgotten, confronted by this sudden eruption. His glasses collided with her face. She recoiled, stood up, and released the record.

"I'm taking off my glasses, Friedichka," he murmured and laughed. "The biggest nuisance of all . . . even for virtuosi."

She stood before him, silent and with no expression of feeling, as if staring into emptiness. He felt everything whirling inside him and the elements changing their courses, blood flowing backwards and thoughts retreating to their hiding places.

"Now, go!" she said in a choking voice. He waited for the obligatory slap, the sudden movement of the body that would belie her words, and since it didn't come, he rose and detached her hand from the neckline of her blouse. She's beautiful, God! He fumbled his way toward her, her blurred image, a blind man seeing through his fingertips. He felt her hands pushing him away from her body. He's a child, a little boy. Everything whining inside him, as if he's lost in a dead world, and it's in his power, Oh God, so much in his power . . .

Suddenly she said awkwardly, with a hint of mockery, pointing to the door:

"Goodnight, sweet prince."

Hatred overcame him. He went out drunk, his legs shaking and his whole being disintegrating to its molecules.

The following evening he sat in the accounts office, the piles of ledgers pushed to one side, trying to devise chapter headings for an article, listening to the thin drizzle outside. It is nothing but naked desire, he tells himself, hunger that seeks a prey. The face staring at the revolving record—a dreadfully funny trap. The prey says "stop," and suddenly, what they call love . . . He feels consoling gratitude toward her: if she had submitted to him, never again would he have been able to float to the violin of Kreisler. He would have sprawled drowsily on her bed and forced upon himself the meaningless sounds. "To storm the defenses with intellectual subtlety and not in the vapor of intoxication"—he writes a new chapter heading. Suddenly the door opens and there stands Frieda, her eyes narrowed, as if afraid of what they might reveal.

"You didn't get to hear the third movement," she says, and smiles again, with great sadness. She stands beside the phonograph, again in the candle light, and talks, as if lecturing to him.

"The third movement—joy of living, rustic clarity, giving you something that's alive, without disillusion, compensation for the second movement, which drains your heart until it's dry, taking it from you." But she doesn't listen to the record.

"I don't want a straitjacket life!" she says, sitting down beside him. "Do you understand? I don't want to know that 'this is what life is.' I don't want the dismal light. I don't want to sacrifice myself to a Moloch full of little eyes."

He doesn't dare interrupt her.

"When I first came to this country, the pioneers' house where I stayed was emptied each night of all those girls who 'know about life' and go out 'to have fun.' Then I would go down to the deserted dining room and there, when I found a suite of Bach on one of the radio stations whose mysteries permeate the darkness, I felt, 'This is it, all that I will ever have—is mine! Everything that is eternally pure, everything I desire. And it fades away, you want to stop it, and it's not in your power to return to it. Yet it belongs to you, a pool of light, a pool that is greater than you and is all yours, no man will steal it from you, ever . . .' "

She sets down the needle on the record, which pensively takes up the theme from the point where it broke off yesterday, and suddenly it springs into that "joy of living" she had promised. She whistles, hums, conducts the orchestra with her hands, and smiles at him, laughing, almost happy.

So they listened, apart, to the third movement. She never again invited him to her room to hear Beethoven, but for many weeks they sat across the table from each other in the dining room and talked about themselves.

Until that morning hour, the
wasteland had extended itself into the yard and had paid no attention to the fence standing in its way, saying: in me the rule of
Nature comes to an end; from this point on, in this enclosed and
circumscribed space of half a dunam, the Elect of Creation will
hold sway—and it sent its children, without fear of the hoe, to
spread throughout the forbidden territory. So the poppies rose and
reddened in the corners of the yard, mustard plants and cruciferae
blossomed, garlanding the wasteland with a crown of purple and
yellow, and on sunny days regiments of thistles advanced, wresting
a livelihood from the powdery limestone soil, and in their impudence bringing with them their guests: black and yellow scorpions and sometimes even a young snake, rearing up among them
calmly and moving half its body this way and that like a man at
prayer.

But this wild and uninhibited orgy lasted only until that morning. The night before the children had been tossing about uneasily on their beds, rolling on their tongues, until their stomachs gurgled, the imagined taste of the goodies, hoarded up a week ago— and the keys interred in Pani-Paula's cleavage. Even those who normally leave aromatic stains on their sheets each morning, the "stinkers" who refuse to shift from their beds until you throw a shoe at them, woke this morning with the first bird's song and peered with sincere satisfaction into their dry beds.

Two weeks ago the Wolfson woman came and said something to the staff in the utmost secrecy. Before taking her leave on the staircase she remembered, ordered the children away, fumbled in her old shabby handbag, pulled out a long checkbook, thought for a moment, her weary eyes wandering in space, then wrote something, tore off a check, and planted it with a solemn flourish in Markovski's hand.

Pani-Paula, her dewlap quivering and her eyes red, cried in a choking, boyish falsetto, "But *meine* Batya, my Batya, when will pay day come?"

"*Goot, Goot,*" said the Wolfson woman. "It will come, it will come! Money is all they think about!" And she disappeared down the slope.

Paula's voice settled back in its original octave. "The old witch! I'd never have believed it if they told me that my Batya . . . how much did she give you?" She glanced at the check in his hand and looked away, grumbling.

Shoshana narrowed her eyes. "When it comes to fighting for salaries, you're all heroes on the sly!"

Everything was prepared for the occasion. Doors were polished until their panels gleamed, giant blowtorches breathed fire into the flanks of the naked beds, incinerating heaps of startled bedbugs, and the smell of kerosene stalked the rooms. The clothes lockers were crammed with starched underwear.

For two weeks the staff had prowled about the rooms, chasing the children off to the yard, carefully examining the laundered blankets and the new pillowcases, until that last day in the morning, when Shoshana raised her arms toward the ceiling and stretched them sideways with a prolonged feminine sigh of relief, padded out to the balcony in her bare feet for a breath of air uncontaminated by cleaning smells, glanced casually down at the yard and suddenly shut her eyes in alarm:

"Look! Just look!"

Pani-Paula and Frieda hurried out to the balcony and Shoshana just pointed down, in speechless horror. The two of them looked and gaped in stunned silence. Then the "estate and inventory manageress" mustered all her authority and adopted a practical tongue.

There was no boy or girl who would dare express protest or astonishment at the peremptory command, any more than they had dared object to the "special ceremony."

"We must make a good impression!" Pani-Paula rampaged from room to room. "They are rich people, industrialists. You can guzzle eggs and roll in goose down—just so long as you make a good impression! You deserve it really, by all means, just give the impression that you're more than cholera cases, you're human beings, God help us! We want to live!"

Thus came the last hour of the wasteland.

All rushed out into the yard, squealing with delight, consumed with eagerness, demented, chasing the weeds without method or logic, frenziedly uprooting everything that came to hand, moving with heads downcast, colliding with one another, forming momentary groups, gulping water from the tap and returning to the attack, until the hoe felt it had no more enemies to strike against. And suddenly the yard was revealed to them in its nakedness, a mass of clodded earth, far stranger and uglier than before.

Then, as they stood staring, disappointment swelling in their hearts, Frieda sprang up from somewhere with her three boys carrying on their backs a great heap of foliage that they laid down in the middle of the yard.

"Now, children," cried Frieda eagerly, beckoning them to approach, "now get this done one way or the other, but do it quickly! You understand? We'll plant all these branches, water them nicely, and we'll have a garden!" She laughed into their faces.

Even the quick-witted ones gaped open-mouthed.

"But it's going to wither," someone protested.

"Of course it's going to wither," she replied. "What do you take me for, a fool? Tomorrow it will wither, but today it's a garden! The guests will see a garden! How lovely! This place works! Why are you standing around waiting? Let's have ourselves a garden. Just so we get a bit of money out of them. Now hurry! It's nearly lunch time!"

They stared long, in disbelief, at the bright figure disappearing into the house, then turned their attention to the heap of foliage and still did not stir, until Abie picked up a pine branch and waved it above his head:

"This is war! It's the battle of the bluffers! Follow me, you *choleras*. Charge!"

The game appealed to them.

When the sun glinted on the new window panes installed in the western frontage of the house, the yard was thick with lush greenery, and little bushes were reflected in its puddles. The girls wandered about the new garden, like matrons with time on their hands, stepping carefully so as not to dirty their socks, and bending over the wet heads of the "plants."

From the doorway of the house Pani-Paula's head peered out at intervals, crowned with a white tiara, like a circus bear. By the gate stood three boys fixing an arch of pine branches, below it a sign that read "Welcome."

Ah! What relief, soothing reassurance, and the heart retaining a modest degree of excitement, gathering strength like a little campfire that everyone has taken care to shield, only the eyes wander at times up the hill, the place where the party of "V.I.P.'s" will suddenly appear. First hats will appear, bald heads, scarves, beards, and after them—the hands. The hands will point to them, to the house. To make the ascent easier, they will approach slowly, resting their palms on their knees, pausing to draw breath. One of the men will support the Wolfson woman, and she will direct his attention to the really wonderful view at the base of the hill, to the sea whose horizons have broadened. All will sigh a collective sigh of wonder, for feasting the eye on the unexpectedly unfolding landscape always has a profound effect on new arrivals on the hill. Then they will adopt the appropriate expressions as they come closer to the house: deep interest, restrained curiosity, and friendly admiration.

At the place where the path up the hill breaks and turns off, a figure appeared moving toward the house. A small flurry in the yard, beginning with last exhortations and instructions and a panic run to the washroom to hurry the laggards, and ending with a distracted, casual standing by the gate, the staff withdrawing into the house, so everything will look "natural."

The approaching figure did not pause even for a moment to admire the view and pressed on toward the house at a run. All eyes scoured the path behind her for the rest of the party.

It was just one woman. Her short skirt flapped between her legs as she ran, and her arms projected forward stiffly, like strange wings.

The girls were the first to press around the gate to see her coming, hushing one another to hear her cries from the distant path. She ran with swaying gait, repeating her brief cries, in which there was a single, insistent sound. So, the grips falling from her disheveled hair, she reached the gate and flung her body against it, her high breasts heaving. When her breath returned to her, she repeated that muffled cry, as if she was still running and calling from afar: "Ra—fi! Ra—fi!" And her eyes on the children's faces, like the wheels of a bicycle scraping to a halt on the edge of a sidewalk.

"Rafi?" said Bat-Sheva alertly, her voice infused with delighted curiosity, and she pointed to the "garden": "Look, over there, look!"

All turned to face Rafi, who stood frozen beside one of the saplings, his mouth wide open and his tongue stuck limply to his lower lip.

For a moment the woman looked. Then she forced her way through the circle of girls and ran to the other side of the yard. And suddenly, beside him, she fell to her knees and clutched the boy to her bosom. Groaning from her heart, she pawed him frantically and showered a torrent of blind kisses on his head, his chest, his neck, his hands, then pushed him away from her to stare at him a long moment, eyes dimmed with tears, and to cry: "Rafi! Oh Rafi! Woe, woe is me, oh, oh . . ."

All this time Rafi was swaying between her hands, limp as a rag doll, his eyes staring above her head, blank, inflamed, and the tip of his tongue between his teeth like a broken doorbell, refusing to ring.

The boys grinned to themselves furtively, as if seeing their friend take a beating.

"Rafi, Rafi," she bared her upper teeth weakly. "Don't you recognize me? It's Mother. Rafi, answer me, Rafinka, say something to me, to your mother!" A swath of hair fell across her face.

Frieda approached suddenly and touched the woman's hand. She recoiled, turned toward her in fear and ranted defensively.

"I tell you, this is Rafi, I tell you! All this time I haven't come. I didn't know where he was. I'm taking him! You must give him to me!" she said, forcing on her voice a tone of composure, to prove to this woman-in-authority that she's worthy of him, of Rafi. "You must give him to me! I'll take care of him, lady, already I . . ."

The instructor gently parted her scattered hair and looked into her face. "Everything's going to be alright!" she assured her, and with her hand she motioned to the children to move away.

The cook appeared in the doorway, stared anxiously for a moment, and at once gestured to Frieda with a twist of head and shoulder, an urgent signal that this woman must be brought inside. "The guests!" she said.

Gevalt! The guests! Frieda put an arm around the woman's waist to draw her after her, but she wouldn't take her eyes from Rafi's face, and suddenly she slumped, fell back against the rail of the fence and spoke softly to the new, irrigated saplings.

"Is this Rafi? What have you done to him? What eyes! What scars on the head! Bald! He's bald!"

Frieda bent down and said that other children in the place had shaven heads "for reasons of hygiene." Look, this one, this, and this . . . But the woman went on talking to the saplings.

"Why doesn't he talk to me, why?" And in a panic, as if the reason was suddenly clear to her, she sprang to her feet.

"He can't speak, is that it? He's never learned to speak!"

Frieda bent toward her again and with restrained impatience promised her that Rafi *could* speak, *had* learned to speak, that he spoke very well. And again she tried to draw her into the house while she twisted her mouth into a grimace of helpless inquiry at Paula, who waited for her in the doorway.

"Look, look what you've done to my child," said the woman, unaware of Frieda's touch. "So pretty he was, a fat little baby, one year old! Where has he been these eight years? Where have you been, Rafi? Where have you been these eight years?"

Hearing the last words, the girls could not restrain their laughter. For a moment she crouched there in silence, swaying her torso back and forth, as if reckoning up Rafi's lost years, clumps of ragged hair falling again over her brow.

Paula's voice broke into the interval of silence. She strode decisively toward the stranger, and the two women, murmuring soothing words and conversing between themselves in Polish, grabbed her by the waist to pull her up.

"No need!" she said with sudden composure. "I . . . I can manage. I understand Polish."

The beauties of the garden were forgotten. All trailed silently after the three women, and the boy who dragged between them, to see what would become of him. The first floor, scrubbed and white-washed up to the ceiling, was full of the silence of anticipation. Only from the second floor, to which Frieda had ascended lightly, slapping Rafi's nape to hurry him on, came the sounds of running water and the jubilant cries of the last to take their baths, those who had missed the beginning of the episode.

A short while later Rafi returned, slowly descending the stairs, groping his way between the two lines of children, who pressed against the banister and the wall to make way for him. His face was flushed with ugly patches, on his thighs flapped new exercise shorts too big for him, and under his arm, a bundle wrapped in a clean sheet.

Halfway down the stairs he stopped; from behind the eternal film of inflammation, like unpolished lenses, peered the eyes of a tame rabbit.

"Children!" cried Frieda, following in his footsteps and her voice striving to urge them on, to get this over quickly. "Children, Rafi is leaving us, so say goodbye to him right now. Be nice to him and wish him all the best in his new life . . . Don't get yourselves dirty! And don't forget to keep an eye on outside."

Maya stared at Rafi's dreadful face, as if seeing it for the first time. He has a mother, this stinker, born on a garbage heap, so the slander went, a unique configuration of gutter maggots . . .

"Isn't he staying for the ceremony?" someone asked.

"Now he's got more important things to think about than a ceremony," said Frieda, and she hurried to the office from which raised voices were heard. The pleading voice of the woman, the voices of Markovski and Pani-Paula, arguing between themselves in Yiddish, rhythmic thumping on the table, and finally also the vibrant voice of Frieda. In this office they only shout at parents when money is being discussed. The door closed behind Frieda's back and the voices were muffled.

"He'll be alright now," said Yaffa thoughtfully, a flush on her freckled cheeks. "And maybe he'll live in Jerusalem."

Rafi stood limp, motionless, in the middle of the staircase. The tip of his tongue on his lower lip and his hand clutching the bundle to his middle. It was plain he wasn't going to fulfill the suppressed desire of those who scrutinized his face with the eyes of hunters, expecting tears.

"Rafi," Salomon suddenly broke the silence, clearing his throat noisily, "who's going to throw bedbugs and sandals at you now, eh?"

Hearing these compassionate, tasteless words, a few of the boys twisted their lips into a scornful smirk. The rest listened in embarrassment.

"If they beat you where you're going to, pay them back the way we taught you," Salomon wagged a finger in Rafi's face, the boisterous tone betraying his emotion. "So they won't think they're dealing with . . ."

A sharp howl, like the cry of an unknown bird of prey, interrupted him. The door of the office flew open, slamming against the wall. In the doorway stood the mother, her hair neatly combed but her eyes staring wide, as if seeking to take in a greater abundance of light, and her hands clutching for support on the lintel of the door.

Frieda's face peered anxiously over her shoulder. She gently detached her hand from the doorpost but immediately moved forward to support her, for the woman was about to collapse like an old mattress.

"Ketzele," said Frieda, a note of hysteria in her voice. "Children! Quiet please! Ketzele, my dear, my sweet, run upstairs quickly, to the bathroom . . . Did you hear me—I said quiet!

Silence! Go at once and fetch Handsome Rafael. Tell him his mother's come to take him home . . . Do you understand? Are we going to have quiet here or not? Not another word! Tell him, tell Handsome Rafael, his mother . . .," she said softly.

Ketzele stared at her in blank amazement, his nostrils flaring frantically and his brow breaking into wrinkles. Then he turned and ran upstairs.

The woman who had come to take her son hurried after him, swaying and stumbling, her heels clattering on the stairs.

Stinking Rafi stuck his tongue to his lip and made way for the woman who ran up the stairs to another boy and did not look at him again, his rabbit-eyes following her in silence, as if seeing her now for the first time.

Anyone accustomed to the melodramas performed without shame on the open stages of reality, attuned to their chaotic colors and to all the embellishments of flowing tear ducts, poorly composed dialogues, an astonishing and somehow artificial chain of events— will guess what was the end of this comical episode.

When Frieda and her pupils heard the brakes of the car stopping outside the house, it was already too late to prevent catastrophe.

When the children hurried out to the yard to meet the "millionaires" and the "industrialists" with those greetings that they had rehearsed a dozen times ("Welcome to the shelter of our roof, dear guests"), they already saw them, the V.I.P.s, standing at the gate in their big hats and staring shocked into the yard, and the Wolfson-woman, like a beetroot plucked from borscht, trying to steer them toward the house.

In the yard, under the eyes of the "industrialists," wandered Stinking Rafi, alone, as if gripped by a frenzy, dragging and uprooting the new "plants" from the muddy earth, carrying a branch, waving it in the air with maniacal triumph and uttering cries of sheer helplessness: "No–o roots! No–o ro–ots! No roots!"

At that moment Maya saw the woman who had slipped away

in silence making off down the slope with her Handsome Rafael, the pretty one with the rosy cheeks, in new exercise shorts and a bundle wrapped in a sheet slung across his shoulder. No one paid any more attention to them.

21
IN THE DREAMING
HOURS OF
THE NIGHT

He has become a youth again.
A feverish adolescent, slipping poems à la Pushkin under her
door. His thought processes, always turned inward, now are transformed into a wavering quest for another. The world is divided
between the lovers and the indifferent. He hallucinates and in
his dream he is someone else, someone more whole, yearning
after this other being that is not himself. Before her he strips off
this borrowed personality, and she reveals in him—him! He is
startled, aroused, illumined by the light of the great understanding. Only a thin wall separates his room from hers. He scratches
on the wall, in his fantasies, on the nights of loneliness that she
has forced on him. The wall is pierced, he inserts a thin thread.
She clutches at the thread and follows him. In his ears sinks again
the grating of the needle on the record that is emptied of its music,
stirring and stirring and stirring in the living flesh.

He turns on his side and lights the lamp again. Night after night he expects her to notice the light. He lies on his bed fully clothed, the writing pad and the big dictionary resting on his stomach, and he writes the letters of her name again and again, in straight lines and diagonally, like a child, forming rhymes, acrostics, anagrams.

He throws the pad under the pillow before replying to the knock at the door. Frieda—in Shoshana's black coat and her eyelashes still wet from the shower, emphasizing the brightness of her eyes.

"I couldn't sleep," she says apologetically. "Everything's so quiet, as if they're all dead." A musical ring to her voice, as if she's been watching, has seen everything, through that thin wall. Without a word he puts on his coat, sensing that his eyes are smiling, his lips fluttering like hers, that the expression on his face is identical to hers.

"Let's go!" He springs up from his bed, as if responding to a signal. "To my place. I'll show you . . ." He's startled when he sees her take off her shoes by the door, as if preparing herself for some mysterious ritual. He laughs and takes off his own, which he's only just put on. Silently, on tiptoe, they creep down the stairs. From the dormitories comes the snoring of congested noses. In the yard they replace their shoes and laugh again. Their faint shadows, shadows in the starlight, flicker before them side by side, touching and separating, bigger and bolder than they are. He looks at her, protecting her with his glance. In the night landscape there is no longer any oppression, any pain; everything floats around him on a film of light ether.

"I love to see you with wet eyelashes," he says to her face. The words become pale. Every tune perfected in his mind sounds like a sick croaking of frogs when he opens his mouth. She narrows her lashes with an air of caprice, looking around her as if she's never been here before. Beneath his eyelids he feels tears. She points in silence to a strange cloud formation rolling above their heads.

His nerves are stretched to breaking point. All of the past races through his mind—running, contracting, swallowed up into one minute point. To walk like this forever, in endless night. The body yearns to tear its own sinews, to stretch them, fill them with air, to leap without weight, to sweep her up, to fly with her and at the same time to clasp her feet. He leads her to the rock, his rock. For a moment he tries to challenge himself, to submit himself to the test, the same terrible hollow sensation that had awaited him here the first time; but everything has become shallow, liberated, without the dread of annihilation.

He spread his coat on the rock to the sound of her lighthearted protests. For a long while he pressed her, with jocular earnestness, to sit beside him—for their time was their own, every moment of sweetness to be savored—adding some nonsense about the opinions of eminent Zionist philosophers on the value of contact with the land, until she submitted with a laugh but sat down some distance from him, sidelong, her coat buttoned up to the neck and her eyes fixed on the sky in an attitude of prayer. He looked at her and at the sky in turns and waited for her to say something about the poem that he slipped under her door last night. There rose a smell of crushed moss, poppies, and sweet broom.

"And what if there's a sudden alarm?" she asked, still looking at the sky. Is this what's on her mind, fear lest their absence be discovered?

"On a night like this everything's quiet," he replied, searching for her eyes.

"An ideal night for an air raid," she insisted. "No moon, and you could slip through the clouds. The village is surrounded by army camps."

Suddenly she turned to him and asked, "Do you really feel no remorse?" He felt wild fear spring up inside him.

"Not yet!" he laughed. "And not ever."

"That you didn't enlist with the rest of them?"

The panic subsided. But now he came to a decision, and as

he had imagined to himself a thousand times and in a thousand ways and fashions, he wound his arm around her shoulders. He felt the expectation in her. His other hand moved on, touching the alien coat and passing over her breast, feeling its shape dimly. Words, words, without limit. From inside him burst a fountain that he could not control, the sensation that they were alone, no one but them sitting like this, like them, on a high rock beneath this end-of-winter night, all other forms of love inferior, lukewarm, their wings clipped.

In the dreaming hours of the night,
In the silence pregnant with desires,
Legends come alive and live,
Legend is life revealed.

She listened, unmoved. "Tchernikovski," she laughed lightly, as if she had outsmarted him.

He pressed home his attack. Her lips were stubborn, sealed, lifeless. The vibration of refusal in her body maddened him. The world retreated, disappeared. "No!" he heard her choking voice beneath him. "Not like this!" Again she recoiled from him, her face blank, tormented. A red surge of anger rose in his brain. To tear this alien wrapping from her! To expose everything to the light of the stars! Her hands gripped his hands tightly, like a vice.

"What is it, this stupid, unnecessary, infuriating, goddamn game you women play?"

"Why have you never married?" she asked suddenly, laughing into his face, his hand in hers, like a mother trying to distract a baby.

"Because I didn't meet you, silly girl!" he laughed back at her.

"No. I'm asking seriously, why?" she laughed, the journalist interviewing.

"I wanted to be a professional revolutionary!"

"Ah," she dropped his hand, her eyes scornful. Everything was calm for a moment. She sat apart from him. Her eyes lost their scorn and studied his movements. Suddenly, as is her way, she told him of a dream she has dreamed. She's traveling on a bus full of men. Her heart knows it belongs to one of them, but she doesn't know to which one. Her eyes wander among the faces. Her heart freezes—will she never know love? Opposite her sits Mark from the high school—could it be him? Her eyes hang on his indifferent face, her heart tries to rouse his embers into life, and suddenly she knows it isn't *him*. Suddenly she wakes and knows exactly, knows for certain!

"What do you know?" he asked, his heart lacerated.

"I know!" she replied.

Unexpectedly she laid her head and shoulders on his knees. He'd never noticed her hair was so long. His hand stroked the nape of her neck. She let his hands invade her sleeves, but then her hands gripped his and trapped them, guiding them to the places of lesser interest. What terrible unsubmissiveness! A statue offering itself for worship and keeping its eyes shut! He took off his glasses and leaned over her face. Her eyes opened and stared in astonishment at his naked eyes. He breathed in the fresh, living perfume, determined now to embark on the greatest journey of all, not to waste more time, not to fall by the wayside.

With curt movements she put everything back in its place.

"It would be a lie!" she said nervously, as if in dreadful pain.

"It would be the one and only truth, the great truth," he muttered insanely, gritting his teeth. With a strength not his own, he pulled her to him, but she defended herself as if her life was threatened. Her face looked different, strange, puffy, almost ugly. He was frantic to wipe from her face what desire and fear had done to it. But she hurriedly straightened her hair, stood up and groped with her fingers for the buttons of her coat, then turned and walked away from him, her head bowed, straying to the edges of the path and slipping on the stones. But he blocked her way, his chest to her chin. Her face expressed hatred, helplessness, shame, and remorse.

"What's the matter?" he said. "What happened? What's wrong?"

"Everything! Everything! Right from the start! Let me go back by myself!" She dropped her eyes.

"Now? Are you crazy?" he wailed. Oh, Virginity! Oh, these stupid, goddam, wonderful virgins! That's it, that's it, that's it! All those experienced and impatient women that he'd had, all those long and short romances became suddenly tasteless, empty, all those surrogate affairs, those forgotten beds. And now—here she is—destiny's woman, the vessel that he will make his own, that he will create anew! That he will bring from simple existence into belonging. He is the one who will beget in her, in this body, the intensity of joy, the great relief after all those years of long and painful expectation. All her childhood, the twilight of adolescence, the treasure house of hope and longing, all these will rise up and permeate his being, melt into his soul. He will stamp upon her the imprint of knowledge, awaken in her the repressed thunder!

Wildly he seized her strong hips, feeling their roundness in his hands. Her shoulders rose like those of a Spanish dancer, and she shielded her breasts with crossed arms, like a little girl. He absorbed all this vibrating stubbornness into his suffering flesh, and his legs betrayed him. Everything melted into whispering sweetness. His knees sank slowly to the ground and with them her body. All those foolish remarks about contact with the Holy Land danced in his brain like devils.

He saw her running, vanishing into the depths of the night. Only then did he realize that she had pushed him away. For a long time he knelt there, breathing in the scents of the trampled earth. Suddenly, his nerves shattered, he fell forward and dug his teeth into the wet turf.

The moment that he had dreaded. Already his heart was heavy with the burden of the future silences, the evasiveness that lay in wait. In the morning he opened the door of the dining room and saw, as he'd expected, Frieda in her worksmock. He felt a surge of malicious pity when she appeared to him thus, in her high padded shoes, in her crumpled apron. Thus she would be day after day, hour after hour, before his eyes, inside this walled citadel. She stood by the open window and sliced a loaf of soya bread on a wooden board. In her face he found no traces of the night.

"I had a strange dream last night," she said.

He forced a cunning smile of complicity. Paula stood in the doorway of the kitchen, and above the steam of the porridge dish she glanced at Frieda with the look of an out-of-work midwife. Frieda slipped away into the kitchen.

The voices of the children were already gathering on the stairs like an approaching storm. Shoshana burst in with them and grinned at him furtively, as if bestowing on him a silent blessing.

He'll go out of his mind if for one moment longer they go on slamming doors, scraping chairs, scrambling for food, banging the spoons about—he'll go out of his mind!

"Dov! More please, more please!" He heard from the table below him the pleading voice of the Quiet Loony. Her hand held out to him the enamel plate, smeared with leftovers. As if in a nightmare, her inflamed eyes followed his movements as he mechanically scooped up the watery porridge with the ladle.

"Chocolate! Chocolate!" Her plea resounded in his ears. He could no longer bear the sight of the anemic face, flushed and dripping with catarrh. Without thinking, he picked up the spoon and sprinkled the precious grains of cocoa onto the extra portion. The girl swooped on the plate, holding it tight to her chest and licking like a cat.

"Why's she got that? Why her?" Aggrieved voices assailed him. "Why her?"

The cook hurried over to the focus of discontent, piercing him with eyes that told him all his weaknesses were known, were known to her and disgusted her. Dimly there came to him the distant music from the army camp, the flowering orchard into which he strayed, the dark waters of the irrigation trench into which he sank his head, the touch of the cold concrete on his face, the unknown thickets where he had wandered all night, the startled birds that flew up before him.

And her old eyes glued to his sallow cheeks, the dark blotches of insomnia.

"Tight-fisted bitch," he cursed through clenched teeth. "Rotten, tight-fisted old hag!" Immediately he felt regret in his heart. Evil flowers sprang open in her narrowed eyes as she repaid his abuse with a complicated Polish curse, full of victorious delight. He saw the faces of the children, curious, fascinated, swallowing every word. He turned back to the table.

"Who wants more?" He raised the porridge dish above their heads.

"With cocoa?" asked a cautious, surprised voice.

"With cocoa!" he replied with a generous smile. "Only with cocoa."

Dozens of plates were thrust toward him, amid a babble of astonished voices. The dish was snatched from his hand. Paula slammed it down on the table so hard that drops of porridge splashed on the children's faces.

"No more!" She pushed the plates away from her one after another. "No more! No cocoa! Nothing! Fifty cows at one manger!"

He expected an angry protest, a howl of disappointment. But they responded with indifference: this is how it must be—a justice beyond their comprehension. They sidled away from the table and crowded around the door, to pick up their satchels from the heap at the bottom of the stairs.

Frieda returned from the kitchen, her eyes on the tray of the Old Man Slonim.

As if in a dream, she heard his voice from the yard, calling her name with impatient persistence—the voice of a normal father looking for his daughter who has gone to play at a neighbor's house. A sort of sick grating in her guts—without warning and without giving her time to prepare herself, he's out there shouting with such naturalness and such vigor as if to fill all at once the great distance, the long time that he hasn't been here, behaving like a privileged member of the family and not knowing that he ought to appear, like those other parents who seldom come, confused, tongue-tied, their faces radiating guilt and a plea for forgiveness.

When she went out to the balcony and her eyes encountered him, she asked herself with momentary bitterness: "Is that him? It's him!" He looked to her strange and different, altogether different. Not like that form which had gradually lost its dimensions and turned into a name, just a name, itself dismissed from her consciousness. Inside her flickered a dim, unworthy desire—let him disappear! Disappear at once! Let him think she isn't here any more, that they've taken her away some place else, or . . . But he went on calling at the top of his voice, and already some children stood beside him and listened to his calls.

"I'm here!" she answered from the balcony, to put a stop to this self-abasement.

"Ah! Mayaka!" He looked at her through narrowed eyes, as if wondering why she had taken so long to answer his calls. Just like the father calling his daughter from the neighbors' house.

As she goes down to meet him there are butterflies in her stomach, as if she were on her way to an exam. She's alarmed by the clear awareness that she isn't pleased to see him, although it's her *duty* to be happy—as if there already has settled within her some fine sediment of not-needing any of these people, and suddenly he comes and stirs and stirs, and everything within her becomes muddied. He doesn't hesitate for a moment but plants on her cheek a kiss full of fatherly possession, in front of everyone. Then he looks at her.

"How you've grown, a proper young lady! Soon you won't give a damn for your poor old dad." He looks at the children and laughs, enjoying the exaggeration. She knows he's waiting for her to contradict him, but she avoids his face with great care and says, her throat constricted:

"Now we go upstairs." That's what they do with all these parents, and he's just like the rest of them. There's a fixed routine. They come, the children lead them upstairs, sit them down on the bed, take from them what they've brought, and try to make conversation as they wait for the moment of their departure.

But Katriel Hermoni marches into the house in full awareness of his own importance. "Hallo, hallo! It's me, Maya's dad, I've come for a visit!" He greets the members of the staff, shakes their hands, wishes them well, beaming with condescension, slaps Markovski's shoulder and hugs him—a king entering his summer palace—making such an exhibition of himself you'd think he was Modi's father, at least, or God knows who else.

She watches him through the eyes of the others. They know just how much every one of these fathers is worth. Her frozen and expressionless face insists that she isn't responsible for his actions, his words, his movements. He will leave his footprints here, and they will be the path that she'll be forced to walk in for a long time to come. More and more she strives to preserve her distance, her critical judgment, standing aside, but at the same time in her heart she prays that he'll shine, succeed, "make a good impression," so that afterwards she can take secret nourishment from pride in him.

His foolish wonderment! Everything impresses him, but she understands that he's acting this way to rid himself of the burden of guilt that all the parents bring with them.

"What a lovely, big dining room you've got! You could dance waltzes here," he says to Maya, and the others listen. He doesn't see anything: the flaccid belly of the bed, the dingy, tattered blanket, the grubby sheets, the springs that have worn loose and fallen to the floor, the mattress that has long since spewed out most of its straw, the patterns of bedbug blood on the walls, the plaster that has fallen and falls with every slam of the door. Maya no longer notices this, for everything by now is so close to her heart that it spreads over her a warm sense of belonging, and her body is familiar with all the lumps and hollows of her bed, so different from those of the others, but he . . . he has an obligation to see, to smell the stink of mold and urine that she herself wouldn't be comfortable without. The boys—"fine fellows" all of them, not the pampered, spoiled type. "You can see they're made of the right stuff." And the girls—"cheerful beauties." He doesn't see the bald patches, the boils, the ringworm scars, the catarrh, the swollen bellies of the younger ones, the bowed legs, the bare feet. Now she looks at everything the way *he* should be looking, seeing that they're all repellent and disgusting and not at all like the charming babies they once were.

At lunch he sits beside Dov Markovski. He's in high spirits, as if there's no other place so invigorating as this.

Pani-Paula suddenly sees fit to comment on the poor quality of the food, which she never does in the presence of the children, and goes on to speak of financial matters, her eyes fixed on him.

"If we do not have the blessing of our father Isaac," she says in Yiddish, "then at least let us have the pot of lentils!"

"Lentils! Everyday lentils!" says Shoshana, who's always anxious to impress on the children their nutritional value.

They listen in wonder.

"Cat or mouse," replies her father with a laugh. "What matters is that there's chicken for the Sabbath." He wrinkles his black eyebrows playfully, as if seeking her appreciation. Maya sees the ping-pong exchange of glances between Markovski and Frieda.

"Everything's rotten here," says Frieda. "Everything's falling apart and broken—there's no money for repairs, the Wolfson woman owes all of us four months' wages."

"Oh, we all know the definition of a philanthropist," says her father, laughing again. "He talks big and does little!"

"Let's go on strike. What do you think, Mr. Hermoni?" says Shoshana, like a bored schoolgirl.

"Comrade Hermoni!" Frieda corrects her.

"That too is one of the sacrifices we make to the angel of war," says her father. And then, seriously, moving his head slowly up and down, his glance embracing all the members of the staff: "In this case . . ." The rest of the conversation is conducted in Russian.

The meal is concluded. In her father's mouth is the fatherly suggestion that she go out "and play with her friends." (As if she'd never played with "her friends." What's all this about friends? Friends! Every word of his enrages her by missing the target.) He leaves the room with Markovski. Before going out she pauses for a moment to listen to the conversation between the cook and Frieda, who are gathering up the plates along with the duty-helpers, sure that this time she'll hear things that she's supposed to hear. She hears them talk of the impudence of the man, turning up like this. Sometime they should send the girl back to stay with him, for as long as it takes to make him cough up.

"A real bird-fancier!" Paula spits. "Poo! Chicken tastier than this may he never know!" Then some whispers about Markovski, and suddenly she remembers and turns her head to Maya, who's standing by the door.

"Look at this one! What's this? Espionage? If you've never in your life heard a good word, hear it now! Bad girl! Get out of here!"

Maya doesn't stick out her tongue, as she'd like to do, because she's afraid they might really send her back to the city, back to . . . This Pani-Paula doesn't understand that she wishes, really wishes, he would pay, not be like this, so they wouldn't slander him like this.

The boys are playing football, and some girls are watching them. Maya doesn't know whether to stay with them or go up to the dormitory, as she'd like to do, to sit there on her bed in the empty room, open her notebook and write, and forget he's here. And she won't show him the poems because she doesn't want him to be proud of her, or visit her. She stays in the yard.

Katriel Hermoni comes out of the house, blinking in the light. Oh no, he's going to offer to play, she guesses with dread.

"Well, are you going to let me join in the game?" he asks the boys. They agree out of politeness and resignation, out of a wish for some novelty, or perhaps because they're eager to test his mettle. He hurriedly tells them what a fine football player he was in his youth, what a wizard he is at scoring goals. He strides confidently onto the tiny plot of tarmac, running on the spot, as the professionals do, to warm their limbs before the kickoff. (All these ridiculous preparations, this exhibitionism! Now they'll demand a brilliant, outstanding, stunning performance! What rashness!)

As she knew would happen from the start, he kicked empty air, sent up clouds of dust, missed balls, made showy jumps to disguise his failures, his eyes expressing petty jealousy at the achievements of the more agile players. When he once succeeded in heading the ball, he celebrated his success with a raucous shout, looking about him with an air of triumph, and when the "goof" was especially serious, he exploited—shamelessly—his status as an adult, argued with the referee, and invented a new rule that had never existed before.

He tussled with them with none of the joyful abandon of an adult pretending to be a child, but like one determined to prove his worth at any price.

When he became tired he stopped. The fringes of his trousers, his shoes, his forehead, were covered in dust. She hoped that now he would lightly mock himself, his years, and his lack of agility. That way he'd come out of it with dignity. But all he said to the spectators was: "Your pals don't know how to play. Even the fundamental rules of football they don't know. And they have a lot, a lot to learn before . . ."

She felt an unpleasant taste in her mouth and wished she could disappear into the ground, escape. The boys were more gracious than he. When they realized his weakness, they showed generous consideration to the old man, and this was the worst of all. Ketzele even invited him to act as referee in the next game. "No, no, thank you very much!" said her father with what was supposed to be a knowing wink. "I've already seen the way you play . . ." Then he added some practical advice, "to improve the *niveau*."

Again he left her in the backyard. It seemed to her the players had already forgotten the episode. But she went on staring at the faces of the spectators to seek their impression of what had happened; she wanted to convince them that she shared their suppressed contempt, that she was just a bystander and not obliged to bear responsibility for his actions. But not one of them noticed her. Their eyes were fixed on the ball.

After a short while she was full of emptiness, perhaps because nothing had emerged, neither scorn nor sympathy. At once she set off in search of her father, perhaps so he wouldn't sense her aversion to him, or to hint that it was time for him to go. She found him sitting in the dining room on one of the chairs, talking ingratiatingly to Shoshana, who was setting the tables for supper. The girl seemed uneasy, and she looked up sharply when Maya walked in.

"Someone's looking for you," she said. Her father turned abruptly. She caught in his face a flicker of disappointment.

"Ah! Mayaka! Come, come here, my girl!" He stands up, drawing her to his side with a display of possessiveness, caressing her. "And how is she behaving here, is she a good girl?" he asks the nurse, gazing at his daughter's face with a look of fatherly pride, which makes all her soul rebel. Maya knows that the woman doesn't answer because he isn't worth an answer, but she, Shoshana, has no right to judge! Not she! Then she sees that Shoshana has gone out, and only a clatter of pans is heard from the kitchen.

"Well, are you going to come with your dad to the bus stop?" She nods, her eyes closed.

He stood up to take leave of Frieda, giving her hand a long squeeze and her face a lingering look. Then he exchanged brief words with Markovski and finally confronted Pani-Paula, who blocked half the doorway with her body.

"So!" she trumpets. "The dogs bark, and the baron moves on!"

"Everything, everything will be sorted out!" he replies hastily, turning his body sideways to pass her and dragging his daughter after him. "In a month from now I'll come with the . . ." But the cook hasn't finished with him yet. Her eyes are like twin slits of evil.

"*He* will come! Sure! Like you can put the shit back in the asshole!"

Katriel Hermoni stands outside. He breathes a deep sigh of relief and moans. "It's all give, give!" he addresses the sunset sky. "The leech has two daughters: Give and Give! And everything from the multimillionaire, the well-known profiteer Katriel Hermoni!"

"Am I the first 'Give' or the second?" Maya asks, and regrets it at once. His eyes look at her in sorrow, in baffled incredulity at her outburst, but suddenly his voice rings out:

"Well, why don't you tell your father anything? What is this? Are you cross with your father? You're so reserved."

"I don't know what you mean."

"Have you nothing to tell your father? Nothing? How you're getting on, what you're learning, what you're doing? Nothing! Who are you going to tell if not your father? Oh, Mayaka! When you were little you used to tell Daddy everything. Do you think your dad doesn't think about you all the time? You think your dad doesn't care? You all seem to think I have an easy life, I bathe in rose water. They say that life is the greatest bargain of all—you get it for free! Ha! Everything for free! But afterwards you pay dearly! For all things you pay dearly." (Maybe now he'll make some small statement of regret, something about the end of things, a hint for the future?) "Look, I owe the hostel for half a year! Half a year! I'm broke! I'm in debt up to here! Not one hair on my head belongs to me! This pair of trousers I've been wearing since . . . do you know what?" (What?) "I bought them before you were born. You don't believe me, eh? It's true! I remember! I went with your mother to buy them in Nahalat Binyamin. Anyway," he laughed, "maybe when you're grown up you'll buy your old dad a pair of trousers for a birthday present."

He laughs for a moment and then his face turns grave. "You must explain to them, now you're a big and clever girl, explain to them it isn't that easy . . . Tell Frieda to persuade Batya Wolfson to wait a little longer. Last week I got a letter from her. I'll try to raise it . . . I can't think how! Only just now your little brother's sick, there's the rent . . . You're a big girl now, nearly grown up, you must pay attention to everything they say, everything they tell you . . ."

He waits for her reply, and since she's silent he goes on:

"What's the matter? Aren't you happy here? There are children who envy you, wandering the streets, in the rain and the heat . . . You know how hard your father works so you can stay here . . . Your father gets up at five o'clock and comes home when it's dark, and sometimes he sleeps out in some dirty shack or in a kibbutz, so you can . . . Come on, what's the matter?"

"No–thing!" she cried bitterly.

"Then why are you like this, like a closed knapsack? I don't know you, suddenly."

Suddenly there came to her mind the memory of another, similar conversation between them, when she was perhaps seven years old. Then too he asked: "What's the matter? What's troubling you?" He was polishing his shoes. A lot of things troubled her then, and they were all mixed up, but she chose just one of them and took courage from her desire to hurt him, from her curiosity to expose hidden secrets: "I wish you and Mummy would be . . . together." And she remembered the funny sensation of foolishness and crudity, and the outrageous daring of her request. Then he studied her face in silence, with an unconvincing look of pain, and finally he smiled and asked: "Did Mummy tell you to say this to me?" She denied it at once, but it was like a fist striking her heart. Since then she'd never said this to anyone . . . besides, she didn't want it any more.

She forced herself to smile: "It's nothing, really!"

"Alright, so let's be friends, eh? Do you really think it's better for those girls who dress up in fancy frocks and tinkle on pianos? We must pull and pull like Mendele's mare . . . Have you read 'My Mare' by Mendele?"

"No, not yet," she answered.

"Once you were so cheerful . . . Well, alright, so you don't love your father? Well—you don't have to! You're not forced to love somebody just because he's your father . . . If I brought you presents, or some toy, then you'd be pleased to see me, eh? When we came to this country my sister Vera was just a little older than you, and already she was out working in the orchards. She didn't even finish elementary school . . . and her friend Masha went to work in a canning factory . . . and my father was richer then than I am now . . ."

"Yes, I know."

"You really have nothing to complain about—you go to school, you're taken care of, you have clothes to wear . . ."

"I'm not complaining, not at all."

Down below, by the bus stop, he groped anxiously in his purse and knotted his brows. "Some purses are just a grubby scrap of leather," he said with a laugh. At last he drew out a coin and thrust it into her hand. "Go on, take it, take it. Buy yourself some chocolate or something."

She felt as if it were his last coin. Her throat framed the words of a dignified refusal.

"Take it, take it. It makes no difference to me. I can still afford these few *grushim*." She closed her hand over the coin, just to shut him up. The joints of her fingers guessed its value. The bus flashed blue eyes at them. The bus—the great and good emissary of a hidden god, sitting up there, in the ultimate bus station in the sky.

"We—ell! Give Daddy a kiss, my big girl!" In his voice she heard slighted authority and a homily on the obligations of a dutiful daughter, and with this a plea for conciliation. The gear-shift grated. From under his peaked cap the impatient eyes of the driver peered at her father, and his knees shifted under the wheel. Hermoni stooped and kissed her full on the mouth. For a moment she thought of his pocket close by her hand and the coin that she could slip back into it. Then he was waving to her from the receding, blue-tinted window, until the bus and the waving hand were gone. Now she wanted to wipe from her lips the bitter taste of cigarettes. The path to the hostel rose before her, stretching up to the blank twilight sky.

"How much did you get?" cried the three thin silhouettes standing by the gate.

"I got thirty *grushim*," she said as she approached them.

"Show us!" demanded Yaffa. She will never learn to disguise her envy.

With her free hand she turned out the pocket of the gym shorts under her dress. She put on an aggrieved expression, sure that her game was flawed.

"She's hidden them, the swine," said Yaffa.

"By my life, would I do a thing like that?"

"She's spent it on something," said Yaffa.

"Alright! Take a sniff!" She opened her mouth wide. Yaffa sniffed twice and screwed up her face.

"I had two ten-*grush* pieces and a lot of pennies. I ran, and they must have fallen on the ground or in the bushes, how should I know?" She herself was already upset at the loss.

Bat-Sheva put out her hand and felt the pocket, she even looked inside the gym shorts under the dress.

"Come on then, let's look, smelly fools," she said grumbling, disbelief and disappointment in her eyes.

"How? In the dark?" chirped Hedva.

"We'll see it shining," said Bat-Sheva.

"In the dark," replied Maya, her nose tilted sideways importantly, "you always find the best things." This wasn't the first time she heard herself uttering meaningless proverbs unintentionally.

They went out to search among the bushes. "Just let's not be late for supper," said Hedva, looking back toward the house, the last rays of the sun gleaming on its windows.

The coin, clenched in her hand, she quietly slipped into the pocket of her gym shorts.

23
MARGARITA

This was a pleasant house to live in. The walls, smeared with patches of tar, were constantly full of chalk grafitti—words of wisdom and children's groping perceptions of reality, political dogmas and threats, intrigues, gossip columns and wedding announcements—an eternal newspaper for which everyone makes his own censorship.

Of those who lived then in Margarita's house, which looked full in the eyes of the hostel over the shoulder of the produce warehouse, today not one remembers its charm—except those who were children, who sat in groups on the exterior staircase that clung to its ribs until some irritable adult came and they were forced to let him pass, standing up and pressing against the wall.

These stairs always arouse in Maya a vague sense of purification. They begin with profanity, excrement, and filth, since everyone makes use of them, and as those who need them climb higher and grow fewer, so they become clear and whole, and at the top, beside Margarita's room, they are already pure and clean.

Here, hiding on the stairs, as your eyes absorb again and again, unconsciously, what's on the walls, you get a good view of the yeshiva boys who take a short cut through Margarita's yard on their way to the hill. They stroll past in pairs, coats slung cockily over their shoulders, like giant bat wings, talking constantly and ignoring the girls, thereby inspiring a sense of vague suspicion.

When "Muti" returned in the evening from the factory, her legs heavy from standing all day and from climbing the hill, she would complain bitterly at "these Notre Dame steps" and quietly curse the precarious banister, which was liable to collapse from the tremor of a sneeze.

In these places everything made of iron or tin rusts immediately. "This is the sign," Muti used to laugh, "the sign that here God is very close." Not that she was of little faith, but that her God put on in her eyes the form of her husband, a man with whose depravity fate had acquainted her only too well.

The whole of the neighborhood, sprawling on the northern slopes of the hill, was the creation of a father to the destitute, an astute industrialist who, foreseeing from the start the outcome of events in Europe, began building from the top of the hill and continued his downward progress until the war was at its height. These houses were nicknamed "sugar houses," not out of malicious slander but because they were built with walls of cookies and ceilings of waffles, with sugar dripping from story to story. (Black market activities are a fashionable topic, and none of our concern, a species of subhistory that has no place among the eternal verities.) Rents were reasonable, except that they forced the lodgers, refugees from Hitler who had lost their middle-class status, to promote them to the top of their list of worries. He offered them his two candy factories and another for combs and shell-buttons, which were manufactured in haste, in three shifts, to satisfy the market of His Majesty's Forces (most of whom were young, sweet-toothed, and had unruly hair), and thus he accustomed them to hard work in the name of the war effort.

"This 'Von Button'," Muti used to say, "ask him for a comb—he'll give it you, *bitte schön*, by all means, but first he'll wait till you go bald." But this she said only at moments of exasperation, when the rain came visiting through the waffle-ceiling, instead of the visit of "Von Button"—promised two years since—to conduct a house inspection.

The room where Muti and Margarita sleep is in the highest abode of heaven, with only the hostel overlooking it, but from its window you can scan the teeming life in the North of the world, as far as the strip of the Yarkon and the barrier of the distant trees. From wall to wall brave men with horned helmets were rescuing from mortal danger women clad only in their hair, and their names—Siegfried and Tristan—in letters of gold.

Muti warned her daughter not to reveal the secrets of the wooden closet and the wardrobe, but Margarita could not resist, and once, in the early days, she pulled out a drawer in Maya's presence. Then, when she peeped inside, holding her breath as she remembered the warnings, she found it was made of layer upon layer of compressed paper and "wooden rings," cunningly painted from the outside and coated with varnish.

"Don't talk about this," said Margarita. "We don't need people to know our furniture is made of paper."

Margarita is a "latch-key girl." On her return from school, or from games, she always lowers her neck to the level of the keyhole, a routine movement of stunning and enviable originality. The key dangles over her heart always, like a charm, even at night, a sort of medal of courage and independence. On the table she finds Muti's instructions, written in European script: "Buy bread. Go to the hairdresser. Pay the water bill."

Maya, when she happens to be there, in the celestial abode, helps her to shift the furniture, which is clustered together like a herd of cattle and must be separated and dragged from corner to corner so the floor can be scrubbed. It's a pleasure, too, just to run with her to the shops in the street of the village, to watch Margarita making her choice from among the dainties on the shelf: lakarda or halva, or maybe today peanut butter? How keen is the delight in choosing!

In the big double bed mother and daughter sleep. Sometimes the younger slips out to spend the night in the hostel, but she never reveals who it is who takes her place.

In the girls' dormitory they push beds together, and Margarita lies on the gap in between, padded with blankets. When one of the members of the staff comes visiting, they throw a pillow over her head and cover her body with outstretched arms and legs.

If Muti had asked, they would have let her, but Margarita doesn't want to be the smoke that points to the fire. One time, when her mother paused for a chat with Frieda by the gate of the hostel, the instructor had a suggestion: why shouldn't her daughter stay for lunch with "our girls" in exchange for a nominal fee, but Frau Hellermann, though her daughter pestered her with joyful hints, replied at once with a smile that combined all the proper reactions—gratitude, somewhat forced embarrassment, and respectable aloofness: one of the few pleasures left to her, still, was cooking for the "Restaurant Hellermann," up there on the roof. In the light of day it's still possible to preserve the thin, separating line.

When the girls go out in a group for a Sabbath walk, and Margarita with them, all the pleats of her dress neatly in order from the waist to the knee, they always know she will yet retrace her steps. Muti's voice will pursue her from the roof as they skip among the rocks toward the path up the hill: "Marga! *Taschentuch*! Marga! *Taschentuch*!" Marga will stamp her foot once or twice from a distance, elbows pressed tight against her ribs, but finally she will return and wait until the handkerchief is bound around her head like a pledge of love.

Since her first day in the "Fifth Heaven," when everything was dim and heavy as lead, the image of Margarita had shone to Maya like a beacon flashing and fading, but once the Queen sensed this, she hastened at once to block out the light with her body, or so it seemed to Maya. The truth is, the brooding luminescence of the Queen suddenly dimmed in the presence of the free spirit, as if she too was praying in her heart for an image of equal worth. As if another lamp was lit and the energy divided.

Muti made sure that her daughter chose friends from among the pupils with care, and she did not hesitate to show the signs of her disapproval, although the institution itself she never criticized (something that her neighbors did with relish), seeing that "the same sun darkens the gypsies and bleaches the white laundry," and she need only worry lest her daughter associate with "gypsies."

Sometimes Muti would gleefully mock the "*Ost-Juden*," always dismissing her neighbors at the end of a conversation with "*Also, shalom und Le-hitraot*", but her own accent revealed an origin that was not pure, and because she took so much care to hide it, it was suspected that here there was something malodorous, something requiring a constant sprinkling of scents. Frau Hellermann brought with her a burden of education, but it became light and insubstantial as air when she weighed it against her daughter's Hebrew exercise book. "You can tell she's from an intelligent home," said Muti when Maya came for the first time to their aerie. The girl felt awkward at once because she detected in this remark a denunciation of the quality of her "home." She wondered why this Muti had persuaded her to come and do her homework with her daughter.

On Sabbath afternoons Muti would iron the morning's washing, spreading out the embroidered napkins on every available space, then urge the guest to try her delicacies—stuffed cabbage, strudel, and tea from a pot encased in a patchwork "cozy"—and between courses insistently explain to her that strudel is more tasty when you cram it into the mouth with the left hand, and Margarita protesting impatiently: "Ach, Muti!" But even at times such as these, Maya felt she was being treated not as a girl but as a phenomenon, as material to be probed and studied.

Maya owed something in return, and so it was only natural that she should entrust her own "secrets" to the ears of Muti. Frau Hellermann, sitting on the bed, filing her nails, listened as if entranced, with a cheerful enjoyment unflawed by jealousy or heartache. Thus the girl discovered in her that warm and reassuring sympathy-of-solidarity that arises from an encounter with one "to whom the same things have happened," with none of the outpouring from the full vessel to the empty one that always conceals an intention to impress and to display superiority.

Muti had taught Margarita to tell people how her father had sent them on before him—he himself had not managed to es- cape—but as soon as the war was over . . . From her daughter she did not hide the truth, not wanting her to repeat her own mistakes. The two of them were not fugitives from Adolf Hitler. In the cabarets of Prague the dancers used to boast to one another of the expensive underwear bought for them in lieu of milk for Herr Hellermann's little daughter. And when Muti once asked "How is it going to end, Victor?" he replied, with true nightclub levity, "Stick a knife in your daughter's stomach!" Later he apol- ogized; he'd been drunk at the time.

Yet it always seemed to Maya that everything was still tense and expectant, that inside the big body, somewhere, a little Muti waited, like a pressed and shriveled Rose of Jericho, for a day when the war would be over.

In Marga's cardboard drawer was a photograph: hair combed carefully over the temples, a delicate, almost effeminate beauty, in the style of old movies, so different from the war heroes of today, a white scarf wrapped around his neck, hugging the pillar of a grey wintry palace, and smiling broadly, too broadly. "He's handsome, isn't he?" said Margarita. "It's a pity I'm not like him."

For both of them he was the embodiment of "licentiousness." Sometimes even Marga would forget and say: "After the war, when my father . . ." But at once, when her sobered eyes met those of her friend, their brief eager laughter would mingle for a moment, all-knowing. Frequently Marga would wonder aloud, with cold pleasure, if fathers who are not "licentious" really existed. When Maya and Marga find themselves in a "conventional" household, they look at everything as if at a miracle, but with an air of scornful superiority, and afterwards, outside, they probe the secrets of the father of the family and find whatever they want to find, and when understanding fails, they invent things from their hearts or from books. Another mystery that they seek to unravel: how is it there are women who "put up with everything" and others, like their mothers, who "don't put up with everything," and what's the difference—is it just their beauty?

Muti is very wise, and always she tries to impress on her daughter and her friend that they must prepare themselves for the days beyond their youth. The two of them make faces and exchange gestures of patient resignation. What have such things to do with them, and why is she so determined not to understand that they belong to a different strain, a generation that can't be surprised or deceived?

"Grown-ups make mistakes," Muti preaches. "They tell the little ones only what happens up to the age of twenty. When they say to a girl 'when you grow up,' they're always thinking to themselves 'till marriage.' That's the ideal state of the *jugend*—further than that they're afraid to think. So far it's very nice, everything prepared, but they haven't yet done anything. Like a pretty picture . . ."

But it's impossible for the girls to imagine Muti ever flying with them to this domain of theirs, revealed to them alone, a place that never was and never will be again, where the voice of temptation incessantly whispers: "Grow up, grow up and flourish, you marvelous creature, it will be different, so different, more wonderful than anything."

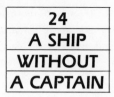

24
A SHIP
WITHOUT
A CAPTAIN

Idleness. Idly she listened to the fading beat of the rain in the tin gutter and slowly gave herself up to the slow dialogue in her bed—the relaxing warmth bubbling between her sleepy body and the sheets.

Her eyes, which had just now opened, searched for the monster. Every morning it grimaces at her with its many-featured face, which never stands still for a moment, bestowing on her the delight of terror free from suffering, but the drizzle blurred the eye of the ceiling and confused its dark shapes. Only then did she remember, and turn her eyes with luxurious relief, to the empty bed of Bat-Sheva.

Now, with everything outside subsiding, rose the voices of the five who had been left with her in the stagnant marsh of routine. The others, the lucky ones, on vacation, were now plunging into a sea of people, seeking the true or counterfeit pearls of love.

Their voices seemed to her to be hovering in the distance, as if carried over from the night before, when it had been impossible to sleep because of excitement at the sudden casting off of the yoke.

The clang of metal springs! Yaffa leaped from her bed into the cold, and from there to Hedva's bed. Casting from her mind the competitive antagonism that had kept them apart for so long, she wrapped herself hastily in her rival's blanket and snuggled against the body of the latest protégée, shivering luxuriously. Dim whispers rose from under the blanket, and at intervals—her laugh, seeking a response, sweet and sticky—as if from time to time the Queen swallowed, outside the blanket, a spoonful of honey and hid it again.

For a long while the room was filled with the sound of her kisses and her chattering, as she cooed and gibbered in baby talk (the same way that Regina, numbed with despair, used to babble in the presence of Kashka's ladyfriends, under the delusion that thus she would magnify her charms at their expense).

"Maya!" they called suddenly. "Listen to a funny sort of dream—d'you hear, Maya?" She gave her attention unwillingly.

Yaffa always dreams of peculiar bodily delights: swinging in a hammock, finding an angora cap on a garbage heap, dipping her finger in a jar full of jam, and every dream is enclosed, with persistent inevitability, in a sweet framework of "good things."

A pity she couldn't remember it all exactly, but when she got up it all came back to her. She was running with her cousin to a kiosk in Mamilla Street—not Mamilla, Ben Yehuda . . . no, it was Mamilla after all—and she told her cousin she wanted chewing gum. This cousin is also Yaffa Matosevitch—in real life that is, not in the dream—and she was born about half a year after Yaffa, but they called her Yaffa too, after Grandma Sheina-Sheindel from Mea Shearim, because the first Yaffa's parents had already split up and they needed to be extra respectful to Grandma's memory. Then the cousin, the other Yaffa, didn't want this, and she said: "I want a cock-a-doodle lollipop!" But she, Yaffa, yelled at the top of her voice: "I want chewing gum and lots of chewing gum!" But the other Yaffa gave her the finger and said: "No! A lollipop!" But she, Yaffa, said: "Then I'll steal your wallet and buy a hundred."

She stopped for a moment and stretched out her neck in suspicious wonder to see why they were letting her prattle on like this, without interruption. But when her glance met Maya's, the collar fell from her neck and her eyes gaped open in intoxication: "My cousin's the one who's got a mother—the most elegant seamstress in Jerusalem. You don't believe it? You don't need to! Even the High Commissioner's wife dresses only from her shop. And they dress this cousin like the doll she got from abroad (the cousin of course—idiot!) from her Aunt Carola when she came from Karlsbaad. Her Aunt Carola is married to . . . and she brought something else even more valuable . . ."

She went deeper and dug and burrowed and burrowed and crumbled the ground. The mole had already disappeared in the earth, but all around were thrown up mounds upon mounds, earthworks of brown-grey dust particles, separated from one another.

Some wild, nervous desire gripped Maya to shout—and to close it!—to push everything inside and to close it, to shout in that voice whose absence from here was suddenly felt, something like: "If not, I'll ram it right down your throat!" But the means of compulsion are given, unfortunately, only into the hands of the cruel. This is our punishment, we who are created in the image, that dark sufferings color our thoughts and the knife of compulsion sharpens our tongue.

Yaffa's prattle, which had not paused even for a moment, simply showed the performer the weakness of her audience. In a sudden flash of inspiration, she sat up and turned her voice on the Quiet Loony, who lay spread-eagled on her bed, apart from the rest, in temporary drowsiness, under the hypnotic spell of the chatter.

The Quiet Loony jumped up, scared: "What-what?"

"Would you be so kind as to tickle my feet?!" said Yaffa with the voice of authority. (This was one of the favors that Little Monkey was often forced to perform to soothe the sensitive nerves of the Queen.)

The summoned one groped, stretching out her fingers before her, to balance herself and to find the thread of the labyrinth between the beds, ominous in their emptiness. When she reached the populated area, her eyes drifted for a moment as she wondered whom to approach, and her hand rose to shield her chin and half her mouth. One quivering fingernail fell between her teeth, a victim of her hesitation.

Yaffa smacked her lips and pointed to the foot of the bed. The Quiet Loony closed her tired eyes and opened them, frightened. The effort of opening her eyes etched a pair of wrinkles, like an equal sign, in the middle of her forehead. She uncovered Yaffa's feet and scratched them clumsily. The girl lying there showed a wondrous gift for mimicry; it was Bat-Sheva's giggles and groans of delight that emanated from between her toenails.

Suddenly, without warning, she kicked her in the chest, as if to show that dominance without the condiment of protest has an insipid taste. The Quiet Loony got up slowly from the floor. Her eyes, already accustomed to not asking whither assistance would come, were drawn together forcibly.

"You want my feet to freeze, you ringworm scab? Is that what you want? Do it under the blanket. *Under*, I said!"

Again blind obedience. It was clear she was still unsure of the identity of her oppressor. Funny, but these things captivated the heart of Hedva, who until a short time ago had seemed to Maya to be lacking simple desires.

With arrogant cries, both of them now gave orders, in turn, lying without movement like babies.

She dressed them laboriously, clumsily, confusing left with right, as she leaned above them. Intoxicated by the ease with which these caprices were realized, they commanded her to run and fetch some trifles from the lockers in the corridor, and when she brought them they tried to teach her to curtsy and say: "At your service, Marquesa." She bent her knees hard together, strangely, as if they too were squinting.

"Put on your glasses, blind bat, then maybe you'll hear better!" cried Yaffa. "Are you going to say what you were told or not?"

The Quiet Loony didn't flinch from the blow. It was clear she didn't understand that all this was a novelty.

"Come on, let's examine her head," enthused Yaffa. She sat up and adjusted the order of the buttons on her blouse. "You see? She doesn't even know how to do up buttons! We'll have to see if her skull bones have closed up."

For a long time the two of them probed with their fingers the proffered scalp. The skull had been shaved not long ago because of ringworm, and the hair was just beginning to grow—dirty brown nests around islands of iodine stains.

Apparently they found that the bones had closed up, because then they decided to "see if she feels the same as the rest of us." She didn't. They couldn't get out of her any sound of response to pinching parts of her body, and she didn't even burst into sweet tears when Yaffa crushed her arm, blue with cold, between her hands in an Indian burn "to show her what thorns feel like."

Bored, devoid of satisfaction and imaginative flair, Yaffa left all this and jumped onto Bat-Sheva's tidy bed. The tensed springs were on the point of breaking and dust rose under the high leaps.

The Quiet Loony retreated carefully. Beside her bed she hurried to put on her owl-rimmed glasses. From within the black celluloid frame she now looked out at the world with a new, armored look.

Yaffa attacked the enamel headboard and began shaking it and wrenching it. Somebody shouted from her bed in panic.

"Little Monkey, are you crazy? *She'll* kill you!" Nira hurried toward her, to prevent her.

"I don't give a shit! I don't give a shi—it!" She shook the hand from her arm and sang to the rhythm of the shaking. No aged monkey, rattling the bars of his cage in a frenzy, could have imitated so closely an aged monkey, rattling the bars of his cage in a frenzy.

"She'll murder you!" yelled Nira.

Yaffa kicked with all her strength at the face of the painted girl. Pieces of enamel flaked and fell on the blanket. "I don't give a shit!" she sang and kicked again and again. Hedva watched her as if mesmerized.

The face of the painted girl seemed to be smiling cheerfully under the hail of blows.

Maya sat and watched, covered up to the neck.

The feeling of release gave way to a vague depression: a parched sponge expecting rejuvenating refreshment and getting soaked in slop water.

Yaffa wearied as suddenly as she had flared up, collapsing on the bed and panting in hatred over the rumpled blankets.

"Please!" She looked up suddenly. "If you please!" (Just like Pani-Paula, when she flings the supper tray at the Old Man Slonim after climbing four sets of stairs.) "I'm gonna get myself an album an' I'm not gonna give it to anyone! I'm just gonna stick my pictures in it, an' I don't care what anyone thinks!"

At once, as if scared by the isolation that she'd forced on herself and in the same old wheedling voice, she turned to Hedva, who stood by the top of the bed: "An' just yours too." And when her eyes met Nira's, she added: "An' just yours too . . . An' yours Maya . . . Batya too."

Maya felt a shock of revulsion, but protest would be like provoking a sick dog.

"And mine too!" the Quiet Loony piped up suddenly. Because she'd been involved with them just now, perhaps she assumed she'd earned herself some rights.

"Hear that?" cried Yaffa. "Did you hear that? Hers too!"

"So what?" grumbled Nira.

"Any photographer would have to be as crazy as her mother to take a picture of that scabby ringworm-face!"

"Shut your mouth, creep!" Nira's voice was full of dutiful protectiveness, but her eyes stared in fascination at the victim, who had frozen in her tracks.

Bat-Sheva herself never broke the taboo of speaking in the Loony's presence of her mother. But Yaffa, her conscience a little bruised, demanded: "What's the matter with you? Why should you care? What's all the fuss about? Scabby ringworm-face!"

"Girls, hey, what's going on today?" came Frieda's impatient voice from the stairs.

"Who wants your stinking porridge?" snorted Yaffa. "Who needs it, anyway?"

Angry that she'd overstepped the mark and driven herself ig-nominiously from the Eden of her delights, she muttered a stream of confused obscenities, to cloud with them the crudities that had gone before.

It all began that day, in the evening. Four girls were crouched in the corner of the yard, kneading with painful and frozen hands the clay soil swept in by the overnight rain from the garden of the German doctor. They chattered pleasantly in the cold and breathed in the scent of the rain-drenched pines coming from the grove of the yeshiva. The sound of the bells of the cattle, returning one by one to their masters from the pasture, came and went from the silent grey distances. Everything around was clean, with-out shadows.

Someone spoke her name, with hatred—and hit the switch!

"The *Queen* stole my sunglasses!"

They were shocked with anticipation and dropped the cold clods from their hands. And suddenly, there's no remembering how, they all found themselves pushing and being pushed into a big red furnace!

Everything that had been hidden and trapped in a heart contracted with fear, with dread of malice, gossip, and evil exploitation; everything that had been repressed and whispered in pain to the rustling of the straw pillows—everything was shaken and uprooted and thrown into the furnace, bubbling and hissing in the fiery molten mass. Until everything turned to emotional, strident happiness, and the layers were exposed. Lionesses confessed in the ears of vixens. Attackers consoled victims. Now it became known, amid whispers of pained joy before eyes full of spirit.

That new album of the Queen's, it's—yes, yes—it's the one and only present that Yaffa ever received from her father, the one she wrapped in Bat-Sheva's American silk dress when she gave it back to her. The robbed one was forced to abandon all claim to the album, pretend it wasn't hers; anything else would be interpreted as a demand for gratitude.

They raised a chorus of protest (even though they knew the whole chain of events and all the motives behind this secret gift), until a single honey-tear glistened in Yaffa's eye. With strange voluptuousness, as if lamenting over her own corpse, Batya interrupted Nira to describe, in a whimper, how she had been forced to steal figs. That Jezebel had hidden behind the big rock where they once found the nest of yellow scorpions. From there she watched her, all the time watching, with a threatening sort of look, so she wouldn't run away. Then the Arab caught her. He picked up the scales from the back of the donkey and hit her on the neck with the crossbar of the scales, here, here beside the shoulder, and then he forced her to put the figs back in the box. Because of this, that Jezebel wouldn't talk to her for a long time—because she didn't succeed.

"A shithouse Jezebel!" said Yaffa.

"Pity a yellow scorpion didn't bite her," said Nira.

"In the popo," said Yaffa.

They all laughed. Oh God, who sets everything to rights, what a laugh!

"And how she locked me out, the Jezebel, on the balcony when it was raining, all night," said Nira, seeking her reflected image in Batya's eyes. "You all pretended to be glad because you were afraid. But it's true you didn't guard the door."

"And how, when her mother slept in the next room . . ."

"Do you know, really, why she told you to steal my purse?"

"And how she wouldn't let anyone cough when her mother . . ."

"Because I wrote for her the essay on the Prophets and she got a 'satisfactory' and I got a 'quite good,' and it was exactly the same essay."

"And she wouldn't let Maya cough with a high fever so her darling mother wouldn't be disturbed, and Maya had to run out every time to cough on the stairs."

"And then you looked for my purse and pretended to find it under my pillow and you said I'd done it on purpose."

This memory! Preservation of what had seemed to rot away, had disappeared long ago! Rumors ripened into stories, aggadic legends of pain and awareness of sufferings that are not the portion of one alone. All differences were reconciled, all vendettas resolved when the motives were revealed.

"So if she doesn't give me back the sunglasses . . ."

"And Little Monkey!" said Yaffa, her eyes on Maya, the one who invented for her the role. She knew it would be enough now to blame it all on "Queen Jezebel," but again that aversion filled her mouth: she too, Little Monkey, demands the spark of purifying cordiality, as if thus she too, Maya, would resemble this salivating flatterer . . . She missed the moment, and the seeds of a new grudge had already been sown.

"I bet everyone's already laid on a surprise in her locker!"

An arrow from the pure air, circles of anguished shock: Margarita. She had been standing there, it seemed, for some time and listening, with this look of vague scorn on her cheekbones, to what sounded to her (so Maya suddenly felt with a momentary flash of solidarity) like bubbles of mutual self-pity rising and bursting. She stared, with a kind of relief, at the one approaching them in the ironed sports outfit, in the gleaming collar and the eternal "*taschentuch*."

"If I was in the hostel," she said, her voice hard, without a hint of sympathy, "she wouldn't be my boss . . . So what are you making here? A Hanukkah lamp—or jugs?"

"But you *aren't*, wise guy," said Hedva bitterly.

"Of course I'm not! Like that it's going to dry and fall apart. You should bake it in a stove."

"I wish we could bake Queen Jezebel!" Yaffa looked at her expectantly, stamping her feet to keep warm.

"It isn't difficult to ride on white asses," said Margarita.

"You've no right to talk anyway," replied Hedva, and Yaffa looked at her with great affection.

"You can say whatever you like to her, then stick out your tongue at her from your roof, you heroine!"

"Smart-ass!" said Yaffa.

"Let's see you open your mouth at her, when you can't get away afterwards with teeth still in it."

Margarita went on looking, with that vague scorn, over the folded crownlike collar.

"I'd say everything to her face," she said. "Afterwards they can take me away in an ambulance."

"That's right, smart-ass," Yaffa grinned at the others, inviting them to grin with her.

"Sure!" said Margarita. "Before I said the first word I'd be beaten to a pulp—by all of you!"

"Not me!" said Yaffa. "I swear, not me!"

"Not anyone," said Hedva. "What's this you're inventing?"

"Do you deny it, do you deny it? Aren't you trying to impress her that you're the best servant! Everyone wants to show her that she's—the mostess!"

"That's right," said Yaffa. "You think I don't remember what you did to me with the broom, Hedva? I didn't want to tell

Margarita before, but now you know what she did to me? She put a broom in my arms in the night, when I was asleep. In the morning they called me Yaffa Broomovitch because they said I'd got married to the broom."

"Bat-Sheva did it," whispered Hedva, her eyes turning in anticipation to Margarita.

"That isn't at all funny," she said. "Not at all. It's very serious."

"You see?" cried Yaffa. "So they can stop calling me that right away! All the time they're making things up! If not—I don't know what I'll do!"

"I know what," replied Margarita. "You'll need a divorce from the broom."

Yaffa recoiled, her weakness exposed, and stared up at the bronze sky.

"Is that what you think?" she howled in pain. "I won't ever get divorced in my whole life!"

The laughter. Again laughter covered everything.

Maya remembered suddenly and ran to the dining room, without enthusiasm, to take her turn at setting the tables. As she distributed the few plates and came to Bat-Sheva's place, she tried to conjure up before her eyes Bat-Sheva's image, radiating dark fear. She saw only the smile of pleasure and the expression of courage. What is it that gives her the power to demand what she wants from another, without fear of the consequences of injury? How is it that she rides on her tongue like a blind race horse and always arrives first at her goal?

She herself, Maya, understood vaguely that the "other person" is a temptation of delusion. Always, in those times of yearning for compassion, for a moment of remission, for someone who'll relieve her, if only for an instant, of this burden of responsibility for herself, as she stretches out feelers all around her, to catch at something that she can wrap herself around—always she feels hurt and diminished. So she is a personality in her own right:

she is the ladder and the climber; she is the bed and the one who sleeps in it. It is only her eyes that look into her eyes. Only when she is thus do they decide she's a "good girl" and leave her alone. This is the only means of making sure that they won't turn against her and wonder about her from a distance, with awe, as if she owes them some debt, to justify her existence—so they won't find in her some excuse to pick a quarrel and oppress her.

It seemed this was her strength, but also her weakness, and Bat-Sheva understood this, as she understood all the others, with that wisdom of intuition. So that the more Maya is anxious to do the other's will—and thus to finish, to escape, to suppress—so the other forces on her fresh processes of pain and Maya can't discover how this thing works; she closes one hole and another, larger one is opened. She shrinks in her presence, making herself small to avoid getting hurt, and this is perhaps the worst thing of all, since she is relieved only when the Queen gives the signal for relief, then is almost happy for a moment, and afterwards, without knowing it, tries to lead everything back to those moments when Bat-Sheva will again give the signal to relax, knowing well enough that any such moment may be paid back doubly.

It is thus perhaps that there was born the supreme assumption that the right of conferring happiness is bestowed on Bat-Sheva, and she looks with displeasure on any happiness that doesn't emanate from her; that anything snatched without her acquiescence or approval turns to a feeling of guilt and impurity; that everything must be shared with her so she can comprehend its full significance; and that it's forbidden to be more successful than her because then the success becomes an enemy, a burden to be apologized for, blurred, repudiated.

From the kitchen came the sound of frying and the smell of Quaker Oats (potatoes had become expensive lately). Suddenly she felt she enjoyed being on duty—here she was, no need to share anything, alone with the gossip of Pani-Paula and Shoshana and the smell of the decayed oilcloth and this sweet, enclosed thing within her that even the Queen cannot invade.

A jump, through the wall, to the world on the other side— shapeless, whispering, hidden—and she feels its expectancy for her. So she has grown beyond the petty details, the horizon retreats and rolls back, and something mighty nods there in her face with a thousand blurred and hovering heads. She prepares herself to meet it and asks "Good?" and it answers her "Very good" while she is still bent over her notebook of poems, and some muffled cry is seeking to draw her to it, wise of heart, bold of spirit: "With us everything will be solved! Between us everything flows freely, only for us is it worthwhile!" Great coils of threads filter out from her brain and her heart to this other side, and somebody—God Almighty—gathers her threads, stretches them, and gazes at them with great eternal eyes.

When she returned to them, later that evening, to call them to supper, she found them yelling at one another, each snatching words from the other's mouth, hugging one another like lunatics and falling on Margarita's neck. To her they seemed miserable and pathetic. A person comes from outside, from the clear air into a stuffy room, and can't understand why those sitting there don't open the windows.

"A stone!" She caught the word.

"Just wait till she throws out her shoes for polishing—then we'll show her! A stone!" Yaffa's hand beat her chest. "Jerusalem stone!"

"*Then* let her try to talk! *Then* let her try giving orders! *Then* you'll see a face!"

Suddenly, in one twinge of the heart, the thing became clear to her, when the word sprang from someone's mouth.

The world gleamed in its hard, metallic beauty: "Boycott!"

"Boycott!" No weapons and no violence! No give and no take, no talking and no listening! Everything simple, everything open, everything permitted!

She jumped over the clods of clay and the puddles. Mud sprayed her legs.

Everything filled with the firewater of freedom!

The drizzle was lit up with the gleam of expectancy.

They sat huddled like rabbits at the half-empty table and served one another with devotion, with melting hearts. Someone suggested that the Quiet Loony should be the one to light the Hanukkah candles.

They looked, excited by their own generosity, at the candle in her hand, the *Shamash*, with which she would light the others. It trembled like a star and was not aimed at the wicks.

Some of the boys urged her on from their places, amused and scoffing good-naturedly, but when one of them stood up to take the *Shamash* from her hand, with an air of dismissiveness, the girls raised a chorus of angry and protective protest, until he withdrew in astonishment. This strong defensive display mounted in response to so feeble an attack immediately aroused the boys.

"What is this?" Salomon stood up defiantly. "What's going on?" And at once he pushed aside the one who had tried to rob her. Of her own accord, the Quiet Loony held out the *Shamash* to Salomon, its flickering light reflected in her bifocals and her chin weak with foolish relief.

"Don't give it to him, Hayyale!" cried the girls. "Don't give it to him! Don't be afraid!"

"Shut your mouths! Old hags!" he laughed maliciously. Genuine malice or false, with him it was never possible to tell the difference.

The half-shadow of Hayyale trembled, hovering on the floor and on the wall, and the candle with it, until Salomon rescued it from her hand.

"Your father's a hag!" Nira snatched it from his hand.

"Hey, what is this?" He wagged his nose at her. "What's happened? Has she had a parcel? Go home, Ninia! Home!" he said and thrust out his hand to her chest to repel her.

She swayed back on her heels but kept a good grip on the candle. "If you don't shift, I'll singe your coxcomb!" she cried.

"I dare you!"

All rose and hurried to watch. He lowered his shining head toward her.

"I dare you! Go ahead!"

"Do it, Nira! Do it, Nira!" cried the girls. "Roast him!" shrilled a thin voice.

The fringes of his quiff flew up and curled backwards. The smell of burning chicken feathers filled the room. She drew back her hand with the candle. Her triumph seemed to defeat her fear of retribution. The Quiet Loony trembled like jelly as Nira again thrust the candle between her weak fingers.

Salomon, who made it a rule never to hit strange women, drew himself up to his full height and laughed. "Next time you come near me I'll make you pregnant! Well? What are you afraid of?" he said seductively. "Come on, this way, baby . . ."

"So?" She stuck out her chin coquettishly. "So? Afterwards you'll have to pay maintenance!"

Everything stood poised on the narrow, dangerous borderline between game and reality.

"Nobody can prove it's me, little hooker!"

She opened her mouth to reply, but he snorted dismissively and leaned his forehead toward the boy closest to him to inspect the damage. He seemed to have won, but the field was surrendered to the Amazons.

"Now light them!" said Nira, her body generously protecting the Quiet Loony.

"Don't want!"

"Don't be afraid of anything. I'll look after you!"

"Don't want, don't like, nathty thmell," she said in a tearful voice.

"Thmell yourthelf!" said Nira and ignited the five angry flames in the Hanukkah lamp.

The Quiet Loony returned slowly to her living space.

When the others returned one by one they were anxious to let them in on the secret, and because they returned one by one to a prepared receptacle, they were absorbed and admitted without difficulty; but as Bat-Sheva approached the house on the last day of the vacation, they realized that they hadn't prepared the shock that was required, and when one of the girls squealed in fright "To the dorms!" Maya answered her with an exasperated snort: "Are you mad? Stay where you are! And don't answer her!" *She* knew she was ready for anything.

"Better up there, maybe, afterwards . . ."

"Coward!" sniffed Maya. Now all the old fears began to rise in her. What's she bringing with her that's so frightening, eh? she asked herself, consolingly. All that's needed is to stand and wait and quicken the pace of the slowly beating heart, until . . .

Bat-Sheva was already climbing the steps to the front door—a venom-bearing hornet.

"Hey, gang!" she cried. It seemed natural to her that they would come to greet her. "Look what I've brought!" she said brightly, calmly, bringing with her an air of carnival, and pointed to the parcels in her hands.

She was wearing the old brown woolen skirt and the old battle dress, looking even shabbier than the other girls. (If she'd come back in something new, fresh!)

They moved apart from one another awkwardly. All the dread stories turned suddenly into fables, the exaggerated claims of overheated minds.

"Oh, there you are Shevale! How nice! When did you arrive?" This was Frieda, emerging from the office, her face soft. "You look, if you'll pardon the expression, like the slaughterer's piglet . . ." She laughed. "Girls, come on, what kind of friends are you? Help her with the parcels! I'll go and set another place for supper!"

A comical moment of hesitation. Everything seemed imaginary, superfluous. Yaffa looked at Maya with a wink, as if expecting her to make the first move. (That's her way of signaling to her, Bat-Sheva, that she, Yaffa, isn't responsible for what's about to happen.)

Bat-Sheva, filled to overflowing with her experiences in the outside world and interested only in the spoils she had brought with her, had not yet put anything to the test. At once she thrust one parcel into the hands of Hedva, simply, without a trace of arrogance, and ran gaily up the stairs.

"Throw that down on the ground, right now!" Nira butted with her elbow the bearer of the parcel.

"I can't!" Hedva stopped dead in her tracks. "I can't," she moaned in despair.

"I knew right away this was gonna happen," snapped Yaffa. Her confidence always grows as that of the other subsides.

The rest of them stared at Hedva—this at least!—and mechanically she dropped the parcel on the damp concrete floor, which showed the brown footprints of the Queen. Now there was no going back, just as the fetus gripped by the forceps cannot escape being born.

"You're all witnesses," said Hedva, bending over the parcel, thinking fearfully of the dirt on its under side. "You're all witnesses that you told me to . . ."

From the second floor they heard the voice of Bat-Sheva chatting casually to one of the boys.

"No talkin' and no answerin'," said Nira, but timidly, without conviction.

A flicker of happiness passed suddenly over Maya's face when she saw the silhouette of the one coming in the door.

"How—did you come—so soon?" Maya asked, feeling much relieved.

"I saw her from the roof, walking along with the parcels," said Margarita. "It's none of my business, perhaps, but if I were you I'd go and play outside."

"Every hole she sticks her nose in," grumbled Hedva.

"Your hole doesn't interest me at all," replied Margarita coldly.

"I think," said Maya, fixing her eyes on the *"taschentuch,"* this time embroidered with little flowers, on the neatly pressed shorts, and on the brooch with the pair of doves in her hair, "I think we should go out into the yard."

"But she'll notice, clever-clogs!" said Hedva. The quivering tip of her nose indicated that were it not for this interfering stranger and all these other geniuses . . .

"But maybe, she won't, anyway . . ." murmured Batya thoughtfully.

"Don't you worry, she'll remember you alright!" she replied.

"You—it's alright for you!" snapped Hedva without fear. Like the rest of them, she knew how to tell the light movements of the weathervane, with those bat-senses of hers—"saying ku-ku-ku and flying off to the chicken coop."

"You should be ashamed!" said Yaffa. "You should be ashamed saying things like that! If you go upstairs, then the boycott's on you too!" She kicked lightly at the parcel, by way of demonstration.

"You'd better shut your mouth," countered Hedva, but she didn't budge. Maya understood her: there's something about this that's intolerable, a scent of degradation, in that it's Yaffa of all people who's waving the flags. An ugly suspicion occurred to her: she's trying to prevent her rival from getting close again to the Queen.

How had she previously imagined the first encounters? Bat-Sheva comes into the house and at once picks a quarrel with somebody—a grievance, a vendetta that she's been hatching all the days of the vacation. And at once ten bodies rush to the defense, and ten tongues! First will come that look of superior impudence. She tries to hunt out allies for herself with the old methods: promises explicit and implicit, forgiveness for past offenses, the blurring of sins. And suddenly—shock and confusion, perplexity, eruption, the revelation of sins, threats of punishment for past offenses; and then—retreat, collapse, dejection. She trembles as they have trembled—sprawled on her side, silent, like a top without a pull string. Like a broken string of beads, she is scattered on the floor, under the beds, in the cracks between the tiles, and no one bends down to retrieve, to gather up . . . Afterwards, when she begins to understand, they offer her, with that generosity of heart that belongs to the oppressed alone, the cord to thread herself upon. Now that she has tasted the torture she has inflicted on others, they forgive her without forcing her to demean herself with repentance. And thus she will learn of the existence of other relationships.

"Lately she hasn't actually done those sorts of things," Maya heard Hedva say.

"And she's protected us in fights with the neighbors," said Batya. "If she hadn't hit that big Persian girl, I don't know what . . ."

"This way we'll just annoy her again, and that's all . . ."

Oh, accursed bellwether! Another moment and the whole flock will drift away to imaginary meadows! Go up! Take flight into the void of the storm, where the clouds collide, to danger and adventure, to the bruised fingertips, to the whirlpool of red and gold! And "Come on, let's go, we'll show her!" Maya cried. Sudden affection for herself, for the righteous stand that she must take, swelled in her.

"No talkin' and no answerin'," shouted Nira and hurried in her footsteps.

"Why do it now?" asked Batya. "Why's it got to be *now*?"

"Now!" croaked Yaffa decisively, and she ran to catch up with them. "Out of my way, I'm first! I'm first, I said!" So Yaffa is again at the head of the line.

"I'm waiting down here," came Margarita's voice from behind. "I can't interfere."

A brief glimmer of regret in the heat of the race.

"If she's got my sunglasses," she heard Batya's whisper in the rear, "take them carefully, so she doesn't notice."

Bat-Sheva stood, her back to them, examining something on

her bed. When she heard the voices she turned, simply: "What a funny thing!" They stopped, panting, their backs against the walls, as if expecting a sudden onslaught. From the corner of her eye, Maya saw those at the periphery slipping away, clumsily, timidly, to avoid the splinters not aimed at them. "Perhaps it isn't so funny after all!" she said suddenly, without thinking, just to get the thing started at last, the sharpened weapons poised to strike. Her guts dissolved in the fluttering warmth of her self-admiration. She felt a silencing pinch on her arm.

"No, it really is awfully funny!" said Bat-Sheva. "In the night we were suddenly woken up. It was scary, such loud knocking at the door—outside some woman was shouting to be let in. Let me in! Murder! Murder! My uncle opened the door. Then she came in all wet, ran straight to my aunt, hugging her and crying and saying two Australian soldiers were chasing her, they'd be here any minute, they must hide her somewhere quick! My uncle went to the kitchen and brought her something to drink. Then he phoned the duty officer at the police station to send someone around. The cop arrived and he had to drag her out to the car because she was already asleep. My uncle knows this woman, she's got a sort of mania, always imagines someone's chasing her, trying to kill her or rape her . . . What he gave her to drink was a sleeping drug, and she was asleep, on her feet! You could've died laughing! Like Berta that time . . ." She turned back to the bed and at once, almost in the same breath, she said: "Just a moment, Hedva, give me the parcel. Awfully funny," she glanced at Maya. "Come on, where's that parcel?"

Hedva blanched, her dread compounded by the effect of this strange story, that was so . . .

"Don't answer!" rose the whisper.

Now it's starting, she thought with a sense of giddy sweetness. But at that moment the thought flashed through her mind: Hedva will be the victim. The joy and relief of one who offers himself, and knows he is not destined to suffer.

"I," mumbled Hedva helplessly, "I . . ." Already she knows she is the sacrificial lamb.

"What did you say?" asked Bat-Sheva. ("Don't say anything!" rose the whisper.)

"It's a bit . . . d–irty."

A tremor passed among them, as if Hedva was spewed out from their midst. Now she was laid, by her own volition, on the pan of the pitiless scales, in dreadful isolation.

"That's alright!" said Bat-Sheva softly. "Give it here."

Maya saw Hedva's eyeball turn toward her, enlarged, and two slow quivers, like the winking eye of an ancient beast. She must atone, she thought. She has to be the victim.

"I forgot, it's downstairs." The dilated eyeball did not budge from Maya's gaze.

"Then go and get it!" Bat-Sheva said in a calm voice.

She saw how, like liquid vaporizing in the test tube over the flame, the fear drained from the faces that surrounded her, until she turned and went.

"I knew it!" croaked Yaffa with a sort of gladness.

She must notice! She *must* notice something! prayed Maya. O God Almighty! Hurry! Give her a quick injection of venom! There she is, delicately arranging her things in their places, as if thus she can exist without them for ever, without thinking of them, without seeing them.

Hedva returned. This was the measure of time: descent, ascent, arrival. She crossed the distance to the bed with head raised high and put down the parcel with deliberate care, as if it were a baby, the wet side up.

"It's dirty here," she mumbled. "I didn't see it before . . . there was water . . ."

"That doesn't matter, it's sack paper," said Bat-Sheva, untying the oiled string. "My aunt packed it for me with sack paper so the rain wouldn't make the things wet. They're building a new shelter at the police station, so they get lots of paper from cement sacks . . .," she said, looking gently at what was inside. "You can use it afterwards to put in your shoes. Come on girls, come and see what I've got for you."

At last she condescends to remember them! Maya stoked the anger in her heart. And it's good she didn't call my name. A moment, if it was possible just for a moment to forget, to peep, like diving into the sea, looking at what's on the seabed and then rising again to the surface.

"Don't answer!" rose the whisper. Why does she have to watch over them all like a dog? Does Yaffa still think she's the boss, the chief boycotter? She winced, bitterly.

Maya felt herself distant from the others on the way to her betrayal. The bed was already within reach of her hand, but suddenly, the friction of a body to her right—a fleeting vision—and to her left the touch of the clothes of another. She turned her head to find them there, by the wall. The wall was empty. Suddenly she realized they were—all of them—on the way. Going perhaps to attack her? Bat-Sheva? Now it's like throwing stones in the open air! Now they are all of them, and she among them, creatures of instinct, more cunning and suspicious than she who waves above the bed, pure and limpid, those brightly coloured objects. Curiosity enfolded her, the novelties and the enervating knowledge that there's no purpose in returning.

They were soft to the touch, bright, pink and smooth, folded into pairs. When she separated them she saw they were whole, almost new, these stockings. All these things that she brought with her were until yesterday the property of cousin Tamarin from Kefar Saba. Now, when she puts on these stockings she'll feel on her legs something that makes her respectable, flawless. Maya didn't even remember to draw a comparison with what had fallen to the lot of the others.

In the yard the games followed one another with the same natural rhythm. It seemed there was no greater relief than that of rebels whose rebellion has failed.

Margarita came down to the yard when she heard their voices. She didn't seem surprised, and in her face there was no sign of recent memories or of scorn, and Maya was grateful to her for this, as she played with them at "new donkey" and "taking the patient to the hospital." As the game progressed she noted the lively, exuberant face of Nira, the incipient breasts of Yaffa, jiggling comically, and the wild and triumphant expression of Bat-Sheva, taunting her and running from her.

Suddenly she sensed that *she* knew. At that moment the affirming eyes of the Queen hung on her. Why on her of all people? Terror froze her to the spot. Perhaps in some careless moment they had chattered among themselves. Perhaps when she stood as "donkey" and they chased one another round the house. And perhaps they have laid on her responsibility for the thing, and a plot has been woven against her, a plot that is already taking effect.

25
FATA MORGANA

In all this there was something ominous and gloomy. To return night after night to the tensions that grind without luster.

They would wander among the hills, prisoners of themselves, descending the road to the village and ascending again, until the cycle led them to her room, to the torments by the flickering light of the candle, to her drowsing and sudden awakening in his arms, as if she's trying to forget and to remember, while the needle grates and grates in the flesh of the record emptied of its music. He could have taken her by force, but there was always the same repressed fear that he would destroy the beauty of things and cause her to raise the drawbridge to her heart. Cautiously, tortuously wrestling with her! God Almighty!

Sometimes she went to the city and returned depressed, ignoring him or looking feverish, and then returning to him, to their "conversations," hinting to him with self-mortification that she isn't destined for his altar. Everything then took on a misty third dimension, its purpose elusive, though it improved his writing. And then one night he let her alone and sat on the bed in his undershirt.

"Talk! Say something! Curse me, revile me! Damn me to hell! One ounce of abuse instead of all these timid endearments of yours! Suppressed passions, contorted face, bodies in the pangs of . . . Are you afraid of the facts! *These* facts are much more demeaning! I hate these suicidal impulses, this *fata morgana*, this false act!"

Suddenly it seemed to him that she was whimpering behind his back. He turned to her, to the lank hair, to the damp dress crumpled by his pawing. He probed with his hand and found the tears on her face.

"You yourself don't know, Friedi," he softened his voice. "You don't know how much . . . these pure, genuine fountains . . . and perhaps it's just because of that. Behold, I bend my knee before you, Madamoiselle Auerbach, black dress coat, butterfly collar, outside awaits the carriage to the stars . . . the horses are stamping their hooves and straining at the bit . . . ah, yes, the orchids . . ." He fumbled with his hands on the chair. "Where are the orchids, damn it?"

In spite of herself, she laughed for a moment with deep affection, opened her mouth to say something, but immediately turned her eyes away.

"No, say it!" He gripped her arm, feeling the roughness of the blisters. "Spit it out!"

"It would all sound funny, theatrical, contrived."

"No more than what's been said before!"

"It's like . . .," she said hesitantly, her face to the candle. "How much time does it take to form a pearl, Boria?" she asked suddenly, ashamed of sounding funny, theatrical. "I don't want this little pearl to turn into a button . . . a button that passes from hand to hand, that every man will try to fit to his shirt cuffs."

"How is it that you have such accurate knowledge of the nature of men, Friedi?" he asked with gentle mockery.

"And then to the laundry!"

"Your analogies are very flattering, Friedi . . ."

"No, no . . . Boria . . . I don't mean . . . not you, Boria. Maybe once people knew how to love," she said suddenly, with warmth. "Once they knew how to love out of ignorance and mystery. Where today is Odysseus, tying himself to the mast of the ship so he won't fall into the hands of the Sirens? Where is Penelope, unraveling her tapestry for him every night? Today you are all so knowledgeable and wise, working out the price for everything in advance and assessing the damage in advance."

"Love," he laughed, "oh, love! Love was created, apparently, on Sabbath eve at twilight, along with writing and the demons. Thus we can explain the fact that we can never distinguish between wolf and dog. The prevailing fashion of our age, Frieda, commands that everything that looks like a wolf is in fact a dog. The one great privilege that it gives him is to be a dog with vulpine complexes." She chuckled with a sort of touching embarrassment.

"And why do you always think of yourself as an object, my pearl? Why? Why not as one who takes?"

"Because I have foolish pride!" And suddenly she was whimpering again: "Foolish, foolish, foolish! I remember how I was a few days before you came here. I went up the hill alone, in the night! Always alone! Because of this pride! There was no living soul around. I whistled some allegretto and felt that any moment I'd fall on the road and not want to get up."

She regained her composure and looked at him, without wiping her nose.

"I'm cowardly, petty, foolish . . . torturing you just so . . . someone will share with me what I have here, in this mad little house!"

She fumbled for her handkerchief and, not finding it, wiped her face unconsciously on the pillowcase.

"Who is he?" he said in a flash of insight. "Who is he?"

She didn't deny it, just closed her eyes and shook her head dismissively.

"I'll prove to you that he's nothing, nothing!" he murmured in a fever of shame. "A delusion! Not worthy of all that you suffer and preserve for his sake. He who has no feelings, whose heart is dead to poetry, who will never sit with you to hear Beethoven."

Guesses flashed through the mind—images of the sentry, of some Tarzan-like divorcé who turns up from time to time and talks with Frieda in Polish. That nameless lover from whom she returns depressed or elated . . . and all of them tormenting themselves with her, like him on the creaking bed, or exposing her fastidious flesh to the light of the stars.

"Who is he?" He squeezed her arm.

"You're hurting me!" she replied and twisted her face away.

He should get up and go. He put on his shirt, his back turned to her and his eyes on the dimmed lamp, on the inner flame that never loses its shape. At the door he waited for a moment for her to call out, but he could not bear the silence and turned to look at her. She smiled at him weakly.

He decided to save himself by willpower. He had saved himself from many things by willpower. Suddenly the awareness that he was mortal formed inside him. Until now Dov Markovski had been an infinite clothed in darkness, and his life a bundle to be used economically. Suddenly he found himself in the middle of the equation, at the equal sign. He must begin to apportion his time, so the value of the unknown quantity will grow and not be dissipated into fractions.

Now, as he thought of her in his room, he considered her thick ankles. She had the potential to age quickly, because of her full, over-ripe maturity. In his more rational moments he would find in her the nervous twitches at the root of the eyebrows, the blisters, the chewed fingernails, and the eczema that periodically attacked her fingers.

. . . He sees her in the avenue, walking beside a stranger. When her eyes meet his she smiles at him with the weak indifference of a happiness that's above that of mere mortals. She even introduces him to the man with good-natured affection. The experience hurts him dreadfully, especially the smile of happiness that at long last she has earned.

. . . No! She's in the theater beside some brute. The face of a butcher and a red neck. Their eyes wander among the rows, and she notices him before the lights go down. In the interval, when he looks again at the empty seats, he remembers the regret in her eyes.

. . . No, no! He's a scarred theoretician. In the encyclopedias— under the letter "M"—you may already find his bespectacled face smiling over two or three dense columns of appraisal. The high-school students curse the day he was born when they must learn his poems for the matriculation exam. With the outbreak of the Revolution, he is freed from Acre prison in a violent action in which he himself takes part. The literary critics always amuse him with their comparisons between his polemical essays and his bitter love poems. Then, at one of his public readings, he sees in the front row a head like dust and moist eyes.

. . . He meets her in the street, years later. On her third finger a wedding ring, clutching a shopping bag. "Oh, I've been looking for you," he says to her with a friendly smile, but she replies with a challenge:

"A boy like you—if he had looked, he would have found!"

She has already learned to be "like all the rest": at home, kosher bread; outside, occasional cream cakes. She is no longer keen on music, and she has come to realize that the miracle in the life of a woman isn't the man. But she clings to him, to Dov, as to one who gives positive weight to her scales. Their lovemaking has the taste of the rejuvenation of withered leaves.

The same week Markovski went down to Tel Aviv and met by chance the woman he intended to meet. Afterwards, as he expected, he felt irritating insipidness as he watched the flaccid body dressing before him in the cold electric light and saw the ludicrous imprints of her girdle.

Before, they exchanged those vulgar hints that immediately aroused their mutual desire. Afterwards, came those standard "confessions," designed to justify her rapid submission, and the cliché of flattering comparison with the prowess of the others. But the comparison fueled his pride and filled him with satisfaction. And it was he who suggested an additional rendezvous. He found in her the lowest common denominator of them all, including Frieda, and his heart was infused with a kind of peace. She was an actress in the satiric theater, darling wife of one of the activists of the trade union movement, who loved the lively atmosphere of the theater more than the theater itself. With great difficulty he succeeded in persuading her not to recite his poetry at her "cultural evenings" in the workers' clubs. "These are poems that can only be read by bespectacled eyes like mine," he told her with a kind of self-mockery.

Now he felt himself immune. Meeting Frieda in the house, he could look into her eyes without emotion, even with light-hearted scorn, which provoked in them flashes of surprise.

As time passed, and the affair with the satiric actress cooled, he began to avoid delving deep into personalities. It was as if now he was concerned purely with limbs: legs, bosom, buttocks, or hips. He found a new and pleasurable sense of masculinity, a kind of delight in the physical. The glorious disdain of one who sits in the National Library and devours detective stories, while opposite him poor lunatics brood their eggs, bowing their heads day after day over the decipherment of some faded manuscript.

These carnal adventures justified for him the new distinction whereby he attributed to others qualities lacking in himself. He always suspected deep down that the sensitivity of others was greater than his, that they too expected some elevation, some contact with the spirit of the Godhead, and perhaps more so than him. Now he cultivated shallowness and moral torpor.

He began, unconsciously, to seek Frieda's hostility, criticizing her speech mannerisms, pouncing on her mistakes, exposing the futility of her opinions, mocking her taste in clothes, encouraging minor quarrels between them. But those covert little smiles, which they used to exchange at the sight of some petty rift between Pani-Paula and Shoshana, did not cease, and with them there would rise again the familiar tension, though he knew that her tension was much greater. He abhors this tension of hers, which always seems to challenge, defiantly, his new perceptions of the nature of man.

"**I** dreamed about the cards," said Salomon when he got up in the morning. "Cards are the surest thing in life." Salomon had gone back to sleeping in the "Casino." Before this he had refused to stay any longer in the "Invalids' Home" and had slept for a whole week on the balcony.

"You just put down the first card—you're lost forever . . . there's no hope for you," said Ketzele to himself, with the regretful wisdom of maturity.

"Only for big money," said Salomon. "I'll only play for big money, not backgammon or any of those kids' games."

"The first card and you're lost," insisted Ketzele in the same pious tone, his hair masking his eyes as he fumbled for his shoes at the foot of the bed.

"You think you're some kind of a rabbi, huh?" the other thickened his voice into the gangster snarl that so enthralls the girls. "Stick around, you'll learn what hands are for! You think cards are just useless bits of paper! You'll learn what hands are for. You'll learn! My uncle from the casino always says: 'That bastard has the hands of a juggler. With those hands he'll squeeze the world out like a wet towel!' Here—look!"

He held out before him bronzed hands with delicate elongated joints, not a trace of grease between them and the back of each finger embellished with the gleam of its inner whiteness.

"Come back ten years from now, you lot!" He turned to the rest of the boys, all of them yawning the mute yawns of early morning, like voiceless choristers. "Come to the casino at night, only at night—two or three o'clock in the morning—and you'll see Salomon! Taking off his diamond rings, putting them down there on the table, spreading talc on his hands, he clicks his fingers—a stack of chips! Turns over a card—another stack of chips. *Halas, ya Effendim**! The day's work over! King Solomon is going to the hotel to sleep (*yawning*)! Now they all start to weep: 'No, no, Monsieur Salomon! Take my wife, take my orchard, only don't go to the hotel!'—'*Silence, ya Effendim!* I don't need your wife now. Tomorrow night maybe. Now King Salomon is going to sleep at the hotel!' Salomon goes, the diamond rings he leaves behind on the table, on purpose, but no one will dare touch them even with his eyes. That's how you'll see me . . ."

Warily the boys pretended to be listening to what Abie called "the morning edition of the Wisdom of Solomon."

"You put down the first card," Ketzele persisted stubbornly. "You're lost. No hope for you!"

"Hope! Hope!" the juggler flared up, like a burning rag dipped in kerosene. "Swallowed a frog, have you? Is your father a detective?

---

* Finished, you landlords!

"Don't you talk about my father, you!" croaked Ketzele suddenly, as if fulfilling an obligation, but he stopped at once.

"Tough guy, eh? If I wanted, I could mash you into the ace of spades!"

The others froze on the threatening brink, hating Salomon for insisting on dislodging the halo of sanctity from his friend's head, but Ketzele had lapsed back into drowsiness, rummaging under the bed with clumsy hands and the mask of hair drooping over his eyes.

"Throw them," they all prayed silently when at last he found his shoes, which had been right under his eyes all the time; but, still crouching, he drew one stiff and twisted shoe onto an even stiffer foot, his fingers groping blindly for the lace holes.

"The other shoe!" The unspoken chorus of hope hung like a vapor in the void of the "Casino".

"He's already telling Salomon what to do! Thinks he's so important! Some kind of Messiah!" The Haifa boy continued the provocation, his body poised to ward off a blow. "Ask in the Bat-Galim casino what Salomon was like at eight years old—no one would believe it! How he beat them all at blackjack, poker, *chemin de fer, chemin de* . . . until the clever folks from Social Aid caught up with him. Who asked for their aid? They take him to a fat socialist bitch. Two eyes looking out of her ass, laughing, thinks Salomon's going to laugh back. What's she laughing at? Does she think I'm her gigolo? Salomon doesn't give a damn. She starts off with flattery: 'I hear you're an unusually glever boy . . .'

" 'That's right, lady, unusually glever . . .'

"Suddenly she takes her cards out of the drawer—so big that you could eat bouillabaisse off them. 'Like to play gards, Zolomon?' Zolomon! Salomon could have made her sell her big underwear in the docks. But I say: 'I never saw papers like these in my life, lady.' Then she says: 'Alright, we leave ziz, Zolomon.' She puts the dinner plates back in the drawer, lays her udders on the table, starts asking questions: 'Ven did Momma die? Vy you not going to zgool? Night und day gambling, poor kid, you must be loosing much on ze cards.' "

" 'Losing? Salomon has never lost in his life!' That's how she trapped me, the fat bitch!"

The boys went on with their morning activities, still praying in their hearts.

"Before they chucked me into this place, my uncle said: 'Ninio, you be a good boy in there, so they don't send you to the 'young offenders.' In there they spoil your hands, but don't forget how to play! It's your fortune!' Lost forever, you say! Is your father a detective? A secret policeman?"

"Ketzele!" said Maya, who stood listening by the door. "Dov's calling you!" She saw the blood drain from the face of the boy, who finished dressing quickly and passed by the juggler with averted eyes. But at the door he whispered to her: "What does he want?" And at once he turned his head and said: "Abie, don't go anywhere this afternoon!"

"Dirdy dog!" Salomon scowled and bared his teeth, in the style of Errol Flynn, watching the flagship of the Armada slip out of the range of his cannons. The door slammed in reply. "Son-of-an-enema!" the Haifa boy shouted at the door. "Australian sperm!"

Taught by experience, the boys slipped like lizards from the "Casino." Poor Salomon—with one hand you can only play "patience."

By afternoon the little flame of the morning had already, as usual, been extinguished and its cinders scattered among the activities of the day.

Now there was a ball between the feet of the boys. How quick they are to forget everything, to spend whole days kicking happily at a mangy tennis ball, or at some leprous scrap of rubber rescued from a garbage dump, and now there was a real leather ball between their feet, a new one (donated by Mr. Glick in place of his sons, whom he took away to live with a new stepmother, and nobody objected to the exchange). They were training to become members of the national team within seven or eight years.

Because of this, they didn't notice the beautiful little woman who stood in the middle of the field—though recently they had become used to visits of women—and paid no attention to the words she said: "*Yozhi! Yozhi! Undeh Yozhi?* Where is Yozhi?"

In the center, by the kickoff line, they finally became aware of her presence, but before the disruption became too much for them she had already managed to intervene in the game, butting the ball right over the keeper's head and persisting with her question, until they gathered around her panting in bemused admiration, rubbing their bruised knees, and some impudent girls even invaded the pitch to sniff at the mascara caked on her eyelashes— a rare species of insect not seen round here since Berta's departure—and to inspect the lace undergarment peeping from her neckline and the leather thongs binding her shoes to her pretty ankles. The regal midget ignored this expert appraisal and her eyes searched blindly among the blurred faces.

"*Undeh Yozhi?*" She asked plaintively, in Romanian.

"*Un—deh?*" The whisper passed round the yard amid clucks of mirth.

"Not here, lady!" said Hedva, and she grinned in her face with admiring scorn.

"*Maman,*" a weak violin-voice suddenly rang out above their heads. The face of a degenerate Ketzele peered down from the balcony, wearing the same angelic expression of the morning— a painted cherub from a child's picture book, his hair stretched back tightly over his scalp.

"*Yozhi!*" The woman screeched and at once waved an admonishing finger at him to warn him not to disappear, as if he were a charmed illusion, and Yozhi did indeed disappear. She threw up at the empty balcony a barrage of sentences in some Babel language, then gave up and began running around the house to find the entrance, all the others scurrying at her heels like the rats of Hamelin.

Beside his bed stood the decadent version of Ketzele, as scrubbed and nauseous as a timid bridegroom, but the pretty woman immediately grabbed his ear and his pockets to look into them, pointing to the stains on his trousers and the fly tied up with knotted thread (how alike are these self-revealing mothers!). But Ketzele-Yozhi, pure-eyed angel, surrendered his body in silence.

Abie approached, a pepsodent smile stuck to his mouth, and at once, as if she'd known from the start he would come, the woman flung in his smiling face everything that bubbled inside her.

"She says you're a dirty stinking gypsy," said Abie (now Maya understood why Ketzele had reminded him to stay with him in the afternoon) and didn't stop smiling. The son looked at the mother with melting eyes, as if the words were very agreeable to his heart.

"What am I to say to her, Yehoshua?" said Abie between his smiling teeth, and they all remembered that he too was Romanian. The woman turned to him impatiently to hear his reply, and he told her, in a grown-up voice, something that aroused gasps of dubious amazement. The pretty woman, still not satisfied, came closer and lifted the shining chin of the angel, and he unconsciously scattered around him eyes that begged for assistance. Disappointed, she let go of his chin and said something long.

"She asks," Abie smiled, "A: Why doesn't her respected son not condescend to look her straight in the eyes? And B: Doesn't her respected son love her anymore?"

The word "love" provoked giggles among the onlookers, just like that, without shame—"love"!

"What's your answer, dear boy? Answer A . . ."

"Make something up, quick!" snapped the angel, the sword of his glare decapitating all the sniggering spectators.

Abie made a lengthy speech. God forgive him for his improvised concoctions and inventions. Just listen! All Europe speaks from his throat! Aramaic and Turkish too!

And all felt dumb admiration for him when a little smile opened on the lips of the pretty woman. But her changes of mood were like the changes of color and shape in a kaleidoscope. She collapsed on the bed with a new howl of desolation, beating the straw pillow with her little fists and exposing the dark roots of her hair (how alike are these self-revealing mothers!). The interpreter looked at her for a moment, like a man who can't endure a woman's weeping, and this look that she caught served only to intensify it. She sat up and smeared the mascara over her nose and chin as if on purpose, to stir compassion in the heart of her son, who stood staring at her foolishly. Gradually her whimpers took on a tune, and the word "Yozhi," which accompanied every stanza, gave them rhythm, like a mournful recitation in memory of the saints in a school yard. One of the girls could bear it no longer; she turned and escaped to those who already stood by the door, clucking to one another "eshtipeshti" before each fresh guffaw of laughter. Maya stayed where she was, always one to enjoy a family scene, but before Abie's translation came the woman had already driven from the door the girls weeping with laughter and was shouting into the hallway: "*Le professeur! Monsieur le professeur!*"

Ketzele-Yozhi stared entranced at Abie, as if through him he could see his mother running and shouting in the corridors.

What was it that drove the shouting woman to climb, for the first time, from the brothels of Hayarkon Street to the top of the holy mountain? A simple story—they threw a stone in the pond and wakened the frogs, and we can't do otherwise than tell it as briefly and concisely as possible, while the woman is out there, shouting in the corridors and searching for "*le professeur.*"

Immediately after Pesach the yeshiva boys set to work and sent gardeners to cut down the young pine grove that separated them from the hostel, so the trunks would dry in time for the festive burning on Lag Ba-Omer. And when they found them suitably dried they dragged them, by the sweat of their black coats and side-curls, down the track leading eastward, toward the valley at the foot of the hill, and as if this valley had been somehow "pledged" to them, they erected in it a great cone, piled up every twig and every scrap of paper that came to hand, and when they finished their work they returned to their evening prayer.

Now this flat valley, which covered a span of one square kilometer, at a modest estimate, was, as we know, the property of the boys of the hostel, who had adopted it for their games. It was also the stadium for the games of the local football league. That very Lag Ba-Omer had been scheduled for a crucial match with a team from the institution for the "educationally subnormal" in a nearby settlement who, it is a well known fact, always make the best football players.

One day before the eve of Lag Ba-Omer, at the hour of pleasant Sabbath repose, a fearful cry of alarm was heard, and when the boys of the hostel rushed in panic down the hill toward the focus of the cry, and with them a party of Hungarian women in Sabbath turbans and flannel dresses who had popped up out of their burrows one after the other, there was revealed before their eyes, down there in the flat valley, a *minyan* of yeshiva boys, yelling at the tops of their voices and gazing with longing at the glorious wooden pyre, raising on high a sacrificial offering to the sun, crowned with a wreath of yellow crackling flame. . . . And before anyone had time to think of the danger to life, etc., the fire had already subsided in a rustling heap of embers. Only then did the boys from the hostel see Ketzele beyond the fire, imprisoned between two yeshiva students, his arms pinioned in their hands, wriggling his body, making faces and winking at them, as if without this it wouldn't have been clear to all who it was who sent up this strange fire.

Of no avail was the atonement pyre that they were forced to

erect at the conclusion of that same Sabbath, with the appearance of the first star, and the league match was a dismal failure, transferred to the miserly backyard of the institution, under the irritating, scornful eyes of the "educationally subnormal." And when the school boys assembled next day, as usual, in the prayer hall, the headmaster, a habitually cultivated and lenient man, spoke and, jutting forth his black beard toward the window that faces Jerusalem, he laid upon Yehoshua Mandelbaum, known as Ketzele, "The great and terrible Ban of the Holy Pillar and all the Curses and Execrations . . . with the Ban of Yehoshua Son of Nun and the Bans ordained by the Sages of the Great Court of Sanhedrin . . . to rid our school of this youth!" And all the excited youths answered "Amen!" The rabbi of that yeshiva, the famous *Mitnagged* Reb Yitzhak Brumberger, bestirred himself and presented his petition to the local council, and at the door of every shop and every prayer house, these words addressed the faithful:

Before the eyes of the Congregation of the Pious and the Godly, Citizens and Leaders, Elect of the Convocation of Israel, sitting in the Councils of the Wise . . . Hark to the mighty Voice awakening, as a jealous Man of War, calling to Arms against all Instigators and Seducers . . . A Voice crying, in the Wilderness prepare a Way, uproot Impediments, roar upon those Adversaries, burn out the Thorns from the Vineyard, trample them with Bow and Arrow . . . Such Men are as the Moth to Ephraim and as the Rot to the Sons of Judah, a Root bearing a Head of Wormwood in our City . . . For they are Children that have not listened to the Law of our Lord . . . And we shall surely drive them from our Boundary and banish them utterly . . .

The words of Rabbi Gaon Yitzhak Yakov Brumberger, may his Light shine, to the Congregation of the Faithful of Kiryat Shkak.

A proper execration! Kiryat Shkak, which until now has bitten its lips and born these piles in silence, no longer has the strength to sit still. By night they throw stones and garbage at the shutters of the hostel, and by day they gather their virtuous offspring home whenever the shadow of the harlots' children walks the street. The shopkeepers of the village loudly remind one another, each at the door of yesterday's hated rival, that these misers have imported even their lentils and groats from Tel Aviv; even food coupons they don't depend on, and all that they need, and on extended credit, are the few loaves of bread and one cup of yogurt between Purim and the Fast of Esther, when one of them has an attack of diarrhea (and they have the guts of ostriches!), and they owe the debts of a *minyan* of Jacobs for a whole sanctuary of Rachels and Leahs . . . not to mention the Red secretary and that whore who used to be there, the hives they have wrecked, green gardens they have trampled, kiosks they have robbed, virgins they have all but ravished, pretending they've no money! Guests who have made themselves kings of the castle!

Never had Kiryat Shkak been graced with a more august convocation of sages than that of the Agudists in black satin coats and yarmulkas and unlaced shoes along with the Mizrachists in English wool coats and yarmulkas pinned on and laced-up shoes, who met in solemn conclave to pass sentence on the hostel. One brings testimony from the Gaon of Vilna and another from Rabbi Kook, and from more sitting comes more wisdom, and as the hand of one is in the frock coat of the other, and the hand of one in the yarmulka of the other, suddenly, miraculously, above their bowed heads, the small Workers' Coalition on the local council has united to sit around the clock with the jubilant Markovski, "to undermine the institutions of theocracy and to leave not one stone standing!" And lo, under every lifted stone, amid the dust of usury, a swarm of lice and deception, worms of "you grease my palm and I'll grease yours," by the table of the dining room the coffee pots exploded and under every beard they found the face: under every sparse beard, a toady; under every heavy beard, a lecher. In the twinkling of an eye, the Righteous Priest becomes a Decreer of Falsehood; all the rabbis, sextons; all the sextons, rabbis, and while they are going barefoot, the village has been filled with the footprints of sons of Lilith and the demons; not to mention the labor taxes, devouring a portion and drinking a tithe, going into the pockets of ten idlers, and before any has had time to probe the defeatism of one, the opportunism of the other, already letters are speeding to the newspaper editors, appeals are piercing the heart of Tel Aviv, and committees of Socialist women in orthopedic shoes come creeping up from the city, wandering about the rooms and saying "tut-tut-tut," and the clamor reaches the heavens until the institutions declare e–e–nough! Have we not enough problems with the time of emergency and the children of soldiers who are walking the streets, that you must foist upon us the children of peace? And all are now commanded to hold their spit until the final cease-fire and to pay their taxes on time to the local authorities and to obey the instructions of the civil guard and not to defecate in the shelters!

And before Markovski had time to slam the door and shout "Conspiracy!" they had already appointed in the local council a deputy vice-chairman from the Workers' Coalition (ha! ha!), and in the hostel, an inspector of *Kashrut* on behalf of the Rabbinate (ha! ha!), and put all the stones back in their places. A lean peace is better than a victory dripping lard! The women in orthopedic shoes stopped coming and the tut-tutting stopped because, anyway, the hostel had been condemned to slow death. The pupils returned to the school and desolation remained in the street of the village, and Ketzele remained. He had been sentenced to go "to the Devil," in Batya Wolfson's own words, and it was his mother who came to plead for his life. And here she is, returning weeping from the corridor and with her "*le professeur.*"

"Look what you've done to her," said Markovski as he entered, supporting the woman who alternately wept on his arm and spoke to Abie. "What's she saying?"

"She says she's going to kill herself . . . she says, all that she's done is so something good will come of him, so he won't be a cruel bastard like his father."

"That's enough, that's enough," grumbled Dov, and he led toward the bed with great care the woman who had now calmed down in a miraculous manner and was dabbing at her swollen cheeks and eyesockets before a small mirror. "You don't have to . . . Explain to her that if the business hadn't offended the religious types, he wouldn't be in trouble!"

Ketzele moved his eyes in disbelief from his mother's face to the face of the secretary, but the woman began uttering dry, piercing shrieks, aimed at the boy, who was faithfully interpreting.

"!!!!!!!!!"

"She says: 'One day he'll need a mother—and then it'll be too late!' "

"!!!!!!!!"

"She says: 'He'll call out to her from the gallows!' "

"!!!!!!!!"

"She says: 'Better to give birth to stones!' "

"Alright! That's enough!" said Markovski faintly, but whoever wanted, listened. "When she says things like that, don't translate, just say 'Same thing.' "

Ketzele screwed up his eyes for a moment but didn't dare move tongue against palate—the gates of a "closed institution" lay in wait for the movements of his mouth.

Henceforward all that came to the ears of Markovski and to the ears of the others from within this bitter soul—pouring out its woes, confessing and seeking support from this intelligent young man, so attentive behind his spectacles—was a short sentence accompanied by the weak smile of the interpreter. She continued to described a world of suffering and hope, a world reduced in Abie's mouth to: "Same thing, same thing, same thing."

The episode was concluded in the days that followed, perhaps after cringing apologies on the part of certain people, and its importance was no longer apparent. It's possible that Ketzele atoned for his deed by performing tasks for the yeshiva, or perhaps by saying prayers of repentence, but the punishment itself had no meaning for him and was soon forgotten.

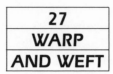

Senya Wolfson had just re-
turned from his tour of the dormitories with Pani-Paula, who
pinned certain hopes on his visit. Hiding behind her corpulent
back, he peeped out and smiled at Frieda, like a child playing
hide-and-seek.

Markovski watched her closely. She ignored the guest, or was
pretending to, but suddenly she turned angrily on Salomon, who
stood there watching: "Shlomo! Go and wash! Go at once, Shlomo!"

"Blackie!" cried Senya to the boy, provocatively. "Come here,
Blackie! Show us what you've got there on your arm. Have you
noticed?" He turned to Markovski. "Have you seen what he's got
there?"

Between the two of them there was a strange entente, unad-
mitted, of two men who desire the same woman.

"Frieda, Frieda, there's no water up there again!" Nira burst suddenly into the dining room. "I soaped myself and . . .," but at once she was silenced by the sight of the Wolfson woman's son.

"There's never any water pressure in the evening," replied Frieda dully, indifferent, or pretending to be so.

"They're watering the orchards," said Markovski. He felt himself isolated, empty, and humorless. "Always, at this time . . ."

"Bring the buckets into the kitchen," Frieda commanded. "But let's have none of your splashing games!"

As she went out the girl peered again at the son of the Wolfson woman, who smiled at her with great friendliness, and didn't know what to do. From outside came the cries of the children as they scampered about gathering buckets.

"So what have you got there?" asked Senya.

"It's a tattoo," Salomon replied with dignity. On the white underside of his arm were tattooed a pair of hands in handcuffs, and above them the letter "H".

"It's very nice," said the guest admiringly, his hand clutching the boy's arm. "But what is it?"

"Did you see the blankets, Sir?" trumpeted the "inventory and estate manageress." "Did you see the blankets? If I had pillowcases, then at least I could send them out to pick grass and fill them . . . Better to cover them with grass than . . ."

"My uncle from the casino has got one exactly the same," said Salomon, looking with hostility at the interfering old hag. The eyes of the guest were fixed on him, encouragingly.

"There was a Greek with them in the prison who knew how to tattoo. All the others wanted girls or Stars of David, but my uncle asked for this, so every time he looks at his arm he'll remember the prison. This 'H' up here," he pointed to the place with the air of a tour guide, "this 'H' is the signature of the artist. Two hands and a chain in the middle. When my uncle came back to the casino he made me and my cousin get the same. At a place on Shemen Beach."

"Did it hurt?"

"Not a bit! Only at the end. They give you a drug, so you won't feel anything. At school I hid it under my sleeve—it's against the Torah."

A column of girls with pans and clanking buckets, like a well-disciplined demonstration, was already crossing the dining room on its way to the kitchen, from which came the sound of vessels filling.

"It hurts only at the end," continued Salomon, his arm still stretched out, trying to remain the focus of attention now that Pani-Paula had succeeded in diverting the ear of the guest, and suddenly, quite casually, he stuck out his foot and a girl sprawled flat on the floor in a pool of water to the sound of clattering tin and the yells of the cook.

Wolfson hurriedly put out his hand to lift her up, then drew back a wet lock of hair from her face. At the same time he laughed without anger at Salomon, who walked out with mincing gait.

"Do you know whose chick this is?" said Boria in Russian, pointing to the girl who was suppressing her tears. The guest, the smile at Salomon still fixed on his face, replied in the negative and without interest.

At that moment Maya took in the triumphant look of satisfaction flashing in Boria's spectacles, and the amused astonishment of the guest who cried, "No, no!"

"Why not?" she replied, cheekily, to carry on the conversation, or to please and amaze, but at the same time she felt offended because she was wet and she'd bruised her knees in the fall, and because she knew she ought to protest when they bring up things that they shouldn't, but the amused astonishment of the man provided her a kind of compensation. Meaning, this is a scandal! All the time there's someone turning up here who throws her into sickly-sweet confusion with his amazement at her being kept in this place.

"Hermoni's daughter?" cried the guest with a pleasure that she almost understood. "How wonderful, dramatic, by God! If I hadn't seen with my own eyes . . . No, now, now I see ex–act–ly! Oh, what an encounter! Hell! The face of Kashka Hermoni!" He laughed again and explained to Frieda things that she already knew well enough and to which she therefore replied with indifference, something that hurt Maya, but she at once set about neatening her hair, with an obscure sense of urgency.

"Don't go yet, don't go, Sir!" bellowed the cook before going out. The conversation was boring her. "I still have things to say to you."

"I know it all!" he replied. Without taking his eyes from the back of Frieda, he said, as she too left the room, "So, so! In a philanthropic institution, ay-ay-ay! Only this week I saw him in the Can-Can with that tall woman, Navcovitch's wife from the Jewish Agency . . . extra fine, with beauty spots on the . . . ay-ay!"

"Could you tone it down a bit?" murmured Markovski in Yiddish.

"It's fantastic, quite fantastic," insisted the guest with a kind of growing wonder. "And how come he has such a fair daughter? His wife's so dark-skinned, isn't she?" he asked in Russian.

He saw her father, this week! Obscure dread took hold of her. "That's his second wife!" replied Boria. Dread and disbelief. The knowledge that he is alive, existing, real, outside the sphere of her awareness, cast on her now a shuddering sense of annihilation, as if she had ceased to be and had turned into a disembodied shape, knowing that they live and exist without her, carrying on their lives without a thought for her.

"Oh, it's true, it's true! Oh, naughty-naughty!" The guest accentuated his mounting enjoyment by sticking hands in his pockets and tossing his head this way and that.

How is it that such people always know everyone and everything? There's no way of escaping, and everyone has a key to this suitcase and rummages about in the rags inside it.

"Not true!" she snapped, disgusted with herself for her lack of understanding. "You didn't see him at all!" He must deny it, deny it! Just so he won't look at her this way, as if she's a symbol of something that pleases and fascinates him, like the tattoo on Salomon's arm.

"He saw, of course he saw!" said Boria, a little astonished that she understood their conversation but trying to put things right. "He sent you, your father, his best wishes and he . . ."

"Best wishes, that's right," said Wolfson, his eyes radiating goodwill. "Your father sent you . . ."

"Run along, run along, little daughter . . . go and change your clothes," Markovski prodded her gently—to stress his closeness to her, she thought angrily. "I've told you a thousand times not to call me that!" she cried, but her voice was mute, as if all this was happening in a vacuum. She was scared by the pure curiosity reflected in the face of the guest.

"I'll be damned!" he said suddenly, the look in his eyes confirming that now she pleased him. "Till this moment I had doubts that this really was her father's daughter . . . now off you go, *cholera!*"

She hurried away to find the other girls, to touch them and hear their voices, but even they seemed unreal.

There were no drearier and more turbid days than the first days of freedom, after the bonds were released. When the Queen went away, suddenly, to live with her mother in the pension, without one backward look at the "Fifth Heaven," they at once became liquid matter, a sewer without banks, looking at their reflections in a stagnant pool.

Wolfson collapsed onto a low chair, stretching out his limbs, full of contentment and delight with himself.

"Well, well! She's sort of close to you, isn't she?" He stamped his shoe on the newly scrubbed floor, to detach something that had stuck to the sole. "Now I remember, Borinka!"

"Better not carry on with this," said Boria impatiently. "The girl is Kashka's daughter, without a doubt, not mine!"

"I remember how you used to chase her mother, damn it, like a torch bearer! Oh, oh, what a complicated world we've made for ourselves!" Wolfson leaped up from his seat. "Have you paid attention, Apache? You always fight over women with your best friends, perhaps because you lack independent taste, eh?"

"It isn't difficult to take the hint," replied Boria. "But in this case it has no substance!"

"Oh, nonsense!" groaned Wolfson. "What a load of nonsense!" He stretched out his arms and yawned, grinning. "And always the same recurring type, eh? Perhaps, then, Borinka, when we spied on the girls bathing, this type was imprinted on us . . ."

"Go and wallow in your wine cellar!" said Boria. He tried to adopt a light-hearted tone but couldn't do it. A string was drawing tight inside him.

"No matter! I give it all up! At once! From the start!" cried Wolfson, measuring out the dining room with his steps. "Being of sound mind . . . Come on, Borinka, let's hold a little emergency consultation: the Wolfson case—local irritation, a little anxiety; the Markovski case—mortal illness, of the guts and heart!"

"And I, for my part, colleague professor, see that the Wolfson case suffers severe hallucinations, induced, if I am not mistaken," he sniffed, "by dissipated drinking."

"From the wine vats of foreigners," added Wolfson. "And because still, as my aged eyes tell me, the malady follows the treatment and not vice versa, it is as clear to me as the numbers of my uncovered checks that the case is still in the preoperative stage . . . In politics you're more alert, doctor. How long is it since I handed her over to you?"

"Then what is God doing?" said Boria, as the string grew still tighter and uttered indecent sounds. "Since the whole story is a lie, you can contribute half of it to Mamushka's charitable fund and use the other half to cover your checks."

"If that is so, we're already in the age of the Covenant of the Pieces . . . One has a headache and his friend doesn't feel it, ha! I resign from my honorable profession, colleague! My eyes, my eyes betray me."

"Colleague professor, you should turn at once to a different branch of the profession," said Markovski, who succeeded at last in putting an expression of gaiety on his face, pushing his glasses to the end of his nose. "Research is, for the most part, contrary to our favorite illusions, the domain of the unimaginative! From now on I suggest you concentrate on simple operations."

"So you didn't exercise your franchise, did you? And this after I offered the wench of my own free will, being of sound mind, with clenched teeth, as was written in my father's will, and with hands in pockets . . ."

"Hands in whose pockets?" asked Frieda, who came in carrying a big pile of clothes and her pockets stuffed with elastic and spools of thread.

"Whose *not*?" replied Senya, and he watched her as she set the tattered garments out before her and threaded a needle.

"Look, just this week! And what deep pockets! Borinka, you'll love this, it's real Odessa-style *cholent*! Once upon a time, my pure and lovely children, the Hebrew contractors, made a conspiracy to strike a blow at the Mandatory Government, and because this blow was sabotage, they held a meeting at the Café Atara, a secret meeting. And so, our Mandatory Government announces a tender, but the Hebrew contractors stand surety for one another and refuse to be controled by some rabble of gout sufferers. What do they do? They sit in the Atara and decide from the start who's going to get the contract and what payment he'll receive. An utterly simple technique: they'll all offer inflated prices, and he whose turn it is to get it will offer a lower price. The balloon will deflate a little, but his reward will be infinitely greater than under conditions of unrestrained capitalist competition. This is the essence of all sabotage! A deal planned from the start! But pay attention! Who is Wolfson to wait until some Ginsburg or

Pomerovski gives him permission to build the land? His wild heart yearns for the nubile project! How does the saying go? 'God isn't rich, but he takes from one and gives to the other!' Since Wolfson knew all about it from the start, he went and offered the Mandatory Government an even lower price! And so, my pure, my lovely children, the big bad wolf gobbled up all the grandmothers!"

"And what a big mouth he's got!" said Frieda.

"And he came running here to escape the wrath of the hunters!" said Markovski.

"Nonsense, Dov," said Frieda. "Nobody can prove it! And anyway, they aren't forced to accept the cheapest offer."

"Bravo, Friedika, bravo!" said Wolfson. "It's only our Borinka who still always drives in first gear! But what then? Yesterday, at seven in the morning, I found one of those jackals in my office, the most honest of the lot, and he says to me straightaway: 'We know what you're up to, uncle,' and straightaway he offers me a deal: I'll take my hand from the corpse in exchange for a few slices of fat. You understand? Some people get paid just so they won't lift a finger! But this is it—when they kiss you, watch out for your teeth! What would you have done, Borinka, in my place?"

"Hit out and shouted *gevalt*! Taken him to court for attempted bribery."

"That's just what I was about to do, but at eight o'clock the second appeared, and at eight-thirty, the third. All that these two had to say to me was, essentially: 'Swine, why didn't I get the idea before you?' The rest are busy now digging drainage wells, but in ten years from now five of them, at least, will be lying in the same wells with their fathers. The second one I took into partnership. To the first and third I gave a project of mine, a smaller one, guilt money . . . There are ten thousand jackals in the land, but Wolfson—in a class of his own!"

"And on Yom Kippur he'll go to the synagogue," said Frieda.

"And why not?" asked Senya gently. "On Yom Kippur they say 'I have sinned,' never 'I have not sinned'!"

"Dov, why does he come to us to boast?"

"To boast? To humble myself! Pani-Paula is insisting I pay off the debts of the institution. If not, you'll be forced to close within a month! If Ginsburg or Pomerovski had got the contract, maybe he would have settled the debts."

Frieda stared at him blankly and said nothing.

"You've grown ugly, Friedika," he said, smiling at her with much admiration. "You were more beautiful before I sent our Orpheus here . . . She's upset! Terrified at the sight of my black heart! There's nothing makes a woman uglier than thought, but Borinka doesn't think so . . . These are the kind of songs he sings you, the blind bat . . ." Suddenly he jumped on a chair, curled his fingers over his eyes like Markovski's glasses, and, strumming on an imaginary balalaika, he burst into song, in march-time, groping for rhymes:

"O! Beauty is a nifty trick,
    A nasty trap to boot!
By which to grab fat burgers' plundered loot!
    Tra-la . . .
But if you look to future days when red banners fly,
    the prolet-slut will sing—amen!
Paint your face with any shit, or use a stinking dye—
    Tra-la . . ."

"But of rain beware, stay out of the rain! Tra-la . . ." added Markovski, strumming along, drawn into the game in spite of himself.

"Well, what do you think?" Wolfson asked the girl from his perch on the chair. Frieda laughed at them both until her sides split. "Don't you know, Wolfson, all women are bourgeois, without exception?" she said and laughed again.

A laughing icon, thought Boria, failing to be swept along on the wave of delight. A laughing icon!

"Oh, Frieda, Frieda!" cried Wolfson, leaping from the chair. "How beautiful this creature was when . . ."

"No matter," she said. "No matter. To a drunkard no drink is inferior!" And at once she turned to Wolfson, as if to laugh with him again.

"Boria, Boria!" he wailed like a child. "She's starting on me again! For a whole month I haven't drunk a single woman! Poor creatures! I've been busy making money for them!"

This is just the novelty—Boria was seized by hot and helpless anger—it's just the novelty in him. After a few hours he'll start to repeat himself and be disgusting! Everywhere he takes with him his prescripted cabaret! Whereas *he* was forced to sit thus, under pressure, day and night, and always to make the thunder flash, the rain fall and the sun shine, and always—different! Among the fifty fools who rush about you . . .

Frieda went on jesting with the visitor, unrestrained admiration in her eyes. "Not now!" she said, seeing the flask that appeared suddenly on the table. "Pani-Paula! She'll come in . . ."

"Pani-Paula!" cried Wolfson. "Who stole from the municipal museum of Zamosc the divine nose of Bacchus, if not Madam Berger? Have you got glasses, or do we drink straight from the bottle?"

"Wait, Wolfson . . ." The girl jumped up.

What sweetness! What willingness! What grace! Boria's fury boiled up until he was forced to grit his teeth.

"No, no, Friedika, you stay here with our Orpheus. I'll find whatever I need. After all, I too have some share in this institution, to which the leaders of the Revolution send their daughters. Don't I? Hallo, Friedi!" he said softly as he passed by her. As he walked into the kitchen, it was clear he had already transferred part of the liquor from one vessel to another.

Between Frieda and Boria hung an unbearable silence. He returned with two tin cups and a soup ladle. He leaned over the girl, who had gone back to her sewing work, and rubbed his cheek against hers.

"Don't do that!" she cried. Boria saw how she froze in her seat. "You're mixing up my warp and weft!"

"Oh! I just love the warp and weft!" And at once he kissed her on the neck. Boria saw how the blood burst from her veins and threatened to flood her. Senya poured Scotch into the two tin cups, urged them to drink, and drank his own from the ladle.

"Ah!" he sighed. "Since the day they invented whiskey I've been happy! Vodka throws you into the mud . . . cognac, into bed . . . and Scotch, into the 'Fifth Heaven'! That's what you call this miserable hole, isn't it?" He took another swig from the ladle, holding it by the handle and denouncing with his eyes the refusal of his friend.

"Why did you come here, Wolfson?" Frieda looked up at him suddenly.

"What? Why? Why—why! That's the thing I came here to ask," he said over the ladle, partly in jest, partly in deadly earnest. "The question itself is what matters, Friedika."

"What matters is knowing what action is right and what isn't!" she answered boldly.

"Boom! And do you know what's right and what isn't, Friedika?"

"Not hurting the other person!"

"What a woman, Boria, what a woman! This is indeed a terrible threat! But thus you establish the principle that the other is the one who's going to hurt you, my child."

"Perhaps every encounter with the other is in itself potential injury," said Frieda.

"That logic leads to distance, to avoidance!" cried Markovski, unable to restrain his outburst, but trying to smile with grace.

"Come on, let's finish the comedy while it's still like this!" snapped Frieda uneasily.

"Comedy?" Senya swayed as he approached her. "You think this is comedy? It's a disaster, real disaster! You don't know, damn it, what you're got yourself into, Boria! The whole thing's a distorting lens that turns everything upside down! I'm afraid of this monster, Boria! She's so pure, always so genuine. She always puts you in the wrong and you don't know what you've done. This woman's a walking charge sheet! And I won't allow this anymore! No!"

"Dov, tell him to stop!" cried Frieda, trying to restrain her nervousness. "After all, we are in charge here!"

"Yes, yes! Now I know it all! Those who try to propagate in the world the splendid notion that in the end we shall all turn into angels—they are our real devils! Better to wallow on dunghills, Borinka, better . . ."

"Let him talk!" said Boria, almost relieved at the outburst. "Senya loves to drink so he'll be able to talk this way, and he loves talking this way so he'll need to drink."

"Do you see how she's looking at me? Has she ever looked at you like that, Boria, even once? Never! Why, my pure, white-winged angel? Why? Every time I ram a witch, I think at once to myself—with Frieda it would be different, completely different . . . everything different!"

Frieda jumped up hastily and dropped the pile of clothes on the floor.

"Would be, would be!" he cried. "Why do you have to interfere?" he yelled, leading her back to her seat and throwing onto the table the clothes that had fallen. "Would be, I said! A month less, a month more! Oh, I know you all! Lascivious she-wolves among pet dogs!"

"Will you kindly let Dostoievski rest peacefully in his grave?" cried Boria scornfully.

"Grave?" roared Wolfson over the soup ladle. "Who's talking here about the Garden of Eden? I'm concerned with Hell! An angel? Who's going to tell you if it's devil or angel? Only when he attacks, this 'other person' of yours, Friedika, only when he attacks—only then will you know his intention, will he cuddle you or throttle you—or cuddle you and then throttle you! Is it because of this we strive always toward confrontation? Oh, Boria, Boria, you're a redeemed soul. You have your catechism, players in a comedy, but seriously! If you don't say your responses properly, we'll drag them from your mouth like toothpaste squeezed from a tube. Hey, Asmodeus, evil beast that you are, don't you dress up for me in white raiment! Go down half an octave, immediately! Bass, if you please, only bass! And now, pussycat! Hey, pussycat! Wailing like a pussycat—is it me, me, me? It's you, you, pussycat! Yes, yes, and now—this time—all of you! Softly, hush, hush! Just background, background! Softly, I said! Softer! And now all of you—in unison! What are you all? Ha–a–a–appy! Who said 'unhappy' over there? Who said 'unhappy'! Oh, unhappy is he who says it and unhappy is he who doesn't! We're all wandering between the walls! Between silence and the scream. All that you can do, Borinka, is lash yourself to one of the walls and butt against the other in revulsion or pleasure! This is distance, Friedika, this is avoidance!"

"Don't let him drink any more," said Frieda.

"No matter. I've got another bottle with me," replied Wolfson. Suddenly, all at once, he was sober, the sobriety that comes from drunkenness.

"Madam, how was the show? The performance—exquisite! I know! You'll never be able to deny it, but then you'll never know how to distinguish between the game and what isn't a game! You still don't know, my cherub, but the game is my forte. Through games I learn about life, like a child. Very often, Boria, we see ourselves as a kind of symbol. We direct our actions and reactions so we'll continue to symbolize something, to ourselves or to others, so every step will have a logical significance. It is the game that liberates us from this symbolism that we force upon ourselves. You, Frieda, don't know how to play, and that is the worst, the worst, most foolish thing about you! Look at her, Boria. Sitting there and staring, as if she's keeping some secret hidden inside her! No secret—nothing! Empty! Only this symbol that she cherishes like a cactus in a little plant pot, watering it with tears and heartache . . . What will the cactus do without the tears and the heartache? No secret—absolutely nothing! Like my cigarette ven-

dor on the corner of Allenby and Jonah the Prophet. Are you
listening? Boria! Put your hand on her shoulder, protect her from
me! The cigarette vendor. For years he's stood there. Years! A
kind of Russian Grandfather Winter in a turban, white beard—
the lot! And eyes—especially the eyes! Blue and pure and pink
at the edges. I'm always eager to talk with him. It seems to me
his wisdom is deep, unfathomable. If I peep, I'll know it all!
'Hallo, it's a long time since we saw you round here . . .' he says
to me. 'And you're always here, in the same place?' I reply. 'Always
here in the same place,' he answers. 'Why are you asking?' He
waits anxiously. You understand? *He* waits anxiously. 'Do you
like always standing here, on this corner?' I ask. Maybe he'll
answer me with something ancient, wise, that will answer other
questions too. 'Like it?' he says. 'This is my permit from the
municipality, the corner of Allenby and Jonah the Prophet, opposite the dress shop.' In the end he asks: 'What brand of cigarettes,
Comrade?' And I go on staring into those blue, penetrating eyes,
to find some meaning, but *he* is embarrassed and starts looking
at me, as if . . . I always forget and go back to him to search for
something hidden there . . . Shit! You too should drink to the
wisdom of empty eyes!"

Frieda suddenly stretched out her hand to the cup and drank.
She grimaced like a little girl. Why doesn't she defend herself,
damn it—Boria trembled—why doesn't she sharpen her tongue,
why doesn't she protest?

"What are you complaining about?" asked Markovski. "About
what? The two of us here—you make money, and I gain time.
The political fronts are clearly defined. They never were clearer,
and perhaps good and bad were never so polarized."

"That's what you think, Borinka! One moment! Complaining?
That's an insult! What can I complain about? I envy complainers!
Ha, a pretty girl sits and looks at me with eyes full of compassion,
and she bores me! Bores me to death! Already I hear all her
whispers and her groans, how she takes my hand and pleads for

a little love, just a little . . . That's all she needs, Boria, so she can stop being a cactus and remain just a plant pot."

"You're tormenting her!" cried Boria. "You're tormenting her and I don't know why! You don't even attach any importance, any meaning to what you say! The words are said just so they'll be said! To impress, to indulge or God knows what . . . But this girl still takes everything seriously! She takes seriously every word that comes from your mouth!"

"Do you really take seriously everything I say, Friedika?" asked Wolfson, in a mood of sudden tenderness.

"Still . . ." she said in a choking voice and dropped her eyes to the shirt she was patching.

"In that case, you're even more stupid than I thought! Very bad! There's no meaning to the words I say, except meaninglessness. Isn't that so, Boria?"

"Are you now Wolfson the symbol or Wolfson playing games?" asked Markovski. "Have you nothing real to say?"

"Nothing real! But you, the people who have things to say, you haven't yet said anything this evening! But you are the people who have things to say! Day after day you prolong their lives, injecting them with hormones, coloring them anew . . . Prisoners of yourselves! Every day of yours is the prison of the day before. The ideas born in your heart last night are your manacles today, the feeling that blossomed in your heart the day before yesterday is the ensnaring thicket of tomorrow because you imagine, my dears, that man is born to be a nursery for flowering ideas and feelings! But that's how we turn to garbage! A cemetery! Overcrowding! You've no room left in your soul! Hence the self-hatred, hence the choking! You are choked! You must uproot, uproot, destroy the weeds before they take root in your heart! Thus you'll always be able to breathe freely, without the stink of the corpses that you drag with you everywhere! Yes, Borinka, you are my one and only friend and I never cease abusing you and tormenting this lovely creature that you're so eager to screw, and you both bear and endure it all. Why? Because you both love me, eh? No! Because you both belong to the Mesozoic Age! You're dragging around with you a long and heavy spinal column! A few years from now they'll exhibit you in the Museum of Paleontology! I've always admired this spinal column! There they'll admire you, but they'll come running to me to sink into good, frail, soft material— eh, Friedika? Am I rotten, Borinka?"

"Swarming with maggots!"

"Excellent! Soon the cheese will be ready to eat. Well, Friedika? She doesn't answer! She's making plans now in her little cactus tub, wondering how to reform me, make me a human being! Human beings! Even if you let them feed on your liver, they'll dig it out, and then they'll say: 'Poo! This isn't fresh, thirty years old, at least . . .' When shall I see you in my office, my pure angel?"

"Never!" she replied in confusion. "Not ever!"

"I asked for a date, not a manifesto! And this comes about only because my good friend is listening with growing hatred to what's happening here, and you're afraid . . . Nothing to fear! Don't ever try to nourish self-confidence in a man. He'll turn it against you straightaway! Will you come?"

"Never!" she repeated. Her eyes wandered to Markovski and the table.

"That's very good, my daughter. You should always make a point of casting doubts. And a little competition between me and your knight is to be preferred. You'll enjoy it, I promise you! The bottle I leave with you to finish off the night . . ."

"You shouldn't have come, Wolfson," said Frieda at the door.

"Borinka! Take good care of her. Okay?" He laughed suddenly, and as if anxious to appease them, took both their hands in his. "Next week! I'll send a note, Friedika!" he shouted from outside, from the entrance hall.

Markovski closed the door slowly and drew her to him with a hasty, clumsy movement, but she seemed sunk in distant thoughts.

Suddenly she lifted her chin and looked straight into his glasses. Her heart fluttered in his eyes. He stood staring, frozen, hypnotized.

28
"I MUST TALK
WITH YOU"

As he left the house he felt a jolt in his heart, as if he had been called.

Beside the gate he saw Frieda alone, leaning on the fence. The head of her shadow fell to his feet. He turned to go back, but at once lowered his eyes, watched the movements of the shadow, and then could not resist studying the profile of her face.

She raised it to the red clouds, as if reading signs in them, her teeth clenched in concentration. He could see her jaw muscle move as if in rhythm with her thoughts. Again the mystery between her and herself, the enticement in her nondiscernment. Still unaware of his presence, she drew in her hand and bit her thumb hard, then sighed softly and turned her face toward the house. Suddenly she noticed him and at once diligently wiped off her expression, only her eyes remaining like two dark patches.

"Going down to buy cigarettes," he announced in a casual tone.

"I'm coming with you." Lightly she touched the back of his hand.

From the darkened house burst the chattering of the pupils going up to their beds. The background will always be their voices, their breathing, their growing pains.

He drew his hand away and felt the pinch of longing. This time he desired not only her body, those desperate fumblings, but the morbid fastidiousness, the debilitating purity, the perverse insistence on scorning those who flounder in the mud, the painful hints that here there will be to everything the intoxication of soaring to the heights.

She, sleepwalking in the Garden of Eden of endless choice, doesn't know that already in the silence, around the corner, the devils of reality lie in wait for her, the straitjacket in their hands. And it's in his power, his power alone, to rescue her from the mediocrity that awaits her. Without him she will never reach those heights.

"You know well enough, Frieda, there's no taste and smell."

"Tonight the pines have a special smell of . . ."

The dread of a night of loneliness is falling on her again. He must offer his shoulder and his ears.

"This time I want the whole landscape to myself," he declared.

She blinked at him in an astonishment that seemed to him artificial—either that or she was unaware of the pains of his "withdrawal symptoms."

"It's a long time since we talked together," she said, trying an affectionate tone.

He snorted impatiently and felt a sort of relief.

"Something's happened to you," she followed his eyes.

"What delicacy of perception!"

"Something strange is happening in your heart . . . I'd like to know . . ."

"You know of course: with us, what begins in the heart always reaches the hands, and this, surely . . ."

"You'd better not go on," she said.

For a while silence hung between them, until, seeing her eyes fixed on him, he could no longer restrain himself.

"Ah! The sight of a man staring at you with pleading eyes, that's what you need right now! It's a stimulating drug, proving to you that all hope isn't lost, eh? Thank you very much, my Zoshia, the world is full of promiscuous Talimenas."

"If you're compelled to talk like this . . . ," she said with surprising softness.

He didn't like that tone. He would have preferred a swift, heated, violent altercation.

"See how amusing she is!" he cried, as if addressing a jury of like-minded peers. "She feels insulted, she presses charges, because some lunatic who's already recovered—recovered! recovered!—once wrote poems for her on sand . . . because he made placebo love to her at a time of emergency."

"Why are you so bitter?" she asked sadly.

He must guard himself against this sadness, must not pin hopes on what lay behind it. It was as if her movements were borrowed from another person.

"Bitter? I'm savoring freedom, poor girl. What a sweet smell it has after the stuffiness of your room! Oh, pardon me, the maiden would rather I unburdened myself before her in sonnets. Oh, what lovely customs she has developed."

"Leave me alone, *all* of you!"

He jumped down from the steps and turned to the pained bewilderment in her face: "I don't see anyone holding you!"

"I'm going with you," she insisted like a neglected child.

"You'll be disappointed!" he said rudely, throwing off the yoke. "I'm no longer easy to mold!"

Inside him a treacherous stream began flowing, flooding.

The hill, and behind it the road—empty of people. The citizens were shutting themselves away early because of the blackout. Their unmatched footsteps clattered among the houses like nuts pursuing one another down a long corridor.

If she won't reveal herself afresh, he repeated to himself, if she won't reveal herself afresh . . .

"Boring!" he broke the silence.

"Talk," she grinned beside him with a sort of flattery, "you love to talk."

You see, again she's making comparisons with herself.

"It's a pity to waste," he said with childish arrogance, "rainwater on stones." He turned to glance at her. Her face had hardened again. What lightness! A fleeting sense of miraculous balance, the nonchalant freedom of a tightrope-walker.

"A fine night," he said with emphatic generosity.

"It's a pity to waste starlight on dead hearts," she replied.

They both fell silent at once, as if to give passage to the rest of the words.

The scent of the pines pursued them until it was swallowed in the smell of chicken blood and the grimy dust of courtyards.

"Boria!"

Against his will he stopped, and at once, to blur the response, he mocked her. "You look like a mouse after an earthquake. What is it?"

"I must, must talk with you!"

His guesses crystallized into a kind of certainty.

"Oh, your lightning rod," he said with a calmness that surprised him. "You miss your litmus paper! Dip it in acid, change its color, and then change it back again! Red-blue, red-blue . . . "

"Boria. You . . . Boria, you're the only person who . . . ," she said in despair.

"Boria and Frieda are people," he repeated scornfully what she had said to him once, "two people who are similar to one another, both sensitive to Rilke and to a silent and radiant sunset . . . Tell me, tell me, little Eve, what does the apple taste like . . . Tell me . . ." He began humming to himself with an air of equanimity. Another moment and he would be rubbing his hands together.

"Do you know?"

"Your secret is safe with me."

"I had to go! I *had* to!

"I said a benediction for you."

"Did *he* tell you?" she asked, impatient, with a sort of undisguised childish hope. "Have you seen him? What did he tell you?"

Everything became clear for a moment and then went dark with insane speed. He was lost, lost and wailing in the darkness.

"I waited for him to send a note, as he promised, but he didn't . . . I had to go!"

Her desire to tell him wraps her in a sort of willful insensitivity to the feelings of the hearer. His ears, his head, his hands hear; only his guts sink in weightlessness, until she draws him to the stone seat by the roadside, that bench where they used to sit in the darkness, tired from their night wanderings. He is dragged after her, not to miss anything, a word, a murmur. In the darkness that's in his brain, words light up—like a warning—one after another, shining, sparkling: "self-respect," "character," "personality" . . . Yet this is not darkness but brightness, clarity! His ears hear clearly, as they've never heard before, and a sort of cruel delight percolates through him. Her voice drones on, monotonous, restrained—that manner of speech which characterizes her emotion, and in which others find coldness and aloofness. His shoe kicks at the little stones and his eyes follow her movements in the dark.

". . . Suddenly he looked at me . . . like this. You know those looks of his . . . a sort of . . . and then he smiled and said: 'Ready?' And without any 'before and after.' I started to laugh and then I felt I was going to die. And when I told him I still hadn't . . . not yet, never . . . he looked at me with disbelief, and then he said he didn't know whether to pity me or admire me . . . You remember that story he told about the youth of the Wolfson woman, when we met for the first time in her house? He told it again. And then he went on and said he was an honest man: 'A man honest in dealings between male and female is he who has already drunk his fill of the delusions with which childhood equips a man, so he'll be eager to grow up.' That's what he said. Then he told me to look around me, in that café. 'Beside every table—a girl,' he said. 'And it's impossible to ignore this. Every day hundreds of fresh rolls are baked and go to market . . .' And at that moment he stroked my face and looked into my eyes. 'I'm too rich, too handsome and too clever, and my gravitational force is enough for quite a few shooting stars . . . Novices are always drawn toward the dangerous enemy, and diseases toward the expensive doctor. You think I'm a braggart? A professional male? Sick with self-love? No! I'm as sober as a surgeon before the operation! Do you hate surgeons? If so, Friedichka, go home and find yourself a witch doctor who'll whisper spells over you . . .' That's what he said. Only when he wants children—and that isn't yet—will he take to himself an unpretentious wife without pride, who'll carry her soul in her body like a dead tooth in the mouth. He'll kill off all her nerves one after the other, and she'll be happy when he rewards her by giving her his name, nights at the theater, standard of living, appearances beside her in public, and sophisticated household appliances. And he'll give her 'conjugal rights,' so she won't poison the air. 'Most women learn to accept this arrangement sooner or later.' And at once he went on: 'Would you, truly, be willing to dry out on a shelf in my house while somewhere or other I butter some fresh roll that's stimulated my appetite? And instead of all this, Frieda, I'm offering you here and now—without all the lies and conventions, without all the artificial complications—a wonderful lover who'll give you hours of pleasure that you'll carry with you to the end of your days . . . Afterwards you can cook for somebody else *borshts* garnished from these memories . . .' He laughed. 'And he'll thank you for them . . . You're too dear to me that I should want to destroy in you what I like best . . .'

"And then I plucked up courage and said: 'And love, Senya, what about love . . .' He was pleased and he repeated the word several times, and at last he said: 'This concept, Frieda, is something you women have invented, out of fear and selfishness. Even street-walkers carry on in their profession just because they succeed occasionally in wringing declarations of love from their clients . . .' Then he told me about his clever neighbor in Odessa, a well-known anecdote that used to make everybody laugh . . . Before he went away to Moscow, he left with his wife a trained parrot that could screech only one sentence: 'Ludmilla, I love you.' And for the three months he was away Ludmilla didn't look at another man."

Frieda's hand moved toward his hand, a slight inclination and her hand was in his. He found himself striving tensely toward the knowledge, toward the ultimate truth.

". . . But he laughed: 'They stuff you women with literature instead of practical psychology. When a writer goes to a whore, even then he'll call it 'delighting in love,' 'making love.' A timeless dialogue between Romeo and Juliet? The little youth dies on her grave of hunger because he hasn't had time to bite her properly, get her flesh between his teeth. There's nothing more terrible than insipidity of the flesh . . . nothing more terrible than that! But if you really want it—I'll recite to you now an intoxicating monologue on love.' "

" 'You understand, Boria? You understand?' The more he talked like this the cruder he became, smashing everything to fragments . . . I felt that . . . that . . . I felt a terrible desire to turn everything over, to provoke from him some violent outburst, some reversal."

He heard the ripping, in reality. Every layer of skin ripped away with a scream, leaving a burning in the living flesh. She plucks leaves from the nearby bush, and Dov feels every sound. He froze himself . . . to stop everything, to retreat, to let the words pass over him, leaving no scar.

"When we went out of the café," she returned to that flaccid, monotonous tone, "he put his coat over my shoulders and suddenly pulled me to him, like this . . . I thought I'd die, be swallowed up on the spot. I felt every finger on my shoulder . . . But I told myself I must not, after all this . . . but this didn't . . ."

Now she'll describe the experience of her virginity! And he, Boria, will lie with her in the virginal bed and live all the movements, the shudders, the sensations. Stop! Shut it out, shut it all out! Every twitch of the nerves, every spark of imagination. But flight is no better than staying. It's all the same—whether he sees or covers his eyes, roars or whispers, everything, everything the same, unbearable, irrevocable!

He stood up from the seat, feeling the need to gulp the air, to move his body. She walked beside him, absorbed in her words and her memory, as if the two of them had been born and lived in two worlds.

"Then I took off the coat . . ."

Boria was grateful for the walking, the hardness of the road under his feet, the reality of the trees and the smell of dried blood, as if all these elements filtered through themselves his hurt, his imagination, his madness.

"I didn't have to tell you, did I?" she said abruptly, blocking his path. "I didn't have to . . ."

"And now it's back to reality. Back to Boria Markovski, 'the true lover,' who sticks love poems under the door and waits with open arms." His breath was amazingly even. "I've always considered the *jus primae noctis* eminently wise and reasonable. Obviously, henceforward the *seigneur* will leave the young couple alone, and in the morning the bride will bring her blood-stained sheets to the groom's house to prove beyond doubt that she was a virgin!"

The lights dimmed in the nearby yeshiva. A few silhouettes left the building.

She stopped and turned to him. "It was a lie, Boria."

He stood motionless.

"All night he ran with me from place to place looking for someone to sell him a bottle. At the end, in his apartment, he kissed me a few times, drunk again from the bottle, and said, 'I am an invalid. Sorry.' "

The walked down to the village. He held out the coins to the elderly woman in the kiosk and picked up the cigarettes. He felt the tremor in Frieda's hand as he lit her cigarette, holding her wrist without feeling. The golden birds of the imagination had flown.

"And now you must run and find yourself someone who'll skillfully deflower you," he said to her, "and you can give up all the . . ." He inhaled almost with delight the venom of the words. Again he was the Dov Markovski that he knew. He laughed at her shape retreating from him—always in retreat—as it disappeared among the houses.

He felt himself a free man. Gradually the pain conquered him like a strange body.

In the morning he enlisted in the Jewish Brigade.

At two o'clock in the afternoon
the eastern balcony began to fill. First to desecrate its isolation
were those three or four, seeking out a pleasant patch of shade
for a game of "five stones," a game which requires for the sake
of its balance, besides somewhat hot-tempered hands, a pleasant
coolness rising up the spine. For a short while these dominated
the empty balcony from their shaded corner, casting at intervals
into the silence cries of disappointment and malice. But almost
imperceptibly, and without opposition, the place was taken over
by the voices of others, smothering with the anarchic racket of
tuning-up instruments the harmonious sounds of the quartet. The
worn tiles leading from the door to the heart of the balcony cracked
into sharp and opaque scales under the tread of the arrivals. They
joined up into groups, uniting for a moment and dividing again,

their particles wandering off to join others; one stands and spits pleasurably into the yard, and at once—to his right and left— are two who compete with him until all the moisture of their mouths is exhausted, and hence, distractedly, not wishing to waste his spittle in vain, somebody tries to entice a passing cat, and the one nearest him runs to find a bucket, and yet another group is formed. They lean over the rail and make tweeting noises with their lips, with feeling, until all the alley cats are summoned from all the yards, gathering at the foot of the house with tails erect, mewing and raising aloft hopeful, eager eyes. Then that clever one, returning from his quest, quickly tips over them a bucket of water. Now they all swarm to the balcony, leaning over, short of breath, to derive pleasure from the almost human disappointment that peeps out of the wet, offended eyes, darting glances this way and that, not to miss the sight of the damp bedraggled furs in their panic retreat, until they disperse on the ground under the net fencing and disappear. Ketzele is already mounting the wooden rail, straddling it like a horse and clearing from it the hands of the others, and some voice, thickened with importance, speaks about the new, complicated lock of the manageress.

When those sitting in the "five stones" corner see Ketzele's thighs above them, they pretend not to notice, but Ketzele isn't pedantic about manners—he bends down, leans his head on the wall, and rolls up in bashful silence his yellow bangs, watching the mediocre game through narrowed eyes, like a reasonable master hangman, who listens with repressed longing to the last words of his victims. Only when the stones roll into the hands of Stinking Rafi does he venture to offer him some measured advice, and then he is a patron eager to get the best from his protégé. Steadfastly he follows his hands, which have already succeeded in reaching the "fourth," after he's sucked in the whole of his upper lip like an old man chewing, and not before he's fixed his inflamed eyes before every turn on the face of his unexpected benefactor. Now he's succeeded in laying four stones before him in a tight, provocative circle, ripe for snatching. But he is so intent upon them, so entranced at their obedience, that he misses—for a split second—the fifth, the one destined to drop into his palm, the fruit chosen to add the crowning touches to the punnet, and finds himself clutching two handfuls of air, one below and one above.

"No matter," Ketzele consoles him with a tone of reassurance. "Don't worry, Rafinka, you're coming along nicely."

Rafi bares his upper teeth in a grin that hangs on his mouth for a long time to come.

Abie's game is elegant, as are all his actions, his throws judicious and restrained—so as not to exhibit excessive ambition—and thus he succeeds in forming a number of circles, but always he gives you the impression that he's only fulfilling an obligation occasionally incumbent on a young man of his age. When the stone slips from his hand, he seems relieved. Without any of the evasions and indignant excuses that serve as a condiment to the game, he abandons the stones—a sober man amid a gang of drunks.

But all this is the "matinee," the "B-movie." The gathering of the five marblelike stones into the hands of the champion portends the thrilling start of the main feature. Ketzele savors them for a moment between his fingers, probing in each one its curves and the extent of its coolness, then rubbing them between his palms to infuse them with his warmth and lightness of touch, picking out the "marker" with a rapid glance. From here on it is clear to the others that they are entitled to descend gradually from the stage and join the audience, taking their privileged places in the front row.

The first moves he makes with an air of languid carelessness, with gaping yawns between throw and catch, his head resting on his left shoulder, his eyelids slack and his hands moving on the ground like independent creatures, but you sense in him how the wave of enjoyment mounts and swells beneath his skin, until he reaches those places that for the others are the summit of achievement, and for him the jumping-off point. Plip! His legs, which until now have lain together as if paralyzed, he parts like the spines of a fan, ringing up the curtain with a toss of the head—and the show begins.

At first all watch him with sincere admiration, with delight that among us there exists such a living paragon. While he is at a level within their reach, he still arouses in them competitive zeal, but then they are steadily sinking as he sets off for the misty heights, into the common grave of equality, sprawling in vacant idleness, all pleasure gone, and the worms of self-love begin to rustle and bore. But then, behold, comes the resurrection, the miracle, the redemption of the feeble!

Impetuously, as is his way, Yosef flung open the door and emerged in gleaming tennis shorts, which both restrained and displayed his masculinity, and an open-necked mesh shirt. All eyes hurried to his thighs, his calves, his chest, his arms—not only because they are not accustomed to exposure in this village, where all are afraid of contact between eye and revealed flesh, but because of his peculiar physical presence. The flowing, effortless movements, the heaving sinews, like those light, tantalizing movements that the audience notices on the stage before the curtain rises, the warmth radiated from the fit, tanned body, that is never neglected for a moment, this hedonistic body, which is never violent (though, as Abie says, "his second blow is the desecration of the dead"), planted in them an unshakeable belief in the goodness of life, in the value of growth, of maturity.

Very young people are endowed with a sense that adults lose in the course of the years, a perception of the wondrous scent of true manhood or womanhood, their rare refinement and peculiar potency, just as they perceive, because of their closeness to the ground, the tiniest plants and the smoothest pebbles.

A month ago, when Frieda left the institution and went to work in a summer camp, they felt they had been cheated. Then it became cruelly clear to them that all her involvement with them had been the act of an artisan, that she'd abandoned them like a project that has failed and is at once forgotten. One morning, at the start of the long vacation, she was no longer there, and the next day some of them saw her standing surrounded by strange children in a booth of straw matting in the outskirts of the village, singing them a song that they had never heard from her mouth, gesturing to the dimwits and trying to get them to form a circle. When she saw the children from the hostel watching her, she waved to them with a brief smile of recognition and turned back to her dimwits.

Out of a foolish clinging to what will never return, they gathered charcoal in the nearby Arab village, and the day that the new instructor was to arrive, the stairwell was black with ill-omened inscriptions: "Shame on the new instructor! Long live Frieda!"

And when the new instructor came, they saw it was Yosef the sentry. On the stairs he snatched something from the hand of one of them.

"From this day forward," he said with unexpected severity, "from this day forward we'll have no more things like this. What do you think the dining room's for?" And then he showed them what he'd snatched—a half-chewed hunk of bread. Then he turned and went up the stairs. The grumbles and venomous whispers were only the sign of their repressed happiness.

Next morning all the graffiti disappeared. It seemed there was no friction between him and them, only the choking desire to be in his presence that took away the barbs of their tongues.

When Yosef came out to the balcony, their haphazard lingering there was transformed to a solid, tangible reality. He leaned his elbows on the rail, his bare foot on a wicker stool fetched from his room, his body floating weightless among them, a pose stimulating in its casualness, some book or other under his arm and his eyes smiling sympathetically at Ketzele's game, its allure already faded.

Suddenly, like a spring released, he kicked the stool, tossing it in the air and catching it in his hand with a barely perceptible inclination of the neck, then put the leg of the stool on his finger and moved away from the rail. The finger ran after the stool and the body after the finger (the game of the five stones long forgotten). Then he bared his teeth, stuck out the lower set, and lodged the leg of the stool on it, but at once, with a mighty crash, he dropped it on the floor.

"Poo! Here's another little beast that hates washing!"

They all understood his meaning and grinned, liberated, while he wiped his gums and lips with a white handkerchief and then, without bending his knees, chased the stinker with an imaginary net, seized it like a puppy by the nape of the neck, glared at it reproachfully, stroked it with consoling caresses, and slowly wiped its legs with the same handkerchief. Now, the cycle complete, he began again, gyrating in zigzags along the balcony, the book lodged in his armpit and the appeased stool responding obediently to all these indignities, everyone following and squealing with delicious fear whenever the little one seemed about to fall, while Yosef wriggled his hips flamboyantly, bulging out his eyes like a circus clown, his arms clawing the air. And suddenly, vibrating his knees, letting his body sink slowly—and as they are still shouting "Oh!"—they see waddling before them a fat-bottomed duck, flapping his spread wings on the ground, the mesmerized stool stuck to his beak, until he quacks loudly, throws it in the air, stands upright, catches it with two delicate fingers, bows to the spectators and, as he acknowledges the applause, points with one hand to the "assistant" clasped in the other, as if saying, "Your appreciation please for this little fellow!"

A moment . . . and the balcony is full of scraping furniture, objects thudding to the floor, ostentatious yells, bared teeth, mules colliding, moments of victory with brief glances at the youth who again stands with one leg perched on the stool—a maestro allowing free rein to the new generation—his great laugh absorbing them all, his eyes responding to every "Look at me!" his voice advising, castigating the butter-fingered with abuse that extenuates their failures, and suddenly it's clear that he's had e–nough! And for his own pleasure alone he springs into his "*Evivo*" cheer:

"*Evivo, Evavo, Evivo, vavo vu–Hey!*
Lefty-Befty, Billy-Billy Befty, Jingele-Mingele,
Luf, Luf, Luf!"

There's no more need of chairs or ducks or grinding the teeth in dirty sand, just mouths gaping at him and accompanying his dance with doggerel rhymes chanted in unison. And then, as the excitement reaches its climax, his calm voice rings out, as if he's just been cast, sober and healthy, into a cauldron swarming with lunatics.

"Will you do me a favor and let me read this antique of mine in peace—a plague on your houses?" Now he's a vacationer seeking solitude, leaning his stool against the wall of the "pension" and propping his bare feet on the rail, clicking the joints of his toes—a favorite movement of his and of everyone's, opening his book at the place marked and cutting himself off from the vanities around him.

The balcony breathed dust and the rushing of the valiant to the yard.

When Maya returned to the balcony with her book, she found there sitting opposite Yosef, as opposite a fire, a handful of diligent pupils enclosing him like a stove guard, and felt an angry pinch inside her: Yaffa and Hedva, with books in their hands! Two lice eggs that once fell into the eagle's nest and now pretend they're his chicks! She pushed her chair between the two of them, to sit facing him, with a kind of reckless impudence, provoking "Hey!"'s and indignant shrugs.

"Not one chicken to crow!" said Yosef.

"Fine!" croaked Yaffa.

After a while, as she sat opposite him, book to book and face to face, she found herself reading upside-down, in their archaic lettering, pleasing to the heart, the words:

"And she came to that place on the bank of the stream, where Amnon tended his sheep the day before, and her heart was afraid and longing, for she saw Amnon on the bank across the stream, and she led her flock to drink. As doves on brooks so both refreshed their eyes on the face of the waters which filled them with sweetness, for they saw the images of their delight reflected in the waters, ashamed to look upon their loved one face to face . . ."

Her heart quaked. She saw his chin rise and felt his eyes looking straight at her.

"I didn't think you were a Yemenite!" his voice smiled.

Feeling suffocated, she turned her eyes away with a childish "What do you mean?" and met the eyes of the others.

"That's how Yemenite children learn the Torah," he smiled as he mimicked the Yemenite intonation. "That's because they haven't enough books to go round."

She wanted to see if there was some rebuke concealed here but didn't dare to look. She just felt some stunning blow and a desire to escape from the sweetness.

"I only peeped for a moment," she said to his book (he'd get the idea that this was the way she talked, a perpetual croak, like Yaffa's voice).

"And it's fascinating, eh?" he said, and suddenly asked her name. "Wait, wait, the name of a month or something . . . I think . . ."

She felt offended that he'd been here a whole month and still didn't remember her name.

"Maya, Maya," he said thoughtfully when he heard her feeble response. "I once had a friend in high school called Maya. But she was all ginger, from top to bottom," he grinned to himself. "What do you know about these things? From top to bottom! The month of May is in the sign of Taurus. A month of heartbreakers," he laughed. "I belong to the sign of Pisces—just boring faces, so the astrologers say. Do you know what astrologers are?" And at once, without transition, to test her, he asked her the title of his book. She saw the title printed opposite her knees and nodded in embarrassment, ashamed to pronounce this . . . this word. As if it might explode in her mouth! She took a trembling breath and muttered carefully and dimly, "Lo–ove of Zion." She felt a blast of air and it seemed everything was falling apart around her.

Without consulting her, he dragged her chair around and set it next to his, against the wall. Her forehead felt the roasting eyes of the other girls as she stared at his finger, which tapped the page with a gesture of invitation to read.

The words were unwilling to unite into pictures. She tried to saddle them but could see only the legs of the two of them—two angles converging at the point of contact of her thigh and a big, exposed knee, until she flung herself forcibly into that verdant, engrossing landscape, the marauding lion, drawing closer to Tamar, his throat like an open grave and his tongue a flame of fire and . . . But he was already moving on and a dam of pages rose between his fingers, leaving the maiden bound to the rock. She began snatching pages from between his fingers, to chase him, to be there with him—and the dam grew thicker. At intervals she held her breath. To sink and to disappear because of the . . . the . . . everything . . . all this that Amnon uttered to the wondrous unknown woman.

She made it a rule always to make her face blank when she read love stories and an adult happened to be present, or she would skip over the pages and return to the same point when the adult had gone. And now she found the force of the rule melting and she couldn't renew it, and already he knew before her everything that she read and was about to read, as if he himself was running before her and writing the words.

Next day, as it was still morning, she knew she was waiting for that hour when twilight is still far off and the taste of afternoon creeps into her mouth. More than that she dared not tell herself.

As in the cheapest realization of the desire of a rich imagination, she found him on the balcony, without the "members of the book club," alone.

"*Bon giorno*, heartbreaker!" he cried as she peeped out of the door, not knowing what to do next. "Don't you want to go on?"

He shouldn't talk like that, she thought, because . . . But she wanted him to carry on talking like that, and she sat down beside him.

Fragments of the sentences that he tossed to her as they read, his probing questions, her evasive answers, the sweet and derisive blast of air that he blew from time to time behind her ear, the contrast between the repressed mischievousness that typifies his body all the day and this relaxed pose, legs outstretched and the dark chest trapped within the mesh shirt exuding patient, steady breathing—all this wrapped her in a haze of awesome charm.

A few days before, when he was trying with Abie and Ketzele to swallow a whole flight of stairs in one leap, she heard Markovski say to the manageress: "Infantile! Totally infantile!" His words carried such a strong tone of denunciation that she almost understood their meaning. She knew that he adopted the guise of an adult in the presence of the staff, whereas they kept something of themselves hidden from him, the same way that they behaved with the children.

When he stood up and stretched his arms, his eyes wandering in the sky, she looked at the book and saw that the dam had disappeared. He turned his head and smiled at her between yawns.

"By tonight you'll have finished it, okay?" he asked. She nodded with her chin. He handed her the book with the solemn injunction "to give it straight back to him," and he breathed on her neck. Until the evening she persevered with the book, but didn't finish it and decided to give it back. When he wasn't with her his fragrance was absent.

He stood in the doorway fully dressed, in khaki, as if ready for a journey. One of his hands held the book, and the other ruffled her hair. Unknowingly she longed for the breath on her neck.

"Interesting?" he asked, his wide-open eyes studying her. She caught herself looking straight into his eyes. "So-so," she replied, so he wouldn't know she hadn't finished reading it.

"My generation was more romantic," he said. "You are so practical . . . I remember how I dragged this book to the bathroom, the toilet, the workshop . . . This week I found a copy in somebody's house. I wanted to see if it hadn't changed. Whoosh . . . short circuit! I've been spoiled! You should hurry up and swallow these whites before you break out of the egg, eh?"

Never had words like these been said to her, and they seemed to fill empty voids in her. He passed the palm of his hand over the hollows of her cheek and her chin, as if studying their contours, and she was afraid to move while his staring eyes wandered inside her body.

"You must be very careful," his face became serious. "If I was your father, I wouldn't sleep peacefully at night." He closed his eyes as if to prove this, and when he raised his lids, two brown slits opened before her. Something inside her told her again and again she mustn't understand him thus, he meant something else.

"I'm going to town," he said and slapped his back pocket. "What shall I bring back for you?"

She was perplexed by the strange, unconventional offer.

"Well?" he cried. "Does it take you so long to think? Nowadays, one should not behave like this! You must think quickly, Decide! Demand! Accept! Gobble up quickly, before they grab!"

"A notebook!" she replied hastily, just so he'd ask why.

"A notebook?!" He twisted his face into a scornful leer. "That's what you ask of a man who offers you half his kingdom?! *Bene, bene*! A notebook you want? A notebook it shall be!"

Now she thought she had made a serious mistake. He threw the book behind him, into the room that had never yet been revealed to her. His hand gripped her shoulder. "Buzz off," he said gently, and he ran his finger up her spine.

She ran and heard his footsteps behind her.

In the night great grief overcame her, empty voids sucking away her lifeblood, until she saw him again in the morning in the gleaming tennis shorts, tightening the slack net fencing.

The "siesta" on days of the long vacation was Yosef's invention, and he was the first to violate it—aside from those days and nights when he disappeared altogether to perform activities of a peculiar nature, activities that must not come to the knowledge of the British.

Maya knew that at regular intervals he would go off at siesta time to a place unconnected with these "activities," returning to stir waves of obscure envy in her heart.

One day, at the height of the siesta, as she lay on her bed in the heavy silence that was broken only by the rustle of pages and the snores of the sleepers, the door opened slightly. She saw him beckoning her to come out.

"Grab your sandals, old lady, and come at once. We're going," he whispered to her by the door, stroking her chin affectionately and sucking in air between his teeth. "I'll wait down there at the corner! *Avanti!*"

"Where you going?" croaked Yaffa, turning toward her drowsily on the floor, looking at her sandals. "Yosef won't like you going out in 'siesta.' "

"Who's asking you, Little Monkey?" she whispered with venom. A few heads rose from the floor and sank down again.

At the corner she saw his straddled, suntanned legs and his hands throwing stones at a distant electricity pylon. She wanted to . . . but at once she behaved as he expected and put on an expression of excited childish curiosity.

"You'll see," he said with the seriousness of me-and-you-and-nobody-else, still aiming stones at the pylon and not taking his eye from it. "If any of those Pani-Paulas or Shoshanas ask you, say you went to buy yogurt at the dairy. Ping! A hit! Did you see that? Bulls-eye! You'd been abusing your stomach and I gave you permission! Okay? And don't look so serious! Coward!" He gripped her arm close to the elbow.

Her mind clouded for a moment because of the ease of his suggestion to lie, but in his eyes she saw how the lie was converted to a bond.

The two of them went down the hill and paced along the white, blind road. He kicked toward her a fragment of brick with a sideways football kick, and from there on they were chasing after it, kicking in turns, shoving one another lightly and yelling, he without inhibition and she with some embarrassment, perhaps because of the disapproval in the faces of the passersby. His pleasure was the pleasure of the game itself, and she was inwardly thrilled by the strange equality that he created between them.

From the dead, sun-roasted main street he led her to one of those cool alleys where the "athiests" live. This alley, which was like a continuation of the sanatorium, perched on a hill and overlooking it, could have been built just for show, its red-tiled little houses without shops and bowered in ancient shadows and the ground carpeted with a bitter humus of fig leaves.

For some time she had known that on these alleys of Kiryat Shkak there was a kind of unspoken ostracism because its residents lived among themselves an enclosed life, going out on Sabbaths to the tarmac beyond the pale to look for a taxi to Tel Aviv, and walking bare-headed and bare-legged; and everything that was done there was the source for the gushing fountains from the mouths of the devout women of the village. So, when they turned into this alley, the wild jubilation of expected adventure spread within her.

"Where are we going?" she asked hoarsely, against her will.

"*Duce* takes good signorinas only to the best places," he replied and touched the tip of her nose teasingly.

And she didn't ask again, until they stood in a long vestibule covered with ivy and with some white, perfumed flower. All at once she sniffed a pleasant coolness, and as he knocked at a carved wooden door with a bronze knocker, she had time to wonder at the pure strips of sky percolating through the thin foliage and at the rapid pumping of her blood that accompanied the muffled footsteps behind the carved lions.

At first she saw only black velvet, as if the whole of the interior of the house was made of black velvet, and suddenly the face of a woman appeared and even her voice was like black velvet. She stretched out a white hand to her from the velvet, drew her inside the black den of iniquity. Scared, she looked back toward the light, to the strips of sky. He laughed in the light, as if understanding her fear.

Inside hung the smell of canvas and paint and the smell of perfumes and fruit. The dim light, the ancient moth-eaten curtains, and this big lady, whose face and hands alone were visible and who stared at her unblinking with a strange concentration, as if reading her innermost thoughts, made her feel giddy.

"You're really charming, *Duce!*" said the woman, one of her big eyes flashing toward him.

"And you're very beautiful today," said Yosef.

Maya guessed she was older than him.

The woman grimaced playfully, as if wanting to prove to him how mistaken he was, if the truth be known.

"Come on, come into the salon. Come Maya," she said, and led the girl with a gentle hand to a big armchair and lightly pushed her into it until she sank down, her legs sticking up in the air (how did she know her name?). The voice went on enfolding her in swathes and swathes of black velvet. Another moment and she would be suffocated.

"A Madonna, eh?" he said proudly when she turned to him, as if he'd created her.

The *Duce* and the velvet woman were of the same height, and as he spoke their faces were level. She sensed in him a sort of self-effacement and a clumsy, agitating, change of character.

"A bit anemic," said the woman, coming close again to study her face, as if he had brought her a chicken to sell.

"Undernourishment," he said apologetically, shrugging his shoulders. "It's just undernourishment, Carmela."

"It's entirely suitable," Carmela smiled with her big mouth. "Like a dried flower in a book. She reminds me of Dürer—absolutely two-dimensional."

"Wait, she's got time," laughed Yosef.

"It's entirely suitable," the woman repeated.

"*Santa Maya del Fiore*, eh?" laughed Yosef.

From here on the meaning of almost all their words was lost on her, as most of the time they spoke between them in that soft language, the one to which Yosef always turned to lend color to his words, like rolling sweet candies between tongue and palate. She felt the resistance rising to her throat.

The woman's face became more and more clear to her, and

all its details seemed exaggerated and repellent: the protruding eyes, like the eyes of an amphibian, the broad mouth with heavy lower lip, the nose large and curved, not a bony curve but a light, fleshy curve toward the mouth, the forehead high and tensed like a bow and the high, broad cheekbones, as if seen through a magnifying glass.

She saw that they had forgotten her and she began, relieved and irritated, to examine the armchair. She peered at its legs, carved with animal heads and garlands of flowers, and weaved a plait from the tufts of the cover. Suddenly—right there in front of her—she saw the picture. For a moment she wondered if it was a picture or a real form, but the boy, in his total nakedness, did not move from his place, and his hand continued to lean on a long shepherd's crook, beside him a dog frozen in mid-leap. Her breathing stopped in paralyzing fear . . . she turned her face away, but her eyes were riveted to the naked apparition. She withdrew her eyes again, sure that Yosef and this Potiphar's wife, in the velvet gown, were reading what was happening inside her.

"Do you agree to let Carmela draw you?" asked Yosef's voice, coming from a distance. He nodded his head at her so she would do likewise. This is the trap! The nakedness of the boy! *She* painted him! A painter—of nudes! And they want to paint *her* naked!

"So long as she holds that expression . . ." She heard the velvet voice, also approaching. "No, no, Mayale, don't spoil it, go on looking like that . . ." She felt the expectation in Yosef's eyes. The woman disappeared.

"Go on looking like that, like before," said Yosef. "Beautiful here, eh? A palazzo from the Brothers Grimm . . . furniture from the flea market in Rome . . ."

She wanted to ask what was so beautiful about fleas from Rome, but the woman returned in a short gown, paint-stained and with rolled-up sleeves, and opened the curtains. The light fell on her face as she sat opposite her on a low couch and laid a board on her knees, sheets of paper and a pencil between her fingers. Now she saw the porous skin above the cheekbones and the flecks of powder that covered it and the red grooves on her lips, like the little channels of caked blood outside the slaughterer's house.

"She's too tense," said the artist. "*Duce,* can you do something to occupy her? *Du–ce!*"

"So, what games did you play this morning?" said Yosef, leaning on the high wooden shelf and winking to encourage her. A big glass of drink appeared in his hand.

"We didn't play," she replied and sat up, unconsciously, to peep at the drawing. She couldn't make out anything between the lines. She wondered when she would try to strip her.

"That's impossible," said Yosef gently. "Ring o'roses, eh? Farmer's horse, eh? New donkey . . . nothing?"

She hated his servility and the bullshit he tried to trap her with.

"Skin color of a corpse," said the woman, and she hurriedly rolled more candies in her mouth. He moved from the shelf and approached, bent down and put his glass to the girl's lips with an enchanting smile. She choked loudly. The alcohol simultaneously burned her teeth, her nose, her gullet, and cut her tongue and her insides. They both laughed.

"Take an olive," he cried as he laughed. "Quick, take an olive!"

Outside was the stillness of noon.

"Do you love him?" asked the woman, regaining her composure and glancing alternately at her cheeks and her chin.

"Who?" she said, full of helpless fury, not knowing what to do with the olive pit that was left in her mouth.

"What a question!"

"I don't love anyone!" she grumbled around the pit.

"More?" asked Yosef, putting the cup to her lips.

"A generation of clever kids has grown up," said the woman. "Once they thought you had to invest love to make a percentage on it . . . *Duce*, would you be so kind? In the studio, on the table, there are two charcoal crayons, and in the fridge are Alfonse grapes, the kind you like."

"*Duce*" went out. He obviously knew where the studio was, and the refrigerator where he could find his favorite grapes.

"That charlady from Petah Tikvah, the one who scrubs floors for you," said the artist casually, as if to make her talk, her eyes looking up at her and falling to the paper in turns, "is she still with you?"

All her fears at once gave way to pure vindictiveness.

"The charlady from Petah Tikvah? Sure she is! Everyone's crazy about her," she prattled. "She's got *natural* color on her lips and cheeks, and she's ever so, ever so pretty . . ."

"Who's ever so, ever so pretty?" asked Yosef, a dish of grapes in his hand.

"Maya's mother," replied the artist calmly, and smiled at her. "It's no wonder."

"What's that you say?" She froze, a little girl offended. "Shoshana isn't my mother!"

Yosef drew laughter from the depths of the diaphragm. Then he came closer to lay the charcoal crayons on the board, slanting his eyes playfully at the Potipharess.

"She's too tense, your Santa Maya," said the woman with total calmness.

"You're making her tense," replied Yosef. The artist took a bunch of grapes from the dish and dangled them with a smile of appeasement, expecting Maya to reach out her hand.

"I don't like Alfonse," said Maya with childish stubbornness (she'd never tasted them).

The woman babbled again in the candy-language, and the girl guessed that her remarks were negative because Yosef frowned at her with his eyes and lips to confirm that the girl was indeed a little monster. Then he munched slowly at the grapes, as if liberated from the Potipharess.

Everything around was frozen, aside from the movements of the artist who paused from her work at intervals to sharpen the tip of the pencil with a scrap of sandpaper or to exchange it for the charcoal crayon, or to screw up papers and toss them into the corner.

Time dragged on endlessly, until the artist turned one of the sheets of paper toward Maya. Maya looked again and again at the drawing. She saw a slanted nose and two triangular eyes. Was this what her face really looked like?

"Do you like it?" said the Potipharess.

"Pani-Paula is our cook," replied Maya.

"Really? How nice!" The Potipharess curled her lips toward Yosef, inviting him to share a grown-up comment on the comical thought processes of children.

"And she always says," added Maya, "that when you cook with your behind it stinks. She's a strange woman."

"Pardon?"

"You heard," said Yosef, a smile hovering on his lips.

"A generation of clever kids," the woman smiled with a forced sigh of resignation, and went back to talking in the candy-language.

They let her alone again. The Potipharess was walking about the room, talking and laughing, and Yosef trailing behind her, touching her, fidgeting with the ornaments, lifting up statuettes to examine them, raising the lid of the piano and trying to pick out a tune between the keys. Occasionally they stole glances at her, furtively, as if not wanting to be caught. Until they stood before the painting of the nude.

"What, *Duce*? Do you really not recognize him?" she heard her voice. "What a charming man! He studied fresco at the academy near the Palazzo Vecchio . . . who else could it be? In Florence they joked that since he appeared in the place they stopped copying the statue of David. Always when he drew, there was somebody drawing him." She raised her arms and set the picture straight (any moment now she'll touch his genitals). "And what a culture! Here, in this country, you're all vulgar and impatient. Everything withers before it's had time to bloom—art, men, women, love . . ."

It seemed to her she had dozed off because Yosef came and touched her shoulder. She wished the woman would go on talking.

In the doorway the Potipharess took her leave of them. "Tomorrow there'll be ice cream," she said, and Yosef murmured something about how she was buying them both dirt cheap.

"Goodbye, Mayale!" said the woman. "You've been quite charming."

"Beautiful, eh?" asked Yosef among the fig trees, and at once he answered his own question: "A real bitch. The Milanese say you don't need to sniff the behind of a beautiful woman. They're all bitches, old lady . . ."

The girl had noticed before that grown-ups have a flawed sense of beauty, and the older they become, so the number of beautiful people around them grows: all you need is a mouthful of teeth. She listened with wonder to the emotion with which Yosef described meeting Carmela in Florence, where he spent the vacation from his studies. "And then—just imagine it! We meet again here in Kiryat Shkak." There they had been happy together because they both spoke Hebrew, and here Italian was their bond.

"Will you marry her?" she interrupted him. He stopped and laughed into her face, that quiet laugh of his which began in the diaphragm and ended in the moustache.

"Do me a favor, *Bambola*," he said when he had recovered a little. "Just don't be a Yenta like all the other women I know!" But at once he drew her shoulder to his waist. "No, no, you're alright, old lady, you're alright."

She remembered with embarrassment his furtive fondling of Potiphar's wife.

"Ten years from now . . . ," he stuck his finger between her shoulder blades, accompanying each word with a jab, "ten years from now I shall marry the ugliest and richest old widow in the Near East!"

"And Shoshana?" she wanted to ask, but now she managed to restrain her delight.

"Show me!" he said and pulled from her hand the folded paper that the artist had given her, glanced at it for a moment with knotted brows, a look that she interpreted as compassionate scorn, and gave it back.

The shops were already open and they hurried breathlessly up the hill.

"You went out to buy yogurt!" he reminded her before telling her to go into the house before him. The sun was veiled with translucent curtains and the tufts of fabric danced in her eyes. The next day at siesta time she invented complicated excuses for refusing, and almost relented out of pity at the look of childish disappointment drawn between his forehead and his moustache.

The pleasant humming of the airplane, like the sound of a violin, circled above the house. Now it will drop the bomb! She knows it's now, this very moment, and she is waiting. Something rips in the air, at once the walls begin to dance and dissolve, the stepmother streams blood and grinds her teeth, the wall slowly opens, the wind rushes in and whispers:

"Maya! Ma–ya, Ma–ya . . ."

Before her eyes is a field of scorched thorns and a little black lawn, between them small hillocks and filaments of red within white. The white of eyes. Eyes! She panics—Regina! "Ma–ya! Ma–ya," whispers the wind, and suddenly—dazzling brightness and a new smell, warm and laden with veiled memories, a weight pressing down on her and a sudden feeling of weakness when she recognized the voice.

"What's happened? What's happened?" She tried to sit upright and burst into tears.

"No, no, don't get up, *Bambina.*" He leaned over her again with his warm teeth.

Something cool touched her forehead (what's he doing here?) and pushed her into the pillow. "Don't cry, *Bambina*, don't cry, don't cry, don't," said the hand that soothed her forehead. As it had sprung forth, against her will, so the crying stopped.

"I wish you wouldn't stare at me like that." She saw his eyes smiling at her.

"Don't go away!" she said hurriedly as he rose and the bed lifted with her, flying! This was her first thought, with the troublesome awareness that she had no right.

"Of course not," he replied. Everything that fluttered in her sank and relaxed.

And there it was again. Above her brows something whose touch was moist and cool, in the same place where he laid his caresses. She wanted his caresses and not this moist and cool something.

"Now you're feeling better, Principessa, eh?" She saw his big hand drawing up a chair, close to her face, and her eyes fixed on him without embarrassment as the strange words caressed her insides. She looked around her, but without alarm: a new, different light streaming through a new, different window, and a fly crossing the golden streak of dust that quivered beneath the ceiling.

"Where am I?" she asked, although she knew.

"In my room," he answered, as if happy at the thought. "Do you remember anything? You're sick, you're in bed, reclining like Cleopatra, and a very important man is wasting his time on you. Meanwhile, the peasants are in revolt."

A sense of jubilation leaped inside her—sick! The sweetness of release! She's given over to the domain of pleasures and to his domain. She closed her eyes so she could open them and be convinced anew. When she raised her head the old pain stabbed again at her brain—and she remembered. Her neck was heavy and her head bandaged.

"Damn you!" He twisted his lips into a comical smile and punched lightly with his fist at the outstretched hand. "I thought you were going."

"Where to?" she wondered, and listened with amazement to the real concern in his voice as he laid her hand on his knee, lifting a finger and letting go, lifting her thumb and letting go.

"Where to? To Heaven's Gate," he laughed, as if accusing her of something.

The bed! The thought flashed through her mind. The bed is his! Her other hand furtively caressed soft wool. She lowered her eyes to the woolen blanket and the heavy army trench coat on top of it, and felt sure, with pain, that he was no longer beside her, it was all a dream.

She lay exhausted in moist silence, the pain of his absence piercing her.

His body approached again, waving something in its hand, like a signal flag. He replaced the warmth on her forehead with coolness, and his warm teeth flashed again. She saw that he had caught her staring at the trench coat.

"I've no desire to donate my blood," he said and laughed.

She wanted to tell him it was a long time since they had mounted a bug hunt in her room and her blanket was fumigated and all soaked in kerosene, but he raised her hand from his knee and rubbed it against his cheek, on the field of scorched thorns. She had never before touched . . . one of those things she wanted only . . .

"A beard thirty-six hours old," he went on rubbing her hand on his cheek. "Nice. You women love this . . . Only a barber can take it off, and you'll pay it all—plus service, plus heartache."

"Alright!" she said grimly, almost with hostility.

"Hey! A smile! What an old grouse you are! We want to see a smile!"

"Alright!" she repeated, but didn't smile. He burst out laughing, until the tears stood in her eyes.

She felt the place filling up with another body and raised her heavy head. Pani-Paula filled the vacuum and took the place of the man.

"Is she still alive?" her voice asked, in Yiddish.

She saw the fleshy dewlap bouncing above her and the two hairs sprouting like antennae from a black mole.

"Why didn't you say—my ears hurt, why?" she said petulantly. "*Kino! Kino!* No responsibility and no human being! *Kino!* That's all they think about. In Poland they don't even let students go *zum kino!*"

Now she remembered how she went to the movie theater with Margarita and how she lost consciousness when the pain started piercing her brain. But the rest of her thoughts revolved around the quivering dewlap and how to cut it out of the cook's face. I wish she'd go away, away from here, she thought. So it'll be like it was before, before she came and spoiled it, so he'll ask me again to put on a smile.

"Now, Madam, take your tablet quickly! No tricks!"

She swallowed hastily, because Yosef was watching, and the water went up her nose. She felt the pill slithering down, kicking and resisting.

"No tricks. Quickly now, there's no time to waste, hot oil in the ear!" said Paula, anticipating her refusal.

"Tell me who's going to pay for the operation," she grumbled at Yosef, the syringe poised in the air. "I? You?!" she said in Yiddish. "Der Minister still hasn't condescended to appear. Markovski ran this morning to send another cable. What a waste of money, just imagine . . . looking, for *him* they're looking? I hope a bomb finds him first, Lord of Creation! So they can send him prescriptions to the end of his days, Lord of Creation!"

He mustn't come, said Maya to herself as if swearing an oath. He mustn't come, he mustn't, so Yosef won't see him!

"Enough, that's enough!" he snapped impatiently. "Give me the syringe!"

She felt his hand, delicately unbinding her head, the cotton wool removed from her ear and the caress of the liquid. Then he adjusted the compress on her neck, his face close to hers. She followed the cook with her eyes, to see if she'd noticed in his movements something she shouldn't notice.

Then she heard their quiet conversation beside the door. They were talking about her. For a moment she envied the old woman that he was talking with her thus, and at the same time she felt a tremulous joy that she was so important to him that he talked about her to the old witch.

When he closed the door behind her he turned up his eyes in gratitude.

"Don't take any notice," he said, "it won't be long before all these people disappear from your life." He cracked a smile of complicity.

Again he removed the warm towel from her forehead and shook it out in front of him with both hands. It returned to her forehead as cold as ice, as if he'd worked a spell. He told her to do this from time to time—to shake it in the air and put it back—and suddenly he went out and left her.

From time to time she was roused by the echo of muffled sounds, the running of water in pipes, or the regular ticking of a hidden clock, and then she would shake the towel heavily, telling herself his hands had done this, and sinking back into a gnawing slumber of longings, preceded by the brief flickering thought that in sleep she cut short the waiting for his return. She stirred at the sudden touch of cold tin and clatter of dishes in her ear. Disappointed, she gulped at the sour tasting soup, leaning reluctantly against the fleshy, doughlike arm, until she sealed her lips.

"Eat! Eat!" growled Pani-Paula. "You must eat up and get well quickly! There's no time to give so much attention to one girl! These modern fathers!"

The old expectation returned to pierce her, and with it yearnings for what had been, and now she saw, for a split-second, old eyeballs floating in their sockets, and alive within them a fragment of true affection.

"Well, well," the cook sighed, like one whose strength is not enough to embrace what is and all that will be, but at once she went back on herself. "Come on, eat up, time is short!"

Then she became blurred.

He breathed into her eyelids immediately after she felt his coming to her in her sleep. All the expectation turned into a kind of sweet and soft jelly.

"Another bullet!" he said sternly to the palm of his hand, as if some little monster was caught in it. "Pull back the bolt. Open the safety catch! Fire! And the disease is dead."

The evening stole into the room. She saw a shadow and the whiteness of eyes and teeth. Now he supported her bandaged head, put her face close to his neck to give her a drink from the tin cup. To make the time last longer, she drank most of the brackish, scorching water until he lightly drew the cup from between her teeth. The water spilled on her chin, and he wiped away the drops with his finger. Already the room was full of evening and full of Yosef. He switched on the light and blinked before it like a baby. The electric light pleased her with its unexpected strength. She remembered that Yosef had installed a generator on the roof. When she looked back at him she saw that his cheeks were shaved, thus depriving her of part of the experience that belonged only to the two of them. With his bluish face and the smell of shaving soap, he had returned to the domain of the others. Only his moustache—that little lawn—remained hers.

"Come on now, mouth open wide!" He imitated the voice of the manageress. "No tricks, you wild animal! And we'll fill you up with these slops from the kitchen! Tomorrow I'll go down to the village and buy for you a whole chicken coop, and they can all go to Hell!"

She swallowed the rice porridge that he held before her, grind-

ing her teeth on the little stones, but didn't stop until she heard
the scrape of the spoon on the bottom of the enamel plate.

"Tea with lemon!" he announced as if this were the next item
in a show. His mouth moved slightly as she gulped, like the
mouth of a mother feeding a baby, and his eyes fixed on the
spoon and her mouth, on the spoon and her mouth. When he
let go her head she wondered where the pillow had come from
(she remembered him saying how much he hated pillows), while
his moustache hovered for a moment over her forehead, waiting
for its touch. Suddenly he sprang up from his seat.

"*Bambina*! What do you know! The fever has gone! It's gone!
In the morning they'll move you to the infirmary and you'll be
a human being again. Eh? Are you glad? Hey, *Bambina*!"

He's glad!

"I say!" He stretched his arms and his back, as if relieved of a
burden. "No girl has ever yet succeeded in keeping me awake so
long! Ah, Madonna, Madonna! Isn't life wonderful!" He yawned
until his jawbones cracked. "So wonderful . . . but I'm dying to
sleep . . ." Then he wrapped her in the blanket, but with less
careful movements than before, and lifted her in his arms and
put her down in the chair. She watched him as he changed the
sheet and prayed the fever would return.

"I think my temperature's going up again," she said. He looked
at her sidelong and laughed. The–the swine!

He put her back onto a dry and cool sheet, tucked in the blanket
with those less careful movements and covered her again with the
coat.

"If you want to sleep, here's the switch! Just lift your hand! All
the comforts! At last we shall all sleep properly, eh? Then I'll pay
you a lightning visit to check on the fever. But God help you if
you wait for me! Eh? *Adio*! *Principessa, adio*!" he sang cheerfully.
"Tonight my *Palazzo* is at your disposal!"

He went to the other world. He'll smile and sing like this to the rest of them! Everything will melt and sink and disappear. Suddenly he stopped by the door and returned to the bed, and that look enfolded her again, as if unwilling to melt and disappear. Unknowingly, she held out her hand and touched his hand with her fingertips. His hand held hers and let it go at once.

Before she slept she wondered fearfully where he was spending the night, and at once she realized. She clasped with her hands the stiff collar of the coat, as if wanting to strangle him. In the night she missed his "lightning visit," and in the morning the women transferred her to the empty infirmary.

One evening Maya felt the urge to show her notebook of poems to Yosef. Until that moment this had been the privilege of a few children only, sentimental judges who were either flattered by the disconcerting awareness that she was one of them or blinded by envy. Now she laid her sole treasure on the jeweler's table. See how he focuses the light of the lamp, fits the magnifying glass in his shrewd, pitiless eye, takes the stones one by one in delicate tweezers, turns their sparkling faces this way and that, with pedantic patience. His fingertip will probe the flaws, will feel the roughness, and his nail will scratch the surface.

She looked anxiously at his face. The imaginary glass was already sucked into the muscles of his eye, and her guts were full of ice. At first he skimmed through the pages like a light wind, then he flicked their edges three times between finger and thumb, as if this was a deck of cards. Suddenly he was drawn to one of them and read it through hastily, skipping the rest. Now she saw his face in which there was no sign of encouragement or discouragement—neither the sympathetic appraisal of a food taster commending unfulfilled promise nor even the false wonder of one who plants confidence in novices.

"Come on, let's go up to the roof," he said hastily, laying down the notebook.

The roof was always closed. Aside from Ketzele, no child had set eyes on it, and since the time that the burial society stole away the Old Man Slonim, the keys to the lost kingdom had been in Yosef's hands.

She tried to summon up the image of Slonim before her eyes and remembered only that he used to smoke cigarette butts in a little holder, and every match he split into two lengthwise, and when he wrote he would wipe his pen on the black yarmulka on his head. The Old Man Slonim was scared of the children and locked his door against them. Once she peeped inside and saw him combing his beard in front of the mirror, combing it this way and that and parting it in the middle, moistening his moustache with spittle and curling it sideways. Then he sighed and returned to his bed.

When the door was opened she was stunned at the massive expanse of the roof, open to the sky and overlooking the blacked-out city sprawling far away to the west and breathing with the sea. A hidden, menacing movement, cold and blurred. Everything unreal except he who stands with her in the heart of the roof like a lifeguard's flag. A cheerful fire, and if it fades everything will die with it, the cold will sweep her away, and then she'll be dragged from this roof into the brooding vortex below. She paced behind him and saw him sit in a rocking chair that was, apparently, the leisure time refuge of the Old Man Slonim. The city disappeared over the balustrade, leaving behind the darkness and the cold anticipation. A searchlight cleft the sky.

"Where are you?" he whispered (Why's he whispering?) and drew her to him, telling her the legends of the stars and their journeys. The heavens were created for her anew, and he was their creator and the giver of names.

"That star, the blue one, you see it? Yes?"

"That one? Yes," she pointed to the sky, whispering.

"This star is—you. And here, the group beside it, Orion— that's me! You should never point to the stars—they say that it makes warts sprout on your fingers. Show me your finger."

And then it happened, the wonderful, inconceivable thing. He kissed her finger, and suddenly she was in his lap, wrapped in his arms, in the rocking of the chair, and afraid to wake up, inhaling with all her senses the first awareness of a man, a sensation both crushing and healing. She wanted to weep and to laugh, and never had she desired life so much as in this moment of a vision-not-herself. His fingers raised her head from his lap and turned her face to his eyes.

"Crying, *Bambina?*" he leaned toward her, and again her skin felt the rough stubble of his cheek and the soft touch of his lips.

"I'm crazy," he whispered into her eyes that seemed blinded by light. "I'm crazy," he repeated as if consulting her. Disbelief invaded her suddenly. She felt this was only a game, and she hadn't yet learned the rules. "I don't believe it myself . . . I don't believe it," she heard his voice murmuring as if out of the stillness. Suddenly voices were heard close by, he hastily pushed her from his knees, and in that brief instant she understood it was forbidden for others to see them like this, and, therefore, the whole thing was true. These were the voices of strangers.

"*Duce*! I'll bet he's on the roof!"

"Hey, Doctor Doolittle, I need you! My goat's expecting a bastard!"

"Is there anyone here?"

The figures moved around the doorway until he called them to him, to the depths of the roof.

"Ciao, Benito!"

"Hey, look what we have here! Yankele, come here and see something!" shouted a high voice.

"Reading by starlight? Healing the Great She-Bear? Looking for the Milky Way? Romancing, *Piccolina?*"

The hostel had recently been transformed into a place of peculiar activities. At night young men and women would appear, all of them chattering in pidgin Italian because of Yosef. The girls practiced first aid in the dining room, and to divert the curiosity of the pupils, they taught them too, showing them how to cut out and fold triangular bandages, how to apply tourniquets and knee dressings. All these activities were defined as "Rapid response to air bombardment." But from the roof there were then heard the voices of the young men, wrestling in the darkness, or the sharp cracks of the sticks they had brought with them, hidden up their sleeves, and from Yosef's room—secret conversations. The pupils swore not to reveal anything that their eyes saw.

"All signs are deceptive," said the high voice.

"So where are we going to sit?"

For a while there was an awkward silence as they searched for a place to sit, or so it seemed to her.

"All signs are deceptive—that I learned from Elimelech! Don't you mock Elimelech."

"How's it going, Pasha? How long—how far? Haven't you finished this harem yet?" asked a thick, guttural voice.

"Then listen," said the high voice. "We were sitting with Elimelech at the tennis court. Sunshine, warmth, everybody content, nothing to trouble the spirit, only the failure of the team . . ."

"Hey, listen Nahumka, we came here for other business!" said a growling voice from the group sitting around on the black asphalt floor.

"Let me finish, turd. Anyone would think your whole life was business, really . . . Yes, then suddenly there dropped into the court a fantastic pair of melons . . ."

"Again? Friends, do us a favor. Give him a tranquilizer, *Duce.*"

"Go for a walk on the roof, check out the topography . . . that too," said the high voice angrily. "Let me talk seriously for once."

"Okay, okay, just get it over with quick," said the growling voice.

"Then I said to Elimelech: 'Listen, no traffic cop's going to stop me riding that thing!' Then this is what he said to me," he turned to Yosef: " 'That thing reaches right to her bumper . . .' Hey, hey, Lemech! It was just something . . . something that excited my weak nerves . . . 'To that thing I give a guarantee of at least two years!' I say to Lemech. Now you know Lemech . . ."

"Maybe that's enough for today," said the growling voice, and Maya saw that the speaker was the double of Yosef, moustache, eyes full of white.

"Then he gives me a look," the high voice went on impatiently, "like a scythe on a new combine. So I explained to him: 'It's just that . . . you understand? It isn't natural for a woman's breasts to stick out like that for ever! A shape like that you won't find in any animal. It's a state of readiness, it has to be exploited."

"Friends, then why did you say there isn't . . ."

"You understand it too! I got up and crossed over the court. 'What are you doing tonight?' 'Looking for somebody to buy a movie ticket.' I like the way she talked. None of the usual stuff, leading you on and pushing you off until you feel like a wet match. Then we went to my parents' apartment. They'd gone to Tiberias. Good luck to them. She forgot about the movies. Right away I saw Lemech was blind, blind—but he's got eyes. I was livid . . . not so much as a . . . and then I went to sleep in the other room. I left money on the table so she could get a taxi. In the morning she wasn't there. At least she was intelligent. You know who it was? The little hooker, the one that went with . . ."

"What are you saying?" said the growling voice. "What are you saying? I wouldn't have believed it!"

The other men grinned noisily until Maya heard Yosef's voice reminding them of her presence.

"No matter, no matter!" replied the thick, guttural voice.

"As that instructor of ours is always telling us: 'Before you go into battle you must sniff gunpowder.' "

Maya saw that he too was like Yosef—moustache and whites of eyes.

"Let her learn about life!"

"And always stand in a state of readiness!" yelled the high voice.

The laughter spread over the roof, rebounded off the balustrade and returned, creating a strong and dangerous sense of male intimacy. "*Andiamo!*" said somebody, and suddenly they rose and turned to the door. Yosef took her arm and ran with her down a flight of stairs. Outside his room he stopped, fumbled in his pockets, and handed her something solid. It was his dynamo torch. "Don't you go and get lost now, eh?" And he breathed on her neck.

Alone she went down the stairs, calming her bewilderment and fears with the metallic clicking of the flashlight switch.

A whole week—and Yosef had been gone. He didn't even say goodbye.

At that time there were in Kiryat Shkak as many novelty shops as there were synagogues. Do we know a Hasid without fur hat and tobacco? So there is no house without its store of trinkets and notions.

The vista of this street should have an advocate acting on its behalf, if only to prevent us suspecting our brothers in the village of narrow-mindedness and abstinence from thought, among all the other vanities of the world. There is a simple explanation for what has happened. These brothers of ours who have earned for themselves an everlasting name in literature, all these peddlers who used to roam about the villages and the fringes of army camps, equal in number to their customers—when they began to feel boots up their backsides, they closed their trunks and put them on board ship, and once they had kissed the soil of the Holy Land, together with their sucklings and their loving wives, they hastened to Kiryat-Shkak, opened the same trunks, and shook out all the contents before them—in some dingy cell, in some cramped stairway, or in some open intersection between alleys—and eked out an exiguous livelihood selling trinkets in the new homeland. Take for example Reb Fishel Fishmann, the great textile trader from Lodz. He has indeed come down in the world, yet he too says "it's good" in his cut-rate store, whose display window looks out on the main street, and on account of it he even holds sway in the local council.

And it may be that the case is otherwise. This boom in the haberdashery business was maintained and fueled precisely by the mounting poverty of the local populace, just as the ricinus blossoms in abundance on every garbage heap in the streets. The soul, however modest it may be, desires novelties, something that the practiced, weary eye may seize on, and what can they buy, the sons of Kiryat Shkak—pianos, brooches, and earrings? At times, when the soul desires, they will enter such a store, a little place where there is nothing to arouse grief or shame, standing before the sales counter from the morning blessings to the evening prayers, rummaging among the assorted garments, holding them up to the light, testing the embroidery and the stitching with that expertise born of generations, searching for some hidden bargain, turning the stack on its head in a great heap, without any protest from the shopkeeper—because they are all one family, almost— then hesitating, jangling the coins in the palms of their hands; and, finally, when the shopkeeper gives the encouragement of the last "yes," they take up again that worthless trinket—the one they first touched—on behalf of the child of their old age, the elastic ribbon that the proprietor swears, hand on heart, came from Switzerland, on the last ship before the blockade, prewar manufacture and a unique process . . . the soul is gratified, and the money in the palm is almost enough to buy—like sniffing a citron.

Even the children of the "Fifth Heaven" are eager for such trifles. Some fine mechanism of the soul has driven from their hearts all major desires, such as would harden their hearts and diminish their self-esteem, so they are not hurt by their inability to realize them. Consider, if you will, a child mounted on a gleaming tin car, or some bleary-eyed brat who pedals a toy bicycle around the "good" streets of the village: a clip holds his hair in place to preserve his fine forehead until his wedding day, he runs and prattles to his mother of everything, and she splatters his face with wet kisses. In winter he exudes a smell of apples, and in summer of oranges. At school he arrives with a parcel of food neatly wrapped in tissue paper (because newspaper poisons our little body with lead). His homework is always done, arrogantly displayed on the desk, the margins of the paper covers of his schoolbooks are broader than is necessary, he has pencil cases of leather and wood and tobacco tins donated by uncles, and his mother is always galloping there in recess to talk with the teacher, and anyway . . .

All the illusory charms of tin cars, rollerskates, scooters—all are dispelled from the hearts of the hostel children, as every man dispels from his heart awareness of the cosmic void when he seeks to attach importance to his actions on the ground.

But trinkets! This is the world of the hostel children! What a world of trinkets! A pocket comb—a little, personal comb! Its head peeps out from your pocket like a little pet animal, devoted to its master. You draw it out with a proprietorial flourish, casually, so to speak, raising up in your hair what there is to raise and smoothing the rest down smoothly, and no impatient child will yell behind your back: "Hey, you, haven't you finished with it yet?"

Sunglasses! You mount them on the root of the nose, and at once your age is hidden behind them. Mysterious, mature, and sinister, discovering things invisible to others! The dust-consumed delusions dress in dewy foliage; the emboldened fields call out to you with a challenge; the sky, layer upon layer of blue, roof upon roof, and new streams of light flowing and whirling, racing to enfold the birds in their flight; and the sun, in a mood of sudden tenderness, allows you to look it straight in the eye.

A ring! The third finger adorned with a ring becomes important. The third finger has a kind of mysterious wisdom, a power that you may revel in. A ring has so many potential uses, such that every sinew in your body acquires a new significance.

Fantasies! It is not the habit of the hostel children to immerse themselves in the artificial pools of fantasy. Always, when the time comes, somebody will be there to dash the leading raft against the shores of reality.

When they take a short cut to the school they pass by the Talmud Torah, throwing a stone at one of its side-curled pupils and moving on, heads held high, without fear of reprisal, to the little alley, the one that lies between the shanties like a long, clodded tongue between two rows of broken teeth, counting the stunted shanties until they arrive at the fifth of them. Pausing for a moment to decide if this is really the place, until they discover near the roof that special stain of mold: from a rent in the tarred paper, peeling like roasted skin, spreads a patch of mold in the shape of a scorpion. And this is the cut-price store.

Suddenly the eager excitement inside her melted away. Standing alone before the door, whose paint was split and blistered as if consumed by a malignant disease, Maya felt the palpitations in her gut. Snakes of cold crept out from the alien threshold, entwining her ankles, and the little coin bit into her clenched palm. Her ears absorbed the angry, whispered urgings of the boys hiding behind the fence.

Then she touched with her fingertips the handle of the door, but before she could turn it, it seemed to move at the touch of her breath, and already a bell was jangling loudly, as if to scare her off. The door swung slowly on its hinges, and there was darkness.

Darkness and dead air, laden with the heavy smell of fabrics and a kind of labored, truncated sighing.

Opposite her, in the depths, from the mouth of some dark niche, a veiled skull floated up to the surface of the pale, threadbare light. A phantom shape swam before her, wrapped in grey cloth, suspended in space, whispering mysterious spells, dragging with it the illusion of a body and sprinkling bubbles of venom.

When the figure came within touching range of her and stretched out before her a probing worm's head, Maya froze in terror. A nose and a shriveled mouth appeared from inside the grey hood, and the wrinkled, black-lidded eyes of a night bird, the eyes of Hansel's witch when she holds out her hand to test the softness of his flesh.

Now Maya is sure that this is a witch who knows everything there is to know. It seems to her she's been standing here a long time—since the dawn of eternity she's been here and forever and ever she must stand here and look into those eyes, stare at the downy cheeks and the shriveled mouth. With some cruel flash of dread, she knows that this witch is she herself: beyond the mountain ranges of time, beyond the heights that she must cross, will spread before her an endless plain, a plain without tree and without flowers, without any living soul, and she will wander there, in this fearful form, across the ruined ground, will wander, her skin pasty, freckled with huge patches, her fingernails long and twisted, wander and drag with her the illusion of a body until she vanishes into the infinite.

From the quivering head before her there came a weak, suspicious croak: "*Vos vilst du?*" There was in this figure none of the endearing rosy-cheeked benevolence of elderly folk in fairy tales—just intense animosity, bubbling with secret evil.

Above her head, on a thin cord, giant scissors hung from the ceiling, blades apart, grinning coldly with perverse impatience.

Beside the door, behind her, came a hasty rustling movement. The dreadful, paralyzing fear dissolved at once, to be replaced by the alarming thought that she hadn't done what they had instructed her to do, which was to distract the attention of the old woman in some way, purchasing something with the single coin that was hoarded in her hand. And this must be done now. She must discover some . . . But first Salomon, and after him Mikki and Ketzele, and maybe another, had already burst in behind her with profane step, pressing into the feeble light and bringing with them torrents of outside air and outside light, the bell heralding their entry with loud peals, like an imprisoned soul awaiting its deliverance. Now Maya clearly sensed that they came not to do wrong; on the contrary, they came to do justice, to exact a necessary revenge for a misdeed.

Ketzele posed casually by the counter and caressed the assorted trinkets with his hand. At Maya's side was heard a rapid curse, a hand seized her clenched fist, hurting her, and snatched the coin from her grip. She looked at Salomon without anger and felt that now she was breathing, really breathing, from the diaphragm! Salomon approached the old woman (now she's "the old woman"—no more!), raised his voice arrogantly, and, as if it was in his power to buy up the entire stock, asked for a comb. At once he opened his hand under her nose, the two-tone negroid hand, and showed her the coin. The old woman peered this way and that, bowed her head over his palm as if to sniff it, then dragged her body to one of the counters, Salomon slouching behind her in his docker's cap.

And then—like a match in the straw!

Like a swarm of young locusts they flung their bodies against the counter, sprawling up to their waists, hands groping in momentary blindness, and already that sweet release making all the nerves tingle! To fill the void, the void, just to extinguish desire, and already it's mounting, blazing in the arms, the teeth, the palate. Everything—for you, for your body! Snatch the foreign and make it yours, suddenly, at a touch, just by taking it! Oh, yes. And this shining thing, this gleaming thing, this crimson! To satisfy, to satisfy all, and more, and him, the faraway. Just take, take . . .

Suddenly the vortex broke into a straight line, striking at the heart, at the eardrums, and a kind of blinding whiteness, stunning the senses: "Thieves! Thieves!"

She felt their headlong leap toward the door and the bell going ding-dong, ding-dong, ding-dong. Toward her sprang a thick, yellow tangle of hair. Inside it she saw a red wound open, and she felt as if someone had dropped a heap of rags at her feet.

The old man! How did they forget the old man? His hands clutched a massive tome of the Talmud.

She too was already in the white outside, her body outside and her eyes still inside, in the vision of the red wound, and in her ears the ringing of the bell and a voice crying out from the red wound, suddenly mingling with the sounds of outside. A woman's scream, the movement of people, and the pounding of feet.

She knows she has the strength to outrun the interfering strangers, who have no connection with the business. The air is light, silky, a kind of flying in the feet, the delicious fear of the chase. They are far behind or close. Don't look back, better not to know! Run, run, and breathe the air that runs to meet you.

If a hand catches your shoulder, don't respond! New things, new terrors! If you escape, everything will be as normal. There's a wonderful charm in the unknown, and some weird desire to fall into the hands of the strangers. The lungs swell with white-hot air, scorching, scorching, white-hot . . . no further, impossible! Find somewhere to hide and dissolve! Here, this alley? Where does it lead to? A hole in the shoe! Run with leg bent, smother the pain in your foot. Climb over the concrete fence. What's this sign say? BEWARE, VICIOUS DOG! Go back at once! A trap! Where to? Who was the child who ran before you?

Things fall from her pockets, clattering behind her. Why? To have to run and lose things too? Lose everything?

Look. Here, where it's dark. Stand quietly in the unknown

stairwell, pant until the nostrils split, until you faint. Suddenly there are no pursuers. Just running water cascading in some pipe, drumming against its sides and wailing bitterly. Through a closed door the murmur of strange, distant voices, quarreling, the cry of a baby.

A lovely light outside, and all is quiet. You can go. Already here's the top of the hill and the start of the straight limestone path, there's the horizon stretching away to the last Bedouin tent. Now you can burst into laughter! Remember that trembling old man with the big Talmud yelling, "Thieves!"

Next day was one of those mornings when spring kisses winter goodbye. The inmates who were left in the institution played "rounders" in a cleft in the hills—a broad patch of ground where warm pools still glistened. Smells of dried blood from the nearby slaughterer's house stung the nostrils, mingled with the light heat haze and with the honey fragrance of the yellow cassia. In the sparkling, humming air, from end to end of the field rose enthusiastic cries, kicking of bare feet, yells of triumph, and the regular clanging of the ball on the tin "base."

Those "dismissed" from the two rival teams, and Maya with them, sat together, all hostility forgotten, in the shadow of the hill, chattering and blinking in the bright light reflected from the field, waiting to be recalled and at the same time inhaling with pleasure the scent of the cool earth and enjoying its feel on the soles of their bare feet.

In the folds of the hill opposite, on the twisting path descending to the field, Maya saw one of the smaller children stumbling toward them and shouting between cupped hands. She strained her ears to listen—something she wouldn't have done at any other time—and heard his cries: "You gotta come right now! Home! Gotta come home right now!" As he approached, he brought clods of limestone tumbling down behind him and his face, even at that distance, glowed with excitement at the knowledge that he, one of the little ones, was empowered to disrupt the game of the big ones. The game carried on for a moment as if nothing had been heard, but then, all at once, like a shorted circuit, the bulbs went dead. She saw Salomon approaching the rock where the little boy stood, complaining bitterly that no one was listening to the message and raising his head to him. She knew he was questioning him. This was a signal to the others, who clustered together and rummaged in the pile of clothes that had been cast off their bodies one by one in the heat of the game. Then they climbed slowly up the hill, whistling and talking, carefree in the blossom-scented morning air.

Maya looked again at Salomon, who had sent the boy away and was talking to Ketzele, who stood beside him. Now the two of them waited, hanging back together as if by agreement, for the others to leave, and she saw how they picked up their crumpled shirts with a casual stoop of the back. She stood up from her seat and approached them to retrieve her own. They turned to go, trailing their feet in the dust, as if to slow the passage of time with their heels.

As if her whole being longed to sleep, to sink down in some distant place and sleep, she walked before them slowly, expecting them to catch her up, to form with her a close-knit band of initiates, with the strength and insolence to predict whatever awaited them and face it squarely. As time passed and still they didn't come, she turned aside from the path to the edge of the field. She stopped and picked for herself a few pods of wild garlic, squeezing the seeds from them, but her fingers found only their bitter smell and none of the flesh.

The two boys came up to the place where she stood and passed by her, dragging their shirts on the path, leaving behind them the trails of their voices like the horn of a passing car.

Maya bent down and noticed the soft young carpet of moss, hidden away between the rocks and the tall grass. She felt a sudden desire to take it, all of it, to herself, to caress its bright skin. She probed with her fingers and scooped up a handful, but now it was mingled with earth, the skin became brittle and crumbled and its sheen was dulled. All this time there coiled within her a hidden, consuming, tormenting voice, a voice constantly asking, "What will Yosef say?" She made an effort not to think of this and found herself thinking of his eyes shifting above her with contempt and smiling at some other person. She wanted only to take to herself this moss, all of this soft carpet, to put it to her cheek, and then to sleep . . .

In the dining room the tense expectation struck her in the face. Already all were pressed around the table, eyes flashing with the glow of provocation. Unconsciously she turned her eyes to the kitchen door, to find him leaning his back against it, as was his way, in his white shorts and with tanned legs crossed, his face glowering at her in brooding concentration and at once relaxing with the very lightest hint of a smile. But the door was empty. In her nostrils rose the smell of the tattered oilcloth, the rancid smell of stale food and soiled tea towels. And then she saw the back of the old man. He sat apart from the table on a children's chair, like a weird bride being introduced to callers, and the fringes of his faded frock coat trailed on the floor in the mud stains brought in by the children. Even before she entered, she knew he was here. She stood beside the entrance with a strange hope that the moment it was all over, without them noticing her, she could slip away first from the place and everything would pass, like so many things that you only need let pass and they disappear and are forgotten. But she knew this was a vain hope because already Shoshana was calling to her with repressed fury: "Would you mind coming in and closing the door? All the flies . . ." And at once she continued with her interrupted speech, mentioning the police and again: "Don't just stand there, move!" Why won't they let her do as *she* wants, and instead she must walk toward the vacant place at the table, cutting with her body through the expectation filled with warnings, and at the same moment seeing the face and beard of the old man—the wispy yellowish beard, smaller than it was yesterday (yesterday!)—nodding repeatedly toward his chest with a mourner's motion, and his eyes suddenly opening and fixing on her, on her of all people, a look of entreaty, as if appealing to her for support in his calamity. Bemused, she waited for the moment when the dim eyes would come alight with the evil, knowing flash of recognition, and again that big red wound would gape open, yesterday's vision, imprinted on her mind.

The ceiling, Yosef, the walls, Yosef, the colors, the oilcloth, the children's heads, Yosef's eyes, the kitchen door, the ceiling, Yosef's face above her, the yellow beard, Yosef—and everything lovely circles within circles, perfectly round. Everything wanting to sleep. To sleep, to sleep in the circles within circles.

. . . She's walking in the street. In her hand a big collecting-box, jangling, and here is Margarita with her. Margarita has the paper ribbons in a new, brown bag. They knock on doors, climb brightly·lit staircases, and descend strange dark staircases, entering long corridors where the smells of vegetable soup hang in the air. They all take ribbons from Margarita, and nobody slips a donation in the box. They shout, angry and refusing to contribute. A big, thick woman, a filthy down on her cheeks, opens a big pan in her kitchen and shows them little children cooking inside, then takes a handful of ribbons from the bag and hangs them in a row across her mighty chest, like medals. The ribbons begin to sing a very familiar and irritating song. Maya tries to remember what the song is, but the woman doesn't want to contribute to the fund and she shouts at them. She tries an insolent tone, but the woman takes no notice. The woman doesn't understand Hebrew. This makes her nervous. The box is empty, only the chain beneath the slit is rattling inside, until the box is wet, and Margarita says: "Don't worry. This is only a dream, and it's wet." Why is it wet? Eyes like . . . teeth breathe into her face, like warm popcorn, and what a bubbling sweetness! She stood up from her place, and they all stood around her, she didn't know why, and at the same time she knew. And look, here too is Boria Markovski, pale and his chin quivering like jelly. The warm popcorn disappeared. Her teeth began to chatter like the beak of a stork. "Don't excite her!" she heard Boria's voice. She detests him. Always he rushes in to help her and ruins everything. Shoshana supported her and sat her on a chair. She hated Shoshana for treating her so tenderly. Where's that old man? Where's Yosef? Damn them, a plague on them all! I want an air-raid—right now! As she drank the water she saw the faces of the children, one by one. Aside from the naturally indifferent, all were scared, flushed. Tension is the food their souls feed on, like concentrated sugar.

"I'll get it out of her," she heard Pani-Paula yell, "if I have to turn the world upside-down!" Why's she yelling? "Grave robbers! Imbeciles!"

All around her they grinned those grins of pleasure, born of themselves at a time of great tension that isn't focused directly on them.

"I don't believe the girl did this!" she heard Boria's voice. "I've known her since the day she was born."

"But I did! I did! Yes—it was me!" Stabbing, pressure, and everything gushes out, like discharge from an ear infection, and the pressure inside her abates and relaxes. "Of course it was me! You idiot! I'll show you! I'll steal again! Always!"

All the time she knew she was talking nonsense, but the others didn't interpret it as nonsense, so it wasn't nonsense, but words that made nonsense out of Boria's words, and she felt a mounting desire to boast, boast wildly, extravagantly. Just wait, wait! She'll do more! She'll amaze him! To sharpen again and again his astonishment, his trust in her words, his fear and his hatred! So they'll know what she's capable of . . . And again, all the time, she felt she was only playing, toying with intoxicating dangers, until she felt the pincers of Pani-Paula's grip that clutched her arm. The face of the cook was contorted with fury: "Why's she still sitting there like a princess? She won't die of this! Not she!"

"You're making the girl sick!" shouted Boria in Yiddish.

"And you're murdering her! You murder them all with your disgusting sympathy! There! So she'll remember this all her life! She'll thank me some day!"

She felt a blow on her cheek and—singing stars—on the other cheek! The stars spin and sing . . . What a dreamy delight in punishment! What sweet self-pity and acceptance of the powerful sense of sacrifice.

And again—the children's faces, without malice and without complicity. And Salomon in his docker's cap. There's no doubt he's grateful to her, grateful and admiring. And inside her all is lit up! A pity they don't hit her some more!

When they opened her locker it seemed to her something like this had happened before, really. It's amusing the way things repeat themselves. Why is something repeated always funny and apparently less important?

In her locker were thrown and piled up, without any order, all the stolen things that they had divided up yesterday. All in her locker. All the little notebooks that stir the desire to fill them with writing, the sunglasses, the barrettes, pencils, plasticine. Everything, everything inside the special smell of her locker. And when she understood how all these objects had come to be in her locker, they suddenly congealed into an ugly porridge: her sacrifice that was no sacrifice. But at once she reconciled herself to all this, accepted it gladly in the awareness that thus it must be, without tears and without surprise. Immediately she recovered her composure.

"I don't believe she stole all this herself!" said Markovski, staring at her in horror. Again he's messing up the world for her! Why does he have to be so protective! She wants to see hatred around her, hatred and heartlessness!

"It was me, I stole it all!" she said. He doesn't believe her. Why doesn't he? Isn't she capable of stealing it all herself?

Downstairs they gave everything back to the old man. They wrapped everything in a newspaper and tied the parcel with string, but he protested and said this wasn't all of it and he wasn't going to move until . . . What is this? Does he expect to make a profit? He should learn to look after what's his!

They turned out all the lockers, searched the house and the yard, and found nothing more. Markovski thrust a few coins at him so he would shut his mouth and get out. The old man protested again and again, but he couldn't conceal his satisfaction when he yelled that "he never believed that thus he'd sell merchandize to Jews!"

Maya was punished with a three-day fast. But in those days she gobbled as she'd never gobbled before. The only commodity that Salomon and Ketzele didn't steal for her from the storeroom was salt. The three of them went out to a spot behind the slaughterer's house, and there they cooked a pie over a brazier in an empty pickled cucumber tin.

She ate from the tin and laughed. Ate and laughed. She had a strange feeling that she was eating their love.

33
A BROKEN STAIR

The recurrent chirp of the crickets within the silence. The hint of a color of sunset caressed the cheeks of the clouds, doomed to retreat in solitude when the shutters of the sky are closed. In everything stood the fragrance of a holiday and heart-pinching longings.

The voices of the two who were talking behind her seemed to be floating in a void. She knew she must keep silent when they are talking.

"I admire the Eskimos," said his voice.

"But I am bitter, my heart is bitter," said the voice of Shoshana.

"I read in some book," said his voice, "that in their poetry there is no such thing as love. *Amore, liebe*, the voice of my beloved! Doesn't exist!"

"I'm not an Eskimo," Shoshana replied, her voice high and

sharp. Lately a change has come over her, as if she's dried up and lost her ability to laugh.

"And it's obvious why," his voice mocked. "Hunting excites them more."

"And that's why you haven't showed up here for three weeks!" she said petulantly, defeated, arousing a vague sense of compassion in the heart of the girl.

"Not now," his voice replied with a yawn. "Enjoy yourself, look how red the heaven is!"

"Heaven, heaven! It's black in my heart!"

"Have you still not learned, Shoshik, that no man's going to look at your heart if his eyes are fixed on your bosom? Eh?" His voice attempted a playful tone. "You are to blame, you women . . . and this, perhaps, is your good fortune . . ."

"Three and a half weeks," Maya said to herself, correcting Shoshana. In this time she had succeeded in casting all thought of him from her heart. From the boiling mixture there was left a frozen sediment of resentment that he had left everything unsolved and vanished. Now he appeared, and the frozen currents were bubbling again, turning everything into chaos.

She put her cheek to the rail to feel the warmth of the wood and listened trembling to the crickets. Behind her hung a silence saturated with wondrous sensations, confusing the mind and infused with hard envy.

"When I was little . . .," she said suddenly.

"What?" asked Yosef's voice. She turned to him.

"When I was little I thought these crickets were the voices of the stars."

"What, what?" he asked.

"The crickets. Every time a star twinkles, it chirps like this . . ."

"Oh, yes, yes," he said distractedly, and Shoshana grinned bitterly.

"Sad?" he asked, but she didn't know who he was asking.

Shoshana was wearing the new turquoise blouse, the one she had lately been working on so hard, with little buttons sewn on the chest in trios, "like everyone's wearing today."

"The little ones too are moody sometimes," said Shoshana defensively. "Getting an 'unsatisfactory' in a test, or something like that . . . It isn't nice suddenly getting an 'unsatisfactory' . . ."

"Well, Shoshik, is that a fact?" Maya, controlling herself, turned toward the outside. An hour before, at the time of the gloomy, sparsely attended evening meal, her heart had leapt in her when she heard the drone of the motorbike, but she decided to wait so he wouldn't sense her excitement. But now it was impossible to go on swallowing the reheated leftovers from the midday meal, and the taste of saccharine in the tea was stronger than usual. She hurried up the stairs, accompanied by the yells of the cook. She found Yosef sitting alone on the nursery attendant's bed, his tanned legs bare, unwrapping some object that looked to her like a revolver. When he noticed her he hastily hid the weapon under the pillow. Then he looked up with surprise that exuded a hint of bitterness.

"Still sniffing around, old lady?" he said in the voice of a harassed adult. The lump grew in her throat. Those things on the roof. The stars, Orion. Unconsciously she was waiting for the same things, or for him to give her that foxy look and whisper: "What do you think I've brought for you, old lady?" But he wrinkled his brow and looked at her without affection, until she was seized by the impulse to flee, to disappear. "You heard the motorbike, eh? Next time I'll fit it with a silencer."

The door opened and Shoshana came into the room, a fragrant, clean, grown-up woman in a new turquoise blouse, a woman to whom everything was already come in its fullness. Her smile faded immediately when she saw the visitor. A soft whisper. This was an eviction order.

She's a cripple! She has a deformity that reveals itself day and night, exposed to the eye, shrieking! However much she deludes herself that it isn't so, she will surely find it again in the eyes of the others, those who radiate from themselves, without effort, a clear and inexorable maturity! Everything is their property and possession: the streets, the shops, the candies, the cars, the movie theaters, the schools, the speeches, the books, the tobacco, the coffee, the wars, the long nights! Try, little girl, to reach out to their domain, and at once you'll see how they defend what is theirs with meanness, with derision, with jealousy armed with secret weapons, practiced and all-knowing, stuffing your heart with postponements to a hazy future, which you can't be sure exists.

Yosef growled something, but the eviction order apparently was rescinded. She thought him somewhat drowsy, as if he had lost the zest for life. So they wouldn't accuse her of "hanging around," she went out to the balcony, but they lingered inside a shorter time than she expected, which aroused in her weak stirrings of hope.

Now they were both sitting behind her, and their voices continued to collide. She sensed he was sick with boredom. And then she threw the question at him.

"What?" he asked innocently, troubled again. "What should I have brought?" At once he added in a warmer tone: "No, no, please, Maya, remind me . . ." (She's a cripple! Shout it! Shout it to the heavens!) "I remember something. Well, tell me . . . Maya . . ." On his face a contrived admission of guilt. "I should have, but what was it? Oh, Maya, I'm going to burst into tears!"

"It doesn't matter . . . a notebook . . . but it doesn't matter, really . . ."

"What's the problem?" snapped Shoshana. "A notebook?! I've got a notebook lying around. Do you need it right now?"

"I don't need it at all, not ever!" she replied.

So many times she has seen before her eyes the notebook that he'll bring with him! She'll give it back to him full of writing, in laborious and rounded script. She has seen the three stars, the poetic formula, that will illumine the basement of each stanza. Every time he opens the book he'll see her differently, through the lines . . .

"Let's make a deal," said Shoshana softly, as if exploiting her special relationship with the man. "I'll give you the exercise book and you go to bed like a good girl—how about it?"

The young man didn't protest and Shoshana turned to the room and put on the light beyond the closed shutter.

"I didn't really forget," he rose and approached her. She wished that foolish expression in his eyes would disappear. "The moment I went down to buy it they closed the shop, right in front of my nose! I knocked on the door, but . . . Do you believe me, *Bambola*? You don't believe me!" he declared. She knew she must believe him, so she lowered her forehead.

"You know what?" he enthused suddenly. "You'll come to visit me, eh? Let's say in the Shavuot vacation. We'll go together to a matinee. Then it's agreed? And now, old lady, let's see that old smile of yours . . ."

If only he'd stop saying "old lady" like that, it's so false.

The light in the room went out and Yosef moved away from her. Shoshana came out and handed her the notebook. Her fingers felt a simple paper cover and soft, absorbent war-standard paper. The poems will be full of ink blots . . . In the darkness she read on the young woman's face an expression of excessive generosity.

"You see, Maya," said Yosef. "Things always work out. You can always find a substitute." In the presence of others he was careful to call her by her name. She guessed that his words were not aimed at her. But her heart told her there would never again be the blue star and Orion.

"Well, now, be a good girl, as you promised," Shoshana plucked gently at the strings, standing and waiting by the open door of the balcony. "*Duce* and I have let you stay long enough. Don't you know the others have all been asleep for ages?"

She turned to the dark room, but suddenly she was struck by

a force beyond the power of her will: to go back, go back! She returned to them, inside her everything mumbling, pleading, contracting. "There's a broken stair down there," she said with wheedling, grating lightness. "I dare not go down. It's dark." She knew that exploiting her age was demeaning, arousing scornful pity. Shoshana stood there for a moment and then laughed as if amused at her cunning.

"The Eskimos don't understand things like these," she said to Maya, in her face the certainty that she didn't understand what she meant. In the darkness she saw on Yosef's face a grimace of reluctance as he rose lazily, stretching his arms, his eyes fixed on the line of the horizon. "*Bene, bene!*" he yawned, "Oh, these women know how to exploit my good nature . . . But tonight— no stories, no poems, and no nothing! Right?"

"Right!" she replied, tensing her face heroically, making an effort not to smile.

"Shoshik my dear, in the meantime fix me a little snack, okay? You'll find something in the parcel I brought, but don't finish it all off as you usually do!"

They left the young woman on the balcony. She saw his groping under the pillow and realized he'd taken the revolver from there. A strange suspicion arose in her mind. The door closed on Shoshana, and they fumbled their way down the stairs. Yosef struck a match and the pleasant fragrance of the sulphur mingled with his own smell. "I don't want to use the dynamo," he whispered, "so we don't make a noise."

There was no longer anyone sleeping on the second floor, and the rooms stood empty and deserted. All those who were left of the "big ones" slept with the infants. Everything was permeated by abandonment and dissolution. On the silent second floor she pretended to slip on the stairs. She sensed the smile spreading over his face in the gloom. And then it happened again—the star, the big star! Her heart vanished and something else, something gigantic, took its place. Quick as a flash she was drawn into the empty, decaying "casino" that had once been their dormitory. And suddenly she found herself in the center of a different existence, solid, warm, crammed with heavy currents that roared about her and the sounds of the chirping crickets compressing the gloom, the non-place where they were isolated from all else, and some cry burst forth from within her that all this fearful storm was because of her, that it was in her power to awaken in him that crazy, imaginary thing.

"Is this what you waited for, eh?" The whisper rose in her ears. "Cowardly, foolish, cunning little beauty. The stair is broken . . . wicked, sweet little vixen, for this, for this . . ."

Only then was she aware that he was stooping and gathering her whole body to him, into his arms, to the fabric of his shirt and to a chin that crushed and pressed against her neck. And the sounds of the crickets above her head, beneath her feet. She knew this was nothing other than an astounding projection into the depth of the future. She pressed against the fabric of the shirt, to melt into this hard, frantic breathing. And then she was lifted from the floor and was in his arms, giggling softly and kicking with her feet, he leaning over her and his teeth nibbling at her cheeks, her chin, her neck, until he brought her to the first floor. The little ones in the beds stirred uneasily, sighed and snored in their sleep. For a moment she wondered who they were and why they were here. Surely they don't belong to this non-time and non-place.

"We must talk very quietly," he breathed warm currents on her face. The window was open, and he was revealed by its light, sitting on the iron frame of her bed, his hands between his knees, his head inclined with a sort of touching modesty, waiting as she undressed. When she drew the sheet up to her neck, she knew that now he'd approach.

"At Shavuot the notebook will be finished completely," she whispered, in order to hurry him.

He came closer to hear and again she was flooded by that

stunning fragrance of shaving soap mingled with tobacco, and something more. He closed his eyes and smiled as if his strength was exhausted.

"Old lady, old lady . . . six years . . . six years . . . jump six years for me," he whispered. She thought he was mocking. "In six more years you'll have grey-grey eyes and long hair tumbling over your shoulders. Old lady, why didn't you hurry up and get yourself born six years earlier? Then you'd find yourself someone and I'd watch you walking together and die of envy."

She listened to his words in disbelief, in dreadful doubt, afraid perhaps that he was making a fool of her, but every word struck at her heart—new, clean, fresh, like the first rain. She didn't want that other someone, the one she'd have "in six more years." The whisper awakened her to the depth of the empty, unknown silences, in caves that no man has explored, and she wanted, in a way unclear to her, to soothe his grief, to satisfy his will, like the one in six more years, and could not. She just drew his neck to her face.

"Who taught you to love like this?" he whispered and whispered and whispered. "Who taught you, little witch, who?" His hand stroked her neck, rolled back the sheet and slid beneath her shirt to her stomach, moving up her body. The hand trembled, hesitant, as if searching for something. And suddenly she knew, swooning, what it was searching for. And suddenly, in a flash he was alien to her, different, terrifying! Embarrassed, ashamed, seized by compassion and fear, shaken by his disappointment, she recoiled from him and covered herself with the sheet. But he leaned over her, as if held to her by a magnet, as if both of them were not themselves. What is this thing, what is it?

Yosef the stranger, the betrayer of his allies, retreated, ripped from her with dreadful force. She wanted him to come back, to come back, but differently, not so . . . And then she heard his forced whisper: "It wouldn't work, *Bambola*, it wouldn't work . . ."

What wouldn't work? she wondered desperately. There was in him none of the joy of manly pride, only a cry for help, a feeble cry for help, like Abraham before the altar. She longed again for the touch of his hand. And suddenly, in an instant, she understood it all. He had raised the curtain of mystery, and here was the furnace, a blazing fiery furnace. The flames licked her face, but he was protecting her so she wouldn't be swept away by them, only "in six more years . . . in six more years . . ." She sat up and forcibly drew his face to her face. The flames had taken hold of her and already she was different, as if she had crossed an abyss, and then his breath came to her lips, and with it that shapeless, melting tenderness, like a taste of warm jelly, spreading, shaking everything into life. All this is still stored in him, and he is torn from her. She saw his back groping between the beds like a sleepwalker, and the caress of his hand still fluttering on her arm, and his other hand under her head, and his body already gone, and something else missing, something she can't grasp, but can only feel is gone, and is dreadfully missed.

She covered her forehead with the sheet, understanding everything, pinching her lips, biting her fingers and inhaling the echo of his footsteps on the stairs. "He's going up to her . . . he's going to her . . . and he'll tell her," she muttered to the rustling of the pillow.

Toward morning she heard the roar of the motorbike, once and once again, and a cry resounding across the hill, slowly subsiding and leaving her with the darkness and the fading touches on her body. And already everything in her was turned to memory, before which there was nothing.

On the eve of the Shavuot holiday she came down to get travel expenses from Pani-Paula. In the dining room stood the two women who were left in the institution, and there were tears in the eyes of one of them.

"Surely you know by now what men are," said the manageress in Yiddish. "Their feet are in your bed and already their hands are groping someplace else."

The two of them didn't notice the girl coming in, either that or they had lost interest in the niceties of education. Anyway, it was all too hard to bear!

"No, my treasure," added Pani-Paula. "There's no person who arouses more respect in me than an independent woman . . . not because I . . . oh, no *liebes Kind*! Not for the reason you think! I'll show you dresses that I wore twenty years ago! You wouldn't get into them! That's how it is, you come to a different country, to a new place, and they all think you came like this from your mother's belly. Yes, yes, I'm an old woman," (for a moment she paused, the pause of the almost-old, to hear the denial) "and listen to what an old woman says to you: women are not material for marriage; they are made of too fragile stuff! For the sake of this they are broken once, and then it's finished."

Maya stood for a long while beside the door without moving, listening in fear to words that she understood but whose significance she couldn't grasp, yet engraving them within her, to decipher them some day, along with so many other things.

"Here, in this old heart," she smote her bosom, at the same time adjusting her corset, "here there are buried enough plots for ten Shakespeares."

"Then what's to be done, Paula?" said Shoshana in pain, blowing her nose. "What, really, is to be done?"

"What's to be done? There's nothing to be done! No man has yet found anything to do! The Lord of Creation has lost the power of invention, but He's always creating for Himself new souls who don't know the old story, so for seventy years they pursue knowledge and die fools . . . No, no, my child. Don't listen to the babbling of an old woman who hasn't succeeded in life. You're a mere infant, twenty years old at the most, and you have cheeks full of blood; you can still snatch yourself a slice of *real* happiness and gobble it up. For you it will be *different*."

"Ach!" Shoshana waved her hand and dragged behind her the broom and a trail of tears.

"What are you doing here, lizard?" said Pani-Paula, this time to Maya, whom she noticed at last. "Everything she hears, everything she must hear—how the worms spit and the beetles laugh. What do you want, eh? Money! Always money! Look at her, Shoshana, take a lesson from her . . . she's immune to everything! No shame! This one will never shed tears for . . . Take the money, go on, take it, and don't come back! Do you hear?" (He's told, he's told!) "Go on, take your rags and don't come back!" She thrust into her hand the travel expenses, but not before she counted the coins twice. "And tell your father, if his windows get smashed in, he shouldn't be surprised! I'll be the one who's smashed them! And don't you dare come back without money, do you hear?"

Maya traveled to town, to her stepmother's house. Restraining her distaste, she held out a hypocritical cheek for a hypocritical kiss, and at the same time felt a flash of malice when she noticed strands of grey in the woman's hair and the gaps left by two missing teeth.

The two-room apartment was already too narrow for her, and she found in it no remembrance of herself, her existence here in the past. The children of the neighbors, with whom she tried to renew the dawn of her youth, seemed to her foolish, colorless, and horribly dimwitted. The little brother was excessively spoiled, and she couldn't pretend to enjoy playing with him, when jealousy and resentment extinguished any spark of happiness. The father was due to arrive only at the end of Shavuot, and already she felt herself anticipating the meeting with dread: a meeting full of obligatory fatherly feeling.

On the first day of her arrival, when the woman prepared for her a special supper, as if she were a dear and honored guest, she behaved toward her, to her surprise, with strange obsequiousness, as if seeking through indirect means to obtain her goodwill, her advocacy. "I need new shoes," she said, gaily, without any feeling of dependence.

The woman was alarmed and shrank in her chair when Maya pulled off her shoes and turned them over on the table between the loaf of bread and the holiday cocoa. The soles yawned, to her great satisfaction, a luxurious yawn. Now she waited, nerves drawn tight, for the bitter outburst ("Is this proper for the daughter of working people? Is this how you look after new shoes? I only bought those in the most fashionable shop in Tel Aviv. What are we? Rockefellers? That mother of yours does nothing but play around, play around with men . . .")

But Regina was silent, nostrils flaring toward the gaping shoes.

"If I don't get new shoes," Maya trilled with glorious, radiant insolence, "I'll go straightaway and tell my grandmother." Not that the old woman was particularly attentive to the needs of the granddaughter, who gave her neither satisfaction nor pride and served as a constant and vexing reminder of sin, but it hadn't escaped Maya's notice that since the moment the second wife of her only son was co-opted into the family, the old woman had divided the leaven of her strength between two lumps of dough: challah on Sabbath eves and the rest to her daughter-in-law.

"*Du shlak!*" the woman bared her front teeth at last. "Pest! *Shlak! Shlak!*"

The "*Shlak*" waited eagerly for these teeth, too, to crack.

On the appointed day she stood before the door of the strange apartment, trying to calm the wild beating of her heart and looking again at the note in her hand. She glanced at her new shoes, at the American frock bequeathed to her by Bat-Sheva, and at the parcel wrapped in brown paper. At last she found the courage to touch the doorbell. Her finger recoiled, as if bitten. Perhaps this isn't the place, she was wondering with a strange kind of hope, when the old woman in hair curlers appeared.

"Yes?" said the woman, and at once looked at the parcel.

"Excuse me, does a man called Yosef live here?" she asked clumsily. As she spoke the name, she knew she'd given everything away. "But, I think perhaps . . ."

"Have you something for him?" The woman stretched out her hand to the parcel.

"I've come . . ."

"Give it to me, please, I'll make sure he gets it."

"No, it isn't . . .," she said, her mouth heavy. "I've come . . .

he told me to come . . ." She took a deep breath and added, with an effort: "I'm from the hostel."

"From the hostel? What hostel?" said the woman, perplexed.

"Perhaps I've come to the wrong place. Does a man called Yosef live here?"

"Yes, yes, I told you so." Maya realized the woman was angry.

'I'm from the hostel for needy children in Kiryat Shkak," she replied, as if making a statement in court.

"The hostel! Oh! The hostel! Yes, yes! How nice! Yo–si!" (Yosi!) the woman shouted into the apartment. "Some girl from the hostel . . . can you come out here for a moment? She's brought you a parcel. Did you leave something there?"

The girl noticed the scorn in her voice. Maya had never considered the possibility of somebody else in the house.

Her heart squirmed like a crushed caterpillar. He came toward her wearing his short trousers, and the blood rushed to her temples when she anxiously examined his face to find some traces of what had been, and found nothing. He smiled at her, as perplexed as his mother. She was seized by the impulse to hand him the parcel and go, not wanting to remember the presence of strangers, but suddenly he touched her shoulder and propelled her body before him, steering her like a car. In the hall mirror she saw the oppression in her face, the face of a little girl, between the coats and the telephone.

A man like him, and still he has a mother who calls him "Yosi," and doesn't know who he really is and pretends he belongs to her. This was a crude offense against good taste.

"Charming, isn't she?" he said to his mother. (Why does he have to involve her?) And again she felt a desperate desire to flee, and come some other time, some other occasion.

He led her into a cool little room, where there were some objects that were familiar to her and that gave the place an air of masculinity, but when the woman followed them in, the room changed at once to a nursery.

Her voice was strained as she answered his questions about her health and that of the people left in the hostel, as he made room for her on the sofa between a suitcase and a pile of ironed male underwear—a girl who doesn't look up and needs to clear her throat before answering, angry with herself and in her anger choking again—and his questions seeming to her tasteless and petty.

"I must run to the shower!" he said and smiled. "Talk to her, Mama, in the meantime. She's a smart girl." The word "Mama" sounded doubly grating in his mouth. She tried not to see his exposed, muscular shoulders, over which he slung a hairy towel before going out.

She wanted to be left alone in this room and to digest it slowly, along with its objects full of memories, but the mother sat opposite her, her face softer now, and began asking her "those questions": the name of her father and of her mother and what they did and where they were from. She answered, taking care not to get herself confused, and waited with dead heart for the obligatory inquiry: "And why did they send you to the hostel?" She was grateful she wasn't asked. On the other hand, she realized she hadn't succeeded in inspiring sympathy in the woman, and fear arose in her lest she express her opinion of her before her son. At the same time she knew that if she displayed before her what she had in her special bag (the story of her life), the woman would be ignited with gossipy enthusiasm and devote herself with interest to probing the details. To avoid this temptation, she wanted to say something else, find something nice engraved in her memory, but her eyes wandered back and forth among the rows of shining tiles, painted in an old style.

"What a pretty dress!" said the woman, putting out her hand to touch it. "Is it local?"

"From America," she replied.

"A present, of course. Very pretty! You don't see things like that in these parts." Just for a moment she spoke like a lonely woman for whom every new face in her house is a cause for celebration.

"Oh, I forgot completely. You'll want a candy, I expect?"

"No. It doesn't matter," she replied. In fact she longed for a candy.

She chose one of those disguised objects, wrapped in fine paper, and whispered a polite thank you. As always, inside the gaudy wrapper, was revealed a simple fruit candy, one of those meant for sucking or munching. Now Yosef would come in and see her sucking foolishly. Hastily she licked at it between tongue and palate, trying hard not to make a noise.

"And which of your parents are you spending the vacation with? asked the woman. In her eyes she already showed the familiar sparkle that indicated that she knew, but at that moment the young man rushed in, wearing a shirt, his teeth flashing and his brows and moustache moist. He threw the towel on the sofa and teased her chin with that secret teasing of theirs, which clouded her brain with anger. Suddenly he slapped her shoulder:

"Virgin of Israel, *avanti*! I hope at least you gave her a candy?" he turned to his mother. "That's a sign that she likes you," he said to Maya. "It's very rare."

"Where are you going now?" asked the mother without smiling.

"Where do you think? To the bridal canopy! Charming girl, eh?"

How does he manage to show himself so fresh and light?

"That's enough of your wisecracks, Yosi. I want you to come to supper. This at least we deserve after all the . . ."

"Alright, alright," he replied, taking deep breaths as if about to dive into a pool.

"At least tonight show that you . . . if only your father knew . . . if he only knew . . ."

"Alright, I said alright!" he said impatiently, a reply that aroused in Maya both gladness (he despises this woman) and disgust (how can he let himself talk like this to a mother who cares about him so much?).

When the door closed, he took her hand at once, turning her as if on a hinge and studying her with great emphasis.

"Listen, you're looking terribly grand! Where did you get all this stuff? And all for my sake, eh? I could swallow you up—a fresh radish." He squeezed her hand with feeling, but as if warning her it was forbidden to remember or to remind. Suddenly he stopped and made her sit down on the stairs. (Stairs again, and everything from the start!)

"Now listen carefully, *Colomba*, and don't tremble at me like that, and don't pretend that in the meantime you've understood it all," he said forcefully. "You can't understand! But when you grow up you won't find anyone who'll volunteer to say to you what I'm going to put right now into your smooth little brain, they'll all tell you things back to front." He turned her face to his face and breathed softly on her mouth until he coaxed a smile from her. "You know how you solve crossword puzzles. You've already solved a thousand, right? We're all drawn to a blank crossword, but most of us are impatient, unimaginative. One across clue, one down—and we're finished. We decide this cross-word bores us like hell! So we run from crossword to crossword, an across here, a down there, and sometimes, just for the sake of it, we shove in some word that doesn't fit. So what? Let some other clever guy come along and break his head over the rest. But you," he laid his finger on her neck and, in his usual fashion, accompanied each word with a finger jab. "When the crosswords are blank, wide open like your eyes—Are you listening or not?" His voice rose slightly. "Look me straight in the eyes! Like that! Without . . . like that! Until he comes along—not one like me— someone that you're sure is capable, quick to understand. And he'll have the patience to answer everything!" He smiled and put his arm around her shoulder. "To rub out is forbidden! Understand? There must be no rubbing out! Because you have nothing in the world but you yourself! You have nowhere to run to and nobody to run to but you yourself. Otherwise you'll start rubbing out and rubbing out until there's nothing left to see . . . In yourself you'll see nothing!"

"Yes," she said, as if she'd been sent out alone into the desert to find a distant, imaginary oasis, far away from both of them. He sniffed at her a little, like a dog. "And make sure you wash every day."

"Yes," she murmured.

"What do you mean, yes-yes? And you'll let all those fools come along and spoil . . . Already I see the picture. You think it's so simple! You say 'yes, yes'—and that's it!"

She submitted at once to that thing melting on her lips, to his breath permeating within her.

"Is this how you keep promises, eh?" he said and smiled. "Yes, yes, and fall down right away . . . and stop trembling like that . . . I'm scared, Maya," he became suddenly serious. "I'm afraid for you . . . they'll come for you . . . all those . . . come and destroy . . . you fool! I would bind you up! That's all I have to say so you can stop pretending you understand anything! I'm afraid you'll end up ruined . . . and don't start dressing up and painting your lips at the age of thirteen . . . you've too much still to learn . . ."

Suddenly he stood her on her feet and prodded her down the stairs. His words sounded like a will. Down there, beside the entrance, he dropped her hand. A girl, very attractive, was walking toward them, carrying a big handbag.

"What good things have you brought today?" he cried, and snatched the bag from her hand. The girl grabbed it back with an angry snarl, swaying on her heels.

"You can tell right away this is my sister, the jewel of the family!" he said to Maya, who was instantly relieved.

The girl turned up her nose and looked at him for a moment, as if he was a hopeless case, and passed by them. Suddenly she turned her head and snapped in a dull voice, twisting her mouth:

"So this is your way of getting your revenge on mother! You're a dirty egoist! That's what I've got to say to you! Nothing in the world is sacred to you! At last you're going to hear my opinion of you! You're a spoiled adventurer, that's what you are!"

Now she turned her whole body toward them and waved her handbag dismissively.

Maya was alarmed, sure that these accusations came because he was walking with her.

"Yes, yes, I've seen that degenerate, your buddy!" she cried angrily. "Walking in the street in a new uniform and showing himself off! At last he's succeeded in finding sex appeal . . . chasing after every English officer and running in front of him, so he can salute like . . . like a trained monkey . . ."

"It's nice to know they're accepting degenerates for training," he replied, and at once grinned. "Poor girl! My poor sister!" he said to Maya with a radiant look. "She's afraid that when she marries her husband will have to support mother!"

The girl disappeared at once between the sandbags in the doorway.

In Mograbi Square, near the drugstore, a surprise awaited them. Cheerful voices came to meet them: "*Ciao! Ciao Duce! Saluto soldato!*"

At once Yosef was the center of a circle, and young men and women were slapping his back, tickling his neck, greeting him in loud voices and with strange nicknames. Three of them she recognized at once in the confusion. These were the men, similar in appearance to Yosef, who had surprised them on the roof. She was jostled aside toward the window of the drugstore and she stared awkwardly at a smiling advertisement for tranquillizers.

"When?" she heard an inquiring, impatient voice. "When?"

In the window—one face contorted with pain, and opposite it another smiling in gratitude and relief at a bottle of pills.

"Thirty-six hours from now!" replied Yosef's voice from among them. She tried to locate him with her eyes and saw part of his hidden body, as he raised his arms like one casting off a yoke—"Hi–pi–hay!"

"Which?" demanded a girl's voice. Maya looked at her cautiously.

"Transport! Via Sarafand to Libya!"

"To the spaghetti!" a familiar voice growled with pleasure. *"Mama mia!* Straight to the what's-its-name of Maria." This was the thick, guttural voice.

"Good!" they all cried in a wild, triumphant yell.

Suddenly, some of them noticed the beggar, to whom she hadn't paid any attention before, sitting leaning against the drugstore wall, before him a tin plate and between his thighs a ghastly growth that sprawled on the sidewalk as he moaned and ceaselessly stroked the trousers that covered the frightful deformity.

"Girls to the rear!" shouted somebody.

"Look at this Casanova!"

"It's elephantiasis. Leave off, lousy bastards!" she heard the voice of Yosef, which was immediately swallowed up by the others.

"Don't disturb him just now! Take care! We'll be drowned!" cried the high, nervous voice.

The beggar, noticing the attention of so many people, looked up hopefully and rattled the bowl, his other hand constantly easing the dreadful pumpkin between his legs. The girls giggled nervously, one over the shoulder of the other, and two of the boys began throwing coins at the bowl, amusing themselves with the target practice, until they had enough of it.

Again she saw Yosef flashing smiles under his moustache, putting his arm round the waist of a girl, jabbing his finger at the shoulder of a boy, lighting cigarettes, his face tense for a moment, then smiling again.

"Hey!" somebody said suddenly and pointed to her. "Hey! Who's this little thing?" At once he stared at her with mock sternness. "Inquisitive, isn't she!"

"The bride! The bride!" cried the high voice, close by. "The bride of *Duce!*"

The faces in the window stared at her with that dual stare of pain and relief. And then they all swooped on her, as they had swooped before on the beggar.

"This is . . . *Duce's* . . . the bride . . . this is . . ." The girls enfolded her in a stifling wreath of hair and billowing spring dresses, and the boys danced around her, praising her ironically at the tops of their voices, congratulating Yosef on his good taste.

She froze where she stood, as if confronted by someone who "owed her a beating." Her head swam, lost among the sights, the onslaught of voices, the beautiful faces full of manliness, femininity, health, unbounded insolence; and at the same time she peered toward the movie theater. On the entrance steps a line was already forming for the matinee show. She tried to catch his eye, to remind him, but he stood far from her and watched with pleasure as they swarmed around her, and suddenly she felt the touch of his arm clasped around her neck, quite openly, in front of the street and the laughing eyes.

"Hey, friends, listen for a moment! A moment! A moment! Who's willing to entertain this charming creature for me?"

Her heart fluttered as if it had been scraped with sandpaper.

"You rotten lot!" he added in a tone of comical entreaty in the face of their silence, and stretched out his hand. "Human beings! Be human beings for a change! I've got to fly! Already I shouldn't be here! Look after her for a while. You'll see how charming she is . . . a real *principessa*! Spoil her a bit, buy her a fruit juice . . . Well? Any takers? *Donne e cavalieri*! Going once! Going twice . . ."

She couldn't move her frozen eyes from him.

"Well, who's it going to be?"

A solid door fell with a crash between them.

"Nobody?" she heard as if in a dream. "Will nobody do this for me? It really is a pity to put such a treasure in your greasy hands . . ." The voice of a girl volunteered without enthusiasm, and after it another female voice.

"A pair of human beings at last!" He smiled at both of them with great affection.

"It'll be alright, eh?" he shouted to Maya and winked. "Ride these two hard for my sake! Don't let them get away with anything! Do you hear?"

She looked up and stretched her lips into a foolish smile, and already she saw him moving off among them, signaling from the distance with a raised hand, like a salute, and there was no way of knowing to whom.

"So what are we buying for our little girl?" said a contrived, pampering voice. The line had already been swallowed up in the entrance to the theater.

"I'll bet she'd like some chewing gum. Do you like chewing gum? What's your name?"

A compassionate, motherly hand took her arm to lead her to a nearby kiosk. She gripped the parcel tightly between her fingers.

"G . . . go to Hell, all of you . . ." Her voice was almost inaudible. A momentary relief came to her, but she felt the muscles of her face betraying her, and she regretted not saying something stronger. She snatched her arm roughly from the gentle fingers. In her ears a long roar, drawn out like a warning siren as she ran across the road and the square. And within the roar she remembered the voices shouting after her, as if pursuing: "Oh! Oh!"—"What's the matter with her, what's up?"—"One of his waifs and strays . . ."

Thus it was, until she reached the public lavatories. The cubicles were locked one after the other, only the last one was free. She collapsed inside and unwrapped the brown paper. Avidly, angrily, she began ripping out one by one the pages of the notebook, the lovely letters, so carefully rounded, the words that had intoxicated her as she copied them, crumpling them and throwing them one by one into the bowl. And suddenly, only the thin cover was left in her hand. She peered, for the first time, into the bowl, full of the torn, mangled paper, and a silent calm took hold of her guts.

After she had stood thus for a long time without moving, she felt her cheeks wet with snot and tears, and she hurriedly wiped them with the cover. The stitching scratched her face. She threw the cover after the pages and saw how the water rose and was absorbed in it, turning it black.

"It's a good thing I've got another copy," was her first thought, panting to stop herself choking. "It's a good thing I've got a copy back at the hostel."

Batya Wolfson was taken ill.
Markovski joined the army.

The second floor they let to the students of the nearby yeshiva. Now, every morning, some side-locked yeshiva boy would stare from his bed at the devil's face on the peeled ceiling.

Secretly, almost unnoticed and without words of farewell, the inmates slipped away like lizards, and only vague rumors accompanied their memories.

The days were as alike as sparrows. Only toward Rosh Ha-Shanah did something happen, something which speeded the departure of Mikki, who arrived at the hostel just in time to witness its death throes.

One Sabbath afternoon four boys went for a long trek through the orchards to bathe in the Yarkon near the seven mills, and there to find the fish spawning-ground that one of them had once discovered on the river bed.

As darkness fell, two of them returned pale and breathless, afraid to speak, and afterwards, with a sort of nervous laugh, they told Shoshana in the dead of night that Stinking Rafi had drowned. The boys were walking beside the waterfall, and Stinking Rafi, who couldn't swim, slipped, just slipped on the smooth stones. They laughed and watched him, but they heard him crying out in terror, and only then remembered that he couldn't swim and jumped in after him, but the current of the waterfall carried him away from them, and anyway it all happened so fast that it was impossible . . .

"Then why are you so cheerful? Then why are you so cheerful?" screamed Shoshana in fright, and at once she ran frantically to the nearest house to knock on Margarita's mother's door.

By the light of blue-shaded flashlights, Abie and Ketzele brought the police search party and the neighbors who had joined it to the site of the disaster.

At three in the morning they were met by an old Arab who lived in one of the shacks near the river. He watched for a long time, from a distance, the party scouring the reed beds, until he took courage and approached one of the policemen.

"*Walad? Walad?*"*

They all hurried after him to his shack, the policemen with them, in a mood of complacency born of relief and the release of tension. And there, on a mat of reeds, wrapped in a goatskin, they saw the child asleep. Only then did they remember that New Mikki had also disappeared, perhaps because his existence hadn't yet taken root in their consciousness. This was Mikki.

He lay without speaking on the reed mat, perhaps because there wasn't among them a single one who had had time to tie bonds of friendship with him. He lay and listened in silence to the voices

---
* "Child" in Arabic.

of the policemen, who had returned reluctantly to their duty and were searching the banks of the river outside, the click of oars, approaching and receding, the questions and brief answers that rose all around as morning broke, until one of the policemen, standing above him to interrogate him, slapped his cheek. Then the shocked weeping burst forth, the weeping of an alien. From his frightened stammering, in response to the threatening presence of the policeman, there finally emerged Mikki's terror that he was to blame. When he held out his hand to catch him, Stinking Rafi missed it, and when he saw the squirming body and heard the cries that suddenly stopped as the lungs filled with water, he was seized with panic. All night he wandered among the reed beds, and when he returned to the river and tried again to look for Rafi, he suddenly saw the Arab waiting for him. That was all he remembered.

The policemen returned grey-faced into the light of the morning, with their long staves and their extinguished flashlights. The old Arab offered food to the children who huddled in the cold against the walls of the shack. The warmth of adventure faded. All night they had looked forward with certainty to the gaiety that would erupt with the return of the vanished—a game that had been invaded for a moment by life itself—and now they were left with the insipid taste of their loss.

Stinking Rafi disappeared. Even his body was never found. Perhaps it was swept into the Mediterranean Sea, into the war that always terrified him so much. At midday the policemen abandoned their search. Anyway, there was no one to demand his corpse.

A week later a hobbling grandmother appeared, and Mikki fell into her arms and refused to let go. He went with the old woman. Only afterwards did Maya remember that this was the same grandmother who, he had once told her, went through the refuse in the backyards with a bag in her hand—and Mikki with her.

One day Salomon faded away too, until it became known that

he had been sent to a "closed institution," as he and his uncle had feared, until he could return to his "casino" in Haifa.

Only Abie, before he packed his bags to go alone to a kibbutz in the Jordan Valley, came suddenly to take leave of her and handed her a notebook of his poems. They were bolder and more mature than hers, and when she read them her heart was filled with envy and longing, and sometimes she would whisper "Abie, Abie" into the lonely darkness, just so she could anchor her thoughts on some human form.

The girls were taken away one by one, almost in secret, apparently untouched by their recent past. In some cases mothers appeared who had married again, but most of them were taken into orphanages and their traces were lost, leaving no regret in her heart. The more its residents were reduced and its routines disrupted, the more the house became her own.

Of the older children, only Ketzele and Maya were left. Hordes of nameless infants, whose future had not yet been decided, still filled the first floor. Maya staked out a place for herself in the larger of the infants' rooms, and Ketzele in the smaller.

Shoshana stayed on in the institution, unpaid, out of a vague feeling of obligation toward the fate of those remaining, but she tended to them haphazardly, hastily, since they were too many for her to handle and she was already busy arranging for her transfer to another work place and running to public institutions to demand their attention to the fate of the children whose condition was deteriorating steadily.

Even before this, Pani-Paula made her decision and went down to the city, bitter and swollen with disappointment, after working five years for Batya Wolfson. At that time there were many soup kitchens in the city, and Paula Berger found herself a place in one of them, but twice a week, in the evenings, she would climb up the hill, driven by conscience, to prepare free and without payment fifteen portions of lentil soup and bread-puddings from the stocks left behind in the pantry house.

The infants were left in the charge of the older children. By a kind of natural process in which there's no knowing how it began and how it ended—perhaps according to Shoshana's instructions—they found themselves tending these dirty little creatures, rising in the night to hush their crying, and in the morning to wrap them in their stinking rags, gripped by spasms of disgust that gradually abated.

All at once the children grew up and were thrown into an exhilarating state of liberation, without prohibitions and rules and compulsions. There were no more meals, the pantry was empty and ransacked, stripped of its secrets. The infants' bellies were swollen with hunger, and they crawled around on the floor that was no longer cleaned, chewing every object that happened their way, scratching the walls, or lying sprawled in the yard to warm themselves in the dead sand like still little lizards.

For a few weeks Maya ate her meals in Margarita's kitchen and used to smuggle out food for Ketzele, until this source too was stopped, and she didn't even bother to ask herself why.

When Maya first came to the hostel they told her the literal meaning of his nickname: "Alley Cat." The same week that they had pillaged the sacred relics of the pantry, she had the opportunity to understand its plain significance; instead of a mash of broken cookies (a delicacy reserved for Sabbath eves), Pani-Paula then found in the tin box a guilt-offering in the shape of a bony house rat, a corpse clean of all suspicion, and at once she was hard on the heels of the boy, the rolling pin in her hand. It seems that he himself, aside from the pleasure of stealing, was deliberately constructing these circles of crime, just to be pursued by them.

Then Maya saw, amid the gasps of amazement at the foot of the house, one of those things that gave birth to his nickname: how he, like the beanstalk in the fairy tale, burgeoned, rose, burst forth, and soared into the sky. In a flash he raced up the gutter pipe, and already he was suspended aloft like the clapper of a bell, every swing arousing chimes of dread in the hearts of the girls and vengeful roars from the throat of the cook, waving the rolling pin and trying to drive away the boys who were encouraging him. Then Maya caught a glimpse of Frieda, standing at a distance, trying to conceal her smiles from Paula, and then her horror at the sight of the boy floating on the balustrade of the roof in the celestial abode of the clouds, leaning outward and threatening the next moment to drop like a star.

He loved heights, rhythm and loud noises and war movies—one of those lucky ones who know how to control their bodies and don't acknowledge the need to control their spirit. He could waggle his ears, double the upper segments of his fingers, lick the tip of his nose, move his neck from shoulder to shoulder, beat exciting rhythms on his knee with two soup spoons, tap dance, turn two somersaults in the air without touching the ground, and if it had occurred to him, he would have thrown a grappling iron to God and climbed up to Him. Everyone had different predictions of his future—he was destined to be a fireman, a champion racing-car driver, percussionist in an orchestra, a guerrilla leader—but he himself was determined to devote all his talents to a more noble profession: *haute coiffure*. A big salon, "covering a whole floor," and an all male team of hairdressers. In the back room, in an iron safe, will be a store of pilferred ornaments, and the prettiest of them he will present to a woman who takes his fancy.

Ketzele admired the Germans—especially the SS—and resolutely despised the vanquished. He pitied the English, shitted on the cowardly French, despised with all his heart the heroic weakness of the Poles, and waved his hand at the impudence of the Russians. Only the partisans who operated behind the lines earned his solidarity.

Sometimes, to give emphasis to his opinions, he felt the need for a wild display:

Piling up all the chairs he can find into one big heap, there, under the ceiling, he becomes a Messerschmitt pilot doing battle with a squadron of Spitfires. He's the German pilot, firing from above, and he's the propeller, and at once he's the British pilot, replying to his commander on the intercom and firing from another chair. He's the wings of the diving bomber, and again the German pilot, and finally—a direct hit and a shriek and a slow descent from the heights, all the chairs tumbling after him onto his body that sprawls beneath them with limbs spread-eagled. Then he rises, inflamed with enjoyment, piles up the chairs again and waves his hand: *"Herr Oberst! Eins geschlossen!"* Climbing again into his plane, adjusting the pilot's helmet, and at once: "Pow! Pa-pa-pa-pa-pa-pa! Ah! A-a-a-a-a-a!" The excited onlookers flinch, engrossed in the spectacle, and the more they flinch, the more his enthusiasm grows.

Only later, when the news bulletins brought with them signs of the weakness of his heroes, did the chairs begin to tumble on the body of the German breathing his last.

At the beginning of autumn a man came to Shoshana to hire the two children to serve as scarecrows in his fields on the outskirts of the village. After the first laugh, they feared they would have to stand all day with arms outstretched. But they were given empty cans.

They paced between the sprouting furrows under the mellow sun, the two of them alone in the great expanse, and rattled the cans. The starlings descended on the field and rose slowly with the rattling—a kind of game between them and the starlings— and returned some distance from them.

Sometimes the girl would stretch out to rest on a dustbank and watch the boy, drumming on his can and dancing among the growing plants. Ketzele had subdued his anarchic enthusiasm, but there sprang up in him a kind of gay light-heartedness that surprised and delighted her. She would look in turns at him and at the little insects crawling on her legs, or at the columns of ants rustling within their closed world. Her heart beat happily in time to his drumming and to his voice ringing out from the acacia grove to the cypress grove: "Away you go, O *Buzambo!*" A sense of being uprooted from everything, without beginning and without conclusion.

In the evening they would return to the landowner's house and hand over the empty cans, so he could give them back at dawn, and gobble up in awkward silence the food prepared for them by his soft-armed wife. At first Maya's eyes were afraid to meet those of the three children of the house who dined with them, lest she find scorn in them, until she saw them expressing envy and curiosity. When her eyes met Ketzele's he would smile at her, a smile of delight over the buttered bread.

After the meal they would slip away into the clinging darkness, unwilling to provide a target for the speculations and inquiries of the lady of the house.

One evening, when they gave back the cans, she put into their hands a bundle of old clothes and a few items of food. "The plants have grown already," she said in Yiddish. Suddenly she leaned toward Maya as if to kiss her, but recoiled at once and patted her cheek instead. Maya understood why, but didn't bear her a grudge.

Now the guts of the "Fifth Heaven" gaped before them.

The last sanctuary of Pani-Paula, the pantry house, a low and narrow building that leaned on the wall of the rear courtyard, was shattered, despoiled, naked, and empty. And on the back wall, the furthest limit of the hostel, always piled up to the ceiling with sacks and boxes, suddenly a new window was revealed — like the one and only cell of a jail whose prisoner has escaped.

The door—the one that always made the pretense of being an armor-plated iron gate with double locks—suddenly all its illusions were shattered. One day Ketzele, in a distracted mood, plucked away the corrugated tin cover on its inner panel, and revealed what lay beneath it: flattened strips of metal from oil cans fastened with nails to the plank frame of the door, once disguised with such diligence and now rickety and bedraggled. Because of the freshness of the material, hidden from the ravages of time, it was possible to see clearly on every metal strip the name of the Belpetrole company and the picture of a bear squatting on his haunches and stretching out a paw. Thus, for years, the bears had sat, one on top of the other, stretching out their paws behind the covering of corrugated tin, without an eye to glimpse them—the silent guardians of the sanctuary.

In the yard, among the broken glass, eggshells, and dried shoes, an assortment of tin cups, their handles covered in rust, now slept an eternal sleep. On one of them was inscribed, like an afterthought, the name of "Abie." Maya wanted to preserve it for herself, but she wondered what to do with it and threw it over the fence. Suddenly she regretted it, but made no attempt to retrieve it.

From the branches of the grey-leaved cypress tree hung a soup ladle, like a miraculous fruit, and by the threshold of the kitchen back door, like an old woman left alone to die slowly, sprawled an iron bedstead, rusty legs pointing skyward.

One twilight hour, when Ketzele had gone down to the village, the girl went into the laundry house, which before she had always run past with an unexplained aversion, perhaps because of the massive sinks where you could be suddenly thrown and disappear and be swallowed up among the wet clothes, perhaps because of Pani-Paula's dripping laundry pole, waved at them menacingly whenever she was disturbed in her work of stirring the mighty cauldrons, or perhaps because of the Hell-fire seething of the giant primuses. Now the place stood in dead silence.

Then she saw that this had been a hasty piece of brick work. One red stain of oil paint on one of its walls and blue on the other wall, as if someone had once tried to paint it and suddenly changed his mind, deciding there was no point in trying to decorate this ugliness. And pitch covered everything—a black sky without stars. In the corner, where one of Pani-Paula's huge frying pans had always stood on the "Dreyfus" stool, she dipped her finger in pitch and wrote on the white patch of wall: "Here are the graves—here is your grave too." Then she blew out air between her teeth with a sort of self-mockery, a gesture toward her invisible audience, and drew a line over what she had written. Suddenly she knew that something was happening in her, unlike anything she had expected. Instead of the compassion she had hoped to arouse for herself in that imaginary audience, there came a delightful feeling of belonging, of identity, of mastery! Mistress of the place! And a strange and pleasing intoxication swept over her, the intoxication of awareness of the moment—the moment that is now, now, now, and will never return.

The glorious plasticine colors of freedom faded and were mashed into an ugly and amorphous lump. Breathing in meant vapors of urine; breathing out meant the fetid stink of hunger. The infants already sprawled on their beds or on the floor, helpless and smitten by strange diseases, among the pools of liquid excrement. Kind-hearted neighbors had taken into their homes some of the prettier and healthier ones among them, until Shoshana could solve the problem of their future, but Maya discovered in all this a wondrous kind of beauty, a sensation of a unique existence that doesn't fall to the lot of others.

At night Ketzele would go down to Kiryat Shak to listen to the news on the radio in one of the cafes, and she would lie half-awake on her bed, listening to the whimpering of the infants and waiting for his voice to break through the distant darkness, a voice ringing out clearly as he ran toward her on the path: "Maya–ka! Maya–ka! Mayaka!"—as if seeking to dispel the gloom with his voice and prepare her to welcome him joyfully. Sometimes he would already be proclaiming to her from outside, impatient, the news that he brought with him: "The Russians have captured . . . the invasion of . . . has succeeded!" And already the smile was on his face, and he would fling himself from the road straight at her, into her bed, huddling against her to warm his frozen body, rubbing his cold nose on her cheek, as if this was not Ketzele but someone else, someone who no longer charmed her with his impetuous spirit but fascinated her with his strange and childish dependence on her, something she didn't like, arousing in her the thinnest of thin sorrows, and with it a disturbing sense of pitying affection.

Once his body has absorbed the warmth of the bed, the boy tells her softly and gently what he has seen and heard in the village, what people there are saying about the news and their prophecies about the end of the war. And as he does so he takes from his pockets what he has stolen for her—candies that have melted in his pocket and crumbling cookies. She inhales with annoyance the foul smell that rises from his mouth and his body, but at the same time it occurs to her that perhaps her body too is giving off the same smells, and she thinks of the strange expression that she found on her face in the mirror, with the staring eyes and the dry mouth refusing to close, so she relaxes and grabs the candies as they both sit wrapped in the stinking blanket that moves above them from time to time when the boy stretches out his hand to slay a bedbug.

One night, when he returned and found her sitting there, he said suddenly, "You shouldn't sit like that."

"Like what?"

"Like that, with your legs apart."

"Why?"

"It isn't nice for . . . for a girl to sit like that."

"But why?" she said, and almost guessed.

"They'll think you're . . . I'm telling you!"

"What?"

"A girl who sits like that, it's a sign that . . ."

"How come you know so much about it?" she asked, and at once she covered herself with the blanket.

"I'm telling you . . . ," he said impatiently. "I saw what you did with Yosef," he suddenly added.

She was stunned. For such a long time it had seemed to her that Yosef was nothing more than an insubstantial image that did not yet exist.

"What are you saying?" she said. "What . . . what?"

"I saw you from the other room," he laughed with a sort of vindictiveness, "but I don't know if he went all the way!"

"All what way?" She was alarmed. "All what way?" And then she understood and closed her eyes in pain at the memories that rose in her with fearful force.

"You fool! I'm just a girl! I'm too young, you fool! I'm a child!" she cried.

Then it became clear to her that she was indeed a child. With great difficulty, with wonder, with pain and shame and desperate longing, she tried to explain to him, to make him understand.

"He was just caring for me! He was just caring for me!"

"Are you sure?" he asked faintly. "Are you sure of that? If not—I'll bite your pulse till all your blood runs out!"

"You don't need to worry," she said and snatched her hand away in alarm. "He was just caring for me . . . he cared for me an awful lot." But she knew Ketzele wouldn't understand.

He nestled against her again and wrapped his cold legs around hers to warm them, and she wasn't afraid of him, but she knew that some time he would perhaps be something different, and she resented him because he'd seen a thing that belonged to her alone, and it was for her alone to revive the memory or to dismiss it.

She suddenly fell asleep, but woke at once when he shook her shoulder, the smell of the candies strong on his breath, demanding: "Mayaka, tell me a story. Tell me a story. I'm so . . . tell me . . ."

"I want to sleep," she murmured. "I want to sleep."

Ketzele was growing backward now, becoming more of a child from day to day, and he needed pampering.

"Tell me a long story . . . the story about . . . I'm so . . . ," he pleaded.

"Tomorrow I . . . tomorrow I'll tell you," she groaned irritably, her eyelids heavy.

He wouldn't let her alone and he bit her on the root of her thumb until she raised her head without pleasure, leaning on her arm and seeing above his head the apertures of the windows blocked with cardboard and the iron frames of the infants' beds standing before her as still as skeletons.

"Once upon a time there lived a king and a queen," she intoned mechanically. "Once upon a time there lived a king and a queen. The king was wise, strong, and brave, and the queen was as beautiful as the sun and as fair as the moon. One day the king went away to war. The queen sat and waited in the palace in her dress of gold and pearls, and the king didn't return," she said drowsily, her eyes hurting.

"Why not?" his voice demanded, as if from far away. "Why! Why didn't he return?"

"I don't know why. I don't know anything."

"You're always making up things like that," he murmured heavily. "Always spoiling the stories . . . make up something else."

"The queen sat in the palace in her dress of gold and diamonds and waited, and waited . . ."

Her voice faded in the thickened darkness. She felt her eyelids fluttering, until her head sank to the rhythmic breathing of the boy and the rustle of the straw pillow.